Push Away...

Matters of the heart:

Melissa M. Marlow

This is a work of fiction. Names, characters, places, and incidents are products of the author's imagination or are used fictitiously and are not to be construed as real. Any resemblance to actual events, locales, organizations, or persons, living or dead, is entirely coincidental.

Publisher: Poehler Publishing

ISBN-13: 9780983524502

ISBN-10: 0983524505

1

As uncomfortable as I was I still needed to go to the bathroom. This bar, Ty's would not me a normal place for me to be. I know I was getting braver about going out on my own, but this was crazy of me. I could never fit into this world.

Tori, my outgoing friend from work, talked me into this misadventure. She was comfortable anywhere, so this was no big deal for her. It was crowded and we moved very slowly through the people. I looked up and saw the sign. I put my head down to trudge forward with one thing on my mind. I needed to go to the bathroom.

As we inched forward, my shoulder was shoved by something very large and hard. It knocked the wind from me. As I grabbed my chest, this very muscular young man held my arms to look at me. "I am so sorry, are you alright?"

My heart pounded and a thought came to my mind that was completely out of character for me, *yes... boy... if I was only ten years younger...* but my lips said, "Yeah, I'm okay. Just need the bathroom." I looked up to his face and yes he was young, but how young I couldn't tell. His skin was a warm brown that looked like he was exposed to the sun every day of his life. His eyes were the brightest blue I had ever seen, and his hair was a very dark brown, definitely not black. I was breathtakingly aware of his beauty and I must have looked like an old lady standing there with my hand clutching my chest.

He smiled sweetly at me and took my hand and started to move us to the bathroom. He was large enough to push people to the side. I noticed when we passed Tori, she gave me the thumbs up. I rolled my eyes knowing that I probably was old enough to be his mother. Okay, maybe not *THAT* old, but too old for what she was thinking.

I made it to the bathroom, but he didn't let go. He pulled me close to him, but I figured it was only because it was crowded; and it sure was loud. He said something to me and I couldn't hear him. I shrugged my shoulders and gazed in the direction of the door to the bathroom. He said something else, which I still didn't understand... and what could I do? I smiled and nodded and rushed into the bathroom. I was relieved with being able to go. I think I had had enough to drink and I would have to sober up to drive home.

I stumbled out of the stall and Tori was waiting for me smiling. "Well, he was a handsome man."

"You mean boy."

"He was interested in you."

"No, I am old and married."

"I am telling you he was taken with you."

I shoved her out the door and she led the way back to the table. We continued to talk and laugh with everyone from work. Tori's boyfriend showed up before it was too late and they went off to dance. I loved dancing and it had been so long since I danced. Would I even remember how or would I look like a fool out there? I felt myself recess into my own world again, because that is what I was good at; so, I just sat there and watched people dance.

What I really needed was a cigarette, but I hadn't had one in years so why would I want one now? It didn't make any sense, so I ignored the sensation. Soon, this night would be over and I would be back to my life. The emptiness was filling the air around me as I realized how much I missed interacting with people and having a good time. I wasn't being badgered for things I couldn't do right, because it seemed that everything I did was wrong lately.

My mind kept going back to the night a few years ago, when I caught my husband cheating with another woman under our roof. I don't mean I found out about it...I actually saw him in the act. Things have not been the same since then. I wouldn't have sex with him again after seeing that. I don't know why he's even still there in the house. He didn't love me enough... if ever. It seemed that other things always came first with him and I was always supposed to be okay with everything because he was the man of the house. I was no longer okay with anything, and I didn't know who I was anymore. I also didn't know how to do things without someone criticizing me. I was always fighting to prove him wrong. After finding him with the other woman and actually getting sick, I

2

no longer cared what he thought or what he said. I had no respect for him as a man and it was rubbing off on my children. He would have been better off leaving. I feel like my marriage is hanging there by a mere thread.

The band was playing their last song, but I longed for it to continue. I watched as the younger people moved together slow dancing, and still having passion. *Was my life over when it came to love? How was I going to feel when I got home? Could I go another day lonely?*

I walked out with the crowd from work, but I parked a little farther down from some of them. I continued to my car alone. I stopped and leaned against a car taking off my shoes. I dangled them in one hand as I continued to my car. I knew I had another month before we went out again, so I at least had time to work on my body more. Maybe I could lose some more weight. I got in my car and leaned my head back taking a deep breath. I should have stopped drinking a lot earlier. If I got a DWI now, I would have to ask the husband for help and I would hate that. I was finally trying to do things on my own.

I heard a knock on my window. I sat up and fumbled to find the window switch. I pushed it down until my window was completely open. I looked up as I asked, "Yes?"

To my surprise it was the young man near the bathroom. Oh, he was a beautiful young man. Every part of his body was perfect and amazing, untouched by the years that had been unkind to my own.

"You said you would meet me?"

"I did? Oh, no I didn't. I couldn't hear you so I nodded. I was just being polite. I am sorry."

"Are you sorry now?"

"Yes, I didn't mean to..." I looked up to that face and it was weathered into a warm brown. He was very appealing to the eye.

He opened my door, "You look like you need air."

"I was just thinking the same thing, but I need to get home now."

I was so nervous that he was standing here getting mixed messages from me. I was a married woman. I mean I am a married woman with children.

He took my hand to pull me out of the car, "A little air wouldn't hurt."

I followed his lead and stepped out of the car not knowing why I would allow this. He had my hand that held the ring that said I was

3

married. I was happy that he noticed right away and pulled it up to look at it, "You are married?"

I smiled politely, "Yes."

"How long?"

"Fifteen years."

"Where is your husband?"

My heart was racing and my hand was trembling as he held it there to look at it.

"I think I am fine now. I should be going." I turned to get back in my car and felt hands move around my waist to turn me to face him.

"You don't want to answer me...you're not happy."

Okay, none of his business. He was a child in my book. A very handsome, strong, and luring young man, but this was not okay. I could not allow myself to be taken with him.

I smiled politely, "I am going to go, now."

He leaned to me with his mouth less than an inch from mine, "Come back next weekend."

"What?"

"Come back and meet me next Saturday and dance with me."

"I am too old to dance that way with anyone."

"Old, how old are you?"

"Don't you know it's not polite to ask a woman her age?"

He smiled and touched his lips to mine softly. It felt so good. I have not been kissed in a long time. His mouth pressed harder to mine spreading my lips. His mouth moved to mine more; sucking on my top lip. He took my breath away, as his arms moved tighter pulling me to his perfect body. It has been too long since I had this sensation of wanting, but this was a very tempting young man. Why would he be doing this? I pulled away and pushed against his body for him to let me go.

His face was serious as he stared into my eyes, "Come back and dance with me."

I pleaded, "I can't."

"Why?"

"I am married."

"But not happy."

I glared at him. I never said that.

"I am old and you are so young."

"What is your age?"

I didn't want to say, but maybe he would let me go if he knew how old I really was, "I'm thirty-five."

He smiled, "That is maturing not old."

"But you are very young."

"No, not really. I'm twenty eight. Come meet me and dance with me." He pulled closer to me, "I will make you feel good."

I shook my head and pushed him away, so I could get in my car.

He pulled me back to him and pushed me against the side of the car. His mouth came to kiss me hard and his body pushed against mine. I found myself kissing him back. Our mouths moved hard and fast together and my body was begging me to allow him to make me feel good. I have not allowed myself any satisfaction in five years and this enticed my insides as the desire to feel this pleasure with him rose. I was stunned and unmovable. I wanted this and I wanted him. I entangled my fingers in his hair to hold him to me hard as I returned the kissing. I felt a smile grow with his kiss, "Come with me now."

"I can't." I held up my hand with the ring on it.

His mouth moved to my neck sucking and kissing as he pressed harder to me. Oh, did I want to let this happen, but why me? His hands at my sides moved to my front unbuttoning my pants, and his mouth came back to mine, "Come with me now. I will make you feel so good."

I shook my head with my eyes closed. I might have said yes if I looked into his eyes. He moved away from me and I felt his hands raise my shirt and his mouth touched my stomach with a soft kiss and then sucking. His hand wrapped around my leg to lift me from the ground, so he could continue, but making it easier for him to do standing up. I wanted to feel him so bad. How could I want this? It was so wrong on so many levels. He released my leg and came back to my face. The tears were streaming down my face, but he kissed them away. "Come with me now."

I shook my head.

"Meet me next Saturday."

I knew he would not let me go until I agreed, so I nodded. His mouth wrapped around mine and he kissed me hard and long. He finally released me, "Meet me at the end of the bar at 8 pm."

I nodded.

He kissed my lips softly again, "Promise me you will be here."

I nodded.

He slowly let me go, but whispered in my ear, "Please be here. I think I can help you."

"Help me with what?"

"I could feel your misery. I watched you tonight, and you need to relax and release your pain."

I nodded once again. He helped me into my car, because I was distraught. He leaned in and kissed me lifting my chin, so I could kiss him longer.

"Unless... you want to come with me now?"

I shook my head. He was letting me go, and I needed to leave. I didn't want to do anything I would regret latter. Shit, I would feel guilty about this anyway.

I drove home wondering how I was going to explain everything. Why I was out so much latter than bar closing. I felt the need to lie to my husband, and my children because I was betraying them.

I drove home wondering who I was. I am Joselyn Evans. I am 35 years old. I have been married for fifteen years to Ryan Evans. I have three children: Jared is 13, Terra is 11, and my baby Haden, who was our little mistake who is only 7.

I work full time at an advertising agency and I am the lead Sales Agent. I make good money, but I am married to a man that doesn't believe in working for someone else. I think it has to do more with him not being able to commit to a full work day.

Back to me and figuring out what the hell I was doing. Okay, am I happy? *No*, I told myself regretfully. Do I want to pursue this other crazy urge to kiss another man? *Yes*, as the torment engulfed me. Will I go back next Saturday? *NO! I couldn't*. But did I want to? *Oh yes*, my heart and body ached for it. I didn't want to go to bed and cry myself to sleep anymore from the loneliness that filled my heart every night. I didn't want to wake up and gasp for air from the decision I had made in my sleep to never wake up.

I glanced up in the rearview mirror to see hazel green eyes looking back at me. I am not completely unattractive, and I have always been told that I have pretty eyes and great legs. Okay, so I could stand to lose 10 to 15 lbs, but I am not fat, just a little out of shape. Quickly realizing where I could stand to lose the weight, it was all from having children. But that was worth it; I love my children.

The question is, would I give into temptation, or not? I glanced back in the rearview mirror; back to my eyes that now had a slight sparkle in them from the thought. Shaking my head as if to tell myself no, and then the decision was made; *no*, I will not tempt myself, and I would continue to live my life as if it were someone else occupying my body. I would stay dormant in the back of my mind because it was the right thing to do.

2

It was Friday and my work week was over, and I was heading home. We had games all day Saturday, so going out wasn't an option. I wanted to go... I needed to go... but my mind was made up... I would not go.

It was very hard getting through Saturday, as my mind wandered to how he would help me get rid of the pain that filled me. It was becoming noticeable and my husband, Ryan asked, "You seem to be somewhere else today."

"Yes, I have a lot of things going on at work."

"Well, if you could get your head away from yourself maybe you could help your son get his stuff together. I don't want to make a second trip because he forgot his glove or shoes."

I did pull myself away from where I was to find him saying this as he sat in the chair watching the sports channel. I laughed to myself, as I realized he was a jerk...a real jerk. It still amazed me that he was not attractive to me anymore at all, even with his perfectly fit body, those brown warm eyes, and those dimples that I used to love, slightly hidden with scruff. Every time I look at him now, all I see is him on top of her and the look on his face when he realized I was standing there stunned, watching him screw another woman in our bed. To this day, I just shutter with disgust at the thought of this happening.

I went to the game and sat in the lawn chair watching these children playing their game and goofing around having a good time. I looked down the line of lawn chairs and couples were sitting together and talking. I never really talked with Ryan anymore. There was never anything we needed to say to each other except for the occasional reference to the children. I looked back at the bench and heard the coach explaining something to a child, but it was full of positives. Why don't we do that as adults? We need to recognize the positives in others so that they can feel better about themselves. I looked at Ryan sitting there, and I realized since the incident of infidelity I haven't said anything nice. I was going to give it a try, but I would have to search for something, "Ryan, do you ever think about coaching? You use to play and you might be able to help them out a little."

"Are you kidding me? Dealing with our own kids is bad enough."

Well, that worked. *Try harder* is what I had to tell myself.

"So, are you going to work this week?"

"Why are you getting on me about this now? Can't we keep the fighting to our house?"

Well, I failed again in my attempts of dealing with *this jerk*. It was better to keep my mouth shut.

I went back to watching the game, but my mind kept drifting off to see this beautiful, muscular, young man in front of me with the bluest eyes, the high cheek bones, the slenderness of his cheeks, and the sun darkened skin. I remembered feeling the pressure of his lips to mine and my body responding, as I sat in the chair next to Ryan. I took a deep breath and moved uncomfortably in my chair. I remembered feeling the pressure of his body to mine and my desire to feel him. I moved in my seat again. I didn't want to think about him.

"What... is your problem today?"

I didn't say that I want a divorce, but my mind went to that very fact. I didn't want to be in this body anymore. I didn't want to live like this. I wanted someone to love, but my young man wasn't love either. That was passion wrapped up in an amazing body that would make me forget for a short time span of how miserable I was.

"What you're not talking to me now?"

"No, I just don't have anything to say."

"Why do you have to do this here?"

I didn't know what I was doing. I looked over at him, "Ryan, I am not doing anything, but watching the game. I made an attempt to talk to you and it didn't go well, so it would be better to not say anything at all."

"I can tell you aren't paying attention at all. Maybe, if you put yourself and your work aside, you would enjoy this more."

He was right. I needed to keep my mind off of where I wanted to be. I felt the tears flow to my eyes and I got up to walk behind home plate. I ran into a couple of moms and we talked about the kids and upcoming schedules. At least it distracted me from the pain I was feeling.

9

I noticed one mother who was younger than me, so she must have had her son at a very young age. She was vibrant and giddy. Was she happy with her life? I looked next to her and noticed Sue, another mom who I considered to be a friend, was sitting there smiling. Was she happy too? I looked back and saw a bunch of smiling faces all watching this game. Was everybody happy and it was only me that lived in a world outside my body that was so miserable that I didn't even want to get up some days?

3

I found myself lying as I left the house saying I was going to the store. I drove all the way to the Ty's bar again. I pulled in and sat there looking at this tavern. I wanted to run away from my life to my desires so bad, but I talked myself out of it. How would I explain being gone for hours and not come home with anything from the store? I turned around and went home. I walked in and dropped my purse and keys by the door and headed straight to the bed room.

"What did you get?" I heard Ryan yell from the TV room.

"Nothing, I didn't find what I was looking for."

"What were you looking for?"

"I don't know. Good night."

I went to the room and changed for bed.

Ryan came storming in, "So, what is going on?"

I covered my half naked body, because he wasn't allowed to see me this way ever again, "Out! I am getting changed."

"I used to see you all the time. What is your problem?"

"Right now... you! Please leave this room."

He walked closer to me and touched my back looking at me, "I don't know how long you expect me to pay for something that happened years ago, but I am a man and I am still your husband."

I felt like hurling something at him, and my skin crawled as my mind went back to the picture in my head of him holding her leg up with his arm and pushing to her grunting. I remembered standing there stunned into silence, as I watched him push to her again; then feeling nothing like it wasn't real. I cringed away from him with disgust and shivered it away. I think once you have experienced that, you can never get rid of the image that fills your head. I don't know if I could ever get past that.

He turned to walk out but stopped at the door, "If you want me to be satisfied here; you should think about what you are doing."

I really didn't care if he was satisfied here or not, and who did he think he was trying to turn this on me?

Obviously it was working because it did make me wonder if he did that because he felt the way I do now. The thing of it was…how could he do that under the roof of our home where our children slept? Hence… the *jerk*. If I would ever allow myself the pleasure of the young man… I would never bring him here.

I waited until all was quiet. I walked back out to where Ryan had made his bed on the couch. His eyes were closed, and I tapped his shoulder waiting for him to reply. He opened his eyes and smiled with that quirky look and dimples all showing, but it made me sick to my stomach. His dimply smile used to turn me on… now it turns me off.

"Did you change your mind?"

I glared at him, "No, but I have a question."

He sat up moving over to make room for me to sit with him. I opted for the chair away from him. I could tell he was frustrated by the way he ran his fingers through his hair with tense fingers, "What is it then? I was sleeping."

I rolled my eyes with this reaction. He was only nice when he thought he was going to get some. *What a jerk*. I would think he would be begging forgiveness every minute of every day for what he has done to me and our family. It will never be the same, ever. I didn't know how to ask him this, but I needed to know if he felt like I do now.

"When you did it…" He gave me an angry glare and I decided I needed to be more careful, so I put up my hands so he could see I wasn't looking for an argument, "…I mean…What were you feeling?"

His head popped up quickly to look me in the eyes. I could see the anger build that I was bring it up again, but then he was confused because I wasn't angry. I just wanted to know if I left him empty and hurt. He took a breath before attempting to answer me, "I didn't feel anything. It just happened and you were so busy with everything. It didn't mean anything to me."

I didn't know how to take that. "Oh… why did you do it here in our home?"

I could see a slight hint of regret in his face as he looked away from me, "I don't know. I didn't know where else to go. You were supposed to be at work."

So it was my own fault for knowing, because I got off early and came home? Great that makes me feel better. How many times has this happened when I didn't come home to catch him? This wasn't helping me at all. It only made me more angry and sick with the thought of his only regret was that he was caught. I stood up to leave and he grabbed for my hand as I passed, "Jos, what are you doing?"

I looked down at him with the deepest sadness, "I have no idea." I pulled my hand free and went back to the bedroom. It wasn't long when he knocked and entered. I was sitting up in the bed with my arms wrapped around my knees thinking about how this happened. We were, I thought, happy together with our little family.

He walked over and sat down on the bed looking at me, "What are you doing?"

"Trying to understand how and why things happen."

"So, did I answer you correctly?"

"I have no idea. Did you answer truthfully?"

"Yes, but I don't know what you want anymore."

The tears dripped out of my eyes without a warning, "I want this to have never happened, Ryan. I wanted to be in love with you for the rest of my life, Ryan. I wanted to be able to trust you, Ryan, and I don't want to feel the way I do every day of my life, Ryan."

He didn't seem remorseful at all and anger appeared in his eyes as they squinted. He got up and walked out without another word. See how I would feel the emptiness. He never says he is sorry, he never begs me forgiveness, and he never tells me that he loves me more than life any more. I curled up with a pillow and cried myself to sleep yet again. I missed my opportunity to feel happiness for what, Ryan?

I went through another week of being numb to the world. We talked about our next outing with the girls. We picked a different place each time we went out. I wanted to go back to the other place, but that opportunity was gone and I probably would never have that chance again. Saturday morning seem to go fine. Ryan let me wander off in my own world without insults today. He was quiet and he looked at me a lot. I spent most of my time watching out the window and then my mind wandered at the game. I didn't want to feel this way. I wanted to enjoy my children and the day but that beautiful young man kept coming to my mind. The more I thought about the young man the more determined I was on going tonight. I had to do this for myself. I needed to ease my pain. Maybe if I was unfaithful I could get over Ryan's infidelity and get back to feeling good about my married life. I took a shower and got dolled up to head out. I found Ryan standing in the doorway of the bathroom watching me, "Going out again?"

"Yep."

"Are you going with the girls from work?"

"Nope, that is in two weeks."

"So, where are you going?"

I turned to him, "I really don't know, but I need to get out of this house. Sometimes it's hard to be here."

"Jos, what are you saying?"

"I can't breathe here, and I need to go out and get some air."

He walked away. I kissed all the kids and went out the door. I drove to the tavern and I was there in my car sitting, staring at what I was hoping would happen. Would he show up with hopes that I would?

I wanted to go in, but my feet would not move. My mind was telling me yes, my body was telling me yes, but I still couldn't talk myself into it. I tried, boy did I try, but it still didn't feel right. I tried to give myself more time to get up the nerve. I sat there for over an hour and then drove home knowing that was not who I was. I walked in and dropped my keys and purse near the door. When I found the kids, they were all sitting there watching a movie. I smiled at my beautiful children, that I would not have if I hadn't had Ryan to begin with, "Who is up for a game or something?"

Ryan looked at me confused. The kids all jumped at the chance to play a game.

"You guys pick it out and I'll meet you in the kitchen."

I went to get changed.

Ryan knocked and walked into the bedroom. I hadn't changed yet, so I gave him the look to get out. He didn't but he came to sit down on the bed, "Jos, are you going to tell me where you went?"

"I went for a drive."

"For two hours?"

"Yep."

"Why won't you tell me?"

"One, I don't think you have the right to know anything about me anymore. Two, I did tell you. I went for a drive and I missed my kids and now I want to play with them."

"Why do you have to be this way?"

14

"What way?"

"Why do you have to be a bitch to me?"

"I wasn't the one who…"

He stopped me with an argument, "Don't start that again. I think I have paid my debt on that one."

"Really? If you saw me fucking someone in our house you would let it go?"

That pissed him off really good. He glared at me for a moment but then walked out. Good, I didn't want him around me right now.

I went to play games with my children. We laughed and played until it was 11 pm. Haden was getting tired and crabby, so I went to take him to bed. I crawled in with him and read him a story until he fell asleep. I quietly got out of his bed and went to my room. I found Ryan sleeping in the bedroom. I was insanely angry enough to throw something at him, but instead, I rushed to the head board, grabbed my pillow and the comforter from under it and stormed out the door.

Ryan sat up, "What are you doing?"

"Taking my pillow and blanket; I'll sleep on the couch."

"Jos, please come here; we need to figure this out."

"NO, there is nothing to figure out. We will never, ever, go there again."

"As the man of this house, I feel that I deserve some satisfaction."

"Yeah, at my expense."

I walked out and went to the couch. How dare he think he has any right to do that to me? He is such a *jerk*.

I fumed until my head throbbed and I finally fell asleep exhausted.

4

Monday at work we got news that our company was getting bought out. This was going to be great because now if I lost my job there was no end to my misery. The new boss would be in next Monday, and he would be doing reviews with everyone to work out who was staying and who was going. All I needed was this new stress in my life.

I took each day at a time. Ryan wasn't around for anything during the week. I had to run all the kids to their activities on my own, on top of trying to close two really big deals. I was hoping that would ensure my position with the *Buy Out*. Ryan did make it home for games on Saturday, but we didn't talk at all except for him telling me that the car was a mess; that I shouldn't let the kids eat in the car; he needed his laundry done; and I should get the dishes done if I planned on going out again.

I got it all done, and I was going out just to piss him off. I threw on a skirt and t-shirt and then headed out. I really wasn't looking for anyone or anything, but in this confused state, I found myself at the tavern. *Was I looking for something other than pissing Ryan off?* I walked in and went to the far end of the bar. I ordered a tall plain Margarita on the rocks while avoiding looking around. I asked if the bartender smoked and he slipped me a cigarette, so I tipped him really well and went out the back to where they allowed smoking. I leaned up against the wall and took the biggest drag from the cigarette. The young man was not here to tempt me. I went out just to piss off the husband, and I wasn't doing anything I would regret. I felt better already. I walked back to the end of the bar with my drink. I finished half and pushed it to the bar tender.

He walked down, "Did you want another one?"

I shook my head, "No thank you. I am done."

I felt warm air hit my ear, "Are you sure about that?"

16

I closed my eyes while my heart jumped out of my chest. He turned the stool, so I was facing him. That's when I opened my eyes again landing on the bluest eyes I had ever seen. I was instantly scared and confused. Why was I here again?

His mouth twisted into a flirtatious grin, "You came back."

The words scampered from me, "I didn't think you would be here." I was stunned that he was standing in front of me.

With a raise of only one eyebrow he asked me, "If you didn't want to see me, why did you come here?"

I realized I didn't even know his name, and why did I come here again? He didn't wait for me to answer him; he took my hand and led me to the dance floor where we danced. He held me close to him, so our bodies touched with every movement. His mouth lingered so close to mine that I felt every breath against my skin. My heart raced with excitement; my body trembled with fear, and my eyes melted from the way he looked at me.

We didn't take a break all night. When they were playing the last song, he kissed me lightly speaking into my mouth, "Come home with me."

I almost felt insulted with the thought of him thinking I was easily influenced, "No, I am married."

There was the quirky grin again, "You came here."

I decided that I should be very blunt, "That doesn't mean I came here for that."

It seemed that he understood now, because as the music ended, he took me by the hand walking with me out of the tavern. He moved behind me wrapping his strong arms around me, holding me tightly in front of him. I couldn't refuse his embrace thinking, *Oh my god did I miss the warmth of feeling wanted.* When he nibbled on my ear as we walked, I could feel the tingling in my gut. I didn't want this to end, and I still didn't know his name. We got close to my car, and he turned me to face him taking my hands in his. Instead of letting me leave, he started to walk backwards pulling me away from my car. I looked back to my car and then to him, "What are you doing? I need to go home now. This is over."

I could see fire in his eyes, and he lured me further, "You don't want it to be over." He pulled me close and kissed my neck, "Just a little longer, please."

How could I refuse this when it felt so good? I followed him reluctantly to a building that looked like a business office. All the while distracting me with kisses and nibbles to my neck, face, and lips. I was letting him pull me in further to his other world.

I pleaded for him to stop and let me go, "It's late I won't be able to explain. It will make it worse." My mouth and body were giving him mixed messages, because I kept telling him I had to leave, but my body leaned into every touch and every kiss he was giving me.

Words escaped his mouth while they were pressed to my cheek, "What worse?"

I gasped, "Everything."

His mouth moved to trace mine while luring me in further, "Okay, fifteen minutes and I will push you out the door."

The warmth of his hands tracing my back, pulling me in closer, kept me following him where he wanted. We barely made it in the door, and he was kissing me hard and pushing his body even harder to mine against a wall. I didn't even get a chance to look at where we were. One hand held me hard to him, but his chest was the only thing that was pressing against me.

I pleaded, "I have to go."

"You don't want to go, or you would have left." His mouth came to kiss my neck to distract me from thinking. It was working, because the last thing I was thinking of was… The heat of him next to me was intoxicating. I felt his hand pressing in between my legs moving upward, and then pushing my underwear to the side. I was scared and needy at the same time. The next thing I knew he was tracing himself against me. That was when I knew I wasn't going to stop him. I wanted him, and I wanted this. Yes, please I need to feel desirable, and if this is the only way to satisfy my need than I'm giving in to this.

A little bit of sanity did remain as I gasped, "Rubber."

He continued to rub against me but his hand moved away. He took my hand placing something in it. He pulled my hand using it to roll it on him. It made me feel good when I heard him moan with pleasure, as I stroked him to put the rubber on him. He was sucking and licking my lips as his mouth continued to move to mine. Our tongues entangled bringing our embrace to intensity. He rubbed against me harder looking for a way in. He gasped, "How long?"

I breathed out desperately, "Should leave now."

He begged, "No, how long has it been?"

He was getting close to pushing in me and I wanted him to. I grabbed his ass pulling him harder to me but panted, "Five."

I felt the pressure of him so close to penetrating me. His mouth opened to engulf mine but he said, "Months?" just before sucking my bottom lip into his mouth.

That was it. The warmth of him moved into me hard and deep.

I whimpered with pleasure, "Years."

It must have stunned him because he stopped instantly. He moved closer to me changing his posture. He lifted my leg gently to his waist, but then his hands came back cupping my face as he kissed my face and lips so tenderly. He made me feel cherished with his careful kisses and his soft touch, as he moved slowly to and from me. I wanted him harder, but the movements were slow and drawn out. I was panting with the warmth of him moving inside me. His slow movements were making my arousal grow. I didn't know it could feel like this, and I moaned with each push into me, even though it was slow and careful. The tears ran down my face, as I realized that what I was doing was wrong, and I was no better than Ryan. My needs were so great that I couldn't refuse him. I grabbed his shoulders as I was feeling pleasure beyond what I had ever felt. Words escaped me, "Oh... my... god."

His movement went deeper and he moved differently and this feeling was coming over me, "Oh, my... god... what are you doing?"

He pushed slower and deeper and I felt an extreme rush of pleasure as he pushed hard into me for the final time, and we both gasped in our mutual release. In between breaths he kissed my face everywhere softly tracing it with his lips leaving a trail of fire, "You okay?"

I nodded and then shook my head no. He wrapped his arms tight around my body to hold me tight. His mouth came to my ear, "Stay."

I shook my head.

"Please stay."

"I can't." I continued to shake my head.

He pulled himself from me. His hands cupped my face, his mouth embraced mine. I pushed him away, rearranging my clothing, I had to get away from this, from him, and I ran out the door. I hurried all the way to my car. He came rushing after me pushing the door to my car shut, so I couldn't get in. His hand traced down my arm, again leaving a trail of fire, "Did I do something to make you angry?"

I didn't know how to explain how I was feeling; the fear, the confusion, the guilt, and the pleasure of it all. I shook my head trying to open the door. I couldn't hold my tears in, and I couldn't really speak. I was just trying to get away from this. I wanted him, it felt wonderful, but I still felt horrible and how was I going to face my family?

"Do you feel better?"

I shook my head no. He turned me to face him kissing where the tears had fallen, "Tell me you will come back."

I needed to feel this way. I missed it so much that I knew even if I said no I knew I would be back. I didn't want him to wait for me, so I looked directly into his eyes, "No."

"But I was careful. Didn't I make you feel good?"

I nodded, but I held up my hand showing him my ring.

"Tell me your name?"

I shook my head no.

"I will settle for you coming back next Saturday, if you won't tell me your name."

"It's too soon."

"Was it that good or that bad?"

I looked up into his eyes with some relief, as they gleamed with happiness, "Both."

He gently pulled me toward the building again, as he kissed me tenderly. I could get lost so easily again, but I pulled away and made for my car. He let the door open this time, but came to squat next to me looking at me, "Why if you are married haven't you done that in five years?"

I started to cry, grabbing the steering wheel with both hands, molding to it turning my knuckles white.

Pulling his shirt up to my face he wiped the tears from my cheeks, "You don't have to tell me; just say you will come back."

I nodded closing my eyes.

"You can't drive like this you know."

I nodded grabbing his hand and kissed the palm of it. He moved to sit on the bottom edge of the door looking at me. He traced his hand along my cheek, "So much pain." He looked into my eyes searching for what I was feeling, "You will let me help you wash it all away, right?"

I wanted him to, but this was not going to help. I realized now that this was going to make the guilt more painful. He traced his hand to the back of my neck and rubbed gently. He raised his eyebrows, "You are amazing; you just don't know it anymore."

I shook my head no and he moved to get up, but leaned down to me, "Two weeks from today; same place?"

I nodded and he closed my door. I drove off quickly and cried the whole way home. I stopped a block away and wiped the black from under my eyes with my t-shirt. When I had composed myself enough, I finished my drive home. I walked in and gently set my keys and purse down in the entryway. I tiptoed up the stairs and went to my room praying Ryan wouldn't be there. He wasn't, so I grabbed my shorts and t-shirt to sleep in. I went to the bathroom and washed up as I changed. I could smell his cologne all over my body and my clothes, so I washed everywhere. Then I tucked my clothes in my arms to go to the bedroom. When I walked out, Ryan was standing there waiting for me. I didn't have anything to say, so I walked past him to the bedroom, but he followed.

"Are you going to tell me where you have been?"

I shook my head, threw the clothes in my dirty bin and crawled into bed.

I covered up and he came to sit on the bed, "You know this isn't going to help things."

I didn't say anything. My guilt was over powering my anger.

"Jos, things are getting out of control, and we need to make up and let this go."

I sat back up glaring at him, "If you caught me fucking someone in our house...would you let it go?"

"No, but I didn't love her."

"Okay, I didn't love him."

"What?"

"If you caught me fucking someone else in our house, but I said I didn't love him, would you let it go?"

"I already said no, Jos, but we can't keep going on this way. We have to do something."

"I am. I am spending as much time away from you as possible with hopes that I won't want to physically harm you."

He stood up, "Why do you have to be such a bitch about this one little thing?"

Now I was pissed, "Because it isn't one little thing; its one huge thing and a bunch of little things. Shut the door behind you."

5

I woke in a much better mood. I got up and made breakfast. I held Haden as he ate. Haden, my baby, was a skinny brown hair boy with green eyes, taking after me a little. Haden liked to be the baby soaking up all the attention he could, mischievously, get. I kissed him and hugged him a lot while he ate. I think he was getting irritated, but I didn't care he was my baby and I missed him. I was allowing myself to feel again and I was directing it all at my children.

After cleaning up from breakfast I went in Terra's room and played with her hair. She had long beautiful hair that was a mixture of Ryan's and my color. She also had my eye color of Hazel green. This little girl was very independent but yet cautious of people she didn't know. I think she was the spitting image of me at this age. She let me French braid her hair while we talked, and then we had tea with the queen. It was a formal way of saying we talked about her friends. I let her ramble on and on; enjoying everything she was sharing with me. I knew these days were limited.

Next, I moved to spend time with Jared. I lay on his bed and played video games with him. My Jared was the most adorable kid I had ever seen. He had his father's eye and hair color and his dimples. I liked that he didn't realize how cute he was yet so he didn't care that his hair was always messy, but maybe he planned it that way, because it made him even cuter. Jared has always been my quiet and private child. You could leave him in his room for hours and he would play without complaining. I probed him for information about his hopes and dreams. Being 13 he didn't want to open up much, but I got to spend time with him.

Finally at dinner time I had all three kids come help me in the kitchen. Jared was making desert, Terra was helping me while Haden did all the stirring. We were having fun working together.

When dinner was ready I sent Terra to get her dad. He came out and sat at the table with us. I don't think he liked that I was happy, and the kids were rambling on about their lives. I was just taking it all in. I felt nasty glares from Ryan all through dinner, but the kids were very talkative and I let myself be distracted by them. Somehow I had missed the point over the last two years. It was like I had been dead and only walking through the motions.

Ryan decided to be the boss again after dinner, "All of you can help your mother clean up."

I didn't say a word, but they had already given me what I needed from them today, so I slowly got the kids out of the kitchen after he moved to the TV room. My children hadn't forgotten me or that I loved them.

6

The next day heading into work I was feeling so much better that the buyout didn't bother me anymore. I knew I was the best they had, and I would continue to have a job. I hoped anyway. I walked into my office and set my things down and went out to check on the situation. No one had heard anything yet, which was a good sign to me. I asked my boss, Mr. Jenkins, when we would start the reviews.

"Well, he is set up in the conference room, but he is here to watch us for a couple of weeks, and then he will go back to the owner to discuss things and then we will get the final decisions in the fourth week."

"So, he's not our new boss?"

"No, I think he is more like a consultant. You know the type; they come in, watch everyone, they evaluate each person on their job with the company, and then they give them the ax."

I chuckled, "I think we'll be okay." I patted him on the back and went to work. I knew I had to be out-standing.

By Friday, I had three new ads and I used all three of our artists; one on each project. I even referred two more clients to my co-workers. My happiness was showing in my work.

Saturday, I went to Jared's game cheering the whole time. Of course I got the terminology wrong.

"So how many points do we have?"

Ryan was irritated, "You mean runs? We have eight."

Jared was up to bat and I yelled out, "Aim for the sky baby."

Ryan scolded me, "We don't want him to hit it high. We want a line drive."

"How many periods do we have left."

24

I think Ryan was completely aghast with this last one, "You mean innings. Do you even watch the game or listen to anyone?"

He knocked me off my high, but I was still okay. It wasn't until he was telling the kids how many baseball blunders I had made, that I felt stupid. I went back to my own world, because they all laughed at my expense even though it wasn't the kid's fault. I was trying to not let it get to me, but it did.

7

I started my week again with the same success that I had last week. I had two more signed by Wednesday. I guess the new guy wanted to meet me, so Mr. Jenkins came to my office.

"Joselyn, Mr. Reynolds would like to meet with you."

I looked up at Mr. Jenkins. He was a heavier set man in his late 50's. Of course nobody really knew his age. He didn't like people knowing that fact. We even had a hard time finding out his birthday but I was able to sweet talk him into sharing that info one afternoon. He was my substitute father and had seen me through my troubles at home. I did feel like we were family.

"But I thought he was just watching these two weeks."

"Let's go."

I got up and tucked a few things away. I followed him to the conference room and I was sure he was going to congratulate me on what a great job I was doing. I had to convince myself this, because I couldn't handle any negative right now. I was doing so well.

We walked in and Mr. Reynolds had his back to us talking on a cell phone. He was telling the person on the other end to buy this and sell that. He must have been working on trades or something by the sound of it. We stood there waiting and I noticed, even though he was sitting, that he was fairly tall with a very nice suit on. He held his posture very strong as he spoke on the phone. He turned in his chair not looking at us. I was on the other side of a very long table, but I was able to make out that he had very dark brown, not quiet black, hair and the skin of someone touched by the sun daily. It seemed like I had met him before. I watched him move to look through some papers and then he glanced up with a quick smile holding up one finger to put us off. I realized where I had seen him before. He was the amazing young man I had...SHIT. I thought I was going to be sick on the spot.

I turned to Mr. Jenkins, "I must have eaten something bad for lunch. I will have to do this later." I almost ran from the room heading straight for my office wondering what I should do. My heart pushed against my chest, my hands trembled, and I was close to a full blown panic attack while my mind was searching for what I could possibly do. I finally started to write my letter of resignation. What else could I do?

At the end of the day my heart ached with the thought of what I was about to do. I peeked out of my office and check to see if the coast was clear. I went to Mr. Jenkins office and knocked, but let myself in without waiting for a reply. I closed the blinds and shut the door. He watched me with suspicion as I walked to his desk. I took a deep breath and put the paper on his desk pushing it towards him.

"What is this?"

"It's my two week notice."

"Why? I don't think he was letting you go today."

"Well, why wait. It will be easier for me to find a job if I quit."

"But, that isn't what this was about."

"I just think it would be better this way."

He shook his head and pushed it back to me, "I am not accepting this."

I pushed it back to him pleading, "You don't understand. You have to accept this."

He sat back in his chair, "Is there something that bothered you today, about him?"

"Yes, but please don't say anything. I just need to move on now."

His face was grimacing while he shook his head no and finally pushed it back to me again, "Joselyn, you have been here with me for 14 years. I have dealt with you and your child bearing years. You are like a daughter to me." I felt the deep glare like he was searching, "Here is the deal; I won't take that now, wait till Friday and if you still feel the same way I will bring it to Mr. Reynolds myself."

I took the letter back and nodded. I walked back to the door and opened it. I looked out first to make sure the coast was clear.

"Joselyn, what is wrong with you today?"

I looked back and shook my head. I went out the door and didn't work the rest of the day. My mind kept going back to that night and how amazing it felt to be with him. How forward he was and confident that I

27

would want him that he pushed me into allowing myself to have that with him. The way he pushed to me so gently after he knew it had been awhile made me want him more. How he pleaded with me to say I would be back…Oh my god I am suppose to meet him this Saturday. I couldn't have him ever again. The confusion of how I felt made the tears well up in my eyes. I was never going to see him again and I would never feel that way again. I was destined to be miserable for the rest of my life. How was I ever going to make it? I would go back to that emptiness that engulfed my every being.

At the end of the day I peeked out and quickly made my way to the elevator. There were a few of us waiting, so when the door opened I pushed my way to the back. Someone caught the door as it was closing, so it opened again. Mr. Jenkins and Mr., Oh my god, Reynolds came in. They were discussing something and I wanted to die. I pulled out a folder and pretended to read something holding it up. The doors open and I made my way to the furthest side to follow out.

Mr. Jenkin's said, "Oh, you wanted to meet Joselyn, she is right here. Joselyn come here, Mr. Reynolds would like to meet you." I shook his hand that he had extended, but he didn't look up to see me.

I let go, "Sorry, I am in a hurry. Jared has a game tonight." I turned and made a straight line for the door. I got to my car and got in. I adjusted the rearview mirror so that I could check to see if I was still holding it together. I saw the panic in my eyes while my heart was out of control. I glanced back to see the two of them walk out and stand there talking. I backed out and put it in drive to hurry to get away from this unbelievable situation. I looked in my rear view mirror to see if they were watching and I notice Mr. Reynolds was watching me drive away. Shit, he knows my car. Would he figure it out before Friday?

I called in on Thursday. I stayed in bed to let myself fall into my emptiness. I couldn't breathe as I thought about how bad this was going to be. I had cheated on my husband with this beautiful man; that was coming into the company I worked for, chop it to pieces, and now the worst part was everything was going to come out. I didn't' know if I could handle anymore.

Ryan came in around noon, "Jos, are you okay?"

"No."

"Can I get you something?"

"No."

"You're not checking on me are you?"

I glared at him, "No." Why would he ask that? I am laying here in bed being miserable and it was about him again, "Should I be?"

"Jos, no, I told you it was over, I ended it."

"I thought it was one night?"

"Yeah, but I ended it that night."

It was obvious that he had done this more than once, "Did you do that more than the one time?"

He walked out without replying to me. Shit can my life get any worse?

8

Even though I was quitting I couldn't stay home with him here. I had a passion of hate for Ryan, and now I hated my life. I went to work just so I wouldn't have to be here. To my disappointment I completed six more sales, and to make things worse I had contacts from four more companies. I got everything organized and walked into Mr. Jenkins office putting the files to the four leads in one pile. My six completed sales folders in another and the letter in the middle. He looked up at me shaking his head.

"You promised you said you would take this if I still feel this way today, so I am done in two weeks."

He wasn't happy about it but accepted it. I wasn't careful about leaving because my thoughts were not here. I was out in left field wondering what I was going to do now.

I went home with a new depression that I couldn't even explain to myself. I watched TV with the children until Haden was asleep in my arms. I got up pushing him to stand, so I could lead him to the bedroom. I looked at Ryan and told him, "I quit my job. I will be done in two weeks. We will have to figure something else out."

I walked away guiding Haden to his room. I tucked him in and kissed his forehead. I went to my room where Ryan was waiting for me. I took my stuff to the bathroom to change and walked back in crawling into bed.

"You aren't going to explain?"

"I have nothing to explain. We had a buyout and I couldn't stay."

"Did they fire you?"

"No. I quit."

"Don't you think we should have discussed this?"

"No, it's my job."

"Yes, but we can't afford the house without it."

"Okay."

"What do you mean okay. Didn't you think about the children when you quit?"

"Yes, I think of them all the time. But this time I had to do this for me."

"You need to go back and tell them you were mistaken."

"NO!"

"You should have asked me what I thought."

"Did you ask me what I would think about you fucking someone in our house?"

"Jos, you are such a bitch. Why do you have to bring that up? It was a long time ago and it is time to let it go."

"You should have let it go before it happened."

He got up and went to walk out, but stopped at the door, "You are so messed up right now that I feel like I don't even know who you are anymore. You might want to have your head checked because I think you are losing it."

I didn't say anything and he walked away; I was losing it. I got up and dug through my dirty laundry looking for the clothes that had that amazing young man's scent, oh yeah… Mr. Reynolds, but then I remembered it was two weeks ago. I had already washed them. I went back to bed and cried myself to sleep.

The next day was more of the same. I was lost again wondering how I was going to live through this. I didn't want to feel this way again, because I had lost so much time, but what else could I do? I lay around as my children tried to coax me back into being playful and giving them attention, but I couldn't shake this feeling. I ended up in my room crying for most of the day. Numb was better than this. As the night grew closer, so did the feeling of not ever being touché, never kissed, and never feel desired again. It was breaking my heart as I watched the digits on the clock changed. Each number that changed tore a piece of my heart out and ripped it to shreds.

I don't know where the next week went. I ended up taking back the four sales leads and completing them. I walked around getting closer to feeling numb. I was getting back into that state of mind of not having a mind or body. The emptiness was definitely back, but I worried about

31

seeing Mr. Reynolds, the man that I lost control with. How was I going to handle seeing him and having him know who I was?

9

It was my turn to meet with Mr. Reynolds; even though I was quitting, Mr. Jenkins insisted saying, "They have an offer and I don't think you want to pass this up."

I didn't want to have to explain my actions to anyone, so I went along with this whole charade. Mr. Jenkins walked in with me, and I was trembling not knowing how I would feel once he looked at me with those insanely beautiful blue eyes. Thankfully, he was busy talking on that stupid cell phone again. He was turned away from us for privacy, holding on to the file. He was asking the person on the phone if the deal was set up, so he could make an offer. I watched his hand as it held the file strongly, but yet careful to not bend the edge. It made me remember how they felt as they traced down my side. NO, stop it. Don't get caught up in wanting him, not now, and not ever again. It was different now that I knew who he was, and soon he would know me more than a person he had hot sex with from a bar.

He hung up the phone, turning around, moving to stand up with his hand extended to me, "Mrs. Evans." He stopped when he reached my face with a stunned look. I reached out shaking his hand saying his name, "Mr. Reynolds." He stood there staring at me speechless. I didn't know what to do and I gave him a little grin, pulled my hand away, and then the smile fell from my face. He let his hand fall, but didn't say or do anything. I had no idea what Mr. Jenkins was thinking, because I only saw this hot young man standing in front of me, and all I could think about was how badly I wanted to feel that body pressed against mine, those lips luring me deeper into a kiss, and the warmth of him in me.

I needed to stop thinking this way right now. I was at work, and things were different now. To my relief Mr. Jenkins spoke up. "Well... I see... Have you two met before today?"

Mr. Reynolds smiled and looked very guilty, but he spoke softly, like the whisper spoken to me before in my ear, "Not formally."

"Okay… Well this is Joselyn Evans, Joselyn this is Mr. Reynolds."

He was startled by the mention of my name and grinned more, "I think I need to make this offer in private…" He was staring into my eyes making me forget that we weren't alone, "If you wouldn't mind Mr. Jenkins…"

I don't know if it was my imagination, but when he took his eyes off me and set the file on the desk, he traced his hand over it like he was touching me. My body shivered with excitement. *Stop it Joselyn; don't think about it.*

"Of course, excuse me than." Mr. Jenkins walked out closing the door.

Mr. Reynold's eyes came back to mine, "Have a seat, Joselyn." It sounded more like he was embracing the name than what he was saying. He sat back down and put his pen to his mouth and leaned back in the chair staring at me. I was getting really nervous, and my stomach was doing flips inside me. A smile came back to his face as he spoke, "Joselyn, hummm."

I sat there not knowing what to do. I had to stay on task, not get distracted by my thoughts, so I finally asked, "You have an offer?"

He fumbled forward to the file, and opened it, pulling out a single piece of paper, looking at it smiling. He glanced back at me, but laid it down on the desk turning it to face me. Finally, he pushed it forward, "This was written before I knew who you were, so you really need to take it for what it is, Okay?" He sat forward, pushing it to me and leaned on the table with his elbow and moved his hand to rest his chin on it, again staring at me, "I think we should go to dinner to discuss the offer."

I looked up at him, as I tried to pull it to me, but he wasn't letting it go. I shook my head no and then he let go of it. I pulled it in front of my face to avoid his gaze.

He spoke again, "Joselyn…it's a perfect name for you."

I lowered the paper to see him still in awe as he stared at me. I shook my head and went back to the paper but asked, "How so?"

"It's a beautiful name. It fits you."

My heart was racing, and I could feel my blood boiling with desire under my skin.

"Come to dinner with me. We can go over it in great detail."

34

I didn't look at him, and I knew this was going to be a terrible mistake, "I can't. My son has a game tonight."

"You have a son?"

I looked up at him quickly and nodded and went back to the paper. I needed to concentrate on what it said, instead of those naughty thoughts that were running through my mind. I took a deep breath and read the agreement. They were raising my salary, and giving me bonuses based on my clients. It would mean a lot more money than I was getting now. Oh, shit, I can't quit. I would be able to pay for everything myself if Ryan and I couldn't work through our problems. Shit, I didn't want to work through them. I didn't want him to ever touch me again.

I looked back at him, "Mr. Reynolds?"

He laughed, "Tyler." Once he said his name and our eyes met, I forgot what it was that I was going to say. He was amused that he had this effect on me so he asked, "Will that work for you?"

I looked down at the paper and peeked back over the paper at him nodding.

"So, you are staying?"

I nodded again.

"Good, we should celebrate by having dinner."

I laughed with a sigh, and shook my head no, peaking back at him over the paper.

His eyes gleamed with flirtation, "Why don't you have your husband take your son?"

Quickly I moved my eyes back to the offer avoiding his, "He is away with work for a couple of days."

Tyler stood up and moved to the windows closing the blinds.

I shook my head, "You shouldn't do that."

"Why? We need some privacy."

I shook my head no, but he continued. He walked back over to my side of the table; he leaned back against it in front of me. He crossed his legs and then his arms across his chest. He looked so strong and comforting; I wanted to stand up and move to him, but I couldn't. His brows furrowed with a question as he asked, "You didn't come back on Saturday?"

I shook my head trying to avoid looking at him, because every time I so much as glanced at this man, I wanted him. I noticed the way his pants fell along his legs and my body hungrily ached to feel them against mine. Oh shit, this is going to be very hard.

35

His voice was softer, "Why didn't you come?"

The sound of hurt in his voice broke my heart, but he needed to know what I felt, "It isn't right."

I peaked up at him and saw a small grin turn the corners of his mouth upward, "You knew it was me, here." I noticed his eyes squint as he asked this, which made looking directly at him easier. Those blue eyes were covered by those long dark eyelashes. Oops, *THEY* did it to me too, so I nodded without saying a word.

"How many kids do you have?"

I was caught off guard with the change in subjects, "Three, why?"

"It helps me to understand why you avoid this... me."

All I could do is shake my head with disbelief. I couldn't believe that he still felt this way.

"Trying to get you to open up is as hard here as it is elsewhere."

I laughed a little silently.

I handed the sheet back to him, "This is an amazing offer, but under the circumstances I wouldn't feel right about it."

He became more business like, "Why? This was an offer based on your work. I didn't know it was you, or I would have asked for more."

I shook my head with disbelief.

"This will help you...to make some changes that you need to make." The sound of his voice was of concern. What was he asking me? Was he asking if I would leave my husband? I nodded because that is exactly what went through my mind.

"With this job you will have to spend a lot of time with me."

Worry filled me as I looked up at him, "This is wrong, and I can't do this."

I couldn't tell if he was angry, "This, what do you mean this? Work here with me or see me on the weekends, because I know you don't show up when you promise," but then that flirty little grin came back.

I gazed into those eyes that I longed for, "All of it. It's all wrong, and I feel awful about it."

His face went cold as he got up and moved back to the other side of the table, "When is your husband going to be home?"

"In a couple of days," I was so lying to him. He was probably home and screwing another woman while we sat here.

"Okay, get through the weekend, and I have a very important client coming in on Monday. I am taking them to dinner, and I want you to do the pitch for me. I will have the information sent to your office, and you will have a few days to prepare. How does that sound?"

He was back to business so quickly. Was he never going to touch me again? I didn't want to do anything wrong, but I really, really needed to feel his touch. That touch washed all the sadness away. I made my point, and he was going to try to be professional, so I had to try too. I stood up and walked to the door. I stopped just short of it and looked back to say something, but he was staring in a lustful way, and he made me smile. I forgot what I wanted to say, as I looked into those eyes.

He winked at me, "It will work out. Trust me."

I shook my head wondering how this was going to work out, but he did make me smile. I went out the door and straight to my office. Mr. Jenkins came running in, "So, how did it go?"

I looked up at him regretfully, "I guess I am staying."

He gave the air a punch with satisfaction, "I like this Tyler. He hasn't fired anyone. He has found the positive in each person, and he is going to try to work it out, to use those positives and make improvements. No one has lost their job yet."

I laughed to myself. He was an amazing lover and a decent person. Where did he come from, and why didn't he have a girlfriend? Shit, maybe he does, or maybe he is married and miserable like me.

10

On Monday he came into my office. It was the first time I had seen him since our meeting. He was smiling as he walked over, sat on my desk off to the side, and looked down at me, "Are you ready?"

I glanced up at him trying to avoid the wanting, so I handed him the file. He was pleased, "Did you work it out at home, so you could go to dinner?"

I nodded with a slight grin. He started for the door, but grabbed my coat holding it out for me, "Let's go. I don't want to keep them waiting."

I walked over, and he helped me get my coat on. We walked side by side to the elevator. Everyone didn't look at us at all. This was a normal site, but I was uncomfortable thinking how I would like him to be nibbling my ear right now. There was a limo waiting for us at the front door. He was grinning, as he opened the door for me. I got in and he followed, but he sat opposite of me with this great smile on his face, "You look amazing."

I shook my head and looked out the window avoiding everything about him. I needed to get in the right frame of mind to present the offer.

"Are you nervous?"

I was trying to clear my head, so I just nodded.

"You don't talk a whole lot."

I was finding it difficult to concentrate with all his comments and questions. I shook my head laughing with a sigh.

"Do you want to practice on me?"

THAT got my attention, and I gave him a condescending look.

He laughed, "Okay, I know you're the best."

He moved to the seat next to me and took my hand in his. There was an instant burning with his touch, but I had to refuse it, so I didn't turn to him.

"So, tell me about your kids."

I shook my head no, "My mind is on this."

He nodded, "Okay… When can you get away on a Saturday?"

I turned to him with my eyes wide open to meet his, "You said this would work out."

"I am trying to make it work, but you don't talk much. It makes me nervous. I don't know what you are thinking."

"That this is wrong, very wrong, and I can't do *that* anymore."

He ignored me about this being wrong and brought my hand to his mouth. My skin burned with desire where his lips touched.

"Okay."

It broke my heart that he was giving up so easily. I didn't want him to back off. I wanted him to be forceful, so I couldn't refuse him. At least he continued to hold my hand and traced his fingers over it soothing me.

I looked back out the window, trying to get my pitch in order in my head. I was surprised that the warmth of his body sitting next to me was actually calming to me.

We pulled up, and he moved to get out first, and then he gave me his hand to assist me out of the car. When I stood up he leaned to me, "You have amazing calves."

I rolled my eyes and shook my head, as I let go of his hand to walk in. It didn't feel like he was giving up, maybe he was just giving me a little room.

We walked into the establishment; the employees there already knew Mr. Reynolds, and they led us back to his usual table. The clients were already there. He introduced me to them. We sat down and had drinks and dinner. When it came time for the presentation, the waiters came over and cleared the whole table of everything, even our drinks. I looked at Tyler and then back at the clients, worried how I was going to do this when he made me absolutely distraught with desire, "Could you excuse us for one minute?"

Tyler stood up right away looking at me nervously. I got up and walked over to the bar with him following asking questions, "What? Is there something wrong?"

He was looking at me like I was going to bail on him, but I tried to sooth his worry with a gentle smile and a caring look into those eyes, "If I am going to do this...you need to stay here."

"What? Why?"

I didn't want to tell him, but I closed my eyes and let the words fall from my lips, "You make me nervous."

I opened my eyes to see how he took that, and he was grinning from ear to ear, "I make you nervous?"

I gave him my most pleading look while nodding.

He laughed with a sigh, "Okay. I will stay here. Go get them."

I walked back to the table taking long slow breaths. I got to the point right away and they liked everything. They only had a few questions, and we went over them. Their concerns were justified, but I persuaded them in the end. When everything was finished, I gestured for Tyler to come back to the table. He walked eagerly over to the table and sat down.

I handed him my notes, "These are the concerns, and these were my suggestions. If you wouldn't mind figuring them out, I am going to use the powder room."

I got up and so did all of them. It was gentlemanly to get up from the table when a lady gets up. I walked away and went to the bathroom, putting my hands on the counter to support myself. I had killed another presentation, but this one was huge. It was a lot bigger than anything I had handled before. It would gross me about ten thousand dollars. My hands were shaking, and I could hardly breathe. Just when I was gaining my composure, I heard the door open. I stood up composing myself; I took one look in the mirror for a final check, and he was standing behind me with his mouth at my shoulder.

I was floored, "Don't you have any boundaries?"

I heard his whisper, "You are amazing. I want to be there for the next one."

"You didn't hear anything. Why do you think I am amazing?"

His face came up to meet my gaze in the mirror, "I watched you. You were different than I see you here."

A tear escaped me and ran down my cheek. He was right, that was someone else out there, not me. I was a failure at my marriage, at parenting, and in my life. How could I do that when I can't even control my own life? Maybe, because it *'wasn't me'*. I was empty with nothing to lose out there. It didn't matter what they said or did because it wasn't me.

He took my hand in his and lifted it to his mouth, so I turned to him. He kissed it lightly, "Can I stay for the next one?"

I shook my head no, 'You still make me nervous."

"Why?"

"Because of how I feel when you are that close to me."

He looked deep into my eyes with confusion, "I want to show you something."

Before I knew what was happening, he was pulling me from the bathroom walking backwards leading me by taking both my hands. I followed, but I was afraid that I would feel again. I didn't want to feel because it was painful.

He led me down a hallway, down three steps to an elevator. He pushed the button not taking his eyes from mine. If I asked where we were going would I make him stop? Would I walk away? I didn't want to make myself do those things, so I didn't ask. We got on the elevator and his eyes stayed connected with mine. He must have known if we broke the connection I would run away. The elevator doors opened as he pulled me into a studio. His body came to mine quickly pushing me against the wall. His hands were pulling up my skirt fast and pushing down my underwear, as his open mouth pressed against my neck sucking and kissing it with aching intensity. I was pushing his jacket from him and he shook free from it. His hands were undoing his pants while his chest pressed against me holding me there. Our tongues entangled with delight like a force of nature. He took himself in his hand and rubbed against me, taking my breath away. I gasped, "Rubber."

I felt him put something in my hand, but this time left it up to me to do on my own. His hands moved back to my face cupping it while he pulled me into an impassioned kiss with his tongue. I needed him desperately now, so I rolled it on to him myself. I caressed him a little more than I needed to, and he moaned with pleasure. His mouth moved searching for a new place to kiss. I tilted my head back while he made his way down to my neck again. I guided him to me and rubbed him against me until he was in the right spot. He pushed hard to me and I gasped. Again, in an instant, his actions became incredibly tender and gentle as he cupped my face in his hands, to kiss me softly moving his lips around mine, and in between mine, as he pushed slowly into me more and slowly back out with blissful intimacy.

41

As he moved to and from me his hands moved to undress me more. He unzipped the skirt that I had on. He was undoing the buttons on my blouse and was pulling it from my body. I felt the pleasure coming quickly because of his slow erotic movements; I moaned with pleasure as the all-consuming climax came over me. He pushed hard to me to intensify it. When he was sure I had complete pleasure from him, he pulled from me. He slid the skirt down, while pushing my blouse from me, letting it all fall to the floor. He pushed off his shoes and kicked free from his pants and wrapped his arm around me walking backwards. His kissing continued to keep me distracted from what he was doing. He turned us around and lowered me. I felt a bed underneath me, as he let go of me. He finished taking off his shirt, and this amazing body glistened in the light coming in from the windows. He knelt down in front of me looking at me in the eyes. I couldn't help thinking, *what the hell am I doing?* I blinked and realized where I was and what I was doing. I had to leave, but I felt my shoes coming off. He moved between my legs and traced his hands up the inside of my thighs until he reached my underwear. He slowly traced his hands around until he could pull them from me. I lifted a little to allow him to pull them from me. I became self conscious of my body. I was a mother of three, so I had extra baggage and sagging here and there. He didn't seem to notice how out of shape I was. He lifted my chin to look at him, and he kissed my mouth softly as his tongue moved to lick at my lips, so I would kiss him. I was gone again and I would allow him anything because of how good I was feeling.

He lowered me back tracing my stomach with his fingers until he could move so that his mouth could take over taunting me. His mouth remained open on my skin while he traced my stomach back and forth sucking where he lingered. Slowly moving up my body, his tongue glided over me. It didn't take very long before I felt him against me again. My body craved what he had and rose to meet him. How I managed to stay grounded enough to pant out, "rubber!" again, amazed me.

His kisses stopped when his eyes found mine. A slight grin came to his face and then filled with determination, "It's still good. I didn't, but I will now."

He pushed to me hard and deep touching god knows what. He pulled out but lowered his body to mine as he pushed in again. I had to open my mouth to breath, and it took my breath every time he pushed to me. Every bad thought I had, every bad feeling I felt, was all sliding away with every push he made to me. He would rotate as he moved deeper,

deeper until the pleasure came again. I moaned with every movement he made. A smile came to his face, as he held mine to look at me, "You are easy to please."

I closed my eyes and tucked my face into him. He pulled my face back to his. He was full of anger, "Don't do that. You are amazing. Let me love you." He was more determined now and his pushes got harder and deeper. He pulled my leg up around him. I didn't realize he was moving us, so I was on top of him. My body was in complete control of me now, and I moved to him in long slow strokes. I could feel the strength of his hands on my hips as he pulled me harder to him. I was lost in the pleasure of him, so when I heard him moan I had to open my eyes. I wanted to know if this was bringing him as much pleasure as it was giving me. It looked painful for him. His forehead was creased, his eyes shut tightly, and every muscle taunt. This felt so good for me, but if he was in pain I had to stop. I slowed more and he moaned, but his hands pulled me harder to him, as his eyes opened to find me. Quickly he sat up, wrapping his arms around me and turned me over to my back again. His movements were so fast and hard now that I couldn't keep up with him. He pulled my legs up higher, so that he could go deeper, but my body tilted allowing him full access into the depths of pleasure. His breath came out in gasps in between holding his breath. I wanted to see his face when he released, but where he was reaching inside of me brought a new ecstasy. I cried out with satisfaction when his body fell to mine and he moaned out, "Oh, shit, Joselyn." After catching his breath for a couple of minutes, his mouth came back to mine swiftly kissing my face everywhere until he found my mouth. I felt him pull from me, but it was only a second to get rid of the condom, and then I felt the heartbeat of his penis rubbing the folds of me. I was lost in him; I could have stayed here for eternity.

He spoke softly to my lips, "I want to feel you... your warmth around me."

"I can't, I'm not taking anything."

He put his face to my shoulder and pressed against the front of me, "You are so warm and so luring for me."

"But I can't."

He didn't push the issue but continued to press against me with no movement. He was trying to get his breathing in control. He kissed my cheek softly and whispered, "I think you like the way this feels?"

I nodded and tucked my face into him, but my emotions were out of control, as the tears ran from my eyes. I traced his back up and down with my finger tips, because I didn't want him to think that I was crying because of him. Every inch of his body was amazing to touch.

I felt his breath again, "Stay with me tonight."

It was like a slap of reality to my face. I tried to push him away. I had to go. He was pulling me to remain under him, "NO, I didn't mean to remind you. Please, just stay with me here."

I was shaking my head and pushed harder until he let go. I moved to the end of the bed and started putting things back on in a panic. What the hell was I doing? He moved and wrapped his arms around me, "I will take you back to the office for your car. I am sorry."

He got up and threw on jeans and a t-shirt. I was trying to get dressed, and he walked up wrapping his arms around me helping me button up my top. His mouth traced my neck with his breath, "Did I hurt you?"

I shook my head, and he turned me to him holding me close, "I'm sorry. This hurts you?"

I traced my hand along his face and spoke softly, "It's wrong and I am wrong."

He shook his head, "No, I pushed you. It's my fault."

He let go when I was dressed, and we went down without touching. We got out the front door, and he waved for the limo. We got in and he told the driver the office address and then closed the glass. He took my hand in his and brought it to his mouth kissing it lightly. He pulled me to him and I rested my head on his chest.

"You amaze me."

I didn't say anything.

"Two amazing woman in one body; two completely different people, why?"

I didn't have an answer for him so I sat quietly. He lifted my chin to look at him, "I need you to talk to me. I need to understand which one is here with me. I need that one to dominate you."

The tears traced down my face again. He wiped the tears away, "So much pain. It hurts me to see this."

I pulled my face away and closed my eyes. He held me tight until we got back to the office. They drove me to my car, and he got out opening my car door, "Are you sure you want to go home?"

I shook my head no, got in my car, and gave him a regretful grin. He smiled and closed my door giving me a slight wave as I pulled away.

I looked in the mirror as I pulled up to the house. I was a complete mess. I re-applied my lipstick and wiped my face. If he asked; I was crying from happiness of how well it went. No, because then he would really not want to leave. I walked in and set my keys and purse down. I went to the bathroom undetected. I washed myself up the best that I could. I looked in the mirror and I finally recognized the face looking back at me. I smiled softly. There was someone looking back at me that felt desirable. I shook my head and grinned with guilt. I could feel again. I walked out, and Ryan was there to remind me that I wasn't allowed to feel good. I smiled at him and walked pass him. I peeked into Jared's room to look at him. Then I went to Terra's room. She was sleeping like a princess. I went to Haden's last. He was my baby, so I walked all the way in and kissed his forehead.

I traced my fingers over his forehead and he whispered, "Mommy you're home."

"Yes, baby, I am home. I love you."

"Are you better?"

"I am so much better. I love you, and I will see you in the morning."

"I love you mommy."

I started to tear up and bent down to hug him as tight as I could. Ryan came to the door and smiled at me holding my baby. I kissed Haden while I wrapped the blankets around him to tuck him back in. I walked back out and Ryan smiled at me as I walked by. I went to my room and pulled out what I was going to sleep in, but he followed me into the room.

"I take it that it went good?"

I nodded, "It took longer than I was expecting."

"So, you are keeping your job?"

I shrugged my shoulders and went to leave for the bathroom. He stepped in front of me, "I'll leave, Jos. I just wanted to make sure it went okay."

I smiled, "It went fine. If I continue to work there I may have to work late some nights. After tonight he may want me to close more deals."

Ryan's eyes glared, "He?"

"My new..." I had to think about this. He wasn't really my boss, because he was sent in to evaluate, but then why did he have a client that

45

I would have to present too? I guess this will have to do, "... boss, Mr. Reynolds."

He gave me a confusing look, "So, he went with you?"

"Yeah, it was his deal. I just pitched it and closed it, but he only went to dinner with us to introduce us. I pitched it alone."

"Well, that's good. Have a good night, Jos."

I was confused. Why was he being nice to me? He walked out closing the door behind him. I sat down staring at the door. Even if we could get along for the kids, I knew I would never be able to be with him sexually. The picture of him came to my mind once again; hovering over her as he pushed to her with that grunting sound, her little whimper as he pushed deeper, and then the look of fear as he glanced over at me standing there watching completely stunned into silence. I remember the feeling wash through me that this couldn't actually be happening.

11

It was only Monday and I had a long week ahead of me. Tuesdays and Thursdays were game day for Jared, and now Haden and Terra were starting to play on Mondays and Wednesday. I would have to go all week before I would get a night off.

The next day at work I was nervous about seeing Tyler. We got carried away again, and that made me uncomfortable. I was sleeping with this breath taking man that was here to handle the buyout. At least it happened before I started working with him. I was very busy setting up new clients presentations. I went down to work with the art crew. I spent hours telling them what I wanted.

When I got back to my office Mr. Jenkins was waiting for me outside of my office very concerned, "Joselyn, what happen last night?"

I was confused by the worry in his voice, "It went great."

"Then why is he in your office not looking happy?"

That didn't make sense to me, and the thought of it made me cringe, "It will be okay. I'll just go in and see what he wants."

Taking in a deep breath I walked in. He was making himself at home at my desk and tilting back in my chair.

I really didn't like that he was that comfortable in my chair. I walked over to the desk and looked down at him, "What are you doing?"

I loved the way he smiled. His teeth were very white, and it seemed to make his skin look even darker. I wanted to melt when he answered me with, "I am trying to figure you out, because you are driving me crazy."

I felt like a scolding mother when I hushed him gesturing to door, "You can't say stuff like that."

I felt his hand touch mine as if to calm me, "I was leaving you a note."

I caved but only to flirt with him a little, "Do I get my desk back?"

Because I flirted, he pushed further, "Or you could come over here."

I felt this sensation of desire from my gut rise and tingle through my whole body. I shivered a little. He moved to get up and moved very closely around me, whispering in my ear, "Look in your desk."

What was he talking about? I sat down and opened my desk. There was a note and a plain white box underneath it. I tried to stay calm, as I read the note:

Thank you for last night.
This is for selfish reasons. I may need you for a deal on short notice.
Please accept this as a token of my appreciation for your hard work.
Tyler

I pulled out the box, and I looked back up at him.

He must have seen something in my face that told him that this was too much, and he retracted a little, "It's not what you think. I just want to be able to get a hold of you for work."

Now I was curious, as I opened it. I pulled it out and held it up, as I gave him that disapproving glare, "A cell phone?"

"Now, you can't say no. It's registered to the company, and all the phone numbers are by last name. I took it upon myself to enter phone numbers of your co-workers on it."

I felt my motherly look, "And yours?"

"I am here to make things run better."

I couldn't believe it and shook my head, "There will have to be rules." I glanced back up at him.

He was more businesslike, "Okay, we should discuss them now." He was making his way to the door and then closed it. I could see the flirty smile raise the corners of his mouth while he closed the blinds. I raised my eyebrows watching him, while trying to hold back a giggle.

He whispered, "Have you ever done it in the office?"

I tried to play stupid with his little venture, "Did what?"

He knew I understood what he was asking and made his way back to me with a determined grin. Playing it cool, I crossed my legs and leaned back in the chair, but I was getting hot just watching him walk towards me. He made his way behind me pulling the chair back. I tried to keep my eyes on him, as he moved back around in front of me, leaning against my desk in front of me. This was like a challenge of who would look away first; the pulse in my veins was heated; my skin felt moist, as my body warmed, and my mouth was watering.

Tyler chuckled when I gave up looking away, "I had hopes that time."

He was purposely trying to make me uncomfortable, so I was going to be stern, "Rules."

"Okay. If I need to talk to you, I can call you."

"About business."

He glared, "If I need you, I will call you."

"About business."

"Joselyn, I am trying to make this work."

"If you call when I am with my children it has to be about work."

He nodded, "What else?"

I held back my happiness from showing on my face, "That is my only rule."

His face brightened, "That is the only one?"

"Yes. I feel bad enough that I am going to be busier than normal, and I finally am getting back to…" Oops, don't really want to talk about how I feel; that is very personal, and this wasn't personal time.

Urging he begged, "Tell me."

Slowly I set the phone down trying to buy myself some time to get control of my feelings. He moved away from me to the chair on the other side of the desk, "How am I supposed to get to know you if you won't talk to me. Please tell me?"

How could I tell him that he made me feel again, when those feelings were causing a lump in my throat and tears in my eyes?

"Have I upset you again?"

I shook my head. I would beg him to drop it if I could talk, but I couldn't.

"Joselyn, please, I hate that you are in so much pain."

I swallowed and shook my head.

"How about I don't call you unless we have an emergency, and we'll talk about it the next time we are alone, but away from here. Will you tell me then?"

I nodded but blurted out, "It's hard for me." I wanted to know if he understood without me explaining, but all I could see was concern on his face.

He got up and pushed a file in front of me, "Let me know what you think about that one. I will check on you in a couple of days. Will that be enough time?" He didn't wait for me to reply. He was heading for the door, giving me space.

I didn't want him to go, "Tyler?"

He stopped walking towards the door but didn't turn around, "Yes."

I wanted to scream it at him, but my voice could only hold a whisper, "You made me feel again."

He turned around to look at me. There wasn't an expression on his face at all, as he stood there stunned. I think the proper word for it was shock. Our eyes stayed locked for the longest time. I was waiting for him to say something, anything. I wanted him to hold me and tell me what I was supposed to feel. He wasn't doing what I needed him to do.

I had to elaborate, "I mean... I just do better here when I am numb...I think."

"No, that's not true and you know it."

I gave him a pleading glance, "Really?"

His chest heaved with a deep breath, and he looked miserable. I didn't know why this would make him miserable.

"I am going to make my final decision early next week on who is staying and who is leaving. The good news is, I am not getting rid of anyone. With the deal you finished yesterday, I can keep everyone. Please don't tell anyone. I am going to give my reviews and still tell people what I would like to see from them. We still need a lot of work. I am telling you this, because it was you that made it possible. Do you understand that?"

My eyes dropped from him.

"Joselyn, do you understand that?"

I glanced back at him wanting to believe what he was saying.

He gave me that adorable, soothing smile, "I like when I know how you feel, but I don't know how you feel unless you tell me. I am going to leave now if you are okay?"

I encouraged this, because I really didn't want to have a break down here.

"That file contains another really big client. If we close this one, I will be ecstatic. Can I set it up for next Thursday?"

I nodded, "But can we do the presentation before dinner?"

"Yes, of course."

"I will be ready."

He smiled again walking over grabbing a tissue, and then handed it to me, "I am going to leave the blinds shut for now and I will leave, but know this one thing..."

That got my attention.

"I want you so bad right now. I want to make you forget what is making you so miserable. If there is anything I can do for you, please don't hesitate to ask. This is more than business, more than personal. Joselyn, you have my attention, and I want to know more, but I will wait until you are ready."

He walked out of my office closing the door behind him.

I took out the file and went to work on it right away. It wasn't even difficult. I came up with six ideas right away and went down to the art department. I gave each of them two of my ideas and told them they had till Friday to come up with something for me to work with. I headed back to my office. There was another note on my desk:

Joselyn,
This is from the man who adores you. I chickened out earlier.
It does not compare to your beauty in my eyes. I will understand if
you won't accept it, but please do, even if you can only wear it here.
It's a tear drop to replace the ones you have lost.
Tyler

I opened my desk to find that same box. I opened it and it was a very elegant necklace that had a small tear drop shaped rock on the end of it. It was a love, hate relationship with my emotions, as I pulled it out and put it on. I usually didn't wear something around my neck, but I felt like he was telling me it was okay to feel.

12

By the end of the week the phone calls were getting to be too much, with having to get the presentation for Tyler ready. I had fourteen new clients looking for our services. I had to do something drastic.

I went to the conference room and knocked on the door. He yelled for me to come in. He was busy on his phone, but waved me in with a huge smile on his face. His eyes went straight to my neck with satisfaction that I was wearing the necklace. He rushed to end his call.

"You're wearing it?"

I nodded, but I was here on business, "Mr. Reynold's..."

He gave me the dirtiest look, but I shook my head. The door was still open, so I repeated myself, "Mr. Reynolds, is there a place that we could move you to for awhile? I need the conference room this afternoon."

"Oh yeah, for what?"

I looked into his eyes very seriously, "It's one of those things that you can't be around for because I get nervous. Can you use my office or something at 2 pm?"

He was pleased that he still had this effect on me, "Yes, of course. I am going to share your office?"

I was a little more sarcastic, "You can even move in your own desk."

He laughed, "Yes, fine. I will get lost before 2 pm.

"Thank you, Mr. Reynolds."

"Mrs. Evans, I like being on the first name bases with all my employees."

I laughed, "You are out of here before 2 pm, Tyler."

I walked back out not waiting for a response from him. In my office I contacted six agents to make sure everyone was going to be at the meeting.

I got everything organized and made a presentation with my ideas ready. I put everything in a portable file and sat down to take a breath. I hoped my idea would work. There was no way I could do all of this myself and get it done quickly.

Tyler walked in, "So are you going to tell me what you are up to?"

"No."

"Should I be worried about someone killing off the messenger?"

"Honestly..."

"Hey, I was kidding."

I grinned at him, "Do you need anything while you are in here?"

"No, I was thinking I would dig through your desk. Maybe smell your jacket for a while. How long do I have to stay lost for?"

"Until, I come get you."

"Then where are we going?"

I was confused as to what he meant.

He laughed, "You said you were going to come get me. Should I have the blinds pulled?"

I shook my head, but he made me laugh, "Behave, we are at the office."

"Oh, so I am making headway with you?"

I gave him a purposeful look with my lips pressed together.

He was pleased with himself, "Don't you have a meeting or something?"

I grabbed the file quickly, "Shit, why do you have to distract me?"

I hurried from the room. I walked in, and everyone was talking horribly about Tyler. I liked him, and I didn't understand what everyone was so uptight about. Oh, that's right no one knew that none of them were going to lose their jobs. I was irritated by their behavior, but once they find out that he had no intentions on getting rid of any of them, I knew things would be better. I handed out a folder to each of them.

Nick was the oldest one of us, and he didn't seem pleased, "What is this about?"

"I need some help."

"You get all his deals; why do you need our help?"

I wasn't expecting that. I guess I didn't realize that is how they would see it. I continued to hand out the folders to each of them. When I got to the end of the table, I took a deep breath and turned to them smiling, "Well, let's just get what you are thinking out of the way. I am not here to discuss what is going on, but I am here to discuss where we are going. Get it out of the way, because I only am asking for your help, but in return you will get the commissions. I only want to oversee it to make sure it is what they are looking for. So, get all the complaining out now. If you want out, leave the folder on the table and walk away."

I was amazed that when you talk money no one wants to walk away from that. No one complained and no one left.

I smiled with satisfaction, "Nick, since you seemed to be the one that has the most concerns I will start with you. I know your strengths are with Sports, Alcohol, and Gum."

He nodded, "That is right."

"Well, if you look at your file you will see two that I have picked for you should fit what you are good at."

He was reading, "So, what do you want me to do?"

"Whatever you feel is best; your idea and your commission. I would like to see it before we show the client though. I have the meeting times at the top of each one; if those can work for you, I would like to have your ideas by Wednesday next week, and then we'll have a couple of days to make any changes. "

"Seth, you are also good at sports, but you are also good at making women look good. I have picked those two clients for you. Same thing goes with your two. I felt you would be the best one to handle these."

"Kathy, you are good at not making woman look weak and helpless. I also like the way you represent kid's products. I hope those are okay with you.

"Tammy, what can I say? You are the best with household products. I actually gave you both. I hope that is okay with you?" She nodded and opened her folder very happily.

"Eric, do I even have to say what you know best?"

He laughed, "No. What kind of car is it?"

"Well, look. It's not really a car."

"Yes. You did not give me a bike ad?"

I hit his soft spot, "But, you also have a second one you might not like as much."

"Oh, no... this is good. I can do this... a sporting store. I can do it."

I turned to Rebecca who was the youngest of them all. I smiled at her.

"I don't have a specialty."

"Yes, you do."

"What?"

"Teenagers."

"But…"

"No. You are the freshest, and next best thing we have to a teenager. I have two companies that have similar products, and we need to represent both, so I need something completely different for each."

"But?"

"No, buts. I know you can do this, and I need you."

She nodded leaving me confident, "If you want to trade or work together I am all for it. When you bring them to me next week, just let me know who worked on them, so we get the commissions correct."

Nick looked at me, "You are serious about giving us the commissions on these?"

"Yes. I figured that Mr. Reynolds gave me a good one, so I should give you what I have. Don't you want this?"

"Oh, No… I guess… I was just… Thank you."

I proceeded, "If you want any help let me know, and if you don't want help that is fine too. I just need more time to work on the next project Mr. Reynolds gave me, and I needed more time."

"He gave you another one?" Kathy asked.

"For some reason, I am not sure, yes."

"How come he is handing them to you?"

"I have no idea, but I closed 13 deals in the first two weeks he was here. Maybe, this is all a test to see if I can handle it. I will make sure he knows that the only way I could handle it is, because you guys helped."

Everyone was happy with this.

"Well, we have work to do. Does anyone have any questions?"

There was no sign of questions, so I packed up and went down to the art department to see if they had what I asked for ready. It was for my next meeting with Tyler's clients. We reviewed it, but it wasn't what I wanted exactly. We discussed it for a half hour, and I remember I had left Tyler in my office longer than I needed to. I rushed back to my office.

He was kicked back in the chair with his feet on my desk smiling, "Did you forget about me?"

I did feel bad, "Sort of… I was working on something."

"Hum… Do you know how many deals you have completed this year?"

"No. I have no idea."

"You are quiet amazing."

I rolled my eyes and pushed his feet from my desk, as I stepped in front of him to put my stuff away. I felt his hands trace the outside of my legs upward.

I turned around with my eyes blazing to glare at him, "What are you doing?"

He looked like a little boy in a candy store who had just got caught stealing a piece of candy. His eyes were huge and his mouth was drooling, as his eyes came up to meet mine. I melted quickly with his look, "Jos, when can we…"

I shuttered and closed my eyes."

"Hey, what's wrong?"

I was trying to shake that feeling that comes over me when Ryan calls me that.

"I did it again… Didn't I?"

"You didn't do anything, I just can't…" I turned away from him.

"See me?"

I shook my head. I didn't mean that I couldn't see him. I longed for him to pull me into his arms, and make me feel good.

His eyebrows furrowed as he searched my face for answers, "What then? You have to talk to me."

I took a deep breath and turned to put some stuff away. I felt him behind me with his face near my ear, "He calls you that?"

How was it that he could already read my reactions? I nodded with relief that he was getting me.

"I am so sorry."

I shook my head. I needed him to wrap his arms around me and kiss my neck. I needed his hands to trace up my arms so my skin could burn with his touch. I needed those lips to touch mine hard and luring. I needed to forget how much everything my husband did disgusted me.

"What can I do to make it better?"

I turned to look at him pleading with my eyes. I wanted to forget how Ryan's actions made me feel empty, alone, and sad.

He could read me so well, "Now?" He waited for my reply, "Come to dinner with me."

I nodded but replied, "I can't."

He closed his eyes with disappointment and took a deep breath, "Come see me tomorrow. You don't have to answer me now… I will wait all night, just show up, please. Don't answer me because you will say no, but do it anyway, Okay? No, don't say it. I will be there."

56

He walked passed me, but let his chest graze my back as he went by. He stopped at the door, "I love what you did in the conference room."

I looked up at him with surprise. What did he mean *'what I did in the conference room'*?

His grin was guilty, and he raised his eyebrows, "You impress me." He continued out the door.

I fell to the chair knowing he had listened to the whole thing. I shook my head in disbelief, but he did make me smile.

13

I went home with the determination that I would be going out tomorrow night to be with Tyler. I walked in and set my keys and purse down. My night with Ryan went very smoothly with no arguments. The kids were full of chatter at the dinner table. It wasn't until bed time that I was miserable with desire to see Tyler. Why did I need Tyler? Why did I want him so badly? Was it just revenge? No, it was a need of feeling wanted. My husband had wanted someone else and that hurt me, but now what I was doing, I didn't agree with it. I hated that I needed him, but I did. I was happier after feeling wanted, and desired. I had more ambition to do things after being with him. I had to go. I had a meeting this coming Thursday, so I had to feel good, right? No, I was making up excuses to go. If I wanted to go, I should just go.

We had games all day on Saturday. Ryan was irritable today, but I was in a good mood, because I knew where I was going tonight. He would try to take me down with him, but nothing he said bothered me today.

"Did you remember to set an appointment for me at the dentist?"

"Nope, you can do it."

"But I thought you always took care of those things."

"Well, I have been a little busy at work lately."

"Great, so busy that you have no time to take care of things at home, just like something else you don't like to take care of."

I grinned. I didn't care. He was not going to get to me today.

"We have to get Haden in to the doctors too."

"Why?"

"Jos, he has been complaining that his ear hurts."

"Why didn't you tell me?"

"Well, if you paid attention to him when you are here, you would have known."

I pulled out my cell phone.

He grabbed it from me, "When did you get this?"

"Oh, awhile ago. I got it after I closed that big deal. Mr. Reynolds wants to be able to get a hold of me if he needs to."

I took it back and called the clinic.

Ryan was angry, "So, he has to call you when you are with your family?"

"No, I haven't even used it till now. Yes, hello. I was wondering if I could get my son in this afternoon. He has an ear ache."

"Jos, we can't do it today."

"Why not?"

"We have the Smith's party tonight."

"Oh, well this is more important. You said so yourself. Yes, it's for Haden Evans. Yes, he is seven. Yeah, that would be great. Yes, thank you."

"So, what, you're running off again?"

"Yes, I am taking Haden to the doctors at 4 pm. The games will be done, and I can get him taken care of."

I sat pleased with myself for not losing my temper with him.

"So, if you're not going to use the phone, why do you need one?"

"Well, I only agreed to it, with the understanding that it had to be an emergency for him to call me when I am here."

"At the ball games?"

"No, with my family."

"Yeah, right. That won't last."

It couldn't have been any worse timing when the phone rang. I didn't really know how to work it, but it did come up Mr. Reynolds. I smiled and turned away from Ryan.

"Hello,"

"Have you seen the art work for our big deal coming up?"

I laughed quietly, "Yes, I have. What is wrong with it?"

"Nothing, I wanted to know if I could expect you."

"Yes, I will look at it on Monday first thing."

"I have to wait till Monday?"

"No, really it will be fine."

"Oh, you are just saying that. Did I catch you with your kids?"

"Yes, I am at a ball game. I have one sick too."

"You're not coming?"

"It will have to wait."

"Till later, or Monday?"

"Yes, it will be the first thing."

"Oh, you are so good at this."

"Not funny. I have to go. My son is up to bat."

"Fine, I will wait all night just to feel those lips."

"See you on Monday."

"I want to dance with you just to feel your body glide against mine.

"Yep, that will be fine."

"I want to make you so hot that you come before I push to you."

"Goodbye." I hung up the phone.

"Told you."

I looked at Ryan, "You told me what?"

"I knew that was going to happen."

"I don't want to hear it. I am making good money, and if he needs to call me, then we both have to deal with it pleasantly."

"I don't have to deal with it pleasantly. You are neglecting your family's needs now. I should have never told you to stay there."

"It wasn't because of you that I am still there. They appreciate me for what I do."

"You mean who."

That threw me off; did he suspect that I was with someone else? Now I knew I had to end this. I leaned to Ryan, "Like you should talk. I think it's time we call it quits." I sat back in my chair to watch the rest of the game. It didn't feel that bad telling him that.

He leaned to whisper to me, "You wouldn't know how to satisfy a man if there was a chart with pointers."

"I think you have that wrong. I didn't know you weren't satisfied until you slept around."

He glared at me. I felt awful for saying those things. I wanted to go home and crawl into my emptiness. It would be better than hurting him. I didn't want to hurt anyone.

I went back to the numb state and gave up on going seeing Tyler tonight. I couldn't do that again until Ryan and I had ended this relationship.

We got home and the numbness was coming back slowly. I walked around like a zombie. I took Haden to the doctors, and they said he had a slight ear infection. We stopped and picked up the medicine on the way home. I gave him a dose and curled up with him in my bed to watch a movie. Ryan came in sitting on the bed looking at Haden, "Is he okay?"

"Yeah, he will be. He had a slight ear infection."

Haden took Ryan's hand and pulled him, "Daddy, come here and cuddle with me and mommy."

He crawled in next to Haden on the other side of him. How could I refuse if it was for my baby? We stayed like that for hours. Haden finally fell asleep a little after nine. I felt Ryan's hand touch mine and I looked over. In that moment I felt awful for not wanting to love him anymore and the tears were coming to me. I didn't want him to touch me. It actually hurt with the thought of being with him. I wouldn't know how to make love to him after seeing him with her. I closed my eyes trying not to think about it, but the thought wouldn't stay away. The look on his face when he realized I was standing there stunned, the way he blurted out 'shit Joselyn', the way he pushed away from her covering her up to protect her from being seen by me, and then moving to me quickly to pull me from the room, but standing there naked as he tried to turn me to go out the door. I hated that I couldn't close off my brain from that, and I pulled my hand away shaking my head. I felt awful that I couldn't love him that way anymore; he was the father of my children, and I couldn't be with him. After noticing my reaction, he got a degusted look on his face. He moved away from the bed and picked up Haden to take him to his room. He stopped at the door and whispered, "Jos, I will be right back. We'll just try, okay?"

He walked out. I couldn't be with him; I had to do something other than throwing up. The sight just came to my eyes. I was panicking. What was I suppose to do? I wanted to leave, but he came back very quickly. He crawled up the bed and laid next to me touching my hand. I closed my eyes and tried to not think about him and what he did. His hand traced my face, and I saw him push to her. I felt him touch his lips to mine, and I heard him in my head moaning as he was doing it with this woman. I pushed him away, "I can't." I got out of bed and walked out. I went straight to the door and grabbed my keys and purse.

"Jos, where are you going?"

"I don't know."

"Then why are you going?"

"Because, I can't do this anymore. I see it. I hear it. I try not to, but if you even look at me sometimes, it comes to my mind. When you try to come onto me, it makes me sick."

"We're still married."

"Then I don't want to be. I think we have to be done."

"Are you saying you want a divorce?"

"Yes, I think I am."

"You better be sure. This isn't something you can say because you think it's what you want. I am not going to stick around if you can't be with me."

"Good, you shouldn't."

"You want me to leave?"

"No, tonight I am leaving. I will be back before the kids are up."

"Don't bother coming home at all."

"You don't have that power anymore, Ryan. You gave up that right when you did what you did."

14

I walked out. I looked like hell. I drove to the tavern, but called Tyler when I was almost there.

"Please don't tell me you're not coming."

I couldn't talk. I held the phone while the tears streamed down my face.

"Joselyn?"

"Uh un."

"Okay, you can't talk to me?"

I didn't say a word.

"Where are you?"

I still couldn't talk. I kept driving, but the tears were blurring my vision, "Hold on."

I set the phone down and wiped my eyes with my sleeve and then picked up the phone again, "Sorry."

"Joselyn, you are scaring me. Are you at home?"

"No."

"Where are you?"

"Just pulling in."

"At home or here?"

I could see him walking out, as I pulled in and parked. He saw me, and I hung up my phone when he came running towards me. Relief filled me when he pulled me from the car wrapping his arms around me tightly, "Are you okay?"

Knowing I was going to be okay now, I let my whole body fall into his, resting my face on his neck. He pushed me away from him against the car forcefully. His hands came to my face to look me in the eyes. His hands moved to my chin, pushing it up. Next, his eyes scanned my arms while his hands glided down over them. I got the distinct feeling that he was looking for something. My wonder was satisfied when he asked, "He didn't hit you?"

I shook my head no. He pulled me back to him and tucked my face to his neck. His heart was racing, and his arms were shaking. His breath was rapid against my ear, "Are you okay?"

I shook my head, but said, "Yes."

He laughed lightly and pulled my face back to look at him, "You have to tell me what happened."

I shook my head, "Dance."

He smiled, "You want me to dance with you?"

I nodded, but he just stared into my eyes. Confusion passed through every inch of his face, as he looked at me for answers, "Dancing will help?"

I gave him a slight grin, "Yes."

He hugged me so tight and kissed my head, "Tell me he did not harm you."

I shook my head.

I felt his breath as he sighed with relief. He pulled his shirt up when he let go of me, and he wiped my face, "Do you realize I have never seen you in jeans before?"

Why would he bring up what I was wearing? I glanced up at him as a grin came to his face, "I'm sorry, but you are hot."

I don't understand why he makes me feel so much better in every way possible, as corny as that was.

"Oh, that is so much better."

I rested my face on his chest and hugged him. He wrapped his arm around me, and we started to walk in.

I glanced up to him, "How bad do I look?"

He smiled and his eyes glistened, "You look amazingly breath taking."

I knew he was lying. I turned to face him, "You are not telling me the truth."

He smiled and touched my face raising his eyebrows, "You are the most beautiful woman in the world."

I grinned slightly, "You, Mr. Reynolds, are not a good liar."

He pulled me wrapping his arm around my waist and holding me close, as he started to walk me backwards towards the tavern. His mouth came to my ear, "Who says I am lying, Mrs. Evans?"

I frowned and tucked my face in.

"You don't like to be called that either?"

I shook my head.

"Then who are you?"

I looked up at him, "I don't know."

He stared into my eyes and continued to walk me backwards until we got to the door. I turned, and he took my hand to lead me out to the dance floor. Before we started to dance he stopped and whispered, "Do you want a drink?"

I only wanted to dance with him and feel every inch of his body next to mine. We went straight to the dance floor. It was salsa night. He held one arm around my waist, and placed his other hand in mine. He moved us to the music. His body complimented me, as his leg moved in between mine. When he pulled me close, I gently rubbed my face against his. When he turned me, I traced my lips to his neck. He was getting wild with the dancing, and I started to forget that I was unhappy. He even made me laugh with the playful seductive looks, when he pulled me close. As he tipped me back, his mouth followed the angle of my neck. I didn't react the way he wanted; it tickled and made me laugh more.

"You know, it's not supposed to do that."

"Well, maybe you should try harder."

He liked that idea, continuing his playful flirtation and seductive dancing. Spending time with him; not having sex, was getting easier. I liked the touch of his hand to my body. I liked the way he looked at me, with desire in his eyes.

He stopped and pulled me closer, "I can't go anymore. I need a drink."

I followed him to the bar. He sat down on a stool and waved for the bar tender, but pulled me into him deeply, gazing into my eyes, "What do you want?"

I raised my eyebrows, with eyes questioning. A grin came to his face. "Sam, can we get two, plain Margarita's on the rocks?"

"You remembered?"

He was mischievous, "If I knew more, I might forget something."

I was confused, "What do you mean?"

He handed me my drink and took my hand, explaining further as we walked to the back of Ty's, "I know so little about you, that I haven't found anything forgettable."

This was more of a lounging area. It wasn't as crowded as it was the night I first met Tyler. He pulled me to a sofa, and he sat down. I moved to sit next to him curling up close to him. We sat there quietly sipping on our drinks, but I noticed he was staring at me. I shied away from his gaze, but he didn't want to allow that. His hand came up to trace under my chin. Not pulling up, but to feel the contour of my jaw bone. His face was so strong and stern, and his mouth came close to me. I felt his warm breath, as he spoke to my ear, "Feeling better?"

I took a large sip of my drink and nodded. His hand moved down to trace my neck, as his fingers skimmed lightly over it down to the top of the t-shirt. His finger hooked to the collar of it making me laugh. He was giving me what I needed the most. I felt desired and special. He wanted to be here with me. I knew it would be better for him to find someone that didn't have this much baggage, but right now I needed him terribly.

He tipped my head back to him, "Open your mouth."

"Why?"

He pulled back my head, and he started to tip his drink to my mouth. I leaned more to him and tipped back further. He smiled and tipped the glass to me and it dripped into my mouth. I smiled and giggled. He gave me that confusing look like he was trying to figure out something.

He finally pushed me up, "You have to drink up. I need to dance with you more."

I took my drink and drank it as fast as I could, while he was pulling me in the direction of the dance floor. He set his down on a table, and I did the same, as we moved out to the dance floor where the music was loud and zesty.

His dancing was more freely moving with the sound of the salsa music. I traced my hands over his body as we moved. I had forgotten just how much I loved to dance.

He pulled my hands around his neck, "How long can you stay?"

I shrugged my shoulders.

"We need to go."

I shook my head, "I like the dancing."

He grinned, "Come with me. We'll dance more." He was pulling me back to the bar.

"Can we get a pitcher of margarita's to go, Sam? We're just going to my studio."

His studio? Did that mean he lives here? I wanted to know what he meant by studio, but I was afraid to ask. Tyler's eyes were oceans of blue luring me into this escape.

Sam came back with a small pitcher, "Sorry, this is the best I can do."

"That's great."

Tyler took the pitcher in his other hand and pulled me out the door and back to the building that looked like an office. I couldn't wait for him to be forceful, and push my misery away. We walked in, and I couldn't wait to kiss him. He held me tight, looking at me, but wasn't forceful. He was smiling at me with a quirky little smile. He pulled me to the kitchen and pulled out two shot glasses. He poured a little in each glass. He pulled out a salt shaker and stared into my eyes. Finally he lifted my hand turning it over. He licked my wrist and poured salt on it, slowly licking the salt off of it, and then took the shot of margarita. He wanted to play a drinking game. Okay, good way to get my mind off of everything. He set me up on the counter and moved between my legs giving me the other shot glass that was still full.

I squinted my eyes, wondering where I should take my shot from. I pulled his collar out from his neck and licked it. I put salt on it and then licked it slowly and took my shot of margarita. His mouth came to mine and he kissed me deeply. Our mouths moved together hard and fast. I wrapped my legs around him, and he pulled up my shirt. The smile on his face was sinful. He tilted me back a little and licked my chest, right in the middle below the collar bone. He put salt on it. He looked at me briefly and then licked and sucked slowly before taking a drink right from the pitcher. I rubbed my legs against him until he pulled me closer. I pulled up his shirt and slid off the counter to stand in front of him. He was smiling as he stared into my eyes. I squatted down and licked the middle of his stomach. I grabbed the salt shaker and put some on him. He looked down shaking his head. I licked and sucked slowly and he moaned. I took a drink and smiled at him, but he wasn't looking at me. He had his eyes closed because he had really enjoyed this. I saw his chest moving in and out and his mouth opened to breath. I reached up and kissed his lips lightly, and his mouth returned the kiss very hard pressing my lips apart so our tongues could do the salsa. The kiss was hard, deep, in a way pleading for more. He was undoing my pants folding them back. He handed me the salt shaker and he grabbed the pitcher but started walking me backwards to the bed. He was smiling at me, and then set down the stuff next to the bed. He lowered me to sit, and he stood there looking at me. I didn't know what to think. By now we were usually done, but this time he was just standing there. Why was he looking at me like that?

Was he wondering what would come next? Where would he go from here?

I undid his pants and pushed them down, but his boxers lowered with them. Oh my goodness; I guess I had never really looked at him. His body was so perfect; there wasn't an ounce of flab anywhere, and his muscles were not overly bulky, but just perfect to enhance his posture. Of course his whole body was complimented by the sun, which allowed for shadows contouring the etched muscles of his chest, stomach, arms and legs. I think he looked better completely nude than he did with clothes on. I stroked my hand against him, as his eyes closed. He went down to his knees in front of me. I was desperate for him to say or do anything. Please tell me what to do?

He traced his hand against my face, "What happened?"

I was shaking from wanting him so badly. Why did he bring this up? I undid my bra and let it slide from me. I needed him to push the thought away from me and not bring it up again. It made me not want to be here. His mouth came to me and sucked my breast. I thought this was where he was going to take the next drink from, but his tongue taunted my nipple making me want him more. I traced my hands from his waist upward across his abs. That was it, we were completely gone. He pulled up to me and kissed me hard. Our mouths moved quickly as if we couldn't have enough; I wanted him and he wanted me.

He was so much more playful than forceful. I could feel the heat of him, as his erection rubbed against my moist folds, but he was busy being mesmerized as his look went deeper into me. I slowly traced my hands against his skin eager to entice him into me. He pushed to me slightly and pulled away with a slight smile on his face. I think he was teasing me. He did it again, and his eyes closed when he pushed to me, but opened when he pulled away. His lips glided against mine with sheer delight. I wished he would just push all the way in. I needed him to push away any ounce of sadness that was still in me. I felt his hand slowly move down my body until he reached my thigh; that's when his intensity grew. He pulled it up and then the push came deep and hard. I gasped from the pleasure of the warm stroke of him inside of me. My misery was being pushed from me. I not only wanted this; I needed this. I gripped my fingers into his wonderful firm ass to pull him to me harder as he pushed deeper. A smile came to his face, as he kissed me softly. The movements were perfect; as my body rose to meet him he came in deeper; desire for pleasure was building quickly. The grin on his face told me he knew what made me feel good. His face stayed calm and pleased as he moved with me, but when my intense pleasure came and my moans increased with every movement, he plunged harder and deeper into me. Every part of his body became harder and harder until I thought he was peaking, but then he pulled from me. His eyes closed, in a way that seemed to pain him.

"You have to help me with this."

I was confused until he placed a rubber in my hand. I ripped open the little package while his tongue distracted me around my ear. As awkward as it was, I reached down between us trying to find my way, shielded by our closeness. His lips found their way back to mine while his eyes comforted me, "You let me be in you without it, but I can't control myself anymore. I need..."

I rolled the rubber on him while his body pushed to my touch. I barely got it on him and he was in me again. His movements were hard and fast. He pulled my leg up higher and moved around in a way that he touched more spots than I never knew existed. I climaxed again before he could release his desire for me. So when I moaned, he pushed hard and long to me and stayed there trying to push further in. He gasped and then moaned as his body tensed so hard I thought he would hurt me, but he groaned in a deep husky way, "Oh... yes..." and melted in my arms.

His body relaxed into crushing me, and his mouth rested at my ear, "You make me feel so good."

I smiled and held him tighter tracing my fingers along his smooth silky skin. I turned my face to his a little and we kissed for what felt like forever.

He finally smiled while he mouthed to me, "I am crushing you."

I pressed my open mouth to his top lip, "Yes."

His face glided against mine, "I don't want to move."

The pressure of his body felt warm and satisfying, "I don't want you to move either."

"What if I..." Whatever he just did made all the juices in my body flow making me squirm with shivers. He had given me so much pleasure that every movement was like an arousal. I shuttered as he moved again.

"You feel that good?"

I nodded. Everything he did drove me crazy.

He pulled from me and I gasped, "No."

A sinful grin came to his face, "You want more?"

"No, I just like the way you make me feel."

69

He traced his hands along my face and continued to kiss me softly on the lips, cheek, chin, and my eyes.

A slight smile came to his face. It seemed to have a question behind it, and I was right. He pulled himself up a little more and looked directly in my eyes, "I need for you to tell me why you were upset earlier."

I grimaced, "I was just..." I didn't want to say that Ryan tried to touch me. I know he is my husband, but my heart, body and soul belonged to Tyler. I was in love with everything about this man I had just made love to.

"Please..."

"I'm trying to forget. If I talk about him, than I have to think about him or it or..." I shuttered, but this time it was from disgust.

He must have understood because he let it go. A smile came to his face, and he kissed me playfully. I was confused; he was letting me off on telling him so easily. He nibbled on my lips to taunt me. I furrowed my brow again. He laughed and sucked on my bottom lip. When his lips moved up to caress my top lip his arms wrapped under me and pulled me to him and he rolled over. I scooted down and rested my head on his chest. I felt his fingertips lightly gliding up and down my back. I think this was the first time in a long time that I was completely relaxed, so relaxed that I started to doze off a little.

As I lay there, my mind wondered off. I was feeling the guilt seeping back in to my mind. I slipped away from him and went to the bathroom. When I came back to get dressed he was awake sitting up with the covers barely covering him.

He gazed at me with that longing look, "Joselyn, can you stay just a little longer?"

I didn't want to leave either, so I crawled into the bed to be with him, but he guided me to lie in front of him on my stomach. He laid his body against mine and slowly traced his hand and fingers along my back, "How long do I get to keep you?"

I smiled, "I have to be back before the kids get up."

"He isn't going to wonder where you are?"

"Yes, but I left a little angry."

He leaned forward and traced his mouth against my shoulder, as they pressed here and there with a light kiss.

"Joselyn, what happened with you and your husband that makes you so sad and miserable?"

70

I whispered, "I saw him…" I didn't want to think about this because it was so painful. The picture came to my mind and I shuttered. He kissed the middle of my back, "Saw him what?"

"With someone else."

His mouth traced up my back, and he kissed slowly between my shoulder blades, "I'm sorry."

That's when I let it all out, "In my home… and in my bed."

I felt the heaviness of his breath against my back and his lips touched gently, "That's why you came looking for someone?"

"Wasn't looking, I was just trying to get on with my life and forget what he had done."

I felt his breath move against my skin again and then the light touch of his lips to my back again, "So, what happened tonight?"

I felt awful and this wasn't going to come out right anyway I said it. The hollowness of my heart was engulfing me even with Tyler lying here next to me. It was making me cold and distant. If he wanted to know this, then maybe he would understand what it is that I am afraid of.

"He tried to touch me."

His lips came to my cheek so soft and gentle, as he glided them against me, "Do you still love him?"

I shook my head, "but…"

"But?"

"He is the father of my children, and I love them."

I turned to face him as the tears tracked down my cheek. I didn't want to feel this way, but Tyler was making me feel again. He slowly wiped them from my face, as he stared into my eyes. There was a gaze of concern, but he didn't speak. He moved down a little and wrapped his leg around mine. His hand continued to rub my back gently, and his mouth touched mine softly, kissing me tenderly. We stayed there kissing for a long time. His face would change expression from sadness, to a slight smile as his gaze lingered.

He moved to sit up, and I watched him carefully. Was this the end? He pulled me up and pulled my legs around him. He pulled me to him and I could feel his desire again. He must be young, because I was so worn out, but his erection told me he was ready to go again. He lightly rubbed his face to mine and kissed my neck gently. His hands traced up my back pulling me to him.

He pushed into me so carefully, but this time his eyes stayed open locking me into a trance of only seeing him. His posture changed and not only was he adoring me, but it was like he was letting himself feel every pleasure of every movement we shared. His mouth stayed open against mine; I could feel his breath moving off of me, as his movements gave me so much ecstasy. I felt my hands gripping his arms pulling me to him more. I had already had so much pleasure today that no matter where he touched me or moved to me I was already trembling from it, but this time I wasn't the only one. His body jerked and trembled from rapture with me. It seemed different; he seemed different.

We clutched together in an embrace, not wanting to ever be apart. I held tightly to him, as our hearts beat together working their way to slowing down. Our bodies caressed with every breath until they calmly halted together. Our tranquility was interrupted by him, "Joselyn, I want to make love to you every day of my life. I want to see your face when I wake in the morning, and I want you to be the last person I see."

I felt all of the air in my lungs escape me with each word he said. He was taking me to a new level of awareness, giving me everything I needed in one large package, and it felt like love. I was scared, because the love I've known seemed to hurt so much right now.

I closed my eyes and leaned my face against his, when I felt the tears escape my eyes to trickle down my face. I couldn't tell if I was happy or sad. He shouldn't feel this way about me no matter how bad I wanted it to be true.

I felt his breath as he held me tighter, "Tell me what you are thinking."

I opened my eyes looking deep into his. I wanted to break down and really cry, "I'm scared."

He reassured me with a slight smile, "Of what?"

Our breathing was heavy and my heart was racing. Not only was he giving me bodily pleasures, he was also making me feel, and it was so confusing because it felt good.

I let the words fall from my lips watching for him to shy away from me, because I was going to say the *"L"* word, "To let myself love you."

He kissed me hard at first but then gently everywhere; there was a tear that had touched my face, but this time it was not mine. He moved to me as he cradled me in his arms, making love to me again. It didn't take long, and he was pulling away from me enough so that he wasn't in me, but close enough to rub against me so I could feel the warmth of his pleasure spread over me. He pulled me close and held me tightly, as he calmed in my arms. His face came back to mine and his smile made me feel warmth in my heart. He pulled the sheets up around me and held onto me, as he moved from the bed.

I didn't know what he was doing, but I couldn't refuse him. He pushed up still holding me around him, and I kissed his lips playfully. He walked into the bathroom which confused me more.

"We need to get you cleaned up if you are going home."

I felt the pain shoot through my heart. He wanted me to go now?

"Joselyn, don't look at me that way. You will leave anyway, and I don't want to give him any reason to be mean to you. Not till we can figure *this* out."

I was full of emotions, and... yet... I wanted to run from him, "*This*?"

"I want to be with you. If you don't love him, than we have some things to take care of. Don't worry. I will set up an appointment with my lawyer... like a regular client, so no one will know."

I swallowed hard. I looked at him panicking.

"You do want a divorce?"

I nodded, "but my..." I couldn't even say that I was worried about my children. They loved their dad too. I was so scared.

He smiled gently and pulled me into the shower, "Hold your hair up."

I did what he told me and he took soap and washed me everywhere. I pushed him back a little looking deep in his eyes searching for answers. He shouldn't feel this way about me, "Tyler?"

It was like he was surprised to hear me speak. He stopped, "Yeah?"

"You shouldn't feel this way about me."

He laughed, "Too late for that."

"How old are you, again?"

He had a glare to his eyes, "Age doesn't matter."

"I have too much baggage for you to feel this way about me."

"Stop that right now."

I stopped and looked at him. I was so scared of getting hurt.

"Okay, you need to go slower. I understand that, but you know how I feel now, so don't you dare push me away."

I nodded and he reached out grabbing a towel. He wiped me off, as I watched his beautiful body move around me. He came back up looking me in the eyes, "Are you checking me out?"

I nodded sinfully. He kissed me quickly and pulled me to the other room. He helped me find my clothes and watched as I got dressed.

"I feel like you are pushing me out the door."

73

"I am. If he gets angry with you, I will suffer. I see how hurt you have been, and I am not going to allow you to feel that way anymore."

I laughed with a quiet sigh. He pulled me out and walked me to my car, "I hate that you have to leave at all, but if you want your kids, than you have to trust me on this one. You need to go home and try to get along for as long as possible."

I didn't understand what was going on here. I was stunned, as I stared at him. He smiled and pulled me into a deep kiss before letting me go. He tucked me into my car squatting by the door, "No more pain; trust me."

I nodded, but was afraid to believe him, afraid that my faith and my heart would be trampled.

15

I drove home wondering what had just happen. Did he just tell me he loves me? How could he love me? He doesn't even know what I like for breakfast. A lawyer? Oh, shit, what did I just do? Do I really want this right now? Do I want to stop him from helping me end my dismay over my relationship with my husband? Oh my god, I have a husband. This is not going to be good.

I pulled in and laid the seat all the way back. I curled up on the seat and closed my eyes, as I let everything run through my mind again.

I heard knocking and yelling, "Jos! Jos, what are you doing?"

I looked up, and it was Ryan yelling at me from the window. I opened the car door and tried to get out of the car stumbling.

"Were you drinking?"

I looked up at him and shook my head trying to walk around him to go inside.

"What are the neighbors going to think?"

I turned on him, "I don't care what they think. Maybe you should have thought about what they would think about you screwing around."

He moved out of my way, and I was able to go inside. He followed me all the way to my room. I quickly crawled onto the bed, pulling the comforter around me, and closing eyes to avoid what I knew was coming.

"Where have you been?"

"Nowhere. Everywhere. Then in the driveway in my car."

"Why didn't you come in?"

"Because, sometimes it is hard to be here."

He sat down and rubbed my back, "Jos, I don't know how to say... I am sorry. Is there any way we can work this out?"

Don't be nice to me now. Please don't do this. I don't want to be nice to you. I turned to him, but the tears escaped me slowly making a trail against my skin. He closed his eyes, so he didn't have to see how he hurt me.

"Jos?"

I shuttered. I hated that he called me that. It once was cute, but now I found it very annoying.

"Jos, promise me one thing."

In his attempt to being brave, he finally opened his eyes to look at me. I didn't want him to know he could still hurt me, so I frantically tried to wipe the tears away from my eyes.

He pleaded, "Promise me you aren't going to do anything yet. We can go to counseling or something. It wouldn't be fare to the kids if we didn't at least try."

I couldn't promise him that. I knew I would never get over what I had seen. He just feels like he is losing his family and now he wants to hold on to it? What a jerk. I knew it in my head and in my heart, that I would never feel that way for him again. You just don't recover from seeing something like that, ever.

"Jos, say something."

"I don't know if I could ever get over that."

He closed his eyes, "I will do anything. I will stay on the couch forever, as long as we stay together for the kids."

"But I need more than that."

"Okay, I am willing to do whatever you want."

"But I don't want that from you anymore. You hurt me, and I don't think I will ever get over it."

"Please don't say that."

I shrugged my shoulders lying back down with my face away from him. A wave of relief lifted from me, as he left the room. I realized I felt good this time, and even though I thought about Ryan with someone else, it didn't play out in my head the way it always had. A picture of Tyler came to my mind instead, with his beautiful blue eyes looking deeply into mine. The tears seemed to stop. I enjoyed the thought of Tyler, even giggling to myself until I could fall asleep.

16

When I forced myself up and away from the wonderful dream I was having, I made my way to the kitchen where I made breakfast for the kids. We ate, they talked, and we all laughed with the chatter at the table. I was going to make it a day to spend time with my children, so we made plans for games and cuddling all day. This new *"me"* felt good.

Monday I walked into work with an agenda at hand. I wanted to start meeting with the other agents to see how things were going, but there was something odd about today. I walked in and set my stuff down to go investigate all the construction that was going on. I walked into Mr. Jenkins's office, "So, what is going on?"

He shrugged his shoulders, "I guess he is staying."

"He?"

"Mr. Reynolds."

My heart was racing. He wasn't going to leave. He was making an office to stay. I slowly walked out of Mr. Jenkins's office feeling a little weird. Was he staying for me? I walked into my office and tried to not think about it. I pulled out the list of accounts that I had everyone working on.

I called Kathy first: "So, how is it going?"

"Oh, I am so excited; you should see what Tori has done with these. We have some really good ideas and they are coming together just fine. Can we come up and show you...." She seemed to be thinking about it.

"Kathy, when is a good time?"

"How about 3 pm today. Tori said she wanted to talk to you about something else, but she will discuss it with you after we show you what we have."

"Do I need to get the conference room?"

"NO! Um… we can show you in your office."

"Great, see you at 3 pm."

I hung up and went to Nick next:

"Nick, how are things going with the Lucia Rum?"

"Well, I think I have something ready on that one."

"And the new gum, Wistaste?"

"Yeah, have you tried it?"

I laughed, "No, I haven't."

"Well, you might have a hard time if you did. I think I will need more time to figure this one out. Can we have till Wednesday?"

"We present it Friday, so maybe have a couple of ideas, or we could meet early Wednesday in case we need more work."

"That sounds good. How about 10 am."

"Sounds good, do we need the conference room?"

"No, we can use your office."

"I will see you then."

As I hung up, Tori came storming into my office, "We need to talk."

I looked up at her worried. She came and grabbed my arm pulling me back to my seat and sat me down in my chair. She was leaning over me looking at me right in the face, "I know where I have seen Mr. Reynolds before."

I laughed, "I thought you were going to talk to me about this later."

"Are you kidding me? No way. He is the…"

I put my hand over her mouth and pushed her back, so I could stand up. I kept my eyes on hers and she realized I knew. She was walking backwards, "Does he know?"

I nodded, but I didn't know what to say. I didn't know how much she had figured out.

"So, what is going on?"

I shook my head and pulled out more paperwork trying to avoid the gaze. I was trying to make it seem like it wasn't a big deal.

"That is why he is feeding you the big accounts?"

"No, that was before he knew. I avoided him for a long time. The offer and the first deal were all set up before he knew. That is why I was going to quit."

"Why would you quit? He was hot for you that night. I think you should pursue it."

"No! I don't want it to be that; everyone would think it was… well, you know."

She was holding her hand over her mouth laughing, "You are hot for him."

"I am still married."

"Yeah, because that is going so good for you.

"Mrs. Evans, can I see you in my office." Tyler had poked his head in.

We both looked at him and instantly; he was uncomfortable, but he tried to recover, "Is there something going on in here that I should know about."

I kicked Tori gently, but kept my eyes on Tyler, "Um, no. I will be right there."

He stepped in further with a questioning looked, "What are you two up to?"

Tori turned around, "We were just talking about a night out. We do that once a month. Mr. Reynolds, would you like to go with us next time?"

I was flipping out in my mind. He was completely grinning from ear to ear, as he was moving in more, "So, where are you going?"

She was all smiles, and her attention was on him, "Well, we haven't decided yet. I could send you a memo."

I was shaking my head behind her back until she turned back to me. I gave her a scolding look.

"Yeah, I would love a night out. Hey, don't plan it a week from this Friday. I have a work celebration that night. I have some announcements to make, and your family or significant others are invited. Mrs. Evan's, when your done in here, I expect you in my office."

I wanted to take the smile off his face, "You mean the conference room?"

"No, my office."

"And where might that be?"

Now he wanted to be playful, "Right next door to you."

I nodded and picked up some papers, "Yes, I will be right in."

In a flirting tone he said to Tori, "Hey, is it Tori? I will be waiting for my memo."

"Yeah, I will let you know."

I took a deep breath as he left the room. Tori turned to me and studied my reaction. She got this grin on her face, "You are hot for him."

"What? No."

She glared at me, "He finds you challenging, and you don't back down to him."

I shook my head and turned away. I didn't want any expression from my face to show her any different. I felt her hand pull me back to look at her. Her face was so close to mine, and she was glaring at me. I popped my eyes out at her, "What?"

"I think there is something going on here and you're not telling me."

I shook my head no, "I do have work to do."

She shook her head, "I think we should plan something this weekend."

I shook my head, "Um. I wouldn't be able to go. I have some things I need to take care of at home."

"Oh, come on, Joselyn, you need a night out."

I smiled at her, "I went out Saturday night, and I wouldn't be able to get away two weekends in a row."

"You went out without us?"

"Yeah, I do have a couple of old friends tucked away."

"You are so lying to me. I will get it out of you at 3 pm today."

I shook my head and grabbed a couple of files. We walked to my door together, "I have to go."

She nodded and went on her way just as happy as could be.

17

I took a deep breath and went next door. I knocked because the door was shut.

"Come in."

I opened the door and walked in; Tyler wasn't at the desk in the room, so I began to look around. The door closed behind me and before I turned to him, his body came at me full force pushing me against the wall with his body. His mouth consumed mine to which I returned playfully. I had missed him in the short time we were apart. I was completely into him, but he was pulling my skirt up, so I had to stop him.

I smiled with the kiss, "I can't do this."

"Why?"

"We're at work."

He slid the skirt back down but didn't release his kiss. He was trying to distract me from everything. His body moved and pushed against mine with urgency. His hands came to cup my face, "I missed you."

I nibbled on his lips a little with a grin. His intensity lessoned, and he rested his head on mine. He took a deep breath, and then ran his nose against my neck, "You smell so good."

I laughed, "So do you, but I probably smell like you now."

He grinned and his eyes met mine, "I have a meeting for you on Wednesday at 10 am."

I shook my head, "I already have a meeting at that time."

He closed his eyes, "This is more important."

"No, work is more important, and this has to deal with two accounts."

"But this is your life."

"Tyler, you do have to check with me on appointments before you make them for me."

He shook his head, "I am your boss."

"NO, you are the evaluator."

He smiled, "Okay, when is a good time for you?"

"Next Tuesday."

"But I have a meeting with the next big account that day. How about this Thursday?"

"No, I am finalizing everything for Friday. I have to give out my final decisions Thursday and Friday. So, it will have to wait."

"I don't want it to wait. I want you in my bed every night."

I smiled, "But... I still have kids, and it wouldn't be every night. I have responsibilities to them."

He glared at me, "You don't want this?"

"Oh, I do, I really, really do, but if this is going to be real, we have to let it develop slower. I need to feel this is real, and sometimes it's over the top."

He got a very guilty grin and reached down tracing his hand up between my legs until he touched me. I was feeling the heat, and I pressed my lips hard to his.

He was more determined pressing his body to mine, "I have to stop, or I am going to take you to lunch right now."

I laughed and shook my head, "You needed to see me about something?"

"Yes, this... I needed to feel you. I wanted to make you hot, so you would make time for me this week."

I raised my eyebrows looking into his eyes, "You don't have to worry about that."

He smiled, "Okay, when?"

I took a deep breath and pushed him back a little. His hand moved away from me, and I relaxed a little. I traced my hands along his face looking into those eyes, "We have to go at this slower."

He nodded, "When?"

I grinned and walked away from him. He followed wanting me to reply. I turned back to him, but he was right behind me.

"You're scaring me."

"How?"

I walked back towards him looking deep into his eyes as he backed up. His face came down letting me be in charge of him for once, and I put my hand to lift his face to mine, "You make me want to do things that I am not comfortable with. I have had a very empty five years and having

82

this much this fast is too much. We have to go slower. I need time alone, and I don't mean without you in it, but I need to learn how to do this."

He nodded and took my hand.

I smiled as I gazed into his eyes, "Please take this slower."

He kissed my hand and he asked, "So, what was with Tori?"

"She recognized you from that first night we met."

He smiled, "She remembered me."

"It took her a while, but yeah."

"So, does she know?"

"No!" I snapped, "But she thinks I should pursue you."

He laughed, "See I am not the only one."

I shook my head, "Do you have something for me? Because if you don't I have work to get done."

He laughed, "You know you work too hard."

"Yeah, well someone keeps giving me some big accounts. By the way, people do not like that."

"Oh, well things are going to be changing around here, and then they will understand.

"What do you mean?"

He grinned and walked away from me, "You will have to wait like the rest of them."

I glared after him that he wasn't telling me what was going on. I think he was trying to get me back for not going to the meeting with the Lawyer.

18

I went back to setting appointments, meeting other agents through Wednesday. Everything was working out perfectly. I was set on Tyler's big meeting on Thursday, and I went home Wednesday very satisfied with myself. Making time for Tyler this week was just not going very well. I needed to be with him, but I was doing okay with getting things done, so I didn't want to push my luck.

Thursday I walked in with my head held high and sat down at my desk reviewing my presentation for Tyler's new clients. He walked in at 10 am with a sinful grin on his face, "Are you ready for tonight?"

"Of course, but we are doing the presentation first."

He was pleased that I remembered, "Yes, then dinner and drinks till late. I know what he was thinking, but I just gave him a smile. Jared had a game and I didn't tell Tyler I wasn't staying yet. I didn't know how.

He had the limo waiting for us, as we headed down. I got in, as he held the door for me, but when it closed he moved close and started to unbutton my shirt. I glared at him with disapproval.

"What, you need to relax a little. I could calm your nerves."

I laughed with a sigh and shook my head. He grinned and buttoned them back up slowly, "I just want to help."

"I need to stay focused."

"Do I get to stay?"

I shook my head and looked out the window.

His whisper came with warmth against my ear, "I still make you nervous?"

I nodded and he backed off with satisfaction, "I will make you very nervous if you let me."

I turned to him to see what he meant, but he was looking out the other window and all I could see was his strong jaw with his mouth turned up in the corner. He was so hot in every way that I looked at him, and he made my insides do things that I didn't think it remembered how to do.

When we got there, Tyler introduced me to the new clients, and then he excused himself from the group. I gave a great presentation. So there were very few questions and only one very small concern. They did pick the one that I liked the most, and I was pleased with myself. It was the one that I had worked the hardest on. I motioned for Tyler to come back over. He came with a full staff to set the table for dinner and drinks to be served. He handed me a margarita not looking at me, but he did have a grin on his face. He held the chair for me to sit, but I moved to the side and looked directly at the clients, "I am very sorry, but you will have to excuse me. My son has a game tonight, and I have to run. If you have any more questions please feel free to call me." I nodded at Tyler, as he stood there staring at me with astonishment. I smiled sweetly at him and walked away. I hailed a cab when I got outside and was getting in when Tyler came running after me holding the car door open, "What are you doing?"

"I have to go to Jared's game. That's why we had to do this before dinner."

"Don't do this to me, Joselyn. You promised to make time for me this week."

I smiled with regret, "The week isn't over Tyler."

He just stood there pleading with his eyes. The guilt was over whelming to me, but I had never missed a game, and I wasn't about to start now. I got back out of the cab and a grin grew on his face. I took a step towards him, "We just hit the deal of a life time. Please don't blow it on me."

I took a step back as he stared. I got in the cab and he closed the door for me. I was miserable, as the car pulled away from him. I was afraid that this would end the relationship. I had put my kids before him.

19

I rushed to my car and drove like a mad man to the game. I ran up to find that I had only missed the top of the first inning. Jared waved at me noticing that I was there. Ryan got me a chair, and Haden came to sit in my lap. This was such a different world then where I had just came from.

"So... how did it go?"

"I have no idea. I left before the papers were signed. I think the presentation went okay, though."

"When will you find out?"

"I guess tomorrow."

"You really left before things were done?"

I didn't want the chatter between Ryan and me, so I scolded, "Yes, game please."

I kissed Haden multiple times which made him giggle. I held him tightly, because I knew my time with him being cuddly was limited. I wish I could hold Jared like this for just 10 minutes.

I didn't say anything stupid at the game, or at least they weren't being pointed out to me, to which I was relieved.

I started dinner right when we got home, and I had Jared and Terra sit down for their homework. Not much left of school this year, but they still had to do their homework. Haden was with his dad down in the den watching some sporting event.

I heard the door bell ring.

"Ryan, will you get that?"

I heard it again.

"Ryan, I am making dinner." I didn't hear him move, so I went down the stairs to answer it myself, but yelled down the stairs, "It would be nice if you could help a little."

86

I opened the door and Tyler was standing there staring back at me. I didn't know what to do or say, but a grin grew on his face. Haden came running up, "Mommy, who is it?" He looked at Tyler, "Who are you?"

I laughed, "Haden, this is Mr. Reynolds."

Tyler laughed, "You little man, can call me Tyler."

Haden took him by the hand, "Mommy where would you like him?"

I laughed because I wanted to say in my bedroom, but wouldn't that be completely inappropriate, "The kitchen is fine."

He was dragging Tyler up the stairs, as I watched the two of them together. Ryan came up the stairs to the entryway, "Your boss is here?"

"He's not my boss, he's the evaluator."

I shrugged and started up the stairs, but he pulled me back, "What is he doing here?"

I glared, "I have no idea." I pulled free to head up again, but he stopped me again. I could see Tyler out the corner of my eyes, and I just prayed that he wouldn't do anything.

"He is in our personal lives; get rid of him now."

"Why don't you go back to your room? This doesn't concern you."

"It does when he interrupts our family time."

I glared at him, "What family?"

He let go with surprise, and I headed up the stairs. Haden was trying to figure out what to do with Tyler. Tyler was so adorable in his suit holding hands with Haden.

"It smells wonderful... what are you making?"

Haden spoke for me, "Shhh, mom's secret recipe."

Haden pushed him to Ryan's seat at the table. Tyler was talking to him and then did a magic trick for him. I laughed, as I watched him interact with my baby. Was he here to impress me that he was good with children?

Tyler looked over at me watching him and smiled, "You didn't sign any of the paperwork."

I came out of my little dream world, "Oh, so it went good after I left?"

"Yes, they couldn't stop talking about you and what you did. They are very excited, and want it published nationally in the next two weeks."

I was very pleased with myself.

His grin grew, "I just need a couple of signatures."

I nodded and walked over, but Haden was trying to get him to do anther magic trick. He complied, so I excused myself to go get changed.

I came back out in jeans and a tank top, and now Tyler was picking on Terra. She had come to the kitchen to check things out and was giving Tyler nasty little looks. I scolded, "Terra, please be nice to Mr. Reynolds."

"I don't know him. He is a stranger and you always tell us not to talk to anyone we don't know."

"Terra this is Mr. Reynolds..." He leaned to her, "Tyler. Your mom doesn't know how to use my first name very well."

Ryan walked in, "Why would you be on first names anyway. Aren't you her boss?"

"I like to be on first names with everyone in the office."

"Well, isn't that just nice."

I was getting so irritated with this whole situation.

"Haden... Terra... go get washed up for dinner. Ryan, could you please help them?"

"Yeah, because you are so busy with work."

I glared at him, as he walked out.

Jared had moved to the table and was asking Tyler questions "Do you like baseball?"

Tyler smiled, "I like to watch it."

"Football?"

"To watch."

"Hockey?"

"Not really."

"Basketball?"

"I love to watch basketball."

I went back to stirring dinner, and I heard Tyler say something to Jared, "I like money."

He laughed, "Yeah, doesn't everybody?"

"I like cars."

"I do too."

"Do you want to see mine?"

"Yeah."

Next thing I knew, Tyler was handing my 13 year old a set of keys to his car. I intercepted him at the door of the kitchen taking them from him. I walked back over to Tyler who was now standing, "If you want to show him your car that is fine, but you don't give a 13 year old car keys. You may never see the car again."

He laughed, taking them back and going down the stairs and out the door after Jared. I followed and watched them get in his car. I didn't realize he had such a nice car. Jared got in the driver's side and Tyler smiled at me, as he got in on the passenger side. He did know how to put a smile on my face, but it made me nervous that he was here in my home.

I felt Ryan walk up behind me wrapping his arms around my waist. He hasn't been allowed to do that for 5 years; why did he think it would be allowed today? I pushed away from him and stepped outside, but he held my arm tightly. I looked back with a glare.

"You are still my wife."

I pulled my arm from him, "But you don't have my permission to do that."

His glare was long, as he held my arm tight, "Do you want to make a scene in front of your boss?"

I looked down at his hand holding my arm, "He is not the boss, and there won't be a scene if you let go of me, but don't push me."

I heard yelling from the car, "Joselyn, is everything okay?"

I looked back to see Tyler standing with the car door open. I reassured him with a nod, "Yeah, can you send Jared in its dinner time?"

I walked back in and set the table.

20

Tyler

I wanted to pull her from the house right now. He was not allowed to touch her; I could see that, but he was pushing a line with her. I sat back down in the car, stunned on what I should do, and then there was wisdom from her oldest, "It's okay you know. It's always like that."

I looked over at him confused.

He smiled, "Dad did something really bad, and mom hasn't been happy for a long time. She cries a lot."

"She cries a lot? Do you know what he did?"

"She spends a lot of time alone in her room. I don't know what he did, but she seems happier lately. She even played video games with me one day. I think she is getting better."

"She said it was time for dinner."

Jared turned on the radio, "This is so sweet. Does she make a lot of money... like enough to have a car like this?"

I laughed again, "Yes, but she would rather have a house and kids."

"You don't have any?"

"Nope. I only have my businesses."

"How many?"

"A few."

"Do you know what my friends say?"

I turned to him, "What is that?"

"My dad doesn't make her happy anymore, and then they joke about wanting to make her happy. Sometimes I wish she wouldn't show up in her work clothes, because they say things... I got into a couple of fights over it."

"Have you talked to her about it? I am sure she wouldn't want you getting in fights about how she looks."

"Well, that's the funny part. She doesn't even know she looks good. My team calls her a MILF. Do you know what that means?"

I laughed slightly, "Yeah, I think I do," as I thought about what that meant... *'mother I'd like to f—'*.

"I don't see her that way, because that is how she has always looked to me, but my friends they notice."

"Would you like me to say something?"

"NO! She doesn't cry or get upset with my dad when she is dressed in her work clothes. It's like she is someone else, and when he says stuff to her... she can blow it off easier."

"She is really amazing at work. A lot of people look up to her."

He laughed out loud, "No wonder she would rather be there."

"She wouldn't. From my understanding, she would rather be here with you. I hear her talk about your games; a smile always comes to her face. Maybe it's just what happened with your dad that makes her sad."

"You really think so?"

"Yes I do. I will try to control my urge to steal her away for work just for you little man, but she does make me a lot of money."

He opened the door, "I better get inside for dinner. She will make me do the dishes if I am late."

I laughed and followed him in.

When we got to the kitchen she was standing by the counter putting a forkful of food in her mouth. She wiped her face and scolded after Jared, "Guess who gets to help with dishes?"

"Awe mom. That isn't even fair. See, Tyler, I told you if I was late." I laughed, and she came toward me, "We'll go down to my office."

Ryan looked over at me, "Joselyn, what about dinner?"

"Eat; I'll just be a little bit."

She glanced back up at me and walked pass me. I looked at her family sitting at the table, and my eyes fell back on her husband. He was completely glaring at me. I retreated with a chuckle and followed Joselyn down a couple sets of stairs, "You have an office at home?"

"Yeah, my plan was to work from home, but things changed that. I do better when I work with others anyway."

She walked into a room that was small. There was a computer on the desk, and the walls had tons of shelves filled with pictures and books.

I walked around looking at them, tracing my fingers over the books to see if there was something I could learn about her in this brief moment. I picked up a picture of her and her husband. She walked over closing the door and then to me taking the picture from my hand laying it face down on her desk, "You had paper work for me?"

I laid it on her desk, but turned to her and cupped her face in my hands kissing her desperately. I was surprised when she responded to me. I was afraid she would push me away. I wrapped my arms around her, and pulled her body to mine, as my mouth moved to hers more.

She did stop pushing me away a little. She gave me that look that killed me, "I can't do this, not in this house."

Her family was up stairs, and she didn't mention them. Oh, this house. "Joselyn, this is a great house."

She shook her head, "This house makes me sad, and I can't do this in this house. It makes me feel like its revenge. It's not revenge, Tyler."

My eyes brightened up. This was not just an affair, because she was not doing this on purpose. I scanned her face looking for anything. I didn't want to leave yet. I missed her, and this was supposed to be my night.

"You left before dinner?"

She smiled at me guiltily.

"I thought you were staying. How come you didn't tell me?"

She sighed, "I was hoping that I would talk myself out of it, but when it came time for the game I had to go."

"But you wanted to stay?"

She nodded, and glanced back up at me. She just made my night with that cute little smile. If she looked at her son's little friends like this, she would eat them up alive. I would have done anything she wanted me to do right here and now, "What do you want, Joselyn?"

She leaned her head to my chest, "I want you to push away all these feelings that I hate."

I traced my hands down her back, and pulled her to me, so that she could feel that I wanted to make her forget right now. I kissed her neck and squeezed her tighter. Her mouth came back to mine kissing me hard and desperately. I started to undo the button on her pants, and she pushed my hand away shaking her head smiling, "I can't. Not here and not now."

I nodded, but moved closer to her. I kissed her and pulled away to look at her again. She was making my heart race, and I wanted her right now. I could make her so happy, right now, if she would let me.

She smiled slightly, "You have paper work for me to sign?"

I closed my eyes and nodded. I let go of her while she walked behind the desk. She opened it, and the smirk on her face told me she knew I had lied. She looked up at me, "This could have waited."

I nodded, "but I couldn't."

She laughed and then so did I.

"See me early tomorrow morning please. We have a lot to do."

She nodded, so I turned opening the door to her office. I hesitated, "Aren't you going back up for dinner?"

She shook her head, "I need to file a few things first." She was patting her heart to tell me she needed to calm down. I didn't want to take my eyes off of her, but I turned to head out. I went out the front door, but to my surprise Ryan was sitting on a bench in front of the house. He stood up, as I walked a little further. He finally stepped in front of me as I tried to leave, and I was forced to stop. I guess he wanted to talk to me.

"I don't appreciate work coming home with her. This is her family time, and it just doesn't seem right to have the boss show up here."

I smiled realizing he was marking his territory. I nodded, "I will keep it to a minimum."

He shook his head, "No, I think you should keep it to the office."

I smiled and leaned into him, "No, I don't think you understand. Your wife makes me a lot of money, and I want her happy." I pulled away looking at him directly into his eyes, "I mean very happy."

He took a step back looking at me with this horrible look; maybe like he wanted to punch me or something. I could only grin, because I had no intentions of getting in a fight.

"When she is happy, she does amazing things, and my clients cannot tell her no. So... I plan on doing whatever I can to keep her happy."

"She is my wife."

"Yes, and I know what she makes." I looked at the house, "You like it here in this house..." I looked back at him, "I suggest you try to keep her happy too."

I got in my car. I knew I had left him stunned. Maybe he would keep his hands to himself now. I drove away feeling good about threatening him a little.

21

Joselyn:

I couldn't believe that Tyler would over step the grounds in my own home. I had to deal with Ryan all last night: First the questions, then the accusations, and finally the blown out fighting and yelling. I really didn't even want to talk to Tyler. I didn't know what he said or did, but whatever it was, it set Ryan off.

I started with my first appointment with Tammy. We had a 9am and a 10 am appointment. Both went fine and we signed both. She was ecstatic and couldn't wait for another chance to work on some of my stuff.

Next I had Nick. We had 11 am and a 3 pm, so I met with him and the clients for the 11 am appointment. Nick did great with the presentation. The clients had a few concerns, but we worked them out and had them signed by 11:45 am. I was going to run out of time today if I didn't get this working faster.

Seth was next and we had 12 noon and a 1 pm. We wrapped up both early, so I tried to get a salad in between the two.

Tyler poked his head in at 1:40 pm, "You were supposed to see me early."

I looked up, "Kind of busy today. I still have a 2, 3, 4 and every half hour after that, and I still won't get out of her till after 8 pm."

He walked in, "Can I help?"

I shook my head, "No, I've got this, but you need to not be here."

He looked at me funny walking in further and sat down, "Did I do something wrong?"

I shook my head and went to put my jacket back on. He stood up coming around my desk, "What is this?" He had grabbed my arm and was evaluating the bruise on it.

I stopped and looked where he was pointing. I closed my eyes taking a deep breath. He walked quickly over to the door, closed it, and turned on me for answers.

I shook my head, "I don't have time to deal with this now, Tyler. We'll talk later if you're still around after 8:30 pm."

He walked over to me and looked at it closer. He put his fingers to my arm and then pulled my chin up to look at him. I pulled away not to have to look into his eyes. I couldn't handle a nervous breakdown right now; I had too many clients to get through today.

"Talk to me."

I shook my head, "If I get upset, I will blow everything. Give me till later, and I will fall apart then."

He glared at me, "Joselyn!"

I glared at him, "Out now!"

He walked away from me but stopped at the door, "Did I cause this?"

I couldn't say anything, and he locked the door. I took a deep breath begging him, "Please, I have too much to do. I can't talk about this. Please don't make me feel now."

He unlocked the door and quickly walked out slamming it hard. I sat down and took a deep breath. I made it through everyone by 9 pm. There was a lot of commotion in the conference room, so I wandered down and looked in the windows. Everyone was still here and it was like a party. Tyler walked up behind me, "I thought you may need some food, and with this day being big for everyone, I catered in. Can you stay awhile?"

I nodded, as he walked pass me into the room and everyone cheered. I pulled out the cell phone to call home.

Jared answered, "Evans residence."

"Well hello, Jared Evans."

He laughed, "Hi mom, when are you coming home?"

"Um, I kind of had a big day, and I just got done. We're celebrating a little bit, so I will be home later."

"Dad wants to talk to you."

"Joselyn, we talked about this last night. Don't take time away from your family for this."

"I just wrapped up 12 accounts and signed them all. Mr. Reynolds catered in food for everyone. I will be home later."

"How much later?"

"After last night... before the kids get up."

"Joselyn, don't do this."

"You over stepped the grounds last night and I can't be there."

"Fine, don't come home at all."

"Sorry, you gave up the right to tell me what to do, and if you want to push the issue I took pictures."

"Yeah, well... so did I."

I took a deep breath, "I will be home when I get there."

"Fine, whatever."

I hung up and walked back to my office. I grabbed my stuff to head home. I really wasn't in the mood for a party. Then, of course, I had to hear his voice, "You're not leaving are you?"

I nodded.

"But you haven't eaten."

I shook my head and turned to him, but the tears were already streaming down my face. He closed the door quickly, "You weren't kidding when you said you had to wait until you were done."

I shook my head as he came over, wrapping his arms around me, and held me tight. He stroked my hair lightly, "Where are you going?"

I glanced up at him, "I don't know."

He pulled out keys, "Meet me at my apartment in the city. Give me an hour to get things cleaned up here; I will get there as soon as I can."

I did need time to release my emotions, so I agreed. He wiped my tears and kissed my cheeks sweetly. He helped me put my coat on, and then walked me to the elevator. I didn't say anything, as I got on. Our eyes met, but the door slowly closed.

22

I got to the city and walked into Ray's bar ordering the largest Margarita that they had. I walked back to the elevators and pushed the button.

"Did you order two?"

I turned with excitement and disbelief that he was here already, "No, I wasn't expecting anyone this soon."

He walked up to me taking the drink from me, took a huge drink, and handed it back to me, so I tried to finish it quickly. When the elevator door opened, he backed me in, but not taking his eyes off of mine. I took another drink trying to hurry, but he moved closer to me.

As the elevator doors opened, he took the glass in one hand and my hand in another leading me into the apartment. He set the glass down and then started to push my jacket from me. I lowered my face as his mouth came to my ear, "I want you."

I moved to kiss his neck and his ear. I needed him to be forceful. It would help to push things out of my mind. He was so good at reading me, that he was unzipping my skirt, and pushing it from me immediately. His breath came swiftly to my skin, with his urgency to be inside me. I needed him too. I undid his pants, helping him out quickly, so I could have what I needed. He took my hands in his pulling them over my head while he rubbed against me hard. Without hesitation he forcefully gripped my hands in one of his, but only to free his other, so he could push my underwear over. His mouth pushed my chin back as he nibbled and gnawed at my neck, while he eased into me with a deep thrust. He pushed harder, and I wrapped my leg around him. It was amazing, the effect he has over me, and I felt the pain slowly leaving, as the satisfaction moved in. His hand released me, but only to press against my breast followed by his mouth. He sucked and nibbled hastily, as if he was craving every inch of me. He gasped as he thrust into me rapidly, so fast and hard that I just held on. He was pushing away all the bad feelings that had built up in me since yesterday. I saw pain come across his face and fear crept into my mind, "Is something wrong?"

"Yes, I hurt from wanting you so badly."

I wrapped my other leg around him and pulled myself to him more, so I could feel his plunges move deeper. He had an agonizing look on his face.

"Is it that bad?"

He nodded as the moaning and groaning emitted from him.

I felt him pull away and press against me, as his warmth spilled against my skin. His face came to rest against mine, as a whisper escaped his mouth, "I'm sorry. Did I hurt you?"

I shook my head with a slight smile on my face, "I needed it hard today; it pushes away the pain."

He smiled and lowered me to the floor; then he took my face in his hands and kissed every inch of my face until he found my lips. His kiss engulfed me; our tongues entangled, obligated to fulfill the desire, not wanting to be done. I was unbelieving when he said, "God, I still want you. Can we take a shower? I need to do this again."

I nodded with satisfaction. I wanted more too.

His efforts, to bring me new excitement, were a little scary for me. I was not expecting what was coming next. He was rubbing something over me and over himself. I felt awkward and curious at the same time. He held my hands in his as we stood there with this pink crap on us, and I was holding back the giggles that wanted to escape me. This beautiful man was standing in front of me with pink stuff on his testicles, "What are we doing?"

He was smiling and moved to distract me with kissing and touching, as he whispered to my lips, "Five minutes and then surprise."

"Okay, what are we doing?"

"Surprise, you have to wait."

I shook my head in disbelief, but his distraction was wonderful; the kissing, the nibbling, and the licking. I really didn't care what he was doing as long as he was distracting me this way, but every time I looked down he was covered in pink.

I let a snicker escape me; I knew I hurt his feelings when he turned away from me, "If you are going to laugh then you can't look anymore."

99

I traced my hands up his back and then down slowly kissing his back to entice him into play. I took my finger tips and crawled them along his sides to his front and glided them up to his chest pulling my body close to his, "Can it come off now?"

I rubbed his chest with one hand, and kissed his back, all the while running my other hand down his leg muscles. I wanted to play, "Now?"

He shook his head.

I lowered my body against his and reached around his legs tracing my hands up his inner thighs pleading, "Now?"

"Oh, god. No, it's supposed to be on five..."

I moved my hands to cup him and rub him into play.

He moaned, "Oh, shit."

I smiled with satisfaction that he was going to give into me soon. I messaged my hands against him; as his body tensed, I kissed the lower part of his back allowing my lips to glide over his skin.

He turned to face the water, and I washed it off by messaging him, as the water ran down his front.

"How can I try something new if you can't control yourself?"

I laughed and messaged him more. I could hear the satisfaction in his moans, as I pleased him into hardness.

He pulled me in front of him, as he slowly moved his hand over me to wash it off. I looked down realizing he had put hair removal on both of us. I laughed, "This is what you wanted?"

"I had something else in mind, but your touch got me going. It will have to wait for another time. I need you now."

He shut off the water, grabbed a towel, and wrapped it around the front of me, but held it around him. We walked back to the bed, but he stopped. He lowered the towel to the floor, "Kneel down."

"Why?"

"Please, I need you now."

I knelt on the floor leaning over the bed, and I felt his hands rub against my thighs as he pushed into me. It was different and not as pleasurable, but he still felt good to me. His hands traced my back up the middle and then back to my hips to hold me as he pushed in further. He wrapped his arm around my waist pulling me back to him. One hand traced my body, while his mouth kissed my shoulder and neck. His other hand reached for the front of me to help me tilt back as he pushed to me. His fingers rubbed against my labia as he pushed back. The duel pleasure was amazing and I was moaning with satisfaction, as he pressed and

100

moved to me at the same time. I called out his name to make it stop, but he knew that what he was doing was rewarding to me. He did it more until I shuttered with enjoyment in each movement. He pulled from me, but grabbed me around the waist pulling me to the bed and rolling over to rub against my body, as he exploded with pleasure against my legs, stomach, and everywhere he touched. His kisses came deep and full of passion, his touch gentling, as he spasms gradually decreased.

When we settled a little his voice came soothingly, "You have no idea how much pleasure you give me."

I felt like a real woman again in my ability to please him. Especially after being told that *'you wouldn't know how to please a man'* I was finding it incredible that he was finding enjoyment with me. Those stupid thoughts on inadequacy seeped their way into my brain, and I started to feel some anxiety. I tucked my face into his chest with uncertainty and doubt.

He pulled my face up so that he could search for my insecurities that had moved back in, "Why do you do that?"

My eyes filled with tears, "I was told I couldn't please a man even if I had a pointer. Are you sure I give you pleasure."

A slight grin came to his face, "That is coming from a man that hurt you. You shouldn't listen to him. I find you incredibly fascinating in every way possible."

He pulled me to him wrapping his arms around me to hold me close. I hope this is love because he was working his way into my heart.

23

I got up in the morning to start my day with a smile on my face. Even when I looked at Ryan I had to smile, because it was like a little secret that I could still make a man feel like a man. We got ready to go, but Jared walked in to the bathroom as I was getting ready, "Did your boss talk to you?"

I stopped doing what I was doing and turned to him, "Honey, what are you talking about?"

I was so worried that Tyler said something that would upset my children. He was still smiling, so it couldn't be that bad.

He shook his head, "It's just that... you look nice today."

I was confused. I was wearing a t-shirt, long shorts and tennis shoes, "Did you want me to put something else on?"

"NO! Mom, you look good. Thanks mom."

I didn't know what I did, but he said I looked good and he thanked me. Wow, what did I do that was good this morning?

At the ball field I got my own chair, and I sat where I wanted to this time, which was closer to the back stop. I think I threw Ryan off because he followed me, "What are we doing?"

"I wanted to sit here today."

"Why?"

"I don't know, it's just different."

He set up his chair and leaned down to me, "You're not going to start anything are you?"

I looked up at him and smiled, "No, sorry we can sit down further." I grabbed my chair and waited for him to lead the way. Haden was asking a lot of questions as to why we were moving, but I didn't say anything derogatory, "Honey, daddy wants to sit down further. It's no big deal."

102

He stopped and looked up at me, "You wanted to sit over there?"

"Kind of, but it's not a big deal."

"But you never say what you want. I think we should sit where you want today."

I laughed and shook my head giving him the biggest hug. Everything was going way too good to be true today. I laid out the blanket for Haden and Terra to sit on.

We were enjoying the game when I heard this recognizable voice that instantly made me nervous, "Mrs. Evans, do you know how hard you are to find?"

I closed my eyes. Shit, what was he doing here?

"I need to borrow you for a couple of minutes at my car. You didn't sign the tanning lotion account yesterday."

I stood up and went to walk away from my family. Ryan grabbed my hand, "Hey, family time?"

"I will be just a minute; please let go."

He glared at me and watched me walk away from him. I chuckled to myself, as I looked into Tyler's eyes and saw that sweet young hot guy that I wanted to have sex with as soon as I could get away again. He turned to walk with me to his car.

"Tyler, what are you doing?"

"I had to know he was being nice after getting home late."

"It's going good. We're not really talking, but this is extreme."

He laughed and pulled a file from his car. He opened it to a single piece of paper. I looked it over and laughed as I read it:

I find you the most amazing lover I have ever had. I missed you too much and I couldn't stay away. Please forgive me that I want to be around you every day.

I looked up at him and shook my head, as I leaned over the car to sign it. I wrote out:

I am hot for you right now and I am glad you came, but this scares me.

I handed it back to him, as he read it with a smile on his face. We walked very slowly back to the game. Haden came running to us, "Do you have a magic trick for me?"

Tyler stopped and did one for Haden. I laughed, as he talked with Haden. I found it very enjoyable that he didn't mind spending time with my kids. Haden took Tyler's hand in his and dragged him all the way to the game. He offered my chair to him but looked up at me, "Is this okay, mommy?"

"If Mr. Reynolds doesn't mind then I don't."

I heard Ryan huff and grumble. I laughed that Tyler was doing this right under Ryan's nose. Terra came over to me pulling on my shirt, "I have to go to the bathroom."

I looked at Tyler and he smiled, "I'll just hang with your husband if he doesn't mind."

Ryan grumbled, "Yeah, you can stay here."

I shook my head and worried the whole time we were gone to the bathroom.

24

Tyler

"So, who is winning?"

"Our team. That's Jared out in the center field."

"What inning?"

"Top of the fifth."

"So, we're the home team. That's great. I always liked being the home team, because of the last at bat."

"I thought you didn't play?"

"I did when I was young."

"Yeah, aren't you young now?"

"No, and it sucks. It's always business, business, business. I hardly ever have time to just relax and watch a game."

"So, if you are busy, shouldn't you be going?"

I looked over at him, "Actually, I wanted to talk to you."

"Yeah, what about?"

"Remember how I told you I want her to be happy?"

He huffed at me with a laugh, "Yeah, your point is?"

"She had her jacket off yesterday. She has a bruise that looks like fingers on her arm."

He turned to look at me laughing, "Yeah, they call that self defense."

I was confused, "What do you mean?"

"Sometimes I have a drink and I get mouthy, and she went to hit me, so I stopped her."

"Oh, well then... when she crossed her legs I noticed a bruise on her thigh. It resembled the other one."

105

"Yeah, and then she tried to kick me. Why am I explaining myself to you anyway? It's none of your business."

"Well, if she is unhappy it affects her work, so I was concerned. So, you are telling me you two are okay?"

"Yeah, we're just the greatest." He was full of sarcasm.

"Well, good. So, how is Jared doing?"

"He hit a line drive to right."

"I hope he gets another one. I would love to see that."

"You would?"

"Yeah, he is a pretty cool little dude."

Ryan laughed and I noticed Joselyn coming back over. She was so adorable and those shorts that were perfect for what Jared wanted. I wanted to talk to her about what she was going to wear to his games, but I guess no work clothes on Saturday.

She sat down on the blanket in front of us. Ryan offered me a beer, but it wasn't the right place for one. Not with a bunch of kids around, it just didn't seem right. Haden was sitting in Joselyn's lap, but he asked her if she would take him to the park.

I was waiting for a chance to impress her, and this was my opportunity, "I'll take him."

Joselyn:

Both Ryan and I looked at him like he was crazy. Of course he melted me with that grin.

Ryan was stern, "No, his mother will take him."

I started to push him up, but Tyler grabbed his hands and pulled him up. Terra had to go with too.

"I'll just walk with you then. I will play with them at the park, and you can still supervise. That's what you are good at."

Ryan glared at him, "I thought you wanted to see Jared hit the ball."

"Oh, I do, but it's more important for the two of you to see him, so I will play with them at the park and Joselyn can still watch the game."

I laughed. Ryan would never think about letting me watch instead of him

We started on our way with Haden and Terra running ahead of us to the park. I kept my eyes on them, but I had to ask, "Tyler, what are you doing here?"

106

"I couldn't stay away from you. I wanted you to see I want the whole package not just the steamy nights."

I laughed, "Really, you would give those up?"

"No. I didn't say that. They will have to see their dad sometimes."

I laughed even more.

"Joselyn, I love to hear you laugh, and that smile is incredible."

"You're embarrassing me."

"No, I am telling you the truth. Your son's friends even notice you."

"What are you talking about?"

"Well, I was going to talk to you about this at a better time, but he talked to me when he was sitting in my car. His friends call you a MILF."

"And what is that?"

"Mother I'd Like to ..." He raised his eyebrows. My smile dropped from my face, as I realized what he was saying. I felt horrible.

"He just wishes you would dress more like a mom when you come to the games. The boys don't harass him as much when you look like this."

"What, I look dumpy and old?"

"You are adorable to me, but to a little boy, yes this makes you look old and not sexy."

I had to laugh, because of the way he said this. He still made me feel desirable to him.

We were at the park, and he took off running after my kids. I turned and watched the game. I peaked back to check him out a couple of times, but I tried to keep my eye on the game.

I heard Tyler tell them that he needed to rest, and I chuckled to myself, but he came to stand by me facing the park, still keeping an eye on my kids.

"I am throwing a small party to celebrate and thank everyone for all their efforts on Friday. They worked really hard for you, and I like the team effort, so I am announcing my final decisions."

I nodded to agree with him.

"It's for employees and their spouses. Do you suppose you will bring your husband?"

I shook my head no.

He smiled greatly and continued, "After that I will be asking for a lot of your time. If it would make things easier, you should invite him."

I shook my head no.

"Joselyn, I will endure my jealousy for one night and one night only. You need to bring him so that he can see who you are working with and what you are doing."

"I don't want to be around him."

"Joselyn, I am ready to be with you whenever you are, but until then you have to keep up appearances."

"I don't care what he thinks."

"You do because you want your kids. Just say the word, and I will set up the appointment again."

"This week."

He turned to me with a confused look on his face.

I smiled slightly at him, "I can't do this anymore."

He glared, "What exactly are we talking about?"

"I can't pretend to be happy in this life. I will talk to the Lawyer this week, anytime. It will be a planning week."

He smiled at me and ran out picking up Haden and put him on his shoulders, "I think your brother is going to be up soon. We should go back to show him we want him to hit the ball for us."

Haden wasn't too happy with this, but Terra came along happily. We walked and just as we got back Jared hit a double. Tyler cheered louder than Ryan and I put together. I was so pleased with him in every way. He waited until Jared made it home, and he walked over to him giving him a high five and telling him what an awesome job he did. Jared leaned to him and said something and Tyler shook his head. They both looked back at me and smiled. I shook my head and sat down on the chair. Tyler walked back over, "Well, I have taken up enough of your family time. We'll see you on Monday."

I grinned at him, but he wasn't done.

"Ryan, we are having a celebration on Friday at the office. It's for employees and their spouses, so I am expecting you there."

I was furious and Tyler laughed. "See you Monday, Joselyn."

"Good bye, Mr. Reynolds."

"Hey, one more thing. Can you walk me to my car?"

I got up, but I was not happy. I walked with him not saying a word.

"You are angry?"

"Yes, I told you *No* and I thought if I agreed to see the Lawyer you would drop it."

"No, he will feel better about the late nights if we invite him to a work party. I wasn't trying to make you mad. Plus, Saturday I will see you because that is the day Tori set up for all of us to go out."

I whispered, "I would rather be with you alone."

He grinned as he opened his car door, "Joselyn, I want you to see I want the whole package. Everything, not just… well you know."

I shook my head as he got in and looked back at me smiling. He was going to cause more problems, and he didn't even realize it.

25

My week was less stressful than the previous one. I had only six new accounts to work on, and I decided to share them with the other agents, so I was just going to help them. I was sitting in my office relaxing, looking out the window taking a breather, knowing that Tyler would have another one for me soon. It was the only way to keep me out late for dinner. Hopefully, he kept in mind when Jared's games were. I did find it odd that he hadn't come in to tell me when I was meeting with the Lawyer. It was making me nervous thinking about it.

Friday seemed to be here in a heartbeat. Tyler walked in smiling, "Are you ready for tonight?"

"No."

"Joselyn, it will be fine."

I continued to look out the window. I didn't want to be tempted by looking at him. It was not our night to be together.

"Joselyn, what are you thinking?"

"I'm trying not to think at all."

"Is he coming?"

"Not sure. You asked him, so he might."

"You really don't want him here?"

"No, I don't want him to know anything about me. He lost that right."

Tyler walked over to me and leaned against my desk, "Everything will be fine. You will see."

"What about my appointment."

His eyes got wide, "Shit."

"You forgot?"

He grinned, "No, I was just trying to get you to smile."

I looked up at him not smiling. His eyes glared a little, as he evaluated me, "You are hard to read like this."

I gave him a smirk, "The key is to stay cold and distant so that I don't get..." I stopped. He should be able to figure out what I meant.

"Are you busy next Tuesday?"

I looked up at him, "What time?"

He got that grin on his face like he was thinking of something. I shook my head, "Don't tell me you have another client that I have to be ready for. I need at least five days to prep."

His smile dissolved, and he huffed shaking his head, "You are in a mood today."

I glared up at him again.

"No, if you don't mind I have that set up for Wednesday at noon. In case you have a game to go to, I wanted to plan it early."

I went through my calendar, "That should be fine. Do you have the file?"

He laid it down in front of me, but didn't take his hand off of it, and his voice came across in a whisper, "Joselyn?"

I glanced up at him with wonder.

"I need for you to not look at this until after tonight."

Why? What did it have to do with tonight? I didn't have anything to do right now.

His voice came in another whisper, "Joselyn, promise me."

I stood up and looked at him desperately wondering what I should do with myself, "I don't have anything to work on."

He smiled, "Good, go buy yourself a new dress."

I wasn't happy with his solution. He gave me that cute little grin that made me melt, "Joselyn, you will get your commission check today. You can afford a new dress. I am giving you the day off to find something that will knock everyone out. Please, just do this for yourself."

He got up and walked to get my jacket and held it for me. I walked over to him with almost a smile on my face. He slid the jacket on me and then handed me my purse. He whispered in my ear, "Your smile drives me crazy, and don't think about the price of the dress. You can afford anything you want now, and that is just the first check from your commissions."

I laughed with a sigh, and he pushed me out the door. I walked to the elevator and ran into Tori. I pulled her along with me for the shopping trip. I was going to get her something special too.

111

We went from shop to shop and finally we came across something that looked amazing on her. At first I thought it was a little off, but only because I wasn't used to seeing her in that color, but it was amazing on her skinny little body. It was a short, flirty semi-formal dress with a halter top, ruche bust, black overlay and embellished circle at the bust over a dark celery color. It was amazing.

We continued to shop, because I am much more conservative. I just wanted a plane little black dress.

We ended up at Nordstrom's, and I found the dress I would feel comfortable in. It was a JS Collections Sleeveless Silk Chiffon Little black Dress. It was airy chiffon with an ultra-flattering fit-and-flare silhouette, emphasized by its pleated faux-surplice V-neck and wide Empire waist.

Next we headed for shoes. I had to have the perfect pair and so did Tori. She held her tongue for most of our shopping trip, but when we sat down to try on shoes, she started to ask questions, "So, how is it that we are shopping and not working?"

"Mr. Reynolds insisted I get a dress for tonight, and I thought you needed one too."

"You know, he just wants to look at your legs?"

"Well… now he gets two pairs for the price of one."

"He is paying for this?"

I laughed, "No, of course not."

"Joselyn, I still think he is hot for you."

"Please don't say that, and please don't bring it up tonight. I guess Ryan is coming."

"No way. Why would you invite him?"

I raised my eyebrows, "Mr. Reynolds did."

"Okay, wait a minute. Can you just call him Tyler like the rest of us, and when did he invite Ryan?"

I opened my eyes wide, "Tyler showed up at my son's game last Saturday, so I could sign paperwork and he invited him."

"But if he was hot for you, why would he invite him?"

"My point exactly."

"Oh, I would never have guessed that. Did you tell him that you two don't get along anymore?"

"This is business."

She shook her head, "Don't be an idiot; if he was interested in me I would be pulling him to a closet everyday."

"We are dropping the Tyler subject now."

She laughed and giggled, as we picked out our shoes. I knew she was thinking about what she would do with him, but she had no idea what he was like. I started to day dream about the first night we were together. How forceful he was, but when he found out that it had been five years since I had sex he was careful and gentle. This thought put a smile on my face, forgetting where I was and what I was doing. When I finally made it back to the real world I noticed Tori staring at me.

"You were thinking about him?"

I shook my head feeling a little embarrassed.

"There is more and you're not telling."

"Okay, but if I tell you it cannot be discussed at work, and you have to promise me."

She was grinning, "Yes, okay." She scooted closer to me in her seat.

I looked into her eyes really serious, "I have sex… dreams about him."

She glared at me, "You are full of shit. If you don't want to tell me, fine. But don't lie to me."

I laughed, "Okay, the night we bumped into him he showed up at my car thinking I had agreed to meet him. I told him I was married, and I just didn't hear what I was agreeing to."

"Oh, my god; he is hot for you. So what happened?"

"Nothing, he let me go when I insisted that I was married."

"That is it?"

I grinned, "There is more, but we have to go."

"No way. You have to tell me… now."

"No, I will give you more info later when you can handle it. Until then we have a party to attend.

26

Tyler.

I was in the back room of Rey's, the place under my apartment, setting up for the party. Everything was coming along fine. I still had to run up to get dressed, but I was waiting for someone to show up. It was suppose to be cocktail hour from 7 pm to 8 pm, and no one was here yet. I realize it's only 6:45 pm, but I thought people would be early, especially Joselyn, I needed her here.

I had the hostess ready to greet people, and I headed up to the apartment. I looked around wanting to see my girl... and nothing. She was making me nervous that she wasn't going to show up. Damn, if I have to go get her, I am not going to be happy. This was all for her.

When I went back down stairs, I noticed Ryan was here. I walked over to him, "So, where is your wife?"

He turned to me shaking my hand, "Hey, how is it going? I was hoping you could tell me the same thing."

I was confused. She didn't go home to get him? Where in the hell was she? I searched the room to find Tori; she would know where Joselyn was. When I realized she wasn't here either, I looked back over at Ryan. He looked very nervous, and I chuckled to myself, "Can I offer you a drink?"

"Yeah, that sounds really good."

We went to the bar, and I looked at him waiting for him to tell me what he wanted. I noticed he was looking around the room himself, "Are you looking for Joselyn?"

"No." He turned back to me, "Jack and coke."

I leaned to him, "Don't you say stupid stuff when you drink this stuff." He glared at me and I had to make myself clear, "You know… the bruises."

He shook his head, "No, it will be fine."

I ordered his drink, and he was still looking around the room. He was starting to make me more nervous, "Who are you looking for?"

He leaned to me taking a sip from his drink, "I am looking for the guy who is fucking my wife."

I coughed, choked, and stumbled, "Um, why do you think that she is with anyone?"

He glanced up at me, "My wife is very sexy, and she doesn't come home every night."

I raised my eyebrows. I wasn't expecting to be having this conversation with him. I moved closer to him leaning against the bar looking around the room, "I do spend time with her at work, and she doesn't seem to be like that." I looked at my watch. It was after 7 pm. Where in the hell was she. I knew I had to get this over quickly.

"Yeah, well it's a long story."

I sighed, "I guess there are more problems then what I was seeing?"

"Yeah, you could say that." He looked up at me again, "For all I know it could be you."

I laughed and noticed she was walking in and looked drop dead gorgeous. My eyes met hers and I must have given her a look because she furrowed her brows and I could actually see it from across the room. Oh shit, that new dress was going to give me a heart attack. I turned back to the bar, "I think your wife is here. Can you do me a favor?"

"What's that?"

"I promise we will talk more, but I need this night to go smoothly. Can you please not bring this up tonight while you are here?"

"Why shouldn't I?"

I turned to him, "Go to your wife, stand by her side and be supportive, because I am asking you to, for me."

He gave me a quirky smile and shook his head, "Yeah, I will find out later. I will see it in the guy's eyes when I meet him."

He turned around and saw his wife. I couldn't look at her, because he would know it was me. I was completely in love with his wife, and there was nothing that I wanted more than to walk up to her right now, wrap my arm around her waist, and pull her to me to kiss that wonderful face. I set my drink down and walked away from him without saying anything else. I was afraid that I would tell him right then and there that it was me and that she was done with him. I had to get it together, and yet I needed to tell her what he was thinking. Shit, what am I going to do?

"Hey, Tyler."

I glanced up to see Tori. I smiled, "So, you came with Joselyn?"

"Yeah, she took me shopping." She was twirling in front of me.

I smiled, "Nice dress."

"Yeah, I thought so. Did you see Joselyn yet?"

"Um... Yeah, she has a nice dress too." I was distracted trying to figure this out. Shit, what am I going to do? I glanced at Tori, who was looking at me funny. I smiled, "Stay close to the stage. I have a surprise for you."

She smiled and agreed. I ran up to the stage. I had to get this over with. Once I mentioned the promotions, she will have to come talk to me in private. That was the only plan I had to work with. I ran up on the stage.

There wasn't cheering like I was expecting, but they didn't realize that no one was losing their job. I cleared my throat in the microphone to get every ones attention.

"Okay, I think everyone is wondering what tonight is all about."

Yep, that got all their attention. I took a deep breath and looked around, "Well, I thought maybe you would all enjoy this, a lot, more if I did the announcements first. So, the good news is... No one is losing their job."

This they cheered to. I smiled with satisfaction. My gaze fell on Joselyn and she was smiling. Oh, god, do I love her smile.

"Second, If Mr. Jenkins can come up here?" I waited. The group parted to make room for him to come up. When he got to the stage, he was all smiles and he shook my hand. "Okay, Mr. Jenkins is now getting a promotion. I want someone overseeing the daily activities, so he will now be the business manager."

Everyone cheered. Mr. Jenkins snuffled and tear up. I smiled and shook his hand.

"Third," everyone was cheering now. I knew this was going to be good. I glanced back at Joselyn again, and she was smiling. Ryan had his hand around her waist. She was trying to push him away. Shit, I have to hurry up.

"Tori, can you please come up here?"

She came running and screaming. You would think she won the lottery. I had to laugh.

When she was directly in front of me I announced, "You have done amazing things in the art department, and I like your artistic eye. You are now in charge of all designs."

She was screaming and crying at the same time. She grabbed my hands, "Does this mean I get a raise?"

I laughed and whispered it to her. She didn't scream because I stunned her. She just stared at me.

"There is one more, but I need to explain." I had everyone's attention again. I looked right at Joselyn, "When you buy a company you want to go in and look around to see what you have to work with. Well, I came into evaluate this company, but what you didn't know is that I am the new owner."

Joselyn's face changed to confusion. I wanted to go to her right away, but I had to finish.

"I wanted to see for myself, the quality of people that worked here, and I am glad I did. All of you work very well together, and I am so impressed that I am speechless, so if you wouldn't mind give your selves a cheer."

They did and I smiled as I watched around the room, but my eyes fell back to Joselyn who wasn't clapping at all. Ryan was turned in front of her, and she was shaking her head. Shit.

"So," I had to cough to get every ones attention again. When I had the attention of everyone except for Joselyn, I started again, "There is one more and I think you will all agree with me on this. Joselyn, could you please come up here?"

I watched for her to come up, and instead, she was busy arguing with her husband.

"Joselyn… everyone… could you please help Joselyn to the stage?"

She walked by Ryan, and I could tell he was furious. My eyes fell back to watching her walk up here. She was smiling, but it was a fake smile. I knew the difference. I couldn't help but smile slightly; I watched the bottom of her dress move in a swaying movement against her legs, as she walked closer. I could tell she was taking deep breaths to stay calm, but I noticed because her breast heaved… and I wanted her more than anything right now. She walked up, and I took her hand.

She leaned to me, "What are you doing?"

I grinned and turned her to face everyone.

"Well, what can I say? When I came in I didn't meet with Joselyn for the first two weeks. I tried, but she was dodging me quite successfully; but in those first two weeks she closed 14 deals, so I had to meet her. When Mr. Jenkins came in and told me she was planning on quitting, I had to come up with a plan to keep her. I started to put a package together on one big account to see how she would handle it." I glanced over at her, and she was shaking her head and fidgeting.

I smiled again looking at the crowd, "To my surprise in order to handle the big account she turned to the rest of you for help. The clients were more important to her than the commission check. This surprised me, but she closed 12 deals in one week and was still able to handle the client I gave her, thanks to all of you." I pointed to everyone, and they all cheered again. I laughed before continuing. I took a deep breath, "So, I am sure it is not a surprise that I am putting her in charge of all the agents. I want her in on every deal, so everything will be going through her."

Everyone cheered again, as I glanced over at her. She smiled at everyone.

"So, just to let you know; I will continue to have my office here, but I will also be busy with other businesses, and everyone will be going through these three from now on. Everyone have a good time, and if you need a cab, I have a line of them out front. Have fun and be safe."

Joselyn was walking off the stage before I finished. I looked at Tori, and she just shrugged her shoulders. I watched Joselyn walk all the way to her husband, and they were walking out. No, she couldn't leave. I ran after her.

Joselyn:

I couldn't believe he did this without discussing it with me first. I didn't want it. Everyone was going to know that he gave this to me because…, dam him.

I walked pass Ryan, "I am leaving."

"Why? Tyler just gave you a promotion."

I turned to him, "I didn't want it."

He grabbed my arm, "What is your problem?"

I raised my eyebrows, "More hours! I didn't want that." I pulled away and went to walk out. Ryan came running after me and pulled me to a stop, "That's fine. Quit."

I didn't want to quit and now Tyler was coming down the hall yelling after me, "Joselyn, where are you going?"

I turned to look at Tyler directly, "I didn't want it."

Ryan grabbed my arm, "Come on, Jos, let's just go home."

I turned to him pulling my arm from him, "You are not allowed to touch me ever again." I turned back to Tyler, "I didn't want it."

I went to walk away. I heard Ryan and Tyler at the same time, "Jos." "Joselyn."

I walked out and straight to my car. I didn't know where or what I was going to do, but I felt like I was screaming in my head, but nothing was coming out of my mouth. I drove and drove. I made it to Ty's tavern where I first met Tyler. I walked in and ordered tequila straight up, to handle my night.

27

Tyler:

What just happened? I looked at Ryan for answers, "What is wrong?"

"I guess she didn't want it."

I looked out the door after her.

He laughed, "Well, I guess your plan to keep her happy didn't work so well."

I wanted to punch his lights out, but I had to go after her, "Do you know where she would have gone?"

"Nope, she doesn't tell me anything anymore."

"What happened?"

He shook his head, as we headed back into the bar. He went on to explain; that at first they were young and in love, but when the kids started coming, things started going to pot. He explained that she would work all day, then come home and cook dinner, then she would have to clean up, and then she would get the kids to bed. He would wait till she was all done, but when he would get her in the bedroom she was too tired to give him the attention that he needed. It continued to get worse as the years went on and they had more kids. She wasn't taking care of her family like she had at one time. I couldn't believe what I was hearing. He was blaming her for not having energy to please him. I wanted to rip his head off. I couldn't believe he was this stupid. I glanced over at him, "Did it ever occur to you that maybe if you helped her with all of that then she wouldn't be so tired?"

"Yeah, right. She has always taken care of that stuff. If I helped I would get in her way."

I laughed, "So, that is it?"

"No, she was neglecting my needs, so I found someone who wasn't so tired."

This is what I wanted to hear, "Do you love this person?"

He laughed, "HELL NO! How could I love anyone but Jos? She is the trophy on my wall, and my friends would think I was stupid."

I already knew he was stupid. I wanted to talk to him more to convince him that he should have someone that will give him attention. I wanted him to doubt his feelings for her, so he would let her go easily. Then I could have her every day instead of once in a while. I just couldn't do it now, so I shook my head, "Well, if she shows up at home, can you call me and let me know if she is okay?"

He stood up, "Where are you going?"

"To find her. I didn't want to make her angry."

"Why would you care?"

I leaned into him, "Did you not get what this was all about?"

He was confused by my reaction.

I glared at him, "She is good, very good at what she does. The best I have ever seen. I can't afford to lose her, and I will do anything to get her to stay with the company."

"Are you nuts? She doesn't want to stay now that you did that."

"How do you know? Maybe it was just the shock. She is worth it, so I am going to look for her. What are you going to do?"

He laughed, "I am going home, because I know she won't give up those kids. That is the only thing that keeps her in my arms."

I glared at him and wondered if he meant that they were together physically. No way. She didn't even want him to touch her; if they were together, she wouldn't push him away, would she? I stopped, "So, even after you did it with someone else, you still do it with your wife? Isn't that sick?"

He laughed again, "Yeah why, does that surprise you? I gave her children that she adores, and I made a few mistakes, but we keep holding on trying to make it work."

No way. There was too much pain in her for this to be true. Did he say a few mistakes? I had to find her. I went back in and found Tori. She was going on and on about her big plans with her new job. How she wanted to try some different things, and who would be best to try them with. I was pleased. She was at a party and she was thinking business.

I tapped her shoulder, "Do you have a minute?"

She smiled and turned to me, as we walked a little bit away from the group she was with. I turned and leaned down to talk very quietly, "Would you happen to know where Joselyn would go if she was upset?"

She looked up at me, "She left?"

I raised my eyebrows, "I guess she wasn't happy about the promotion."

"You think?" She was full of sarcasm, and I didn't understand.

She smiled, "Tyler, it is obvious that you are hot for her, and she is afraid that everyone will think you want to sleep with her, and that is why you did this."

I was floored, "Do you think I want to sleep with you or Mr. Jenkins?"

She laughed and shook her head, "But you don't look at me like you look at her. The whole office knows you are sweet on Joselyn."

I took a deep breath and leaned down whispering, "You know I gave her the raise and the big account BEFORE I realized it was her."

She glared at me, "Yeah, but that doesn't matter. Joselyn has a reputation to uphold. She is good at what she does, and she doesn't want anyone to think she didn't earn it."

I was frustrated, "She did earn it.. She does earn it every day. Have you ever watched her?"

She grinned with a scolding smile, "That is what I am talking about. You watch her, and everyone knows it."

"I guess I shouldn't have an office there."

She turned me to face her, "You do know she isn't happy at home. Her husband is a jerk."

I chuckled, "Yeah, I talked to him tonight."

"I haven't seen her smile in years and now... I see it daily. I like that you have an office there."

"Do you know where she would have gone?"

She pulled out her cell phone, "I will give her a call."

I stood there and waited. She must not have told everyone that I had her number too. I was getting impatient. She closed her phone, "She's not answering. Did she leave with her husband? He is gone too."

"No, I was with them when she left without him."

She grimaced, "I could check the office."

I nodded, "You do that and call me." I pulled out my phone and took her number to keep up appearances. I had an idea. She may have gone back to Ty's.

We parted ways, and I started for the long drive. I just couldn't imagine that she would go this far. I called Tori when I was half way to Ty's. She wasn't at the office. She had to be at Ty's Tavern. I drove as fast as I could. If she wasn't there, I was going to go nuts.

I called her house. Ryan answered. I asked if she made it back there yet. He laughed and rubbed it in again that I wasn't making her happy. He made a comment about her being easy, or meeting the guy that she was screwing from work. It made me want to turn around, go there straight to his house, and kick the shit out of him. I didn't like that he was talking about his wife like this. The only reason she was with anyone was because of me; I pushed her into it. I hung up, because I couldn't stand the stupidity coming out of his mouth. I just couldn't believe that he didn't care about her feelings at all; and he hurt her. My mind drifted off to my past, and I just couldn't lose Joselyn no matter what the price was. I haven't been in love with anyone for 4 years, and I couldn't handle a loss again. He just didn't understand how lucky he was to still have his wife and children with him and then to treat them like shit. She has to be there.

28

I pulled in with relief that her car was here. I closed my eyes and took a deep breath to calm myself and try to think of what I was going to do or say. I had to make this right.

I walked in and straight to the bar, "Kevin!"

He came over pointing to Joselyn on the dance floor, "I was wondering when you were going to show up?"

I shook my head. She was dancing with some young guy. I laughed to myself shaking my head, "Margarita's?"

"No, actually, straight Tequila."

I headed out to her. I taped on the kids shoulder, as he turned to me, "No, way…" but when he saw me he changed what he was going to say, "Oh, sorry Tyler. Be my guest."

I moved behind her wrapping my hands around her waist and whispered to her ear, "What are you doing?"

Her face turned to me grazing my chin with her nose, as she leaned to me, "Trying to push it all away."

I lightly kissed her cheek, "There are better ways." Standing behind her, swaying slowly to the music; she reach back to pull me into her more. I was in heaven with her tenderness. I turned her to me holding her with one arm, taking her hand in my other one, and let the music take us. I knew she wanted to forget, but I needed to know what was really bothering her, "Joselyn, why are you mad?"

She leaned her forehead to my chest, "I didn't want it."

I whispered, "Why?"

She didn't want to talk about it, so all I got was silence. I don't know why, but that really irked me, and besides, I had to get something else off my mind, "Your husband said you two still had sex."

She traced her hands along my collar raising her face until those eyes collided with mine, "Did you believe him?"

Those eyes did it for me in every way; I noticed that they were very green at the moment with just a touch of brown in the center and surrounded by a black ring; but yet they were so pure and honest that I knew as soon as I looked into them, that I shouldn't have even brought up her husband, "No."

I saw a glimpse of shimmer in those eyes as she said, "Dance with me."

I continued to hold and move her slowly. I was inching our way to the door. I needed her to open up to me, and I think she would be more comfortable doing that in private. When we got to the edge of the dance floor she looked up at me in a scolding way shaking her head. This was the woman from the office coming out, so I felt challenged. I really didn't understand which one she was at this moment, so I caved, leading her back out to the middle of the dance floor moving with her. Her body moved in ways that were fascinating to me when they responded to my touch. I couldn't help myself; I had to touch those lips. I pulled her close to me and leaned down to glide over her lips with mine. Her mouth came to mine hard and desperate, as her tongue licked my top lip before she pulled me deeper. I took advantage of the situation pleading with her, "Are you ready to go now?"

She nodded, and I didn't hesitate. I was pulling her from Ty's right away. We got outside, and I wrapped my arms around her waist, as she walked in front of me. She wasn't in the mood to talk, I knew that, but how was I going to find out how to fix this if I didn't know exactly what her problem was with it. I understood what Tori said, but no one knows we're sleeping together, so that couldn't be it. I unlocked the door, as her hands wrapped around me grabbing my ass. I loved when she let me know what she wanted. I walked her in kissing her neck, but she turned on me to push off my jacket. I wanted to keep her longer, so I shook my head, "I want to dance with you some more."

I pushed her away from me leaving her standing there stunned. I couldn't help but smile to myself, as I walked over to the stereo turning it on. I sat down in a chair and started to take off my shoes. I was leaving her wanting me, and I was enjoying this. She walked over to me slowly and put her foot on the chair between my legs. I smiled tracing her calf down to her foot pulling her shoe off. I tilted my head looking up at her and she glared at me. Not the response I was looking for. She put down her foot and put the other one up. I didn't even look this time. I ran my hand down her calf to slide the other shoe off but I also traced my other hand along her thigh pulling her to me and kissing her lightly along the inside of her leg. I felt her fingers entangle in my hair; now that was the reaction I was looking for. I slid her leg down and stood up wrapping my arm around her waist to hold her close to me. I slowly swayed with her moving to take her hand in mine. I pushed her away turning her. When she was a full arm's length away, she smiled and laughed a little. I pulled her back to me, as she rolled up into my arms. Now that she was in front of me, I swayed her some more trailing my nose along her face. I lightly kissed her and traced down her neck and shoulder kissing her lightly, as I moved my mouth against her skin. She turned her face to mine and I leaned into her. She whispered, "Tyler, what are you doing? I want you to make love to me." I smiled, because that is exactly what I was doing. I turned her to me and leaned my forehead to hers and held her tight, as I stared into those eyes.

Joselyn:

This was too serious for me, and it was making me nervous. Why couldn't he just push me into having sex, so he can push all these bad feelings I am having away? Please just make love to me the hardest way you can. I had to look away; he was going to make me feel, and I didn't want to. I undid the top button of his shirt, and I felt the smile against my forehead, so I continued to unbutton until he took my hands away from his shirt but held them tightly at his chest. I glanced back up at him wondering why he was stopping me, but his grin was sinful. I took a step back, turning away from him, and slowly reached to unzip my dress. He huffed out a pleasing moan and moved closer to me, so that he could run his fingers down my back. You would never guess with the feel of his tender touch that those hands were very strong and could drive me mad with aspiration. I felt his hand wrap around my waist, as his other pulled the strap from my shoulder. His mouth came openly warm to linger there, as we walked toward the bed. I was pleased now that he was making a movement towards making me happy. Just as we reached the bed, he turned me to him, "Joselyn, why do you want this... me?"

Oh shit he was going to make me feel again. I didn't want to feel, I needed to forget. I reached back to zip up my dress; this wasn't what I wanted at all. I stepped alongside him giving him one last grin before walking away. I reached down for my shoes and headed out the door.

The door was shoved closed while I was trying to open it, "What are you doing?"

"Tyler, I can't do this tonight."

"You don't want to leave; I know you don't."

I turned to him tracing my fingers down his chest and pleaded with him, "I just want to forget tonight."

His face grazed mine in agony until his lips parted, his tongue touched my skin, and his lips moved to suck me into him. I was gone that instant, as he led me back towards the bed. I caressed him hoping to entice an erection, because I did not want him to stop this time. We were frantic in our attempt to discard our clothing. This was what I needed. I was gasping with every breath, as his thick rod slid between my legs, and moved against my feminine folds when we moved to lie down. His hand came to me to entice the feelings I was already having, but... really, there was no need. The moisture from me was more than enough to allow him in easily. I wanted him badly and wanted him now. I could feel the burning from deep within my body, so I begged, "Please, Tyler, now."

His hands moved to my face, as he hovered over me, stroking himself against me again. Why was he waiting? He had to know I was so ready for him. I needed to push the bad feelings away, and I needed him to fill me with his warmth. Please just give it to me hard. I didn't want to wait; I had to help him. I reached down between us messaging him against me until he soared into me.

This was supposed to make it all go away, but I found it more confusing. He plunged into me again, but it wasn't taking the sadness away. He plunged deeper, moving in this incredible way, which felt amazing, and yet the sadness wasn't leaving. He didn't take his eyes off of mine, while he shoved harder and deeper; but now the feeling was unstoppable, and tears leaked out of my eyes. His movement slowed to a tender rhythm, as my body rose to him with each plunge begging for relief. His eyes filled with worry, as he mouthed to me, "You are hurting?"

I didn't understand how I could be so close to ecstasy, and still the sadness took over.

His mouth searched my face kissing me to try to relieve the sadness. My body engulfed him with every plunge intensifying our bliss. I trembled with every movement while more tears ran down my face. He moved up more and pushed deeper but never increasing the speed of his plunge. I gasped as I felt a sensation growing from the bottom of my toes. I arched as he pushed deeper and kissed my chin, "Did I cause the pain this time?"

I couldn't answer him because he was also causing the pleasure. He watched as I released every enjoyment I had with moans of satisfaction. He continued to move to me causing me to shutter as he pushed even deeper. His noises were telling me he was close to climaxing. Realization hit when I thought about feeling him cum inside me. I was scared of what I wanted because the enjoyment would be so satisfying. I was relieved that he was still logical; pulling from me he placed a condom in my hand, "Help me."

I ripped it open quickly and moved to roll it onto him, but he was eagerly pushing to be inside of me again. As he stroked again, I rolled it on the rest of the way, and he shoved deeper into me again. He traced his hand down my leg pulling it up as far as my body would allow, and he moved all over inside me. Then he moaned loudly and his body jerked with a series of spasms. After he came, his body pressed hard to mine and his mouth came to rest by my ear. I was embarrassed by my sadness and when he pulled out to remove the condom, I turned away. His body moved around mine embracing every part of me, as the air of a whisper came softly to my ear, "Are you going to tell me what I did wrong?"

"Nothing, I just didn't want it."

He was soft and caring as he held me firm, "Tell me why?"

I was losing it, as I replied, "You make me out to be better than I am."

His mouth traced back and forth against my ear, "No, you ARE that good. Your strength, your confidence, you believe in what you are doing; it's the honest truth that people are captivated by you. They listen to you and want to hear what you have to say. I would have been stupid to pick anyone else."

"But, they will think it's because we are sleeping together."

His lips nibbled at my ear, "Joselyn, if I was sleeping with you or not… you would have still been my choice. I made that choice far before I knew who you were."

"But it's wrong… I'm wrong… this is all wrong; you are far too young to deal with my baggage, and do you want know what the worst part is?" I looked back at him full of remorse, "I am falling in love with you."

His mouth came to embrace mine heavily holding me tight to him, "That is the BEST part. I am in love with you, too."

Tyler:

As soon as she left for the bathroom I called Ryan, "Hey, I found her. She will be longer, because we have a new contract to talk about."

"That's my wife; asking for more money. Where are you?"

"I'm at the office."

"Hey, I drove by there. Her car wasn't there."

"Yeah, well then we left, and she is eating now. It will be awhile."

I saw her coming back, "I have to go."

I hung up quickly. It rang, as she crawled into bed with me. I smiled pulling her over me.

"Tyler, your phone."

I laughed, "Nothing is more important than you."

She smiled and nibbled on my neck. It didn't take me a second to take advantage of her playfulness.

29

Joselyn:

Monday he must have seen me walk in, because he was in my office almost right after me. He closed the door, so I turned to see why he shut the door. He stood there smiling at me; I think to calm me, but it was making me more nervous. Or, was he going to tempt me here again? Now, would be such a bad timing for this. I was already nervous about taking over as the lead agent. He walked over slowly, and then took my hands in his looking down at me, "This is going to be like a normal work week. Look at who we have to deal with this week. Have a meeting and discuss who should get them, and then put up your feet."

I shook my head. It wasn't that easy. I noticed his smile was a mischievous grin, as he stared into my eyes.

"Tyler, please don't make me do this. I can't do it."

He laughed, "Just do what you did the last two weeks. That is all I am asking. If it doesn't go well, we will discuss it, okay?"

I nodded, but felt sick to my stomach.

He let go and traced his hand on the folder he had given me, "Have you looked at this one?"

I nodded while starting my computer.

He sat down on my desk again, and I really didn't like that he was making himself so comfortable... to sit on my desk in front of me. I raised my eyebrows looking up at him, "There is a chair."

He laughed, "You are going to do just fine."

I shook my head and pulled up the calendar, "How many do we have this week?"

"Six."

"Only six, well that isn't bad."

He shook his head, "And this one. So what do you think?"

"It's Ty's place. The bar and grill where we met. It has some specialty items that are attractive. How hard is that one?" I was confused by his persistence on this one, "We'll do some publicity stuff for advertising."

"Did you look at the whole thing? They already do that."

I looked up at him, "Do you have some sort of steak in this one?"

He grinned, "You could say that."

I pulled out the reports; I plugged into my plan, "This is not the normal run of the mill advertising campaign. I looked at what they have to offer, and then I plugged in the numbers."

He was smiling, when I pulled out the reports, "They make more money when they run these three events on these three nights; and this is when they make their least amount of money and the days they fall on."

He nodded.

"Well, if you know them, you might be able to talk them into building on an addition for future business. I searched the top places, and they make money by offering things at all times of the day... So I drew up a design and if there is room..."

"Oh, there is room."

I glanced up at him, and he looked like a little kid in a candy store. I couldn't figure him out this morning.

"Well, I was thinking of adding softball fields and volleyball courts and running tournaments during the weekend mornings. We could off balance this place as a sports bar, and the guys will come and the girls will follow; but that would be a suggestion not an advertising campaign."

He nodded, "Is that all you have?"

"No, I have a lot more ideas, but this was my suggestion for the future. You don't like it." All I could think was *this was not a good way to start.*

He took the papers with him and walked out without another word. I was not only shocked but speechless. What was I going to do now? Start all over? I needed my reports for the other things I was working on. Shit. I stormed after him and into his office. He was sitting at his desk already reading through everything. I kind of yelled at him, "I wasn't done with those reports."

He glanced up at me, "Can you please close the door?"

Oh shit, I irritated him. I turned to close the door taking a deep breath. No, I wasn't going to let him bully me. I have had enough of that in my life. I saw the blinds close in the corner of my eye. "Tyler, what are you doing?"

He turned me, moving closer to me, tracing his nose close to my ear, "I missed you."

I wrapped my fingers around the back of his neck running my fingers through his hair, "Tyler, I can't do this here. You know that I can't."

His grin was sinful, "I need you... now."

I shook my head pushing him away a little. He took my hand and rubbed it against himself, "I need you, Joselyn. I tried to behave; to not think about you like that here, but just now when you came in angry... this is what you did to me."

I pulled my hand away from him staring into his eyes but spoke softly, "Tyler, please, I can't do this here."

Just then someone knocked. He looked down, "Great, now what am I going to do?"

I covered my mouth trying to hold in a laugh but replied, "How about an early lunch?"

He glared at me and moved to his desk, "You are going to have to get that."

I giggled more, "That is what you get for acting like a leach. No more of that, ok? Can I have my reports back?"

He held them up looking very uncomfortable sitting there. I headed for the door opening it. Tori was standing there smiling, "You are talking. I want lunch with you."

I looked back at Tyler uncomfortable in his chair, "I think I have a business meeting for lunch today; we will have to make it tomorrow."

She glared at me and continued to walk in. She made herself comfortable in the chair in front of Tyler's desk, but spoke to me, "Joselyn, you should come here too."

I closed the door and walked back over. She was all happy with herself; as she sat there. I could see Tyler's discomfort, "Tori, what is this about?"

She looked up at me smiling, "I was helping Tyler look for you on Friday."

I kept my cool and didn't say anything.

She glanced up at me, "He asked me if I knew where you might go."

I laughed a little, because she was acting like a little girl.

She pointed at both of us, "Both your car's were at Ty's place, but neither of you were there."

Tyler frowned, "Of course we were there. I was talking to her privately begging her to come back and give it a try. What is your point?"

She retorted her stance, "You two are... is something going on?"

I touched her shoulder looking at Tyler, "We could really use her on our side."

She was pleased, as she looked up at me smiling and nodding.

He laughed, "Yeah, but you can't tell anyone."

She shook her head no and waited impatiently. I turned leaning against the desk, "I am having Tyler's baby."

He coughed behind me, and I covered my mouth. I could hardly keep the laughing contained. Tori stood up glaring, "You two are not funny. I will get the both of you back for teasing me like that."

Tyler laughed, "Um, did you need something, or should we include you for lunch?"

"Where are you going?"

"To a hotel." He cracked up laughing, and she was even madder.

"You two are not funny."

"Tori, this is what bothers me the most. I don't want everyone thinking that way, okay?"

She glared at me, "You two are so hot for each other, and it's not even funny. We are going out Saturday, and I will prove it."

I shook my head, "You could find out today if you want to go to lunch."

Tyler was laughing again, so I snickered. She stormed away, "I will get the two of you back."

I shook my head crossing my arms. She went out the door, and I didn't move, but I glanced back at him, "Are you okay?"

"Yeah, that helped a little. What do you think she will do?"

"I don't know, but I think I will call her up to my office and confess. She was the one who talked me into going out in the first place, and maybe it will be okay." Then I turned to him leaning over his desk, "You have to stop doing that..." I gestured down at him, as he glanced up at me and then down my shirt.

"Tyler, that cannot help this."

"Lunch, and thank you. I will go early and call you at 11."

I smiled, "Call me at 10:50, so I know where I am going, and I can hurry."

He stood up leaning across his desk to me, "You will hurry?"

I nodded, and he reached to kiss me gently.

Tori walked back in at that moment, "I did have a quest...oops."

She closed the door and glared at us. I walked over to her, turned her around opening the door, and led her to my office. We walked in, and I closed the door.

She was so happy and whispered, "I knew it. You are such a bitch." She pulled me to my couch, and we both sat down. I sat staring at her.

"Well, I want all that nasty details."

I shook my head looking down. This still felt wrong, "You know... this isn't right... no matter what you think."

"You have been miserable for long enough, girl. Tell me the juicy detail."

I bit my lip to explain where I left off, "The night when I insisted that I was married, he kissed me. I tried to refuse, but I hadn't kissed anyone in a long time, and it was amazing."

She scooted closer, "Yeah, you can tell it would be."

I shook my head, "I felt horrible, but he wouldn't let me go unless I agreed to come back."

She nodded, "When?"

I cringed, "I avoided it for three weeks, and when I went back I was angry with Ryan, and I really didn't think he would be there."

"Why not?"

"Because I was suppose to come back in two weeks; but I really felt it was wrong, so I didn't go."

"So how did you meet up again?"

"He was there, and we danced."

"That's it?"

I shook my head.

"You can't tell anyone this, because it's still not real to me."

"You went back to his place?"

"He was kissing me and holding me, and I just felt so good."

"You are in love with him?"

I nodded, "But this isn't good. I need to end things with Ryan, and I am worried about the kids."

She was shaking her head, "They will be fine. It can't be good for them to see you sad and miserable all the time."

"Really?"

"Yes. Are you guys really going to lunch?"

I laughed, "Yeah, we are."

"Are you doing it or eating?"

"Eating."

She glared, "Have you done it?"

I looked up at her regretfully but nodded.

She screamed, "I knew it. He was crazy on Friday, and the only thing he could think about was finding you. He left the party and everything."

30

I shooed her from my office as soon as I could, and got on setting up the six clients folders, so I could meet with the agents. Nobody wanted one of the accounts at all, so I guess I had two this week. I met with Tori and gave her my ideas, and she kept it to business this time. I went back to the office and started really looking at what kind of advertising we wanted to do for a local tavern Ty's, trying to make it. I leaned back day dreaming about what would catch my eye about Ty's place.

When my phone buzzed, I jumped grabbing for it. I hurried to answer. My mind switched like a light bulb to imagining his hands tracing down my back.

"Hello?"

He laughed, "Are you thinking about me?"

I grabbed my jacket and purse and headed to the elevator whispering, "Yes."

"So, am I going to tell you where I am?"

"I guess that is up to you. I am heading for the sandwich shop now."

"What do you want to eat? I can order in."

"I was just going to get a light salad."

"It's on its way. Hey, do you want to know where I am?"

"Yes, but I am in a hurry, so give me the details."

He directed me on where to go and the use of the back door. I went up finding the room okay. The door was slightly open, so I peeked in. He was moving around the room trying to stand sexy and manly in his boxers. All of a sudden, I felt really dirty about this. I walked in and closed the door.

I felt his hands trailing my sides from my hips on up, pulling the skirt with them, "Tyler, stop."

He leaned forward to my ear, "Something wrong?"

I turned to him, falling into his spell, gazing into those marvelous eyes, shaking my head no, "Um, I don't want to get wrinkled. We have to go back to work."

He nodded, as he stepped back. I slowly unbuttoned my shirt, while I melted under his heated gaze. *It was incredible to be wanted like this.* My heart was racing; he licked his lips with desire, "Joselyn, can I help you?"

I smiled slightly, because I did want his hands to glide over my skin, and his puppy dog look was making me forget that it was wrong; so I shook my head no walking to the table and chair. I slid it from my shoulder draping it over the back of the chair. I felt him move behind me wrapping his hand around me resting on my stomach. His mouth kissed my bare shoulder, while his other hand traced down my back. The whisper was sweet and light, "Amazing."

Oh that did it. It didn't matter if it was wrong; I needed him, and I needed him to want me. I felt his hand pull up on my skirt, "Tyler, wait, unzip me."

I stepped out of my shoes, while he unzipped the back of my skirt. I lowered it, as he smoothed his hand over my butt.

"Oh, my god, Joselyn. You're wearing a thong."

I stepped out of the skirt replying, "Only when the skirt is tight. No lines."

"I wish you wouldn't have told me that. Every time I see you in a tight skirt, I am going to go nuts."

I laughed a little, as I draped it over the back of the chair. He unhooked my bra in the back slowly sliding it forward from my body, as his arms grazed mine. I was losing it; my body was heating up with the slightest touch from him. His mouth came hungrily to my cheek and neck, while his hands traced my butt and labia at the same time. I gasped when his mouth came to suck on my ear. When his words came to me I was ready to beg him, but he asked, "May I help you with this?"

Turning to him our mouths linked in desperation. I was preoccupied with our tongues colliding, our mouths separating just enough to collide again and again. Once he had his fingers twirled into the sides of my thong, his mouth released me, but only to explore as he pushed it down. His mouth enticed me with lingering caresses, which started by nibbling at my neck, moving to my chest sucking my breast, and then licking my abdomen. I couldn't handle the taunting, so I entangled my fingers in his hair to pull him harder to me. His mouth continued to move lower and lower, stopping at the inside of my thigh, just so he could help me step out of my thong; but the biting there took my breath away and made me weak in the knees. He directed me back to the bed, kneeling down and slowly pushing my legs apart and then moving between them. His curious fingers played within the labia. I knew what he was going to do, yet I couldn't really believe it; not until he pressed me open further, and his mouth came close to me breathing warm air against me. I fell back knowing he was going to give me something I had not had in a long time. The warmth of his mouth, the play of his tongue against my clitoris, and the nibble on my clit caused a moan that escaped me without my control, "Oh Tyler."

I groaned more from the pleasure that was escaping me, as his tongue taunted more. I whimpered as I climaxed into an orgasmic shrill, like I had never done in my life. My body was spastic, and trembled beneath him, while he slowly kissed his way up my body. He allowed my body to rise to meet his mouth longing for more. When his eyes finally made their way to mine, I saw a burning fire within him. The hardness of his erection pushed deeply into me filling my wanting desire with a stroke of scorching pleasure. His hand pulled my leg up further, as he plunged deeper, dancing within me to stroke every internal part of me. His moans were full of gasps and whimpers. A man's body becomes hard and taunt when he is close to climaxing and Tyler's body was as hard as a rock. He groaned my name over and over, as he rotated inside of me. I wanted him to feel what I was feeling, so my body contracted internally to tighten around him, not letting him escape the depths of satisfaction. The more my body enhanced his, the more sporadic his breath came as he dove deeper and faster. I whimpered again, as I felt an explosion within me that made my body orgasm with complete release. His body pushed to mine hard one more time, and then his mouth came to find mine, "I am so in love with you."

"Tyler, this is sex; really good sex."

He grinned and nibbled on my lips, "It wouldn't be this good if I wasn't in love with you. Please tell me this is more than sex for you?"

I nodded as the tears leaked out.

"NO! No, Joselyn, please don't cry. It's supposed to be wonderful not bad."

I shook my head wrapping my arms around him, "Why do you feel this way?"

"I love the way your eyes sparkle when we make love, but there is one problem."

I knew it, he was married too.

He lowered his face to my ear and whispered, "I came in you."

I closed my eyes with chagrin, "Shit."

His mouth traced mine, "I couldn't stop. You felt so good."

I whimpered. This was not a good thing, and definitely not good timing. I needed a calendar now, but I didn't want to let him go or let him move away from me; he felt so damn good.

31

The first thing I did, when I got back to the office, was pull out my calendar. I counted and recounted the day's closing my eyes with worry. It was mid cycle for me, and this would have been the perfect time to have sex if I wanted a child, but right now this is NOT what I wanted or needed. I counted again but slower... anyway I counted this was not a good time for this.

I heard a knock and the door opened. I glanced up to see Tyler peak his head in, "How is 10 am tomorrow?"

The funny thing was I had my calendar up. I looked down and said, "Great. What am I doing?"

He stepped in and closed the door walking towards me whispering, "Lawyer."

I smiled at him, "Okay."

He moved closer, "Really?"

I raised my eyebrows with my response, "Yes, of course."

He glared at me, "No tearing up, no hesitation, and I have another appointment?"

I shook my head.

He sat down on the desk looking down at me, "Are you okay?"

I nodded but I couldn't look up at him. I was too nervous thinking about how bad it would be to be pregnant right now in my messed up life. I felt his hand trace under my chin, "Joselyn?

I could only swallow deeply and stick to business, "Tomorrow is fine."

"Joselyn!"

I smiled and looked up at him, "I am fine, tomorrow is fine, and I have a couple of things I need to work on."

He laughed leaning down, "You are so strict. Does your boss know that you work to hard?"

"I think my boss gets easily distracted."

He laughed again, "No, he is crazy about a woman."

"You should really get him help. Woman are full of trouble."

He kissed my cheek soft but quickly whispered to me, "I hope so."

He got up heading to the door, but glanced back at me before opening the door. I shook my head and pointed as he went out.

I was determined to get this out of my mind. I took his file and went to Mr. Jenkins office. I knocked and he was more than eager to let me in, "I am so glad you came to see me. No one even talks to me anymore. I don't like this job."

I laughed, "Yeah, I don't like my job either, and I need some ideas."

He sat back relaxing in his chair, "Oh, the sweet smell of a new account."

I laughed as I sat down.

"So he talks to you a lot?"

I nodded and gestured to the folder, "Yeah, his next big account, but its local and I can't figure out how this one would be a big account. It's a local company and they don't have the revenue to be big, like huge, so I am a little confused on how to make them bigger."

We continued to talk for a few hours. He gave me some things to think about which usually triggered some ideas in my head, but this time my mind kept wandering back to Tyler's sweet and adoring face as he said 'I came in you'. I really had to forget about this before I went home.

After working all day on Tyler's big account, the rest of the day I thought I had come up with some good but simple ideas for him. I knew we had an appointment with a lawyer early the next day, so I wanted to be prepared before Wednesday. Tyler walked out with me and walked me to my car, but only because he parked two down from me. He stopped, but looked around and noticed there were a few others leaving work at the same time. I could tell he wanted to sweep me off of my feet but couldn't. I watched him stand there nervously putting his hands in his pockets looking down and talking quietly, "Are you ready for tomorrow's meeting?"

"Yes, it will be fine."

"I am just worried about you."

"I know. Thank you."

His eyes came up to meet mine, "I am not doing this for you. I am completely selfish."

I was caught off guard, but grinned, "I should go."

"I don't want to walk away, Joselyn."

I smiled, "We will find out tomorrow how long this will have to go on this way, okay?"

"Just, can't you come home with me now?" He looked around to make sure no one was within hearing distance.

I opened my car door, "Would it help if I said I wanted to."

His face dropped, and he kicked something on the ground. He looked like Jared when he wanted something, and I told him no. I wanted to wrap my arms around him and tell him everything was going to be okay, but right now I didn't know that. I didn't even know how to tell him that his timing for coming in me was bad.

He huffed a little saying, "No." His eyes came back to meet mine, "I don't want you to be around him. He makes you sad."

Okay, now he was breaking my heart that he actually cared about me. I whispered, "Tyler, I have to go."

He took a step closer and saw a few people coming our way and he stepped back. They yelled at us to have a good night. I waved and replied and so did Tyler, but his gaze came back to me, "I hate this."

I took a deep breath, "Are you going to stay with me tomorrow for the meeting?"

He was concerned, "Do you want me to?"

I nodded.

"I will stay with you."

I got in my car and rolled down my window. I slowly pulled out and stuck my hand out to him, "I love you."

He squeezed it, but let me go as I drove off.

32

I felt awful my whole drive home. I hurried into the house grabbing Haden's and Terra's stuff for ball. I yelled for them, but they weren't coming. Ryan walked up the steps, "Where were you today?"

"What? Hey, Kids we have to go. You have to be there in a half hour." I was rushing up the stairs to get changed quickly.

Haden came out of his room crying.

"Hey, what's wrong? You have to hurry, or we will be late."

"Daddy says we can't go. You two have something more important to do."

I was so angry with Ryan at this moment. It wasn't up to him on when we were going to discuss things, if it was going to affect the kids.

"I asked you *where you were* today."

"Work. If you want to come with us, I suggest you help us get ready."

I stormed into my room grabbing clothes to change into. He came storming in, "I asked you where *YOU were* TODAY?"

"What do you mean?"

"I went to your work and they said you were out. I waited for an hour and a half but you never showed up."

"Yeah, so... I had a lunch meeting, and then I met with a prospective client. What is your problem?"

"You. Tyler wasn't there either."

"Yeah, he was with me for the meeting and then took me to meet a new client."

I stormed from the room and went to the bathroom to get ready. At least that door had a lock on it. I saw the handle turn, as I got dressed quickly. He pushed on the door and hit it hard, "Open this door."

"No."

God I hated that he was this way. There was no way he would sit around waiting for me anyway. I knew he was bluffing. I stormed out of the bathroom grabbing the bags, "Haden, Terra, Jared; come on guys, we are going to be late."

Ryan grabbed my arm, "They were told to not listen to you. They were told to stay in their rooms, because we need to talk about something."

I calmed myself, smiled at him and removed his hand from my arm finger by finger, "I don't know what you are upset about, but this is not going to help you or me, and it is definitely not good for the children. Do you really want to do this now?"

"Yes."

"Well, I am sorry, but I do not. I only get a few nights to spend with my children, and I would like to do that now."

I walked over opening Jared's room. Terra and Haden were curled up with Jared. I smiled at all of them, "It's okay guys. Come on; we'll get something to eat on the way. Come on."

They looked scared out of their little bodies, as they came slowly to me. I touched each one as they passed me and their father, "It's okay. See… daddy and mommy are not yelling, and we are going to go have some family fun; right, Ryan?"

I was very determined to get him to ease up. The kids were scared. He walked away grabbing his jacket and keys. I followed pushing everyone out but taking a huge breath before walking out the door.

I wondered as we drove how anyone could have so many different emotions in one day. I turned to look at my babies and smiled. "I see the letter A" I waited a little bit for someone to kick out the next letter, and no one said a word.

I had to try again, "I see the letter B."

Haden spotted the letter c d and e. Terra was next with the letter f, but Jared found g. Then it became a race who was finding the next letter. Ryan's face stayed firm and distant. We got to the ball field and the two youngest rushed from the car. Jared got out slowly and kind of stood there. "Hey, baby, would you get the chairs? We'll be right over."

He looked up at me with a determined face to not leave me. I smiled at him, "It's okay; we're fine."

He didn't like it, but he got it and walked away. I watched until he was a safe distance away. I looked back in the car at Ryan, "Don't you

144

think you could have done this a better way? They are all scared right now. What if I came at you like that after I saw you with..."

"This is not about me."

I tilted my head implying really, but I didn't say a word.

"You don't come home some nights; you go out for lunch disappearing for a couple of hours; you work late, and you go out. I know what you are doing, and I will not allow it. You are my wife."

I smiled, "Your wife I am, but look what you did to your wife. I am not trying to be mean. I care about you, but only because you are the father to my children. I did love you up to that moment, maybe even afterwards a little; but I was empty and full of regret thinking that it was my fault. Clearly, it wasn't all me; you don't like that I have figured it out, and now I don't want to live like this anymore. I am sorry if I just can't do this anymore. Now, if you can try, maybe you could be the dad I know your kids need."

He glared at me getting out and slamming the door shut, "This is not over."

I headed over, and we sat with Jared between us. Ryan talked to him and he relaxed. We stopped for McDonalds on the way home. I knew the kids were hungry, and I didn't feel like making dinner. We went in the house as the kids were heading up to their rooms, "Guys you have to shower and clean up before going to bed."

They were fighting over who was going first. Ryan walked in and went straight down stairs, so I was relieved. I went to the kitchen writing down a few ideas for the small campaign I was doing that nobody wanted. I then went back and drew up a huge advertising campaign for Ty's place. It was like it hit me in the midst of everything in my life. "Escape to your Haven. Ty's place... where the Mi-ty's are calling."

It was cute and an escape for people to go to. That is what I used it for. I laughed to myself as Ryan walked in, "You are working again? Can't you give it a break?"

"It hit me, and I didn't want to forget it."

"I think you should be helping the kids."

"Yep, I'm done now." I folded it and tucked it back in my brief case and walked to the kid's rooms, making sure everyone was showered and teeth were brushed.

When everything was winding down and the good nights were said, I finally headed to bed myself. I quickly fell asleep with Tyler on my mind, the way he held me, the feel of his hands tracing my back, the way he kissed my neck, the way he… I opened my eyes to find Ryan on top of me. I was scared instantly, "What are you doing?"

"You weren't turning me away."

"I am now. Get off me and…" I was struggling to push him away, but he had my hands held down and he was smiling, "Jos, you are my wife, and you will fulfill your duties to your man."

"No, never."

He pushed away from me, "Joselyn, I know what I did was wrong, and I am so sorry. I wish I could take it all back. What can I do to make it up to you?"

"Nothing, I can't love you that way anymore."

He reached to trace his hand along my neck, "Come on Jos, you know you miss being touched." He lay down close to me and whispered, "Do you remember when we were playing around before Haden came along? We were exploring new ways to touch each other."

I turned away from him, "I can't anymore, because I see you with her. When you look at me I see the way you looked at her. When you try to touch me, I see you tracing your hands against her back. The worst of it, is when you try to kiss me, I see you gasping for air as you f…"

"Jos, stop. Why can't you forgive me? I am a man, and I made a mistake. You know you have always been the only woman I have ever loved. That other woman was just sex. You will always be my perfect partner… my soul mate."

"Then your soul should have told you how bad this would have hurt me. It has ended our relationship forever, because not one day goes by where I don't see a picture of it in my mind."

"Because you aren't trying to forget."

"Oh, believe me… I have tried. Can you please leave now?"

He got up and took my hand pulling it to his stomach, "I am still a man and the reason it happened was because of neglect on your end. Please don't keep it up. I don't know how long I have to go to prove to you that I only love you."

"Forever, that's why they call it marriage."

"Marriage also means the union of two people, Jos. We don't have that either."

"That is why this has to end. I cannot give that to you anymore."

He stormed from the room. I knew that was the wave before the storm, but I just didn't know how bad the storm was going to be.

I was surprised when he came storming back in, "I think I should get the bedroom for a while."

I laughed, "Fine, but it will start tomorrow."

He glared at me, "I have one more question?"

"What!"

"Where were you today?"

"I already told you, and I am really tired. I am done having this argument."

"Are you Fucking Tyler?"

"Would it make you leave me alone?"

"What do you mean by that?"

"If I say yes, will you leave me alone?"

"You are such a bitch, Jos. Why can't you just answer the question?" He hesitated and got a huge grin on his face, "You want me to think you can do better than me. Let me just tell you right now. No one would want a worn out mother of three, and that is exactly what you are, Jos, a worn out, used up woman that can have her fantasies but will live lonely if she is a divorcee. Do you get what I am saying?"

"Yeah, at least I know how you feel."

"See, you are just being a bitch."

"Leave!"

He stomped out again. I was waiting for the storming in again, but it didn't come. Of course his words hit me harder than I should have allowed. I knew that they weren't true, but they felt true enough to make my heart ache; he was such a jerk.

The more I thought about this the more I realized that love is really amazing. I love Tyler so much that I could let him go right now without any regrets, because I wanted him to be happy; I wanted him to have a family of his own, to have someone love him the way he deserves, and to give him all of their time; I truly loved Tyler in a way that I couldn't explain, and yet I would be devastated to not have him in my life

Ryan knew how to get to me and he did it again. I cried myself to sleep once again, but this time thinking about not having Tyler in my life. Glancing at the clock one last time at 4 am, I knew tomorrow was going to be a very long day.

33

When Tyler called me into his office by phone it made me nervous. I walked in, but Tyler walked to the door and stepped out for a minute. I noticed there was a sandy brown haired man that I didn't know, sitting behind the desk. I heard Tyler direct Lindsay to hold his calls, and no one was to interrupt us; this was a very important meeting. He came back in closing the door and shades. I shook my head laughing with a sigh. He usually only did this when no one was in the office with us.

He held the chair for me, "Joselyn, this is Shane Winchester, Shane, this is Joselyn Evans." I shook his hand and sat down while Tyler sat down next to me. I laughed because Shane was in Tyler's seat behind the desk or maybe I was just nervous. I waited because I didn't know what to say or do.

When he finally spoke he was looking down at something, "So, you have three children?"

"Yes."

"Does your husband work?"

"Yes, he's a sub-contractor. He makes up his own schedule."

"So, would you say he is home more than you?"

I looked at Tyler but answered, "Yes, I guess."

Tyler smiled and nodded for me to continue. Shane asked a lot more questions as we sat there. It was getting to be an hour and I felt drained more than I was expecting. Tyler traced his fingers across the back of mine. I looked down feeling stronger after his reassurance. Shane stood up abruptly and irritated, "Tyler, I had no idea that this was going on. I can't represent her if you aren't truthful with me."

He started to pack up his stuff. Tyler stood up, "Hey, wait. We need your help."

He looked at me from around Tyler's shoulder, but whispered to him, "You are having an affair with her. I can't support that."

I whispered, "He did too."

Tyler's attention came back to me, "Joselyn, you don't have to talk about it. We can take care of this another way."

I shook my head, "Tyler, I am not divorcing my husband to be with you. I am divorcing him, because I can't be with him anymore. You came into the picture after I was messed up for a long time."

He was struggling internally, "Are you sure you want to talk about this?"

I shrugged, "I have to be. I'll be okay."

Tyler was such a distraction for me that I forgot Shane was in the room until he spoke, "Tyler, I just think you are replacing..."

It was if someone had hit Tyler, because he was all over Shane that instant, "This has nothing to do with that. Now, please help her."

They seemed to be having a stare down, and I didn't understand what he meant by the word 'replacing'. What did that mean? I watched Tyler, even though he kept his back to me.

Shane sat back down, "Fine, but I think that Joselyn and I should discuss this in private, Tyler. Will you please excuse us?"

Sadness filled his eyes, as they came back to mine, "I said I would be here."

I had to let him off the hook, and I needed to do this for myself. He always says I am strong, so I should be able to deal with this, "Tyler, it's okay."

I could almost feel the pain that this was causing him, "Are you sure, because I don't care what it does to me."

I tried to be firm and strong, "It matters to me. I will be fine."

He took my hand kissing it softly, but turned to look at Shane, "I love this woman, and you will treat her respectfully."

"Always Tyler. You can be such a..."

Tyler laughed, "Yes, I am a pain in your..." He took one last look at me before heading out the door.

It was silent for so long that I felt like I needed to explain something to him, "I know what you are thinking."

There was no acknowledgement from him, but I could see a slight grin.

"I don't want his money, or anything else. I know he's very young, and he deserves someone his age, and a family of his own, but right now I need him."

He finally glanced up at me, "That isn't what I was thinking."

"OH?"

"No, but I am glad that you are honest. It's just that I think he is so busy helping you, he is forgetting that he might need some help."

He might need some help? He was so successful at such a young age. Having this advertising business is huge, so what could he need help with? I swallowed, opening my mouth to ask, but couldn't let the words come from my mouth. I watched him carefully trying to figure out what Tyler needed help with; I hoped Shane would let something slip.

After that, things started to move along quickly. He asked about Ryan and all the details of the nasty affair. I could hardly talk about it without getting sick to my stomach. Shane kept neutral without much facial expressions at all. I knew we were getting to the end of the questions, because he had flipped the last page. He scanned it and handed it to me, "Well, because Tyler is my college roommate, my biggest client, and one of my best friends; I will give it my best."

"Okay."

"But there are a few things that I am going to ask of you that might be hard."

I was waiting for him to tell me to stop seeing Tyler. I knew it was coming even though I didn't want to hear it.

"First of all, you need to spend as much time with your children as you can. You want equal time for custody; then you need to show the judge that you have time for that."

I was more than happy to spend time with my children, so that was going to be easy to follow.

"Second, do you want the house?" I shook my head as he glanced up at me, "That is understandable considering, but you are the bread winner in the home, is that a correct statement?"

I didn't understand where he was going with this, but I halfheartedly nodded.

"Okay... The point I am trying to get at is this: Do you make enough money to pay off the house, let him stay there, and still have a home where you can house the children when they are with you..." He paused searching my face, "...without Tyler's help?"

It did make me feel good that I could take care of myself and my children.

"My goal is to prove infidelity on his part. The good news is that most people that cheat will cheat again. I am going to ask for 50/50 custody with no spousal support on your behalf. If there is infidelity, and I can prove that it has continued, then maybe that will be a given, but I have to get an investigator."

I asked softly, "You think he is still cheating?"

Avoiding me; he just nodded.

I asked the question I didn't want to know, "You think I am a cheater, and I will hurt Tyler?"

That got his attention, and his eyes came back meeting mine. His eyes were a golden light brown. Instead of being cold and distant they brought warmth and understanding. "I wasn't implying that. With woman it's a little different." He hesitated but asked, "Do you love him?"

I didn't know how to answer him; out of fear of what I was really feeling, but being honest with myself I was in love with Tyler. He was too good to be true and I knew it; my eyes welled with tears while I nodded. He stood up handing me a tissue, "Okay then. I will get started right away, but there are a few things I need for you to do for me."

Now, he was going to tell me to stay away from Tyler.

"Start house hunting. Keep it within a mile of where you are living now, because it will look like you are trying to keep things normal for your children."

I was surprised that he wasn't getting back to Tyler yet; I guessed at this one, "But don't buy, right?"

"Right; if you find one you like, let me know and I will try to detain the sale until we get the court date set. Second, you have to put Tyler on hold. No more meeting him, or however you two do it."

He was just going to slide that in there thinking I wouldn't notice what I was agreeing to. I knew it was coming, "But can you tell Tyler, because I don't want him to think it's me not wanting to see him."

He gave me a compelling grin taking in a deep breath he said, "You really do love him?"

"I can't explain it completely, but he helped me feel again."

"Yeah, you did that for him too." That came out as he was turning away from me. I wondered if heard him right. What did he mean? He looked at me one last time offering me another tissue. I stood up and went to the door, "I'll just get Tyler, but you will explain?"

"Hey, Joselyn?"

I stopped; glancing back at him.

"Does Tyler talk about himself much?"

I shook my head no but asked, "Why?"

"It's nothing, but when you resume the relationship take your time, there is a lot to learn about Tyler."

"He's not going to freak out and kill me, is he?"

Shane raised his eyebrows and laughed lightly, "No, nothing like that, but he had a broken heart for a long time, and that is why he understands you. I think he needs to talk to you about it, before you two continue."

"If you tell me, I would know what I am fishing for, and I could be more careful."

"If you love him; you will be careful."

"Thank you."

I proceeded out the door. Tyler was playing basketball with paper balls and the waist paper basket with the girls at the receptionist desk. He stood up anxiously, "Did you get the deal?"

I nodded handing him a fake folder, so he could finish the deal. He passed by me in front of everyone, going into his office. He closed the door, and I took a huge breath. Lindsay walked to the counter, "A tough one?"

I nodded with eyes wide open staring at her. She smiled as Mary and her both giggled at the counter. Mary spoke up, "He says you won't let him sit in on your presentation. He usually goes to the bar or something."

I did get a giggle from that, but only because the thought in my head was different from what I was going to tell them, "Yeah, I don't want him to get any ideas. I have to keep my edge, otherwise he won't need me."

They both laughed, Lindsay replied, "I wish he needed me."

Mary spoke up, "Yeah, me too."

I laughed sighing right along with them, so they would think I thought he was dreamy just like them. I thought this would be an added touch to the charade, "Oh, I better get busy; I have another one tomorrow."

"He gives you a lot of accounts."

"Yeah, but I think it's only because I usually close the deal if I present. Mr. Jenkins helps me also; I wouldn't have come up with it

without him. You guys should buy him lunch; he misses the interaction."
I slipped them two twenties, "My treat."

I went to lunch with Tyler, but only because he caught me walking out of my office. We had a very comfortable discussion about not seeing each other outside of work for a while. It didn't seem to bother him, and that surprised me, but I understood why it didn't bother him when we got back to work when he said to me, "It's only temporary."

That made me happy. Something else made me very happy. I glanced into the conference room to see Rebecca and Kathy having Chinese for lunch with Mr. Jenkins. They were laughing and talking.

I heard a whisper in my ear as I watched, "You are a very good person in your heart."

I smiled and watched a while longer as I saw them laughing and joking. It did warm my heart to see him happy.

34

I was a little nervous about my meeting today with Tyler's big local client. I was thinking this was another one of his close friends, for us to be handling anything this small. I started by showing Mr. Jenkins what I had, because everything should go through him. He was delighted and gave me the approval. Because it was Tyler's client, I went to him next before I presented to the client.

"You know you don't have to do that. I completely trust you and everything you do."

I gave him that disapproving look, so he would sit down and look at what I had. He did pay attention and ask question. He liked my main idea, but I advised him I had to pick up the artwork for the presentation. He was fine with that, having confidence in Tori. I was looking at their financials and suggested a five day work week to make the necessary cut backs to maintain a profit. He nodded and hummed and hawed. I rolled my eyes, because he was asking questions that didn't even pertain like: 'So what kind of panties are you wearing today?', 'Does your bra match?', 'You are going out on Saturday with people from work?', 'How long do you think we have to wait?'

I finally left his office feeling that tingling yearning crawling up my body. My breasts were heaving to be touched by him. I was moist with longing to feel him. My lips ached to feel his touch mine. Oh, I had to put this out of my mind. I gazed out the window thinking of being off somewhere alone with him. I made one last phone call before having to head for our meeting.

"Mrs. Evans, how can I help you today?"

"I am looking for an appointment for tomorrow morning."

"Awh, is this an emergency?"

"No... but I was hoping to meet and talk with the doctor."

"Well, I can schedule you at 9 am. May I put down what this is for?"

"Check up and birth control."

"You are 35 now?"

"Yes."

"I see. You and Ryan are done with having children?"

"Yes, we broke the mold with Haden."

She chuckled, "He is a dreamy little one. We just love him here."

"Thank you. I am a little prejudice and I think he is just perfect, but molded after the other two perfect children I have."

"You must be a great mother?"

"No, but I like to think I try hard."

"Yes, I have that set up for you. Is there anything else I could help you with today?"

"No, thank you. See you tomorrow."

I saw Tyler walk in, and grab my jacket when I hung up. He was grinning from ear to ear, "You don't know when to stop working do you?"

"I was setting up a doctor's appointment."

"Are the kids okay?"

"Yes."

His eyes got wide, "Are you okay?"

I nodded sliding into my jacket, "Everything is fine."

"You know I hate that word. It doesn't mean good or bad... it's like in the middle... it's settling for."

We were heading to the elevator, as Rebecca was heading out to lunch. She always took the early lunch.

Tyler turned to her, "When someone says they are fine, what does that mean to you?"

She giggled, and acted all giddy that he was talking to her. I rolled my eyes at her stupidity, but I reminded myself that he was young and gorgeous, "Well, I think that means that it's okay. Not great; not bad."

He turned to me, "See. Fine is mediocre."

I laughed, "So you would rather me say, I'm mediocre today."

Rebecca laughed, "That sounds totally ridiculous Mrs. Evans."

I cringed. I just hated being called that, "Well, that is what I was pointing out to Tyler. If you are okay you say you are fine."

"Yes, but that doesn't really tell how you are, or how things are."

We argued all the way out of the building and into the Limo. He said Ray's and then closed the window. He sat opposite me and stared with a grin on his face. I tried to look out the window, trying not to get distracted from the task at hand. He laughed, "I like to watch you before a presentation. You like transform into this killer instinct and you have one thing on your mind."

I whispered, "I didn't earlier."

He raised his eyebrows, as I glanced over to him. I couldn't help myself, but smile with a smirk on my face.

"Should we skip this meeting and go to the hotel?"

"Tyler, we are not supposed to do that for awhile."

He crawled onto his knees in front of me, "I know but it is driving me crazy." His hand came up my skirt to message my thigh. I was still hot from thinking about him earlier, so I turned to him opening a little more. I rapped my arms around his neck and nibbled on his lips. His hand came to rub against me and this deep groan came from this mouth, as his face traced mine in agony, "Joselyn, the more I try to not think about being with you the more I think about it."

I agreed, "Me too. It's like someone said no, and now I want you more."

"Can we do it in the car?"

"No, Tyler, no we can't."

He pushed away and sat on the seat across from me again. I crossed my legs and looked out the window. My body was aching for him, and the burning desire was making the moisture between my legs very uncomfortable.

I heard him moan, "Oh, Joselyn, you have beautiful legs."

I smiled and continued to look out the window without a word.

He led me from the car into Ray's. They led us to his regular table. He ordered our food right away. I was pleased that he remembered what I had last time. The food came, and he picked something from my plate, and then I took what I wanted from his plate. We didn't even ask it was so natural to eat with him now. I looked around when I was close to being done, "So didn't you plan on having lunch with the client."

He leaned closer, "About that. I kind of have a confession. Would you mind presenting it up stairs?"

"Tyler!"

"I mean it. I have the chart boards up, and I have everything set up to make it easy."

We headed up stairs, and I was getting more nervous. He walked in, took off his jacket, and sat down watching me. I walked in and looked around, "The clients?"

He laughed, "I have a confession."

He took off his shoes, and I glared at him. He unbuttoned his shirt and his chest peaked at me as he continued. Oh how hot I was getting watching him slowly undress. He raised his eyebrows, "Well, go ahead."

"What?" I stood there glaring at him.

He laughed again, "Go ahead with your presentation."

"What about the clients?"

He smiled, pulling his shirt from being tucked in. He undid his pants and took them off. He was now standing there in his boxers, with his dress shirt draping open inviting me into him, and of course he still had his socks on. I laughed, as I looked at him standing there, "What is going on?"

"Okay, confession." He moved closer to me and started to unbutton my blouse, "Well, you see Ty's place is short for Tyler."

I watched his face, as he concentrated on undoing the buttons, "I like to be close to what I own. I don't stay there to make it convenient to pick up beautiful women; it's convenient to watch over my business."

He slid my blouse from me and carefully laid it on the chair. He looked back at me moving closer. He traced his hand down my chest from my collar bone to my cleavage. My chest heaved from wanting him.

"I should have told you sooner, but Shane wants to protect my assets more than me, so I have an agreement that I keep my mouth shut if I meet anyone, but..." He looked into my eyes, "I am in love with you, so I don't have to worry about that."

Tears welled in my eyes, as his gaze went back to my body hungrily. He traced his hands around my waist and unzipped me, "Since I have already seen everything, I was torn on what to do."

I glared at him wondering... torn about what?

He slid the skirt down talking to my body, as it slid down leaving a trail of hunger, "You see I really want to see you present an idea to a client; hence me being the client, or make mad passionate love to you."

I held back a grin, as I stepped out of the skirt. He gasped as he watched my calves. He handed the skirt up not taking his eyes off of my legs, "You have amazing legs."

I smiled as I draped the skirt over the chair, "So, I take it my approach remains a secret?"

He nodded in a drooling way, as he traced his hand up and down my calf, and then slid my shoe from me. I stepped down, and he slid the other one off. He put his hand on his chest looking up at me, "Can you just turn around for me once?"

I laughed and turned around once stopping facing him. He slowly stood up taking in every inch of my body, as he came up to meet me.

I looked into his eyes but reached back to undo my bra. He gasped, as I slid it from me, "What are you doing?"

I grinned at him, "Protecting my secret."

He lunged forward like a wild cat; his mouth came hungrily to my body, licking and sucking, as his hand cupped my breast, just to protrude it out enough to run his fingers gently against my nipple before nibbling gently on it. Yep that did it. The heat was coming from my inner core. There was not going to be any stopping what was coming next. I wanted to feel him and the heat of him in me. I knew he would harmonize the tingling feelings that I was so enjoying. My mind had been on him all morning, and I wanted to feel him hard and full of desire. I walked closer to him until he stepped back falling to the bed. I slowly traced my bosom against his body moving my body against his until I felt him hard between my legs. I lowered to just graze him and he moaned, "Please don't tease me. I have been like this since you walked off the elevator this morning."

I lowered to him again and he rose to grind against me. I engulfed him into my body and he gasped. I pressed my hands against his chest to move away, leaving him exposed, but only for a moment. His deep growl from within released, as I rocked to him again, pulling and sucking him into me more. His body reacted on instinct, thrusting upward to meet me. His hands gripped my hips to pull me harder with each thrust. I was losing him to the abyss. His gasps, groans, and trusts showed he was climaxing much faster than I. His body came to entangle every part of us together, as he rolled us to our sides. We breathed in each other's air, as we inhaled and kissed frantically. He stopped kissing me to whisper, "Joselyn, I have to stop."

"No... you don't."

"Oh, god. I have to..."

He was pulling away, but I want to feel the orgasm again, "If I was going to get pregnant I would be already. Please do it."

"What do you mean?" He tried to not push, but his body moved on its own accord; pushing deeply causing a wave of delight.

A new sound escaped me and I was in need of ecstasy. I would do anything to keep this going. I reached to nibble his lips begging him to forget any logic he was trying to have, "Please, Tyler?"

He gasped, "What do you mean?"

Gasping with each word I tried to explain, "Yesterday… mid… cycle… Oh my god… would be… yesterday."

Rolling over, he held his body away from me, hovering; he thrust his body quickly into me a few times then emitted, "Are you saying that you could be having my baby?"

I wished he would quit thinking about it and focus here. He needed to keep it going, not slowly; he was going to drive me insane, I declared, "Sorry… should have… stopped… yesterday."

It was making love to an all new man. His determination had changed his drive. His body seemed to rotate, move, push, plunge, rock, and thrust in every direction, moving deeper into me. Each time a grunt would escape from him and a plea, "yes, please, yes," from me.

The feeling was so powerful that I felt dryness in my throat and then tears well in my eyes. This was really stupid, why would I cry for something as wonderful as two people being this loving.

One long stroke in, and Tyler let out a long drawn out moan. However, I not only screamed with the orgasm, my body trembled and shuddered uncontrollably. I tucked my face into his body thinking about what I just told him, "I am sorry, I didn't know until I checked the calendar."

He gripped my face kissing everywhere and mouthing, "You are not kidding me?"

I shook my head as he continued to kiss me everywhere, "I know… it's really bad timing, and I don't know if I even want to do that again."

He kissed me deeply and huffed, "I do."

I was relieved, as his arms wrapped around me.

"But we're supposed to abstain from this, and if I am pregnant, it isn't going to look so good."

He laughed, "I don't care." His eyes came back to mine, sparkling with glee, "If I have to use every dime I have to help you keep your kids, I will. I don't care what anyone thinks or says. It's about you and me now, and I will do anything you need me to."

The thought of this was too much. How could I believe he was happy about it?

"I am going to treat you so good; you will think you are in a fairytale."

The words that he was saying took me to a new level of delight, "I am already."

He laid me back, moving away from me, kneeling next to me all excited rubbing my stomach, "When do we find out?"

I was surprised by this much excitement, "I guess in about a month."

"I have to wait a month?"

I laughed, but didn't share in his excitement. I did wish he would react like this, but I really wasn't expecting it. I thought maybe because I wouldn't be all sexy he would be turned off.

"Can we have a girl?"

I glared at his enthusiasm for a girl, "Why a girl?"

A little more serious side of him showed as he lay down next to me, "I guess I have to talk about more of my past."

I thought I was going to die. He was married and has a little girl. I watched him reach over to the night stand, so I rolled over to rest on his chest wondering how bad this was going to be. He pulled out a picture slowly handing it to me. It was a picture of a lovely young woman hugging a little girl. She looked about three or four. I traced my finger over them, "They are both beautiful." I glanced up at him as tears filled his eyes.

He was slow to respond this time, "...That was my wife and child."

Was? ...Was? What did he mean? I laid my head down on him wrapping my arm around him. I didn't know what to ask, what to say, or even how I was feeling at this very moment.

The warmth of his fingers trailed up and down my back, "I suppose I should explain."

Quickly, I wanted him to know that I was okay with whatever he needed to tell me, I kissed his chest and then put my head back down. I just needed to know one thing, "Are you married?"

"I was."

The pain in my aching chest eased a little, "You love your daughter?"

"Yes, I do, very much so. That was taken four years ago, she would be 8 now."

Okay, now to the real question, "Do you still love your...?" I couldn't say it. I wanted to, I needed to, but I couldn't ask. I needed him to love me, and love me more than her. She was so beautiful.

He sighed, "In some ways I do."

My throat closed off, and the pain in my chest was pulsing to beat me from the inside out. I let the words escape me with a breath, "You don't see them?"

"No." He seemed very certain of that.

I lay very still wondering if I should tell him how I really feel. Yes, I have to say it, "This scares me."

The warmth of his hand cupped my head; fingers entangled my hair. His chest rose underneath me in one heavy breath, "They are not in my life, Joselyn. You can ask me anything you want to about them."

They weren't in his life. Shane said he had a broken heart; I guess that was enough for me at this moment, "No, I'm okay."

"You don't want to know more?"

I did want to know more. I wanted to sit up and hit him for not telling me he was still in love with his ex-wife, but I couldn't get what Shane had said about the broke heart that I couldn't be angry at him. He so understood when it came to my marriage and my children. No, I am going to let him tell me in his own time, "Not unless you want to tell me. If and when you are ready, I will still be here if you want me to be."

He took the picture from my hand and put it back into the drawer. He pulled me up cupping my face and kissing me everywhere.

In my confusion of today's events I laid in bed wondering about things. How was it that Tyler, if he still loved his wife, why wasn't he with her? If I was pregnant, how were my children going to take this crazy mixed up problem? Did I really want another baby? The only conclusion I found was that I really didn't want another baby, but I would deal with it if it turned out I was.

35

I was getting a little frustrated with Tyler. After spending the day with Ryan, all I could think about was going out, dancing, and then drinking heavily. We were meeting at Rey's place, because Tyler could get a round of free drinks. He even offered the Limo for moving from tavern to tavern. I walked in and ordered a margarita.

He inched closer to me, "Do you think you should have that?"

I turned to him, "No, I guess not. Why did I even come if I can't drink?"

"Because this is what you would normally do. I will get you a virgin margarita."

I glared at him, "Great, but if I am not drinking than neither are you."

He laughed with a sigh, "I'm not the one carrying a baby."

I leaned into him more so I could whisper, "I will go home."

He pulled away surprised, "You wouldn't?"

I glared deeper into his eyes, "You better get two."

When Tyler walked away Tori came over, "You two are going to have to be a lot more careful if you don't want anyone to know."

I pulled her in front of me, "We're postponed until I am divorced."

"You are kidding me?" She was as disappointed as I was.

"Nope, lawyers orders."

"So, no getting hot and wet?"

I had to scold after that one, "Tori, please."

She laughed and wrapped her arm through his when he returned with the drinks. He handed me one and set the other one on the table, as Tori pulled him away from me for dancing; I watched with enjoyment. Just to make sure I tasted his drink and then mine. They were exactly the same.

The ladies all took turns dancing with Tyler. I danced with Craig and Seth, but we did watch each other. Finally they pushed us together, but it was without Tori's involvement.

Kathy was persistent, "You should dance with Tyler; you are the only one who hasn't."

"That's okay, I am too old to dance like that."

She pushed us together and out to the dance floor, "Dance."

He wrapped his hand gently against my waist turning his face away from me. He spoke softly, "Are you finding this as hard as I am?"

"Yes."

"I want to trace your back."

"I want to nibble your ear."

I felt his hand move around my waist a little more pulling me closer, "They are watching us very carefully."

This did feel good, but, "I know, so be careful where that hand is."

"You mean I shouldn't reach down between your legs tempting you?"

His flirting was building an urge in me, "Only if you don't want me to fondle you until you are hard."

Breathing hard he huffed out, "Joselyn, I want you now."

My heart filled with pain, "Yeah, and we're avoiding that."

He leaned down a little, so our eyes could linger, "I need you."

I wanted to fulfill his need. I inched closer so that our mouths were less than an inch apart, my chest heaved from wanting him.

Tori came to our rescue wrapping her arms around us, "Okay, I thought you two were avoiding this?"

He let me go and kissed my hand lightly, "Thank you, Joselyn." He waved at everyone, "You guys have fun. I have to be up early tomorrow; go ahead and use the limo. Kyle will take you wherever you want to go."

I stood there stunned that he was leaving. He glanced at me, "Joselyn, it's too hard." He walked away from me standing there not believing he would do this.

I was so torn apart with the emotions I was having. I knew he was right; I tried to stay calm, but made a mad dash for the bathroom.

I felt really stupid when Kathy, Rebecca, and Tori all came to the bathroom. I was throwing up in the stall and Kathy spoke, "Hey, Joselyn, I really thought he was going to kiss you."

That was not what I wanted to hear.

Rebecca spoke next, "Yeah, I mean we all know he likes you."

163

Tori tried to help me, "He knows she is married."

The agony of feeling like a high school student late with my period, and wondering if the boy still liked me after giving myself to him, was coming to mind. I tossed again. I really needed to talk to him now. If I was getting sick in less than a week than I probably was pregnant.

I heard Mary say, "Is she okay?"

"Yeah, I think she thought he was going to kiss her."

I had to put a stop to this, "No, I didn't. I just don't feel good."

Now I heard Tammy, "Joselyn, we all know you're miserable. If he likes you maybe you should think about..."

This was so humiliating, "Is everyone in here?"

They all spoke at the same time, "Yes."

I felt my phone buzz. I took it out and looked at it. It said a message but I didn't know how to check those. I wish Jared was here, he would tell me how to check that.

I walked out and shooed the girls back out to having fun assuring them that I think it was the lunch I ate. I said my good byes and went to my car calling Tyler.

"Hey beautiful."

"Did you send me a message?"

"Yes, you didn't get it?"

"No, I don't know how to check them."

With that he laughed. "It said I was sorry. If I would have stayed any longer I would have kissed you."

Boy did I love this man. I giggled replying, "Well, the girls are rooting for you, or maybe me. I am not sure, but they all thought you were going to kiss me. We have to be..."

"I know, I know. I just get close to you, and I haven't seen you outside of work since Tuesday and I am going crazy."

"Tyler, I just got sick."

"What, are you okay?"

"I don't know."

"Do you want me to come get you?"

"No, I am going home and to bed, but Tyler?"

"Yeah?"

"You may get that wish of a girl."

"What?"

"The only time I got sick was with Terra."

"Joselyn, where are you?"

"No, I am almost home now. I love you."

"Joselyn, turn around. I need to hold you. I don't care what it costs us."

"But it might cost me my children."

"You're right. I just hate this."

"Me too."

"I'll see you on Monday."

"Joselyn, call me later if you can?"

"I will try."

36

I had new life the following week. I brought snacks for work and cleaned out a draw, so I could keep something in me all the time. It seemed that if I kept my stomach happy, I didn't get sick at all. I had nine new accounts.

I had my meeting with the agents, wrapping up the ones from last week, setting up appointments for presentations, and then getting the new ones handed out. Everything seemed to be going extremely well. Tyler avoided coming into my office, but I noticed him glance in my door regretfully. I was working with Tori on some ideas, and when I got back there was a new file on my desk. I opened it and it was a print out of houses within a mile from mine. I smiled as I went through them. I put a star by the ones I was interested in, and then I called Mary in.

"Can you bring these to Tyler?"

"Um... no."

I looked up at her. She has never refused me before, so I was irritated. I could see that she was uncomfortable with telling me no, so I thought I should see why she refused, "Do you have a problem bringing this to Tyler?"

"No... Yes... well maybe."

I took a deep sigh, "Sit. Tell me what is wrong."

"He has been irritable since we all went out, and you haven't spent much time together this week, so we were all hoping you would go talk to him. You don't have to tell him we all think he is cranky, just about anything would be good, or at least that is what the census is.

The laughter escaped me before I could think about it, "Okay, if you guys insist; I will go bug him."

This was the perfect excuse to see him; I missed him terribly, and I was happy to do this for everyone. I stood up taking the file with me, "I wanted him to have this anyway."

She was giddy, as she followed me out of my office. I walked to Tyler's office and knocked.

"What?"

I opened the door and peaked in, "Can I come in?"

Tears filled his eyes as he nodded. I walked in closing the door and the shades. The girls were leaning over the counter, as I peaked at them before closing the blinds.

"Oh, Joselyn."

I walked over to him; he wrapped his arms around my waist and rested his forehead against my stomach, "I miss you so much."

I traced my fingers through his hair trying to comfort him, or maybe to comfort myself, because I missed him too. I whispered, "I picked out a few houses to look at; if you wouldn't mind."

He kissed my stomach, "I can't handle this anymore."

"Tyler, it's only temporary." I lifted his chin and wiped his tears that now soiled his face, "You're breaking my heart."

"I am going crazy. I can't think or do anything. It all comes back to you."

I smiled sweetly and kissed him gently, "You are scaring the girls."

"What?"

"They sent me in here. They think because we haven't been hanging out that you are a crab."

He nodded, "I am. You are just so…"

"We need to do what we used to. We are going out of our way to avoid each other, and we can't do that either."

He agreed, "I don't want to stay away."

I could feel the pitter patter of my heart being next to him, "Good, because I really need you now."

That seemed to make him happy, "I planned it that way."

I glared at him. "You purposely wanted to make me miserable without you?"

"No, I mean I wanted you to need me."

Kissing the top of his head, I pulled away and made my way to the other side of the desk sitting down in the chair. I gave him as much reassurance as I could and then slid the folder to him, "Look at these. See which one you could tolerate."

He opened it and started to read them. I got up walking to the window, "I need another big account, Tyler. Do you have anything for me?"

"No, I have been pouting."

"If you have more big accounts; that means we spend more time together."

I felt his breath at my ear, "Do you promise?"

"Yes, Baseball season is almost over. Working later a couple of nights wouldn't be that bad."

"But Shane said you should spend more time with your kids."

"Well then, figure it out. I need to be busy, so I don't worry. I need more time with you, because I am miserable without it, and I don't want to lose what I have now."

"You're not demanding at all."

"You know I have control issues."

"If you come with me now, you can have complete control."

I whispered as his arms wrapped around me, "No, I like when you control our love making."

He kissed my neck gently. I turned my head towards him and kissed him.

"How are you feeling?"

Not sure if I really was pregnant, I was still taking precautions, "I have a whole drawer of food in my desk."

He seemed to understand, "So, does that mean you are?"

Saved by the bell; we heard a knock at the door. He let go moving back to his desk quickly sitting down, "Come in."

Mr. Jenkins walked in and sat down. I didn't want to look back, because I was feeling very lonely right now.

"So what is on the agenda this week?"

Feeling the warmth of the afternoon sun I replied, "I have six presentations this week, but I will show them to you as soon as I have them from the agents. I have nine new accounts that I passed out, so we will take care of them next week."

"Tyler, do you have any big accounts this week?"

"No. I got lost in some other things, but I will get on it. I have a couple of ideas that I can get working on."

"So, I heard everyone had fun last weekend."

I turned to Mr. Jenkins, "Why didn't you come with us?"

"Well, the Misses wouldn't understand, and I am getting too old to party like that. I heard that the two of you didn't stay out late either."

I shook my head sitting down next to Mr. Jenkins.

"Tyler, do you think this new set up of yours is working? I feel like I am getting paid a lot of money to sit around and be bored."

Tyler agreed, "Yeah, I am sorry about that. I think Joselyn is complaining about the same thing."

"Yes, I am. I just asked for more big clients."

"Well, I was thinking that maybe..." He looked back and forth between Tyler and me, not really knowing how to say what was on his mind.

Tyler scolded, "You are the business Manager. If there is a problem you have to speak up.

"Things are a little different this week."

Tyler encouraged, "Yes, go on."

"Some of the staff said that they thought maybe there was chemistry between you two." He looked at me apologetically, "I am not accusing in any way. You know I love you, and I completely support you in leaving Ryan."

I took his hand in mine, "Mr. Jenkins, don't worry, I don't take offense to it at all."

He turned to me more taking both my hands in his, "Joselyn, I just... you know... and then the girls were telling me that you two almost kissed last week... and I remembered when I first introduced you... you ran off... then when you did meet, Tyler's mouth dropped to the floor, so I knew... but I wasn't sure."

Tyler stopped him, "Mr. Jenkins, your right. I don't know what to say."

He smiled sitting back in his chair with relief, "Oh, god. I thought you two would be mad, and I know what you are doing."

I was confused, because I didn't realize we were doing anything; he squeezed my hands, "Joselyn, sweetheart, I respect that you two are refusing to act on feelings, but honey I think it is time to divorce that husband of yours. Staying away from any temptation is respectable, but he is snapping at everyone." He turned to Tyler, "I'm not trying to be mean, but you have and the girls are complaining."

Tyler started to laugh out loud. I thought he was losing it, but Mr. Jenkins started to laugh with him, and it made me laugh, too.

169

37

Through the week we had lunch together in the conference room, but invited everyone that wanted to join us. The first couple of days it was quiet just the two of us. I ate off his plate and he ate off of mine. He was making sure I was eating right with all the food groups. By Thursday Mr. Jenkins was having lunch with us. A couple of the girls peaked in, and Tyler invited them in. The five of us had lunch talking and laughing. It was nice, but everyone watched us as we switched food again. There were things I just didn't like, and he let me have what I wanted from his plate.

More accounts came in daily, and I was having fun again. The busier I was the better I felt. I spent a lot more time with Mr. Jenkins reviewing ideas and discussing improvements. Tyler sat in once and awhile, but usually after the girls pushed him in the door to keep him from getting crabby.

The next week was going better yet. I had 16 accounts to work on this week, and the agents were fighting for the chance to get the extra ones. I was pleased that everyone was working so well together. Thursday came and we closed the 9 deals from the week before. I was on a high. Craig even presented his ideas himself, and they still closed. He nudged me, "I think you're rubbing off on me."

I cringed, "I don't think you should close anymore."

"Why, I still got the job done?"

"Because... you won't need me."

That made him happy. "So, is everyone having lunch again?"

"Yeah, everyone is welcome to join."

"Yeah, I am thinking I may do that."

I think all the girls in the office were having lunch with us now. Tyler seemed to get a lot of attention from everyone, and he handled it well. His concern was always on me; I noticed how everyone would catch him gazing at me. Not only did this worry me, but it also made me feel special to him, and I really needed it now. The conversation was usually light, but today it was getting far too personal. The girls were complaining about the boyfriends and husbands. They were bashing, and Kathy glanced down at me, "Joselyn, you know what I mean."

I glanced up not saying a word about the subject of husbands. I really didn't feel like I was married to him anymore. Rebecca spoke next, "Come on, Joselyn, you have been strapped for years."

Craig asked, "Tyler, are you married?"

He looked down at Craig, "Not anymore." He stood up and looked down at me whispering, "You okay?"

It was interesting to me that he said not anymore. To me, that was confirmation that he was not married. I let him know I was okay; but he wasn't and he left the room. Mr. Jenkins saved me with a lecture that maybe relationship discussion should be kept to our night life instead of at work. He helped me clean up and nudged me, "You should check on him."

I glanced up at him feeling ill. I shook my head, "I think I have to go home."

I tipped a little, and he grabbed my arm, "Joselyn, you okay?"

"Yeah, but I feel weird. I think I will..." I put my hand to my head.

He helped me to sit down, "I am going to get Tyler."

I grabbed his hand shaking my head, "No, I am fine. I think I will take a sick day for the rest of the day. If he asks, just let him know I went home, but don't say anything if he doesn't ask. Please Mr. Jenkins?"

He nodded but walked me to my car. He didn't like that I was driving feeling a little off, but I agreed to call him when I got home safely.

38

Tyler

I hated that I wasn't comfortable talking about Meredith to anyone yet. I knew I would have to explain further to Joselyn, but right now she was my main concern. I called the gaming commissionaire that was a good friend of mine, and we talked about representing the cities activities. He agreed to meet with me. I was pleased, because this could possibly be the biggest deal I could have ever gotten for Joselyn. I knew that if I got it, she would close it no problem. She closed everything she touched.

I thought about how she presented herself. She was gorgeous, which got their attention and that melted them into listening open minded, and then her confidence was compelling; no one could turn her down. I loved to watch her go in for the kill. As I thought about her, I found myself smiling. She did amaze me in more ways than one. My mind drifted off to making love to her. She allowed me more than I could ever ask from anyone, yet she was tender and perfect. I could picture the curve of her lower back, and I could see her wonderful butt and awesome legs wrapped around me. The feelings were overwhelming, and I needed to shake off this awareness of wanting her all the time.

Coming back from my day dream was difficult. I answered my phone, "Hello."

"Hey, guess what I am doing right now?"

"Shane?"

"Yeah, dumb ass. Guess what I am doing?"

"Why am I a dumb ass, and what the hell are you doing?"

"I am taking pictures of a said husband opening a door to a hot little blonde."

"Shit. You are kidding me?"

"No, and it is not innocent. I have him."

I stood up walking out of my office to check on Joselyn.

"You are speechless. Come on, this is what we were waiting for."

"No, that's good. I just want to check to make sure she is okay."

"Why, she doesn't know. I will be careful."

I looked in the window, but her office was empty. I turned to Mary, "Where is Joselyn?"

She gave me that approving flirty grin, "I don't know. I haven't seen her since Mr. Jenkins walked her out."

"Shane, I have to go."

"Wait. She isn't there?"

"I don't know. I have to find out."

"Call me back. Do you want me to stay here?"

"Yeah. I will call you back once I know that she is here."

I hung up and headed to Mr. Jenkins office asking Mary, "Is he back?"

"Yeah, he came back a little bit ago."

I stormed into his office, "Where is Joselyn?" I was close to panicking.

"She went home."

I almost fell over, "When?"

"I don't know, maybe 30 minutes ago."

"Shit."

I headed out of his office. He was running after me, "What is wrong?"

I didn't say anything, but I pulled him to the elevator with me. I waited till it opened and turned on him as the doors closed.

"She hired a Lawyer, a friend of mine. He is at her house taking pictures for evidence."

"He is not doing what I think he is?"

I nodded as he closed his eyes. I could tell he felt for Joselyn as much as I did. His reply explained it more to me, "I told her when it happened before that she should walk away."

"I was trying to help her, but I don't want her walking into it again."

"No, you are right."

I took off running as the elevator doors open. He yelled after me, "Good luck. She needs someone to care."

He has no idea how much I cared about her. I called her.

"Hey. I take it Mr. Jenkins told you."

"Told me what?"

"I am not feeling well. I am going home."

"No, he left that part out. You're not there yet, right?"

"No, but I am two blocks away."

"Joselyn, turn around and meet me at the apartment in the city."

"I would love to, but I am not feeling well enough to drive back and you know we are supposed to be careful."

"No, I think Shane would be okay with it just this once."

"Tyler, I am so close and I really need to lie down."

"Joselyn, no! Don't go home."

"Tyler?"

"Trust me. Don't go home."

"WHY?"

"Joselyn, please don't go home." I was driving like a mad man, "Stop at a store and wait for me."

"Tyler, I pulled over, but what is this about?"

"I need for you to not go home."

"I miss you too, but I wouldn't be good company right now."

"Joselyn, I can take care of you. I want the whole package."

She sighed, "I know, but this is temporary. I love you but I have to lie down. My head is swimming."

"Just put the seat back and tell me where you are."

She sighed again, "Tyler, I really need to lay down now. I am sorry; I have to go home. I am only a block away."

"Joselyn, I am only about a mile away. Will you wait for me?"

"Tyler, I can't do this today."

"Is it the baby?"

"No, I don't even know if I am. I only got sick once and this is different."

"How so?"

"Tyler, I am home. Can I call you later?"

"Joselyn, I told you to wait for me."

"I am sorry. I love you."

She hung up on me. She must be really sick. I called Shane back.

"She is there?"

"Yeah, I am heading to her now. How close are you?"

"Half mile."

"Get here."

He hung up, and I was going nuts with worry. I didn't want her to see that again.

I pulled up, and she was pushing past him. I got out of my car running to her, and she stopped to look at me. She didn't look good and she was giving me that look, "He is in there right now with someone else, isn't he?"

"Yes."

She held her hand out for me to back off. I tried to plead with her to just leave with me, but she walked in. I followed quickly behind her trying to step in front of her to stop her from seeing anything. I didn't want her hurt again. We were so close to ending this part of her life. She scolded me to move, but I didn't. He came running up the stairs, "What is going on?"

She looked at him, "In my home... again?"

He moved closer to her, "Joselyn, you are over reacting."

She threw up all over the front of him. I grabbed her, lifted her into my arms, and carried her up the stairs to the bathroom. Shane came in, "I think you may want to get the blonde out of here."

Ryan looked at me standing at the top of the stairs while we heard Joselyn throwing up in the bathroom and then he looked at Shane, "Who are you?"

"I am your wife's Lawyer."

He went white and walked down the stairs.

Shane looked at me and I asked, "You have proof right?"

He nodded, "But you showing up here... isn't going to be good."

I moved closer to talk quietly, "No, it will be okay because Mr. Jenkins knew she was sick, and he knew I was going to check on her to make sure she got home okay."

He squinted, "Tyler, are you sure?"

Was he asking me if I was sure about the situation or about my feelings for Joselyn? My answer would have to cover both, "You have no idea."

The blonde came up the stairs a little shaken, but Shane escorted her out of the house. In the mean time Ryan looked at me, "What are you doing here?"

"Mr. Jenkins was worried that she wouldn't make it home. He asked me to make sure she got home okay." He came up sitting on the couch leaning his head back covering his face with his hands. I almost felt bad for the guy, but he did this to himself, "You might want to get changed."

He looked down at himself, and got up slowly to go down the steps. When he was face to face with me, he stopped to look me in the eye, "It's you!"

I didn't flinch, move, blink, or anything. How do you tell another man that you are in love with their wife? I knew that now was not the time for this. I heard Joselyn again. I glanced back at the door feeling horrible for her and then I looked into his eyes again, "I think you might want to change, because if she sees that she just may do it again."

"The Lawyer, he is a friend of yours?"

"She asked if I knew any Lawyers, so I got her one. I told you... I want her happy."

He almost seemed beaten as he shook his head and walked away.

I heard the water in the sink draining, so I asked Joselyn, "You okay?"

"No."

"I'm sorry."

She opened the door looking up into my eyes, "You tried to stop me, but I wish you would have just told me."

I shook my head wrapping my arm around her waist to give her support, "Bedroom?"

She held her arm out pointing down a short hall. I walked her into the room helping her to sit down at the foot of her bed. I was tempted to explore her room, but she wasn't doing well. I gestured to the dresser, "Which drawer?"

She pointed toward the top, so I pointed to the second one down. She nodded, so I pulled out the drawer holding items up for her to see. She just nodded, so I laid them down beside her whispering, "Do you want help?"

She shook her head, so I stepped out of the room closing the door. I noticed Ryan was walking back up the stairs looking at me, "She okay?"

I shrugged, but I didn't move.

He glared at me, "Did she see anything?"

I shrugged again.

"The bucket is under the sink; there are water bottles in the fridge, and grab a towel from the bathroom. She may need that stuff."

I was confused that he was allowing me to help her. He glanced back at me, "Well, I don't think she will want my help."

I moved as soon as he said that. I grabbed everything and went back to the door. Everything was very awkward with Shane, Ryan, and me all exchanging glances. I had to say something to Ryan, "I asked Shane to stay."

Ryan gestured to a chair where Shane could take a seat. I knocked on the bedroom door, "Are you decent? Can I come in?"

I heard her, but it was faint. Emerging into the room I put the water on the night stand opening it for her, set the bucket on the floor, and handed her a towel, "You okay?"

She shook her head. I felt her forehead, "You are burning up."

She nodded, "Flu."

I knelt down whispering, "Is the baby okay?"

"Tyler we don't even know yet. This is the flu."

I lay my head down on the bed next to her, "I am not leaving."

She traced her hand in my hair, "Okay. How is Ryan taking this?"

I looked back at her. Why would she care about how he was feeling? She gave me a faint smile, "You told him, right? That I love you."

I took her hand in mine and kissed it hard shaking my head. I mouthed to her, "I didn't know how."

It was like everything was wiped out of her, eyes so heavy that they closed sleepily. The thump of my heart was making it hard for me to try and stay calm. I knew I shouldn't be here, but she was my main concern over anything else that might happen.

When she was completely out, I went and sat on the couch with Ryan, but didn't say anything. The three of us sat there for two hours and finally Shane stood up, "Sorry guys, I really don't want to leave the two of you alone, but I have kids to get home to."

It wasn't long when Ryan looked at the clock thinking the same thing as Shane, "So, what am I telling the kids?"

I shrugged my shoulders again. I really didn't know what to say or do. All I knew is that she wasn't doing well and to handle this alone would be too much. He got up, going down to the door, as the kids came home, first Jared, then Terra, and finally Haden. Ryan took them down stairs and explained that their mom was sick. Jared wandered up the stairs to see me sitting there. He walked over to me, "What are you doing here?"

"Mr. Jenkins was worried about your mother. He sent me to make sure that she is okay."

"She came home early?"

I nodded and his lips pressed together in a straight line, "Dad's friend was over again?"

I glanced back up at him. I was confused by his question.

"Well, that is why you are here, right?"

I shrugged my shoulders, "How did you know?"

"I wanted to tell you the other day, but I was hoping that she was getting better. She has been happier, so I thought things were working out." He glanced up at me, "Things aren't going to work out, are they?"

I shook my head.

"Are you going to be around more?"

I nodded.

"Okay."

He walked to the kitchen, so I followed. He took out stuff to make sandwiches. I watched him as he put peanut butter on some pieces of bread. He folded them and poured three glasses of milk. He turned, "After school snack."

I chuckled and watched him go down the stairs. I walked back to her room peaking in on her. She was still sleeping. I went back out to the chair and waited.

Ryan came up about dinner time, "You're still here?"

I nodded and watched him. He walked into the kitchen and looked in the fridge then the cupboards.

I suggested, "I could order for delivery."

He came back out, "That would be great. I haven't cooked in years."

"What do you want?"

He called the kids up and then asked what they wanted to eat. I listened and slowly walked to the kitchen. He was paging through the yellow pages asking what sounded good. They decided on Chinese, but they didn't deliver. I think he was trying to get rid of me, but I didn't agree to go pick up food. He caved and grabbed his coat, "I guess I will go then. Anyone want to go with?"

Haden and Terra offered, but Jared ignored his dad.

"Jared, are you coming?"

He shook his head, "I think I will stay in case mom needs something."

I cracked a smile. He didn't want me to take care of her either. He was very mature for his age. We sat in the living room while we waited.

Joselyn:

I walked out of the bathroom, after brushing my teeth, to find Tyler sleeping in the chair and Jared on the couch. I walked over touching Tyler's hand. He startled awake looking at me, "Are you..."

I put my hand on his lips, and pulled him to lead him out of the room. He followed me out of the house and I turned to look at him, "I am better now. You can go home."

He shook his head, "Not until... no I want to be there when you talk to Ryan. I don't want you dealing with it by yourself."

I grinned, "I don't plan on talking about it with him ever. Shane got the evidence we needed and that is it. Papers can be filed and served. I don't need to explain myself."

The warmth of his lips on my forehead was comforting, "I don't want to leave."

Pressing my cheek to his in agony, wanting to beg him to stay, I pleaded, "It will be okay." The warmth of my inner core ached for him to caress and hold me. His open mouth searched for a good place to rest, but then he whispered, "Jared is watching."

I hugged him tightly, "Thank you so much for making sure I was okay."

"Joselyn, I will leave, but you should talk to him. He knows what Ryan was doing."

I was hurt and upset, "What?"

"He knew what Ryan was doing. I don't know how, but he has known for a while. He even knew that was why you were sad for so long."

Sadness was filling my heart, "How do you know this?"

"He tells me things. I haven't figured out why, but I mostly listen."

I took his hand and squeezed it, but turned looking at Jared, "Thanks. I will let you know how it goes tomorrow."

He didn't let go, "You said you weren't going to talk about it."

"Not with Ryan, but I will with Jared. He seems more grown up."

"I think he is more than you know." He leaned down toward me whispering, "Try to remember that I am in love with you."

How he could make me so happy when I felt so sad was a wonder to me. I let go of his hand, "I hope so."

I walked to Jared wrapping my arms around him. We watched Tyler drive away together, and then Jared asked, "Is he nice to you?"

I hugged him tighter, "Yes."

"So, he is going to be around more?"

"Would that bother you?"

"No, not really, but I don't think Terra and Haden will like it much."

39

Tyler had a meeting set up for me on Wednesday, but I didn't know the details of it. We headed out at 10 am, but he wasn't telling me where we were going. We ended up at the baseball stadium, which I wish I would have know beforehand; I would have worn a much better choice of shoes. As we walked he was curious, but only because I had bought a pregnancy test this morning and did the deed before we left. It was in my purse and I wanted to ignore what it said, so I wouldn't be off when I met the new client.

"Joselyn, let me see. You don't have to look at it, and I won't tell you."

"No."

"I won't tell you."

"I will be able to tell by the look on your face."

"No you won't, because it doesn't matter to me."

"Look at you now. You are all goofy and excited. I will be able to tell."

He finally gave up when we got off the elevator, but he had this goofy smile on his face, like he was spell bound or something. When we walked in, I noticed it was a huge conference room. Everyone stood when we entered, and Tyler introduced me to everyone; then he held a chair out for me. They handed him the folder, which he handed over to me right away. In the folder was a list of events over the rest of the year, and then into the next year. I am assuming we would have the account for a good year. I scanned the list as Tyler spoke to them. I was excited, because this wasn't just one thing. It was a list of 40 events that I would be advertising for over the next year. The variety of events included; having carnivals, the circus, all the way up to sporting events. My mind was running a hundred miles an hour, already working on the first three. I wasn't really paying attention to their talking, but it was light: like the weather, families, and how Tyler liked this new company. It caught my attention when Mr. Cutter asked, "So how many is that now, twenty-four?"

"Yeah, something like that, but you know I only take special interest in a few of them."

I was wondering what they were talking about, because my mind was definitely not here, until now.

"So, why did you get into this type of business?"

He grinned, "Well... I wasn't planning on it, but something caught my eye, and now I am having fun with it. Plus, Jake, if you give us this, I can spend a lot more time at the ball field."

"Okay, okay. How about you come on Saturday for the game? We have box seats, and we'll discuss things a little bit."

I smiled and leaned towards Tyler, "I won't be able to."

He turned to me not understanding, "You are kidding."

I shook my head, "It's playoffs and Jared has his last tournaments, and then the other two have their final games."

This Jake guy asked, "What time?"

"I am sorry, but it will be all day. Sometimes games go until 8 or 9 pm on Saturday, depending on how well they do."

He smiled, "I do miss the rush of having game after game. Your son is how old?"

I smiled, "He is thirteen."

"Tyler, she only has a few years left with him, and it goes so fast. Why don't we do this..." he pulled his phone out moving his fingers about a mile a minute, "Well, since you have a son, why don't we make it the following weekend, and you could bring him."

I was pleased, and then I went for whole gang, "I do have two other children."

"Yes, of course, bring the whole family."

"Did you want full ideas, or just a rough draft?"

He grinned and glanced at Tyler, "She doesn't goof around."

He shook his head, "And you haven't seen her work yet."

40

I excused myself and went to the bathroom. I pulled out the stick now that I wasn't nervous. It said that I was not pregnant. I walked out and Tyler was waiting for me. He examined my face probing for the answer, "You looked?"

I gave him a harsh look, "No."

The way his mouth curved upward made his lips full of temptation, "You're not a good liar." His arms warmed me with an embrace, "You know I will take care of you, our baby, and everything. You can work; I will stay home changing diapers, doing laundry, and everything. I don't have to work."

We staggered onto the elevator still embraced, as he continued, "I will buy the house, so you don't have to think about it."

I didn't have the heart to tell him. I shook my head, but he took it as I didn't want to tell him. I wanted more privacy to let him down carefully.

I stared at him sitting across from me, as he gazed back into my eyes, "It will be okay, Joselyn."

He was taking my actions all wrong. I closed my eyes, "Not that I am not, but it said no."

He crawled across the floor of the Limo towards me, and laid his head in my lap. I traced my fingers through his hair. I could feel the shallow beat of his heart, and the calming breaths that escaped him. The pain came out in his voice asking, "Can I see it?"

"Why, you don't trust me?"

"Yeah, I just don't believe it. You have been woozy in the mornings."

183

"It might be too early to tell, and I haven't gotten my monthly yet, but that might be because of everything going on. You know stress can do that."

He traced his hand along my calf, "You have beautiful calves."

I leaned down kissing his cheek. His playful tone came back, "Can we have sex in the car, yet?"

I laughed at him, "No."

"We could stop at the hotel."

I let my fingers explore his strong jaw, the hollowness of his cheek, and then those luscious lips. He glanced back up at me full of mischief, "Do you want me to start now?"

His hand slid up inside my thigh. He knew just how to touch me to get a rise out of me, and I scooted down more to enjoy what he was doing. The way his fingers played within my folds, the way he taunted my swollen clit; he got me going, but just when I was going to beg him to be in me right here, he moved away from me lowering the window, "I need to make a stop to pick up some paperwork. Stop at TR's." I giggled as the window went up moving to his side quickly to entice him, "Why would they name a hotel TR's."

I pressed my hand against his already protruding mound, restricted by his clothes.

A growl came from his mouth, but he tried to control himself, "It's professional sounding; plus they do have it in their logo as 'your business home'.

I stroked my hand against him knowing I was driving him crazy, "The next thing you are going to tell me is that it stands for Tyler Reynolds." I started to laugh, but it must have irritated him. He took my hand from him, entangled our fingers, and he looked out the window.

"Tyler, tell me I am wrong."

He glanced back at me as we pulled up, "I think I have a little bit more to tell you."

I really didn't know how to take that; I was in shock, as he pulled me from the car. We stayed composed until we hit the elevator where I couldn't stay away from him. I pressed my hard nipples against his chest. His hands cradled my behind pulling me to rub against him. We lost all rationality with the dictates of our bodies, letting them take over and soar into ecstasy. He rushed me into the room, and the heat was on. I was already burning with prickles of electric pulses to all my nerve endings, begging, pleading for pleasure. I was hurrying to get out of my work clothes when I felt his arms around me and his mouth at my ear nibbling. It didn't take much when he reached down to finish what he started in the car. The touch of his fingers felt silky and warm against my heated sex. I was gasping and becoming weak in the knees, as the pleasure rose from within me. I wanted and needed his warmth to fill my body, but my excitement was rising quickly. I reached back to try to undo his pants, but the quickening of his twirls against me had me releasing a moan, as I tipped over the threshold of a completely enjoyable orgasm. He turned me to him undoing my bra, and then pushed down my underpants quickly, as we moved to the bed. He was full of desire, and I needed to please him, so that is exactly what I did.

Pushing him back, I crawled over him to straddle what was already hard as marble. I leaned over letting my tongue touch his skin for a taste before allowing my lips to enjoy the feel of his skin. Moving lower... lower... lower... taunting him with every delicious mouthful I took. It wasn't until I took his shaft in my hand stroking him gently, and lightly placed my lips around the tip, that he begged, "Joselyn, please."

This is not something I would have done in my past life, but with Tyler I wanted to share everything down to every last drop of intimacy. My tongue did things to him that caused a growl from deep within him. His fingers gripped at the sheets below him, and I moved swiftly to enhance the pleasure. He moaned out, "Please just a little..." I sucked harder and pumped faster until he pushed me away. I stroked him to a moaning release, where his body twitched and jerked beneath me. The strength of his hands pulled me up to him where I rested my body snugly to his.

We took a lot longer than I was planning, but only because I was still thinking pregnant thoughts, and wanting to eat something; when I realized that I probably wasn't pregnant, I decided that I needed THIS worse than eating, and I enticed him for more. He was more than willing to continue.

How do you explain when someone cups your face in their hands and the need for them to caress your lips, the desire to feel their body against yours, and that flutter from deep within that makes you want more than you ever want to allow. That is what I wanted from Tyler. When he coddled into my breast again, he glanced back up at me, "Are you doing something to them?"

I laughed, "That is why I think I am pregnant. They are tender and very sensitive."

He glared at me, but his attention went back to grazing the palm of his hand against my nipple, and I felt the ripple in my stomach, and I cried out. He glanced up to see what the noise was about, but when he realized that he was the cause, his intensions went back to pleasing me yet again.

After having this much pleasure at one time, I wondered how I would get back to the office and be able to concentrate on work. We'd fallen into the deepest ocean of pleasure and shared the most intimate sensations of sharing our souls.

41

We, my family and I, pulled up to the ball field ready for all day. I had packed a lunch and snacks, while Ryan had put juice boxes, Gatorades, and waters in a cooler for the day. We started off with Jared's game. It was a win and then on to Terra's game, which they won. Jared played again winning again. It seemed to me that this was definitely going to be a long day. I didn't even try to talk to Ryan, and he was afraid to say anything. I don't know if he was that angry or sad, because he was wordless as we sat there. The best part was that I wasn't getting insulted either.

Finally it was Haden's game, but Haden was angry with Jared for having to leave early to warm up for his game. I reassured him we would keep him here as long as possible.

The game started the same as all of the other ones today, with a toss of a coin to decide who was going to be the home team. Haden got to go out with the coach, and he was all nervous standing there. He looked back at us worried, and I smiled nodding for him to be okay with this all, but looking passed us, he waved frantically. I felt a hand on my shoulder, "Good, I made it."

I wanted to crawl in a hole. Things were going good today with no arguing. I didn't ask him to come; shit what was he up to?

"Hey, Ryan how is everything going today?"

He grumbled, "Why are you here? I'm not doing anything wrong."

Tyler laughed, "I came to see the kids play ball. I looked up the schedule online with hopes I would find the right teams."

Ryan tapped Jared on the shoulder, "Would you get Tyler a chair?"

He stood up smiling at Tyler, but ran to get it. I was shrinking in my seat.

"Joselyn, how are you feeling today?"

I glanced up at him, "Okay?"

He smiled, "Good, so they are just getting started?"

"Yeah."

Jared came back with the chair, but stood there looking at the three of us. I knew what he was waiting for, but I didn't want to be the one who decided where Tyler was going to sit. Ryan moved over, "You can put it here."

This was very uncomfortable, and Tyler smiled at me as he sat down between Ryan and me. Haden came running over to us as soon as they were done, "You came. Tyler, you came to my game."

He laughed, "Yes, I did, and guess what?"

Haden's eyes got huge waiting for Tyler to tell him something, "Yours is the first game of mine today."

Haden was beaming.

Tyler leaned forward, "Are you supposed to be over here? I kind of wanted to see you play, and if you get benched for talking to me I would be sad."

He grinned, and took off for the bench. I glanced at Tyler and mouthed thank you, but I heard Ryan say it to Tyler.

"Thanks, he hasn't really learned that yet."

We sat there for a little bit and Tyler stood up, "What do you guys have for snacks?"

I glanced up at him, "I made sandwiches; are you hungry?"

"No, I brought some snacks. Jared, do you want to help me?"

I stood up to go with, but Tyler shook his head, "No, you take it easy. I am here to help Ryan today, so you can sit back and relax." He was pushing me back down to my seat. Ryan glanced over, "You wanted me to help?"

"No, not if Jared wouldn't mind helping me."

I watched as Jared jumped up to go with him. I turned to watch them walk to Tyler's car, but I didn't see it. He opened the back of a different vehicle.

I heard Ryan, "You don't have to stare, Joselyn."

I ignored him. I wasn't staring; I was watching Jared not Tyler.

They were grabbing trays of food. I shook my head turning back to the game laughing to myself.

"It's all healthy." Jared wasn't too pleased, but did open the fruit tray and start to eat right away. Tyler set down a veggie tray on the blanket in front of me, but handed a smaller container to me. I glanced up at him, but he scolded, "Protein. Eat it and I don't want to hear about it."

He glanced down at Ryan, but only because Ryan was getting irritated moving forward in his seat. Tyler put his hand on his shoulder, "You are going to be so happy I showed up."

Ryan glared, "Oh, yeah. Why is that?"

"Because I can help take care of your family, and you can enjoy the game."

Ryan sat back smiling, so Tyler sat down next to me. I glanced over as I opened the container.

He leaned to me, "It's eggs, spinach, and grotto cheese. I hope you like it. I had it made special."

He stood back up. He seemed edgy. If this was uncomfortable he shouldn't have came. He walked to the dugout squatting talking to Haden. I tried to watch, but after taking one bite I was shoveling it in. I must have been hungry or something, because it was haven to the taste buds.

Ryan wasn't pleased, and grimaced as he spoke, "Oh, Jos, that smells horrible. How can you eat it?"

I was smiling, while I shoved another bite in my mouth. I watched as Tyler talked with Haden about holding the bat and the way he was holding his hands.

Ryan leaned forward, "Why is he showing him that. I didn't want him holding it like that. It will make it harder for him to cut at the ball."

Jared looked back at his dad rolling his eyes. He noticed I saw what he did. I questioned him with a look, but he shook me off and went back to eating. Terra laughed, "Dad, that is how my coach taught me."

I started to laugh, but kept my mouth full of food. I offered Jared a bite, but he turned his nose up at it. Terra sat with her mouth wide open. I fed her a bite. Her eyes bulged out of her head, and she moved closer to me as she swallowed. She opened her mouth again like a little baby bird waiting for the mama to feed it.

Tyler came back sitting down, talking to Ryan, "Your wife is kind of a health nut, and it looks like your daughter takes after her mother."

Ryan glanced at him, "Since when?"

"Since I've known her."

He leaned forward looking at me, "Is that how you lost all that weight?"

I glared at him not saying a word, because it was only 12 lbs. Tyler's finger grazed the back of my hand. I glanced at him as he grinned. I shook my head. Was he trying to make him mad?

Haden was up to bat, so we all moved to the edge of our seats and held our breath. I only noticed this when he hit the ball good and hard, and we all jumped up screaming. He was adorable running with everything he had. He was still going... going... rounding to second. I was worried they were pushing him, but Tyler was screaming 'run' as he moved to the fence. The weirdest feeling came over me like I was going to cry. Why was this making me feel this way? I watched as the coach waved him further, and he continued passing the second base. I covered my mouth, and moved around my chair. I was going to start to cry. I walked away, as they all yelled for him to stop. Everyone was cheering, and I knew he did well, so why do I want to bawl? I am so pregnant, and I know it. I went to the car grabbing my purse. I had to check again. This was my fifth time checking, so I was beginning to think that I wasn't, but with me being this off balance today, I have to be... that or I am going to be really miserable when my period comes.

42

Tyler:

I watched her walk away from us. I wanted to follow her, but didn't know what I would use for an excuse. I wondered if the food made her feel ill. I should have gotten her something simpler than that, shit.

Ryan leaned to me, "I still think it is you."

I swallowed shaking my head more than in disbelief than trying to convince him that it isn't. Reluctantly a grin came to my face, as I thought about how much I loved her. I really didn't want to discuss this with Ryan today, because if she was having my baby, I wanted to make it as easy for her as possible. I looked back at Ryan, "Do you love your wife?"

He glared first and looked back at the game talking quietly, "Yes."

I think that was a good offset, so I smiled and picked up the tray, "Want some food?"

He glanced at me, laughed with a sigh, and then shook his head taking some food. I grinned, and we went back to watching the game. However, I still kept an eye out for Joselyn. I needed to know if she was okay.

Jared jumped up, "Hey, I have to go."

Ryan got up, "Okay."

I looked up at him, "Do you want me to take him? I mean you could finish watching Haden's game."

He glared at me, but I reassured him that I was here to help him take care of the kids today. Jared and I got up to go, but Ryan walked with us to the truck. He was leaning in Jared's window telling him to buckle up. Joselyn came running, "What are you doing?"

"I am taking Jared to the other ball field."

She looked worried, but I reassured her that I would take very good care of him. I glanced at Jared, "We won't switch sides 'til we're out of their over protecting eyes."

Jared was smiling and laughing knowing how they would react. I, however, didn't have a clue, so when Joselyn grabbed my ear and scolded me, I complained like a little boy, telling her to stop and that it hurt, but she was very angry with me, "That is not funny at all."

"I was kidding; you do know that?"

She glared at me, "He is not allowed to drive until he gets his permit. Do you understand me?"

I was taken aback a little. She was the woman from the office. I looked back at Jared, "There, now tell me who could turn her down when she is that direct?" Both Ryan and Jared laughed, as I glanced back at Joselyn, but she still wasn't happy with me.

"I am just going to drop him off, and then I will be back to help Ryan get everything."

She finally smiled at me touching her stomach slightly. I questioned her with a look. She just smiled and backed away from my door. My heart was racing. This was getting more complicated by the minute, and I had to hurry back to try to talk to her. Did that mean what I thought it meant?

43

We got to the field, and I went out with him to warm him up throwing for a couple of minutes until the other guys showed up. We goofed around with pitching, and by the time his team got there he was getting pretty good. I had pitched for a few years, so I knew the basics. When his friends started showing up he came running to me, thanking me, and asked me if I was staying for his game. I nodded as he took off to be with the rest of his team. I heard all the guys asking him who I was, but he just said a friend of the family. I wondered what he would call me after I was with his mother.

I walked slowly to my truck heading back to help Joselyn and Ryan get everything to move to this field. How was I going to get Joselyn alone today? I walked back up just in time to see Haden hit again. He hit the ball solid, and it soared over the shortstop's head. He took off at full speed racing to first base. I was yelling to run, as I moved closer to Joselyn. Ryan was preoccupied by the hit. I was trying to get to her, but he turned to look at me, "Did you see that?"

I nodded, but was distracted with wonder. I cheered for Haden; seeing him beaming on second left me with the oddest feeling. I wanted to pick Joselyn up, hold her close to me, and have her tell me I was going to be the father of her baby. She glanced back at me, and her eyes were full of tears. I decided to not push the issue after seeing her happy; he was her baby too. I sat down carefully in between them, but leaned toward Joselyn. Once we were married there was no way I would let her sit here, and not hold her hand or touch her in some way. I would want the world to know I love this woman in the way I treated her.

The game ended, as I was daydreaming about how I would show her that I cared about her all the time. She touched my arm, "Are you staying for Jared's game?"

I stood up, "Yes." I started to help Ryan load everything up for the move to the next field. I looked at Joselyn, wanting her to ride with me, but I might be expecting too much. She smiled at me, standing by my truck waiting, and then I saw her look at Ryan standing by their minivan. She took Terra by the hand and smiled gracefully, "We are going to walk. We will meet both of you by the other field."

She turned and walked away. I looked at Ryan, and he shrugged his shoulders, but I didn't like that she is walking that far. Haden chased after her taking her other hand. I looked at Ryan again and he smiled, "She won't leave those kids."

Did he think he was winning because of them? He will never win her love again, and I knew that, but his little smirk irritated me. He got in and drove away. *Calm down Tyler; you can deal with this in a mature adult manner. Do not kick the shit out of him in front of his children. They will never like you if you do.*

I took a deep breath, and slowly headed to the other field. I watched Joselyn walk with her children, as they talked and laughed. I watched as long as I could, but when I had a line waiting for me to move on, I had to go and park. I carried up the food again, and then went to help get the chairs with Ryan. I wanted him to know I was here to help her, because he didn't usually help her. He had all the chairs on one shoulder and the blanket in the other hand. He was already heading up to an area for them to sit. I helped set up the chairs, as he went back grabbing the cooler with food in it. I glared at him, as he walked back over. He raised his eyebrows looking at me. He was trying to get to me.

We both sat down at the same time. I crossed my arms, and he crossed his legs. We were having a silent standoff.

He finally broke the silence, "So, why did you come here today?"

I grinned, because he should have kept his mouth shut. I leaned to him daring, "You're the one who told me she wouldn't give up those kids."

He turned to me not understanding.

I raised my eyebrows, "I told you I want her happy. Is there a better way to make her happy other than coming to spend time with her children?"

He was pissed, and I could see it in his face. Shit, this was supposed to be civilized, not a standoff. I caved, "I am sorry. I didn't mean it that way. I really like Jared, he is cool, and Haden, he is inspiring, and I don't have a family anymore… I miss it."

He coughed, "So, you want mine?"

"No, that is not why I am here. I want her to be happy, and she worked hard this week. I thought I could help you with everything, so she could relax."

He glared again.

I shrugged my shoulders, and stood back up looking for Joselyn, "Do you think they should walk that far?"

"Yeah, it's good for her. She got heavy after the kids, and this is good for her."

She was heavy. I don't believe that. She doesn't seem that way. Maybe she gains a little pregnancy weight, but I am sure it would come off quickly. I saw her at the park, and sat back down.

He laughed a little, "She is independent. She doesn't like hovering."

I smiled because in my bed she loves the hovering. I had to say something, "You said you love her right?"

He turned to me, "Yes, I do."

I leaned to him, "Do you love her enough to let her go? I mean… under the circumstances of the infidelity thing, I don't think she wants to stay with you."

"Are you saying you want her?"

"No. I am here to support her in whatever decision she makes."

He leaned forward, "Why do you want to help her, if you aren't sleeping with her?"

I sat forward too, "I will tell you, but it's a long story."

"We have a whole game."

"No, we only have until she gets here."

"I guess you better start."

I glared at him, "I met her before I bought the agency. She was out with work friends."

"So you are meeting her?"

"No. That is not what I said, and if you don't want to hear this then…" I sat back and crossed my arms.

"Fine, I will keep my mouth shut."

I laughed, "When I met your Joselyn I really met her. I ran her over on her way to the bathroom. I didn't know she was married or anything.

195

I didn't see the ring; all I saw was this amazingly beautiful woman who was holding her chest from where I plowed into her. She was on her way to the bathroom, but I felt bad, so I helped her get there. Before I let her go, I asked her to meet me."

"So, she did?"

I laughed again, "No, she didn't. I was hurt; my pride was wounded. I had gone to the bar waiting for her to find me. She wasn't even looking for me. No girl had stood me up when I asked them to meet me."

He huffed, "Yeah, I bet."

"No, it's not like that. You know how girls are. If they think you're interested they come running even if they aren't, but they want their free drinks."

"Oh, that sucks."

I agreed, "Well, I ended up sitting there watching her. She wasn't flirting, dancing, or anything. She was sad sitting there. She was longing to feel happy like everyone else. I could see it on her face, and I felt her need in my heart. It made me want to find out what was causing her sadness."

He stopped me, "Jared is up."

I glanced to see if Joselyn was coming, but she was still at the park watching the game from the fence in the outfield. I was getting nervous about talking with Ryan. I didn't want him to get the wrong idea, but I did want him to know how sad she was. Haden got a double and we both cheered. He leaned back, "So when did you fall for her?"

"I swear you have a one track mind."

"You don't even know me."

"You're right. Forget it."

"No, really, tell me more."

"I have had a few things in my life not go the way I planned, and I knew the feeling that was on her face. It was lonely, longing, sad, empty, and just…"

"Pitiful?"

"Yeah, but I had been there, and I thought maybe if I helped her find her happiness, I would feel better about my own sadness. I followed her when she walked out with all her friends, but as they headed to their cars she ended up alone. She stopped, so I got a little closer, and she took off her shoes to finish walking to her car."

"So, that is when it happened?"

I turned to him raising my eyebrows.

"Okay, I am done talking. What?"

"I did try to kiss her, but she wouldn't let me. She refused showing me her wedding ring. I didn't care that she was married; all I wanted was to make her sadness go away, but that wasn't what she wanted or needed. I backed off, and pleaded with her to come back the following weekend."

"I know she did. She went out the next three weekends in a row."

"No, she didn't. She didn't show up. I went back two weekends in a row, and she didn't show up." Of course, I left out the last weekend. I was hoping that he wouldn't catch that.

"She didn't show up, but she left the house and was gone for hours."

That did confuse me a little, but I still wanted to continue.

"Well, I had been trying to make my pain go away, so I gambled big in business to try to get my life over, but someone didn't want me to go away, and everything I have touched has worked out just the opposite for me. I bought the agency without knowing she worked there."

"You really didn't know?"

"No, in fact, I was supposed to meet with her one day. Mr. Jenkins and Joselyn were standing in my office while I was on the phone. I turned to them, but I still was not looking at them; as my phone call ended, she took off running. At the time, I wondered why we would even want to keep her if she could run off like that."

"So, you still didn't know it was my Joselyn?"

"No. Mr. Jenkins asked me to wait on letting her go and convinced me to give it a little bit of time. He was the one who told me that you two were having problems at home. It seems that Mr. Jenkins knows about your little… mishaps."

He groaned putting his hands to his face. "I knew he knew. He hasn't been nice to me for a long time. By the way, why are you being nice to me if you know what I have done?"

"I am here to make sure she is happy. I need her with my company. Everything she touches works, but we are getting past the point."

"There is a point?"

"Yeah. She avoided me for two weeks and 16 accounts later I found out she wanted to quit. I did some fast planning, and put a proposal together to keep her. When she finally made it to my office I was stunned. I didn't know what to say or do. This was the beautiful unapproachable woman who was so miserable. Ever since then, I just

197

can't help but want to make her happy. Somehow, if I help her find happiness in her life... maybe I will find mine."

"You sound like a woman."

"No, I am a man who has had losses beyond what I could handle, and this is my way of dealing with them. This has nothing to do with making you look bad to her. You have already done that, and I will point it out, that it was before I met her. I just want her to get on with her life, and get passed the sadness. Do you love her enough to let her go?"

He looked at me. I couldn't tell if he was mad or hurt, or maybe he was considering it.

He shook his head, "I think I could make her happy again if she would let me. I do love her, and we have children together. I want her to try."

She was coming now, as I glanced up. I leaned to him, "If you saw her fucking someone else... could you get over it?"

His face flashed to mine with anger. I nodded towards her, "She is coming, but I wanted you to understand. There are some things you just can't get over, and it wasn't just a onetime goof up, and she knows it. She won't be able to move on with her life until this is taken care of. I am sorry, but I am here to help her, because I need her."

The confusion showed on his face, as his forehead wrinkled, "Because she is good at her job."

I grinned as they walked up. Haden came and stood in front of me, "I heard you cheer."

"I did. You were great. How did it feel?"

He was grinning from ear to ear, "Great. That was my first time hitting a double and a triple. Thank you, Tyler."

I leaned forward to shake his hand, but he hugged me. He was actually wrapping his arms around me hugging me. He seemed so small. I felt a lump in my throat, and turned him on my lap. I had to choke down the lump, "We have to watch your brother do the same."

Terra looked up at me, "And then you have to watch me do it."

I was surprised. She didn't like me much, so I had to ask, "You want me to watch your game?"

She laughed, "Yeah. Do you like boys and not girls?"

I was shaking my head, "No, I just thought you didn't like me."

"No, you're okay. We have met you a couple of times now."

I stayed with them almost all day. As I watched Joselyn my stupid desire to pull her close to me was driving me crazy. I needed to know and

I needed to know now. I was saying my good bye to the kids, and Joselyn walked me to my truck.

"Thank you for coming today."

She seemed honestly happy.

"I thought you could use some reinforcements."

She grinned and then laughed with a sigh, as she stood there looking at me.

I had to beg, "Can you try to get away later?"

She shook her head no, "I am a little tired." She stroked her stomach and my heart leapt.

I looked deep in her eyes, "You are?"

Warmth filled her face, and a smile crept to her mouth.

I pleaded, "I need to hold you or something. Please?"

She looked down, "Plan a meeting for Tuesday, a big one that will take us hours to plan things out."

"I can't wait that long, how about Monday?"

She glanced back up at me, "I will have to see the doctor."

"Why? Is everything okay?"

"I'm spotting a little, but it happens. I just want to make sure."

"Joselyn, why didn't you tell me earlier? You shouldn't be here. You should be resting. Let me take you home."

She shook her head no, "It's okay. It happens."

"I am going to go crazy with worry."

She leaned in to give me a side hug. I wanted to die, because I needed so much more than that. I needed to hold her, trace her face with my fingers, touch her belly, feeling for my baby.

She relieved my desire when she spoke, "I will call you later after I get my feet up."

I nodded and let go, "Is he going to be hard to deal with? I could stay."

She shook her head, and turned me pushing me into the truck, "I think it will be fine."

44

Joselyn:

I walked in with my agenda at hand. I had to review the nine accounts for the week, work on some ideas for Saturday's meeting, and then try to fit the doctors in today. I called early, and couldn't get in until 1 in that afternoon. I called and set up appointments with the agents for the week. I was heading to Mr. Jenkin's office to see what we were up against this week. I loved that you could tell he was happy for the company. His face grew to a grin as I walked in, "Have you been working on what we talked about?"

"Yes, but I am waiting on the Lawyer. What do we have for the week?"

Tyler walked in, and I could smell him. Oh, god, did he smell good. I couldn't even look at him. I sat down and crossed my legs. He came to sit in the chair next to me. He traced his hand along his thigh when he sat; my eyes drifted to watch the contour of his muscles stretching against his pants. Noticing his strong but sensitive hands pressing his pants smooth, I imagined them touching me. I bit my lip trying to distract this impulse to crawl on his lap and taunt him, so I fixed my site on Mr. Jenkins, "Do you have a list?"

He stretched out to hand me the list. Tyler moved closer to me, so he could look at it with me. I felt his breath against my cheek causing an arousal of heart beats to my swollen clitoris. I was trying to ignore how just being in the same room was heating me to the core. I casually glanced at him, "I will get on this right away."

I went to get up, but he grabbed the sheet, not noticing what he was doing to me, "How many do we have here?"

Mr. Jenkins was laughing, "Thirty."

Tyler went into business mode, "Don't schedule them all for this week. Spread them out. We are getting too many clients, and we are becoming a hot commodity. We will be picking our clients from now on."

Coming down to earth a little I asked, "But shouldn't we take them all? I mean, if we are just getting big, we should take advantage of that, right?"

I saw a spark in his eyes that made the hair on my neck rise, but he was still business, "Okay, you are right... but if we make them sweat a little, up our prices, and then except them as our choice it will seem like it is more of a privilege for them to have us representing them."

I had to get out of here now. He was causing moisture to form between my legs. I grabbed the paper from him hastily, "It's always a privilege to do business with us."

Mr. Jenkins was laughing, as I walked out. I had to get away from Tyler, because I was getting so revved up being close to him, smelling him, and thinking nasty thoughts, that I didn't know how long I would be able to control myself.

I walked into my office shuttering to try and wash those feeling away. I cleared my head as much as I could and went through the list prioritizing them according to our specialties, and then according to what I liked about them; mostly, the commissions that the agents would be making. Tyler walked in full of self confidence and planted himself on the corner of my desk, "You are feisty today."

Avoiding his captivating posture I reproached, "No, I'm not."

He was so unaffected by me, "When is your appointment?"

I rolled my eyes, "One."

His perky little smile enlightened me, "Can I go with you?"

"Tyler." I gave him that scolding tone, but the grin on his face was adorable, those warm lips tempting, and that bulge in his pants was calling to me. I shivered with the thoughts but told myself *I have to stop this.*

He was still clueless to what I was feeling. He definitely thought I was shrugging him off because I didn't agree with him about spacing the new clients out, "The reason I don't want you to plan all of them for this week is, because I don't want you to overdo it."

That was an open invitation to play on his feelings; I stood up moving closer to him, "Do you think I can't handle it?"

He shook his head, "Oh, no. I know better than that." His eyes met mine; finally a spark of interest, "Are you flirting with me?"

I gestured to the door that it was still open. He stood up wanting to comply with my desire, especially since I moved closer to him. With his eyebrows raised he whispered, "I think I should close the door, so we can discuss this further."

Feeling ashamed of my desires here at work, I shook my head no, but my eyes fell deep into his making the ache in my loins almost unbearable.

"Why not?"

I didn't want to have these feelings at work. I didn't want to have people thinking that he was giving me work because I was giving him sex… but I did want him. I did want to feel the hardness of him rub against me. I wanted his mouth to warm my breast. I heaved with a deep breath, "It wouldn't be a good idea."

Resting my hand on his chest to keep the distance between us didn't help with my wanting. My fingers explored the muscles beneath the cloth. His chest caved, his stomach contracted, and he appealed, "Joselyn, what are you saying?"

I pushed away, and my feet followed until I could pull myself away from him. I shook my hands frantically trying to get rid of this feeling. I was at work and the feelings I was having were not appropriate. In a way, I snapped at him, "Nothing."

He stormed to the door, "I am the boss, and you have to explain yourself, now!"

He looked out the door, "Mary, we are discussing something will you please hold our calls?"

He closed the door and then the blinds. He pushed the button in on the door to lock it. He turned raising his eyebrows in question, as he walked towards me, "Do you want me to go with you?"

I shook my head. He was not getting this at all. I didn't want him to get it, but I didn't want him to be hurt either.

"Why didn't you want me to close the door?"

I shrugged, trying to play it off with no inclination.

He moved closer to me lowering his face and traced his hands along my hips, "Do you need something?"

I felt horribly distracted by every inch of his body. I reached up gliding my hands along his neck wanting to taste him. I rested my forehead to his chest in misery. I hated that my hormones were wild with wanting him right now.

"Why Joselyn... I think you're horny." He sounded like he was impressed that he was getting it.

I shook my head no with determination until I looked up into those inviting blue eyes, like an ocean wave pulling and sucking you out into its depths. His eyes searched my face, as if looking for the answer. I needed to feel his hand, that glorious hand, which did things to me that left me boneless, remembering the pleasure it would bring. The tender touch of his fingers traced down my neck causing my skin to burn, lowering to my chest making my nipples hard. His fingers lingered on my skin, but exploring lower... lower... until they glided slightly, grazing the top of my breast. I closed my eyes, as I felt the warmth growing in me. This was not good. I begged, "Tyler, I can't."

Getting it; I felt the warmth of his fingers, the heave of his chest, and the desire from him, "I know, but you want to."

I didn't want to answer him. His movement was so fast that he caught me off guard. He captured my face in his hands, and kissed me with a passion that seemed to have been building in him since the beginning of time. I parted my lips to engage in the pleasures of feeling his tongue tangle against mine. He finally let go taking a step back. Quickly he spoke, "I could go with you to the appointment."

I felt ashamed for even wanting him to, "And what would you use for an excuse?"

Playfully he spoke, "I don't care, anything. Do you have an idea?"

I shook my head taking another step back. He reached for my hand, "You were almost there; don't change your mind now."

I knew I had to stay focused and put this out of my mind. I turned to move back to my desk, "I have work to do."

His arms came around my waist, and his mouth came to my ear, "Joselyn, you are confusing me."

I nudged him with my elbow, "Don't make me hotter."

He turned me quickly to him, pulling me into his body, tracing his lips against my face, "Hold this thought, Joselyn, because this is the only way I am happy." His mouth kissed my forehead, but then he released me, and walked to the door. He stopped just before unlocking it, "Remember, anything you want it's yours."

The thoughts that were running through my mind were sinful. I only grinned, because I wanted him badly.

He laughed with a sigh, "You should see your face. I swear you are so horny right now."

I pointed to shoo him out, and he laughed.

I took the deepest breath to calm my nerves after he walked out. I am so glad that a woman's desire didn't show like a man's, or everyone would know what it is I was feeling right now.

45

I don't know what possessed me, maybe it was how horny I was earlier or the doctor's appointment that confirmed my pregnancy, but I had to call Shane to see how things were going.

He laughed when I explained who I was, and then explained why I was calling him.

"Do you realize that Tyler just called me?"

"Why did he call?"

"The same reason you are. Um, let me see. Can you give me a couple of minutes?"

"Yes." I sat on the phone listening to elevator music. It was an upbeat song maybe a Michael Jackson song without words, of course. I started to sing along trying to remember the words, but he had so many great songs that I was entangling the words from different songs. I gave up, telling myself that I had to have the children listen to his music, as a musical history lesson.

"Joselyn, I have talked to Tyler a few times; has he updated you at all?"

"No."

"Okay, I spoke with a judge, and he advised me to get better evidence."

I wanted to throw up, "What?"

"Don't worry. I have him a few times, but I was trying to make it a closed case, so I want to follow him a few more weeks. I have an appointment for arbitration set up for August 16th at 9 am."

"But that is a month and a half away."

"Yes, but by then I will have plenty of evidence."

"I don't think I can wait that long."

"Why is that?"

"I am pregnant."

"Shit. I am assuming it's Tyler's?"

"Of course."

"Does he know?"

"Yes, but I don't want to be showing at the meeting."

He took a deep breath, "I will see what I can do. Relax... I will take care of it. I really wish Tyler would have told me."

"I just found out Saturday."

"So, you are not that far along?"

"No."

"Okay. Stay calm; we wouldn't want you to worry with that little bundle. Has Tyler gotten possessive yet?"

"What? No... Why?"

"Joselyn, you have to let him tell you about his life, but be patient. He has had a rough few years, and when he told me about you I knew he was serious, so it's nothing you should be too worried about, but he has to be the one to tell you."

"Okay, but couldn't you just tell me?"

He chuckled, "No, Tyler will tell you in his own time."

"Are you sure you just don't want to tell me?"

"No. Relax, I will see what I can do, and I will call you back by the end of the week."

"Okay."

I was surprised that Tyler hadn't updated me on things, but maybe he was trying to keep me safe from worrying. I appreciated it as much as I didn't like it. Tyler wasn't the only one that was struggling with my two personalities, and not being able to make up my mind which one I truly was. Someone who needed to be taken care of and loved, or the business person that was too busy to make time for personal needs.

46

We went with Tyler on Saturday. I was meeting with the board of directors for local activities, but we were meeting at the Baseball Stadium. We meet in the box seats, and I set the kids down in the seats asking them to stay put and be quiet. Tyler scolded me, "I didn't ask you to bring them with to sit there."

I was confused by him. Three larger men walked in. Tyler shook each of their hands. Jared looked back, "Oh... my gosh, Josh Williams, Seth Grant, and Jake Monroe." They were all famous baseball players.

Jared was moving to them as Terra and Haden followed. They all shook hands and I stood there impressed. The guys entertained my kids while Tyler introduced me to the committee. I sat down with them, and we started to discuss things, but Tyler interrupted, "Joselyn, the guys are taking us down to the field; is that okay?"

I turned to him, and my kid's smiles were so big I had to laugh, "I guess so."

They were out the door so fast I couldn't help but worry. We settled into our meeting again, and started going over stuff. There were eight people on the committee, and I spoke with each one discussing their agendas for the remainder of the year. The first one was a woman, Mary Roberts. She was very sweet to me, and we got along fairly well. I had a good understanding of what she was looking for. I continued to the next gentleman, Craig Turmone. He was in charge of benefit events. We went over his lists, and it was exciting to see the stuff involved with this. It was a little more challenging, but I was excited to do this. I continued to the next one and the next.

I would look out the box window down at the field to see my kids playing with these grown men, while Tyler was out helping Terra and

Haden. He even picked them up twirling them around. My kids were going to like having him around.

I went back to work with the next one and then the next until we were completely done. I glanced back out, and they were gone. My heart leapt, but someone from the back of the room spoke to me, "Tyler just called, and they stopped for ice cream on the way up."

At the completion of our meeting I shook everyone's hand. I was excited to get started working on this, but I wasn't ready to end our time with Tyler.

He walked in with my kids, "Are you ready?"

"Yeah, I guess so."

"Good, the game starts in a half an hour and we have… over the dugout seats."

I stared in amazement as my children went nuts. He held the door for me, as I followed the kids out. Jared occupied all of Tyler's attention; asking about the guys, how did he set that up, and could they do it again. Haden heard the 'again', and then let go of my hand grabbing Tyler's hand. Tyler looked down, and the smile on his face was priceless making my heart fill with joy. Can this even be reality; because it just didn't seem possible to be happy, and have someone who enjoyed being with my children as much as I did.

Terra tugged on my hand distracting me from the boys. Her face glowed with a gleam in her eye and a smile on her face.

I had to ask her, "What is this about?"

"He is nice."

"Yes, he is."

"He is your boss, right?"

"Yes, kind of. He owns the company I work for. Mr. Jenkins is my boss."

"But… then… why does he come on these business deals with you?"

"Well, I think it's so I could bring you guys with me, but get the deal for him." I leaned down to whisper, "I am very good at what I do."

She covered her mouth giggling, "He needs you."

I put my finger to my lips to hush her, but she laughed more. I loved spending time with my kids; it was like experiencing stuff for the first time, but through their eyes.

Jared and Haden took up both sides of Tyler, so we sat with Haden between us. As we watched the game, Haden was up and down from his seat whenever he was excited. I felt Tyler's fingers playing with my hair, but only until Haden would catch it and then take his hand and move it to the arm of the chair. Haden wasn't upset or irritated at all. I really didn't know if he just thought it was okay because he does it sometimes when we cuddle.

When the game was over, Haden was worn out, and I almost had to drag him from the stadium. He had no energy to walk for himself, and he was fishing for me to pick him up. He was getting much too large to carry, but Tyler picked him up. Haden glanced at me with a grin and gave me thumbs up. I laughed that Tyler fell for the oldest trick in the book.

He handed Jared his phone, "Hey, press the number six. Tell the driver that we will meet him out front."

Jared looked at him, "Driver?"

"Yeah, I will help you guys home, and then your mom can ride back with me to her car, or I will pick her up for work on Monday."

"So we are getting a ride in a limo?"

"Yes, if you call him."

He was quick about it then, because he was going to get to ride in a limo. Tyler got in, but didn't let go of Haden. The rest of us followed. Jared asked me if we needed the car on Sunday, but I was okay without one. Tyler also offered to come get me for it tomorrow, but I said I would call if I needed it.

Tyler crawled out of the limo still holding Haden. He was really out now. I followed them up to the house, as the other two ran ahead to tell their dad about their day. Jared was going on about the three guys that he got to hang out with. Ryan held the door for Tyler, "I will take him."

Tyler pulled away, "Just point the way. He is out."

Jared was demanding Ryan's attention, so he pointed Tyler in the direction of Haden's room, and then went back to listening to Jared. I followed up the stairs and into the room. He laid Haden down, and I moved in to tuck him in. He leaned into me putting his hands on my hips, "This will be normal soon."

I turned taking his hands from my waist, "Not here. It's not revenge."

He grinned, "Do you want to go get your car?" He raised his eyebrows wondering.

My heart skipped a beat, "Let's see what we can do about that."

He laughed as we walked out of the room. I closed the door carefully, "Ryan what are you doing tomorrow?"

"Why?"

"I was wondering if I should go get my car."

"Where is it?"

"Down by the stadium. Tyler gave us a ride in the Limo, so that he could help me get Haden in."

He glared at me. I could see the wheels turning in his mind wondering what I was up to. I took a deep breath, "If you aren't going anywhere, Tyler said he could pick me up for work on Monday, and I didn't need to worry about my car until then."

He glared more, "So what does this have to do with me going anywhere tomorrow?" He looked at Tyler now pushing the kids away.

"Nothing, I just didn't want to be left without a car."

Tyler grinned evilly, "Well, if you want... Ryan if you decide to go somewhere; I could always come get Joselyn tomorrow and bring her to her car."

Ryan was very angry now, "No, I am not planning on going anywhere. Joselyn, weren't you going out with work friends? You haven't done that for a while."

"After today... no, I am bushed. I am going to bed, read a book, and sleep."

Tyler looked at Ryan, "Did you have plans? I could stay, and keep them company until you get back."

Ryan was about to lose it, "No. You can leave."

Jared grabbed Tyler's arm, "Dad! He took me to meet famous baseball players. Don't you think we should be nice to him?"

Tyler patted Jared on the back, "It's okay buddy. I am going to go, but we will do that again. I had fun."

Terra wrapped her arms around him, "You are the best. Thank you."

He cupped her head with one hand, "You are welcome." He put his other hand out to Jared, but they just hit knuckles. I pulled the kids from him, "Tell your dad more about your day. I will walk Tyler out."

Ryan wasn't pleased, "I thought you were tired?"

"I am, but I am walking Tyler out." I passed them both walking out the door. Tyler followed me to the car. I was steaming, "I should just leave with you now." I turned to Tyler, furious.

He grinned, "You know there is nothing more that I want then that, but I also know you love your children, and I won't let you harm your chances of being with them."

My heart raced. He was thinking about me long term. How could he be so perfect? What was wrong with him? It was almost making me angrier. I glared at him to see what he was up to.

He laughed, "Don't get mad at me. We just had a great day, and I didn't do anything wrong."

I stomped my foot, "That is what is irritating. You are supposed to be on my side."

His eyes went soft and tender, "Joselyn, I am on your side, but I am on all of your sides, and you wouldn't be happy with me if I swept you off your feet, and you could only see your kids every other weekend."

The tears came to my eyes, as I stared at him.

"Is this a hormone thing, because you are breaking my heart?"

"I don't know."

"Okay. Take a deep breath, call me if you need your car tomorrow, and if I don't hear from you, I will see you at 8 am Monday morning."

"I don't want you to leave."

His glance came back to meet my gaze, "I don't want to leave either, but you need to rest, and if I stay here I am going to wrap my arms around you and kiss you until your toes curl."

Why was he so perfect? I knew he was right about the whole thing, but I just didn't want him to leave yet.

After getting in the car, holding up the driver, he spoke softly, "Take care of my baby, and my unborn child."

Tyler directed the driver to go, so I watched until the car turned the corner. I could not wipe the grin from my face, as I walked back into the house. I strolled up the stairs and towards my room; I had one thing on my mind, to go to bed.

"Where are you going?"

I looked back at Ryan, "To bed. I am so tired."

"I got something today."

I had no idea what he was talking about, so I turned to find out what it was. He was holding a large envelope.

"What is it?"

"Papers. You are served papers… papers."

I was confused. Shane didn't tell me that he was delivering those today.

"I'm sorry. I didn't know they were coming today."

"I think we need to talk."

"No, Ryan. I think they say everything. Have you looked at them? It's a really good deal for you, and we would share the kids 50/50."

"I'm not looking for a deal, Joselyn. I want to talk to you... I mean really talk."

"I am really tired; can we do it tomorrow? I will set up play dates for the kids."

He just stared at me. I walked away to my room. I tried the messaging thing on my phone to let Tyler know that the papers were served. He didn't message me back. I lay down with a book, but didn't get but two pages in, and I had to close my eyes.

47

I was groggily waking up, but I really was not feeling well. I thought if I just lay here a little while longer, maybe this feeling would go away. I curled up with my pillow more, hugging it. It just wasn't comfortable.

"Joselyn?"

That was Tyler. Why was he here? I opened my eyes a little, but my head was pounding.

"Hey, just relax. I will get the doctor."

I tried to blink, but everything was light and foggy. I mumbled out, "Too bright."

I saw him move to the window and pull the curtains, "Is that better?"

My head hurt so bad that I didn't move my head, "Yeah, what happened?"

"I don't know."

I looked around noticing that everything was white, and bright, "Why am I here?"

"When I came to pick you up for work you were in the shower, but you didn't answer me. I broke the door in."

I think I heard him right, but the tiredness was coming over me, and I couldn't stay awake.

The next time I woke, Tyler was sleeping in a chair. I tried to look around, but it was dark now. I tried to pull myself up, but my stomach was cramping.

"Hey, you need to rest."

"How is the baby?"

"There is no baby."

"Yes, there is, Tyler."

He smiled softly at me, "No, Joselyn. There was no baby, but if you want one I am sure we can make one."

I was confused again, and laid back down frustrated. Ryan wasn't here, but Tyler was. I know I was pregnant, so why was he telling me I wasn't? I didn't like that I didn't know what was going on.

"Tyler, can you get my purse?"

"What do you need from it?"

"Just hand it to me."

"I didn't grab it when we left. We were in a hurry."

"Why?"

"Don't worry about it. You don't remember anything?"

"No, just... I was reading and fell asleep."

"That was on Saturday."

"What day is it?"

"Wednesday."

This was too much to process right now, and my head was still pounding. I had to sleep more, so I could figure this out.

The next time I woke up, I was pleased to see Tyler sitting there, "What are you doing here?"

I was comforted by his smile when he replied, "I think I should ask you the same question?"

I looked around realizing I was in a hospital. This was so weird, and my head still hurt. He got up bringing my purse to me, "You said you wanted this."

I tried to sit up, but felt really sick. Tyler grabbed me and raised the back of the bed, "What are you looking for?"

I dug to the bottom and felt the pregnancy sticks. I smiled, "I was pregnant."

I pulled one out; it was negative. I pulled the next one out; it was the same.

Tyler was looking quite awful, "Joselyn, it's okay. Don't worry about it."

I pulled out another one. It was negative, "I know I was Tyler. Don't tell me I wasn't."

"How many did you do ?"

"Five... including the last one at the ball field."

"So, you remember?"

"I remember this. What about my doctor's appointment. She would…" I pulled out another one, and it was negative. I dug and dug, but it wasn't there. "It's not here."

"What?"

"No, I know I took five, Tyler. What about my doctor's appointment that you wanted to go with me to?"

"I haven't been able to get your information. Shane was going to try, but the red tape is a mile long."

I put my face to my hands, "Why am I here?"

"When I came to pick you up, you were in the shower. Ryan let me in, but you were taking a long time. I knocked, and you didn't reply. He laughed, and said you like to sleep in the tub sometimes, but the floor or carpet was a little wet, so I broke in the door. You were in the tub, leaning over the side with the shower running, but the curtains were open."

"You couldn't wake me up?"

"No, um… you were bleeding pretty badly."

"Where are my children?"

"At your parent's house; Shane took care of it. He didn't like the way things looked."

"What do you mean looked?"

"The house… you… just everything."

"I have to go."

"Oh, no you don't little lady. You are staying right here."

I tipped over, and he tucked me back in, "Joselyn, are you sure you were?"

"Yes."

He swallowed hard, "You're not anymore."

For not wanting to have another child; the guilt spilled over into loss, crying my eyes out. My head began to hurt again so bad, that I thought it was going to explode. Tyler rubbed my forehead and temples until I fell asleep again.

48

I just had the worst nightmare. It was so weird, and I felt yukky, but maybe if I get up and make breakfast everything will be better. I rolled over to get out of bed, but my nightmare continued. Tyler had moved to the side of the bed, tracing his hand along my forehead leaning over me, "Hey, is your head better?"

"What happened?"

His caring eyes gleamed at me, "It doesn't matter, baby. When you are better, I am bringing you home."

"What about the kids?"

He smiled, "Them too."

"Tyler?"

"Hey, it's okay. Ryan, the kids, and your mom and dad are coming up today, so I have to leave for a while."

"No, it's okay. Please don't go?"

Being firm but careful, he reassured me, "It will be better if I do, but Shane will be here and so will Mr. Jenkins."

"Why are they going to be here?"

"I want to keep you safe and comfortable. We should see if you can take a shower before the kids come."

"I look horrible, don't I?"

He smiled, "You might scare them a little. Are you okay if I go get the nurse?"

I nodded, and watched him leave the room. I felt my head where it had been pounding, and I had a huge bump there. Shane walked in with some flowers, "Hey, I guess you are stuck with me today."

I tucked my hair behind my ears, self-conscious about how I looked. He grinned again, "I am just setting these here, and then I will wait in the lobby for Tyler."

"Is there a reason you are staying with me when Tyler leaves?"

"Yes."

"Are you going to tell me why?"

"You really don't remember anything?"

I shook my head, and gazed at him with pleading in my eyes. He shook his head, "Right now it might not be a good idea to remember, so why don't you just take it easy, and I will stay while he is here."

"He?"

"Yes, Ryan."

A flash of a large envelope in his hand crossed my mind, and the pounding in my head became excruciating; it hit me so hard, like a ton of bricks... that I was blinded. I grabbed my head in pain, "You served the papers?"

He stood up moving closer, "Joselyn, don't think about anything. Shit, you are in pain. Don't think about it."

I heard someone come in, and the next thing I knew was, this someone was sitting next to me rubbing my temples lightly and whispering to my ear, "Shhh, it's okay. Don't try to remember, not yet. Just relax and get better."

I opened my eyes to the brightest blue gaze that made you feel like you were surrounded by the Caribbean waters. The warmth rose in me, while he tried to comfort me. Something wasn't right about this, "Tyler, what happened, exactly?"

"We really aren't sure other than what I know."

I gazed into those eyes, "Please tell me?"

Those blue eyes darkened just a trace, "I have told you everything that I know. When I found you, what the doctors are telling me, and what Ryan has told me. They really don't want to tell me a whole lot, because I am not your husband. Shane is here to show them you don't want him to know everything either. He presented the staff with the papers that were served to Ryan, so they are at least telling him a few more things than they will tell me."

I traced my hand along his face, "See, too much baggage, Tyler. You deserve better than this."

He did not agree, "Nope, I was hooked from the time I plowed into you."

The fingers on my temples and the warmth of his hands radiating against my cheeks calmed me. Slowly, he helped me to lay back down,

"The nurse is going to help you take a shower. Do you have makeup in your purse?"

I was surprised that he would bring that up, "Do I look that bad?"

"No, it's just that we think you passed out in the shower and fell. It seems that you hit the side of your face. It's not that bad, but the kids might worry."

I covered my face embarrassed, but he moved my hand to the spot he was talking about, and then put his hand over my face more. His eyes met mine, and I realized it was worse than what he was telling me. His mouth twitched a little, as he tried to smile, but he was nervous about it. He tried to make me feel better, "It's already healing though."

"Great."

49

Tyler

I handed Shane a cup of coffee; he has been here almost as much as I have, "Thank you."

"Tyler, we have to discuss some things."

I sat down. I knew he was going to tell me I had to stop seeing her until the divorce was final, but how could I now? She will feel badly.

"First of all... I think you should leave for the day. Mr. Jenkins and I will keep a close eye on her."

"No."

"I need you to stay away from the room while Ryan is here."

"She said she was pregnant, and she is missing the test thingy from her purse. HE KNEW! Did the doctors give you any more info?"

He looked away from me. He didn't want to tell me and was avoiding me, as he stood up. He walked over to Mr. Jenkins, but only to ask his help with me. Mr. Jenkins moved to my side trying to convince me to leave, "Tyler, it would be good to get out of here for a little bit."

"No. Tell me what they said."

Shane took a deep breath, "Tyler, go look at the house. Tell me if that is the one. We need to get that going if she isn't going home."

I glanced up at him, "Ryan did something, and you're not telling me."

Mr. Jenkins turned to me, "She has miscarried twice before, once with twins before Haden and once with a little girl after Haden."

"So what does that have to do with this time?"

He took a deep breath shaking his head, "You know it's just weird. One minute she was fine and then it goes. She had some tests run, and she was accused of trying to get rid of them herself."

219

"She didn't want them, and she took something to get rid of them?"

He grabbed my hand, "She wanted them, but they found traces of something that might cause her body to reject the pregnancy in her system."

"Okay, and that means what to me?"

Shane was irritate, "Dumb ass, he is getting rid of them without her knowing."

Mr. Jenkins raised his eyebrows, "He takes pride in having a 'trophy on his mantle' is what I think he used to say to me."

I wanted to kill him. I remembered Ryan making that comment to me when he came to her promotion party, "Are you sure, or this is what you are thinking? Because if I am going to kill a man; I want to know I am doing it for a good reason."

Shane shook his head, "You are not killing anyone, and we're not sure. We were talking about the report I got from the doctors that says that this herb was in her system. The thing is, there is no law against it if it is early enough in the pregnancy."

"She just found out the Saturday before... Shit. She thinks he knew, because the test thing wasn't in her purse."

Mr. Jenkins shook his head, "You know, I knew something was wrong after the last one, and then she caught him with another woman. She just shut everyone out." He looked up at me, "She has been with me for the last fifteen years and I love her like a daughter. I really don't think it was her."

"Did this report say anything else that I should know about?"

They both didn't look at me. It was if they were both ashamed of what they knew. Shane handed me the report, "You cannot say anything, because they won't give me any more details if I share them."

I walked away reading through the report. It was a few pages long, so I sat down. Things didn't make sense to me much, but I kept reading. I was on the last page, and I think I finally came across what it was they were trying to tell me. The word 'Semen' jumped out of the page at me. I went back reading the line over, as I heard the kids coming off the elevator.

"Tyler, what are you doing here?"

I glanced up avoiding looking at Ryan. I tried to wipe my eyes free from the tears that filled them and hugged her kids. Terra was the only one that commented, "Is she that bad?"

I cleared my throat, "No, she is doing so much better. Mr. Jenkins there told me a sad story that is all."

Mr. Jenkins laughed and got up to bring them to the room. Shane was in front of me as Ryan passed me, "Tyler."

I glared at him, "Ryan."

He avoided my glare, and continued to the room. I stood up to only find myself restrained by Shane, "You have to control yourself. Sit down."

"I don't want him in there with her."

"You don't know if she consented to it."

I looked back at Shane, "Yes I do. She wouldn't."

"You don't know that."

I felt the rush in my face, as the blood pulsed under my skin, "Yes, I do know that. She wouldn't let him touch her."

"Okay. I will go in there, but you have to get control, or they aren't going to let you be here."

"I promise I am just going to read this again. I don't think I get it the whole picture."

I could tell he didn't trust me, so I took a deep breath and sat back down. The only thing I saw was his feet turn away from me, as he headed to the room.

50

I was trying to make out what this was telling me. I wish I had more understanding of medical terminology. This really sucks, because it was just so confusing.

I felt someone hit my foot. I glanced up hoping it wasn't Ryan. I didn't know if I could control myself from killing him. To my relief it wasn't. Jared was standing there looking at me. I knew he had something on his mind.

"Did you see your mom?"

He glared at me just standing there. I didn't know what else to say, so I tucked the report away waiting for him to speak up.

"You like my mom?"

I sat up more, and put my hands in front of me glancing up at him, "Yes, of course I do."

"Do you love her?"

I couldn't breathe, talk, or anything. My eyes locked on his. He didn't seem to be angry just curious.

His eyebrows rose as he asked me again, "Do you love her?" He was more determined for an answer. My heart pounded, as I contemplated on how I should answer him. My mind tried to search for the right words, the right thing to say. My answer came out without considering how he was going to react, "Yes."

I braced myself for what was coming, but he sat down next to me without a word. He leaned back, so I glanced at him, "Don't you think your mom wants to see you?"

"I needed to talk to you."

I wiped my face from the tears that had filled my eyes; this kid was causing me to sweat. I sat back waiting for him to start; the silence was killing me.

"I don't think he hit her."

My gut turned over doing a summersault, "We don't think that."

He took a deep breath, so I glanced at him. He didn't look up at me but he spoke again, "The baby was yours?"

I lowered my head. Was this kid a *'know it all'* or what? I didn't even call her that often. After I caught my breath I had to ask, "Why do you think that?"

His reply came back quietly, "She wouldn't do that with him."

I lifted my head and watched a few people walk by before he continued, "She didn't allow dad to even hold her hand, so I knew they weren't doing that. He sleeps on the couch down stairs."

I nodded. I knew he was trying to make me feel better, but the more I heard the worse I felt. She was staying for the kids, and this wasn't healthy for him; Jared who has understood all of this without any of us talking to him. I didn't know what to say to him, "You know a lot."

"Yeah."

"Is there something else that you want me to know?"

"You have to promise me something first."

"Anything."

He touched my hand, so I looked at him, "Promise you won't hurt my dad?"

I felt the strain coming back to my eyes, but I had to promise him, "Yes, I promise."

He leaned forward picking at his fingers for a long time. I wanted him to tell me what he had to say. I held my tongue, not wanting to push him. I could tell he was really struggling with what he wanted to tell me.

"He made us have a slumber party after the day with you."

So why did I have to promise to not hurt him?

"He made me keep Terra and Haden down stairs no matter what we heard."

I closed my eyes knowing this was going to get worse.

"He spent the night up in mom's room."

I nodded without a response.

"I heard her yell at him, so I turned up the TV and went up to get popcorn. I didn't get popcorn."

I swallowed hard knowing I had to let him off the hook on telling me, "Jared, you don't have to talk about this if you don't want to."

"I love my dad, but I love my mom. She wouldn't let him touch her but..."

223

I leaned forward to be even with him. I peeked over to see one tear slowly tracing down his face.

I put my hand on his knee, "I know. It's okay; she doesn't remember any of it."

He broke down crying. I pulled him in and hugged him tight, "It's okay, buddy. It wasn't your fault."

His words came muffled, "No, he used us to keep her quiet. I should have stopped him. Is that why she lost it?"

"No, no. NO! That isn't what caused her to lose it. You didn't do anything wrong. I bet there was a part of you that wanted them together, and you are feeling guilty."

His cries came harder as he nodded.

"No, I understand completely. They are your parents, and they are supposed to stay together, but you want them to be happy too?"

"Yes. He said that she would be happier once they were together, but I knew something was wrong when she was in the shower, and we had to get ready for school."

"How long was she in there?"

"That night, all day Sunday, and Monday morning."

I closed my eyes in misery. She was dying in her bathroom, and he let her stay there.

Jared looked at me, "He felt bad. He felt really bad, Tyler. She locked him out, and he sat in front of the door the whole time trying to talk her out of there."

"Why didn't he break the door in?"

He looked at me with his face so red, his eyes blood shot, "He sat with his head in his hands and kept repeating that he blew it. Tyler, you said you wouldn't hurt him."

"Yes, I did say that."

"Are you going to tell my mother?"

"No, what you told me here today is between us. I will not make you repeat it or remember it. It wasn't your fault, and if she remembers what happened, then I won't be able to lie to her, but I also won't encourage the remembering. I think it would be better for her to not remember."

He hugged me again. This time it was so tight that the tears that filled my eyes leaked out. He let go and sat back down, "So what do we do now?"

"She can't go home with him."

"I figured that."

"Shane is buying a house a few doors down from yours for your mom. That way you can see them both every day."

"I don't want to see my dad."

"But you said you love him."

"I do, but I don't like what he did."

"Okay, but you might have to explain why to them. I don't care what you tell them. You can say anything you want, and I will keep my mouth shut."

He nodded and we both sat back, then we both took a deep breath, and now we waited together. I think we were both feeling the same thing, but with guys... you don't have to talk about how you are feeling.

51

Joselyn:

Tyler was going to bring me to a new home. I was nervous because we really hadn't discussed anything, and I was not good at spontaneous; it made me uncomfortable. He sat with me waiting for the discharge papers. He had assured me that everything was going to be okay. The house he purchased was less than four houses from my home. He said I could stay there, or I could pay rent, whatever I wanted to do. I didn't know how to take that, but he just assured me that he didn't want to make me feel helpless and trapped into something, so he was leaving it up to me. The only reason he offered to let me stay there without paying anything was because I was going to pay off my house and leave it to Ryan with the divorce. I really didn't want to be in that house anyway. It felt cold and distant like something was very bad there.

"Hello. I am looking for Joseyln Evans?"
"Yes. Are those my discharge papers?"
"No. I am Susan Mullen a social worker, and we want to make sure when we let you go that you are going to be okay and safe."
I grinned but I had no idea of what I would need to be safe from.
"I see here you are not going to your home?"
"No. Tyler here has a house, and I will be staying there."
"Um, if you don't mind, I would like to talk to you privately."
I shook my head, "No, I do mind. He can stay."
I looked over and Tyler was already moving to the door but stopped when I said he could stay. He moved back to me and took my hand looking into my eyes, "It's okay. She just wants to talk to you privately. I can wait outside."

"I don't have anything to hide, Tyler. You can stay."

He gave me a nervous smile but stayed. He sat down on the bed behind me.

"So Mrs. Mullen, what is this about?"

"Well, we have some concerns."

"Okay."

"Looking at your chart, we noticed that you miscarried twice before."

"Yes." I glanced at Tyler and he gave me a reassuring grin. I have never told him this, but yet it didn't seem to surprise him. I turned back to Susan waiting for the next question.

"You have been asked about some chemicals that we found in your system before."

"Yes, but I don't understand what they are."

She raised her eyebrows, "Well it is not clear, but some of them can be found in herbs and they cause the body to have contractions pushing all of the contents in the uterus out.

"So, is it something I am eating that I need to stay away from?"

She shook her head and I didn't understand. Tyler traced his hand down my arm whispering, "Joselyn, it's something that you would have to know about and take a lot of."

I glanced back at him, "You knew about this?"

"Yes."

"Why didn't you talk to me about it?"

"Because I don't think you were taking them on purpose. If Ryan found the pregnancy test that was positive, he might have been desperate."

Susan gasped, "You think it's her husband?"

Tyler looked into my eyes, "Joselyn, did he even want more kids? Because, this happened to you before."

I couldn't breathe let alone answer him. I stared at the floor trying to trace things back in my mind. I was looking for anything that would have given me any indication that he didn't want kids.

"This stuff you say that is in my system. How would someone get a hold of it?" I was grasping for something to make sense.

Susan stood up, "I really don't think I have any more questions for you, because it is obvious that you really didn't know anything about this."

I looked at her saddened that she wasn't answering me, "How could someone get their hands on these types of herbs?"

She shook her head in a way that told me she didn't have an explanation. She stopped and looked at me, "There was one more thing?"

"Yes."

"When you came in and they were checking you out there was semen…"

I gasped looking at Tyler full of panic. I didn't expect that. He took my face in his hand, "Joselyn, it's okay I knew."

I shook my head, "No." I pushed him away and stood up pacing, "You are telling me that…" I looked at Susan.

She stood up waving for Tyler to leave. He stood up watching me as I paced. He walked to the door, "It's okay, Joselyn. Its better if you don't remember."

I shook my head as tears were coming to my eyes and slowly spilling over. I looked at Tyler with a question on my face, "How did you know if I didn't?"

He cringed, "I read the report."

"Why didn't you tell me?"

"You didn't remember and if you blocked it out, I figured you didn't want it to happen. That is all I was thinking. I am sorry, Joselyn, but that doesn't change how I feel."

I ran to him, and he swept me into his arms. He held me tight trying to calm me as I apologized over and over again. He wasn't angry with me at all, and I was so relieved. It hit me like a brick wall what the flash I had was, "He got the divorce papers that day."

Tyler huffed with relief, "Yes. That is right. I think maybe he was trying to keep you, and he was desperate. Joselyn, did you want to try to make it work one last time?"

I pushed him away far enough to glare at him, "You have to ask me that?"

He huffed with a laugh, "No, but I would understand if you wanted to make it work because of your kids."

"That isn't even a possibility. He wasn't allowed to come near me for any reason."

He traced my arms up and down, "Okay. Everything will be okay. The house is ready and I will take you there. Anything you want we will do. I am here if you want me to be."

Susan put her folder together, "I guess I will do a little more research, but I suggest that you be careful around your husband."

"What about my kids?"

"Well, right now we have no proof and until we do he will have partial custody."

I nodded, "But I don't feel safe leaving them with him."

"Well, I think if we try to keep them from him he might do something desperate. As long as you cooperate then I think he will be civil. He was very calm during our interviews, and he didn't point a finger at you at all, so I think Tyler is correct that he didn't want you to have his baby."

"But what about the other ones? We are talking about three lives."

She looked down, "I am sorry for your loss, but we don't have any proof."

I nodded but I didn't like it at all.

52

The house was wonderful. He gave me the grand tour, and it was a lot larger than my house. I had never been inside this house, but it was amazing. The kitchen was off the entryway. It had a breakfast nook at the front of the house that extended outward to let in more light. The room was octagon and easy to move around in. The dining room was off of this, but it had no furniture.

"Do you want to go up or down first?"

I shrugged and he grinned, "Down first." He took my hand leading me down a set of steps into a smaller room. There was a fireplace, and he explained where he would put a couch if he had one picked out. It had a patio door on the other side that lead to the back yard which he had to point out that there was a swing set and a play house. On the other side of the room was a very large bar area with a sink and fridge. He turned to me, "Work gatherings."

I shook my head, "It's good to keep personal life separated."

He laughed, "Too late for that. It is going to be a family business soon."

He really knew how to please me. I shook my head, but with a grin on my face. He led me down another set of steps. This room was very small. It had the hot water heater, washer and dryer in it. There was also room for a table for folding clothes is what I thought. He pulled me back up the stairs and back further on this level. There was a full bathroom with lots of storage, then back to another very large room. It was open and had large windows. He looked at me, "Home office for two."

I laughed as he wrapped his arms around me from behind. His mouth came to my ear, "Are you ready to see upstairs?"

I nodded. He seemed really excited to share this with me. We went up the steps, and then continued up to the next level. The living room had a large couch with duel chases on each end. There was also a TV on one end of the room.

"Furniture?"

"Very little. I didn't know what you liked."

I was impressed and he pulled me down the hall. He opened the first door, the second door across the hall and then the third room. He looked back grinning, as we went to the end of the hall. The smile on his face was priceless. He pulled me into a larger room with a large bed in it. There was a dresser and armoire in the corner. He walked in and opened the armoire which was actually dresser drawers with a TV on the top shelf. He was nervous and unsure, "I didn't know if you like to watch TV in bed."

I laughed as he led me to a Bathroom that was amazing. There was a whirlpool tub, duel sink vanity, and a separate shower in the corner. He pulled me through another door and this room was smaller, smaller than any of the other rooms. He was reluctant to show me this, "I guess we won't need this for a while, so you could use it as a walk-in closet."

"What was it supposed to be?"

I could see the pain as he grimaced, "A nursery."

I turned and walked out, but he was quick to follow, "I am sorry, Joselyn. I bought it before I knew that you had lost it."

I really didn't want to talk about it. For not wanting a baby; it had grown on me. The idea of that baby powdery smell, the wiggles of little fingers and toes, and then the little face, had grown on me.

Tyler tried to change the subject quickly, "We can buy the kids beds and stuff tomorrow if you are up for it. I just didn't want to do too much without you."

I didn't know what else to do, so I nodded.

"Shane got all of your clothes; they should be here somewhere."

"Where are your clothes?"

"I didn't know how you felt, so I left them where they were. This is the first home I have had in..." He looked at me, as sadness swept his face.

"Since you were married?"

He nodded but pulled me to the living room. He grabbed the remote and laid down on the chase pulling me to him. I curled up in his arms, and we cuddled without a word.

About dinner time he ordered delivery for us, and we went down to the kitchen. We did our ritual of exchanging food, but as we sat there he was grinning from ear to ear. I noticed and laughed a little and then he did too.

I glanced up at him, "Are you staying with me here?"

"That is up to you."

"I don't want to be alone."

That put shine in his eyes, "Are you hitting on me Mrs. Evans?"

"Not really." I bit my lip before continuing, "Are you keeping the other places?"

He smiled taking another bite of food, but reached into a drawer. He pulled out a key chain. He handed them to me, full of satisfaction.

I was confused by this.

"They are all labeled. I have three places besides here. You are welcome to any of them at any time. You have been to all of them."

"So, there are no other secret places that you have?"

He was shaking his head, "If you get mad at me, you can escape to any one of them. They are as much yours as they are mine."

I shook my head, "No, you may need to get away from me if you have to live with me."

"Are you saying you are difficult to live with?"

I felt horrible, but I needed to get this out, "I don't know how anymore."

For some reason that made him happy, "Good, we will learn together. It's been awhile for me too."

"No sleep over's with some young hotty?"

He shook his head, "Nope, I have only asked one girl to stay since I lost my wife."

"Lost?"

His gaze rushed to meet mine. He hesitated, but after swallowing deeply he explained, "I'm not divorced."

I just stared at him. I didn't know what to say. I was getting a divorce and he was still married. I didn't know how to feel, because he was so understanding with me.

"You have nothing to say?"

I shook my head, "I can't judge you, because I don't know anything about your relationship. For all I know it was as bad as mine, and if it is then I understand."

He gave me a slight smiled, "I am glad you feel that way. Do you want to know?"

Wanting to be careful I nodded slowly, "If you want to share."

His face dropped, so I knew it wasn't going to be good, "There was a car accident." There was a long pause, and I thought maybe I should help him, but how? I waited for him to continue.

"Merideth said my name, and that was it; she was gone. Katrina, my baby…"

He stopped; closing his eyes a tear dripped out. I moved closer to him taking his hands in mine. I had no idea that he was widowed. He continued, "She still looked perfect, but the seatbelt that held her seat let loose, and she was tossed all over. They said it was like the shaking thing, and she was bleeding internally. She lasted four days, and I still couldn't say good bye to her." I moved to him, and sat in his lap cupping his face to my chest. I felt awful that I have been so selfish in our relationship that I didn't even know this. The pain and sadness would be terrible. I have only lost babies before I met them. He lost a wife and a child that he loved. Words escaped me without thinking, "They would have had to put me in a padded room."

He held me tighter as we sat there, and then he spoke softly, "I knew you would understand. Let's go up to the couch."

I nodded getting up pulling him up the stairs after me. He sat down on the chaise again, and I curled up in his arms resting my head on his chest, "Tyler?"

"Yes."

"I love you."

His mouth kissed my head, as he pulled me closer, "I am in love with you too."

53

Mr. Jenkins was on his way over with some accounts that they needed help with. I was still straightening the kid's rooms, now that we had furniture in them.

In the back room of the basement, we had his and her desks with a large table in the middle. He set it up for working at home. He was worried that I would be irritated by people at work, and all the gossip that was going to fly around the office.

My kids were coming home from their grandparents today, and I was doing much better now that everything was healing just fine. My mother wasn't happy with me, and she was hardly talking to me. Thank goodness for fathers, because he was very supportive of me, and my decision to leave Ryan. He said it was good to have his daughter back, which made me feel better about this whole situation.

"Joselyn, can you come down here? Mr. Jenkins is here." I went down the steps quickly throwing myself into his open arms. I missed him. He was like the wise old owl that comforted me in every way.

He had a large brief case the size of an easel and grinned at me, "I need you to look a few over and give me some ideas. We have only closed seven deals in the last three weeks without you and I just can't go another day without you."

Tyler took us down stairs and laid them on the table for me to look at. I stepped back looking at each one. I smiled taking a step towards the third one.

"Allure perfume. What did they come up with...? Never mind. Try this: 'When a woman has needs... Allure will get her what she wants.'"

Tyler smiled, "What do you picture?"

"The bottle out front, with the silhouette of a woman who is spraying it on her body but behind the bottle, and then a man moving into the picture, but completely frosted so the picture of the people is not clear."

I moved to the next one. "Illumina, which was an assortment of light bulbs. I squinted my eyes and giggled, "Give us a chance, and we'll brighten your day."

Mr. Jenkins asked, "What do you see?"

I grinned realizing these two were up to something. I huffed, "People walking into different rooms turning on lights and showing happiness; in the kitchen, bathroom, and maybe a lamp by a couch to sit and read by, everyone smiling, but only after turning on the lights."

"Okay, I got that. Next..."

I moved to the next one. I glanced back at both of them and they weren't paying any attention to me. They were looking at the product. Mr. Jenkins was standing there with the notebook in one hand and the pen hanging out of his mouth, as he stared at it. Tyler was grimacing, as he looked at the product. It was a type of lip gloss... lip stick. I picked up the info sheet and read. I set it back down, "The sweetness of a kiss will last all day long."

I peaked at Tyler as he said, "You should see if it works."

Mr. Jenkins laughed.

I stepped to the next one.

"Wait, what are you seeing for it?"

I stepped back as Tyler's hands came to my waist to catch me. I glanced back but spoke, "Show someone starting their day with it, then checking it at lunch time, after that when the work day is done, and finally when she is making dinner, her other half walks in kissing her commenting on how sweet the kiss is."

Tyler whispered in my ear, "You should see if it works first."

Mr. Jenkins was shaking his head, "This is going to be hard to get used to."

Tyler kissed my cheek, "Well, you're going to have to get used to it, because it's going to be a family business soon."

Mr. Jenkins leaned to me and kissed my cheek, "I am so pleased that you are finally going to be happy."

I shook my head moving to the next one. Tyler let go of me and walked to his desk. This was an enhancement product for having sex. I have never used such a thing, so this was a little more difficult for something off the top of my head. I laughed with a sigh, "Why do they even make these kinds of things? They wouldn't need them if people just took the time to spend with each other."

I heard Tyler laughing by his desk. I glanced back, "Are you finding this funny or difficult, because you aren't helping over there."

Mr. Jenkins laughed, "Joselyn, you are the professional. Let him be; he's not very good at this."

Tyler got up coming back over to us, "I am too. She's good, but this I will have to see."

I put my finger to my lips thinking about this one. How could I word this? I tapped my finger to my lips thinking 'Inspire' what does it inspire? Well, I know the answer to that, but how do you relate that with cleanliness.

"When there's not enough time to make time... Inspire."

Mr. Jenkins laughed out loud, while Tyler just shook his head, "Where do you come up with this stuff?"

"Don't heckle her. She is good, and you know it."

Tyler brushed against my back wrapping his arms around me again, "And what do you picture?"

"Well, most people lose it when they start having kids, so... how about lying a baby down asleep in his crib, and on the way into their room one of them grabs the tube of Inspire?"

Tyler whispered, "We could see if it works."

I elbowed him looking at Mr. Jenkins. He wasn't looking at us, but I could tell by the grin on his face that he was enjoying Tyler's playfulness with me.

Tyler kissed my neck, "I need you at the office."

I turned to him, "Can I please have the rest of the week off? I haven't even seen the kids yet."

He stood there just smiling, as Mr. Jenkins collected the stuff. He was putting it in the large briefcase as Tyler turned me to him, and pushed me toward Mr. Jenkins stating, "Mr. Jenkins you're the boss; what do you think?"

He coughed and then replied, "I think it's a good idea to take the rest of the week, but I will be by tomorrow with more."

I gave Mr. Jenkins a hug, "Thank you. He is a bully."

He kissed my cheek softly and then headed back to the office.

Tyler pulled me in close after seeing Mr. Jenkins out, "Do you have any idea of how hot I find you when you are so focused on your work?"

I bit my bottom lip with a slight grin. Tyler must have taken that as me flirting, because he came at me full force pressing his lips to mine forcefully while pulling me from the room. Not separating for the climb up the stairs, we tripped up the first couple of steps, with me landing on my back. Bracing himself on the steps, he lowered to press his body gently to mine. Darkness filled his eyes, muscles tightened in his arms, and his tongue licked his lips to moisten them. His body glided against mine making me fully aware of the erection he was experiencing, "See what you do to me when you talk all business."

Stroking him gently in the attempts to distract him seemed to work, because I was able to squirm my way out from under him crawling up the steps quickly. He followed catching up to me in the living room, where he pulled my feet to a stop, crawled over me letting his body glide and graze every inch of my body. I was enjoying this playfulness and wrapped my legs around his waist.

Leaning down as if to entice me, but he pleaded with me, "How am I ever going to behave with kids around?"

Laughing out loud and then restraining myself I scolded, "You will have to control yourself better than this."

His hands came to me aggressively as he undid my pants, frantically moving back to pull them off, swiftly coming back licking and sucking at my stomach. The warmth of his breath, the twitch of his tongue, and the smoothness of his lips was driving me crazy. I grabbed at his head, entangling my fingers in his hair, letting my squeaks of pleasure escape me. His eagerness to please me intensified, and he crawled upward until his nose nuzzled into my neck tickling me with his breath.

Flash… This was something uncomfortable. I yelled, "Stop."
*Flash…*I was pushing away from something, someone.
Flash… I had to get away from him, "Please don't do this."

I felt hatred, pain, and a sickness was coming over me. Someone was forcing his way on top of me. I had to hurt him, I had to get away, I was not going to let this person hurt me, "Ryan, you jerk, leave me alone."

Tyler:

There was a transformation in her. She was looking at me, but she wasn't seeing me. I have never seen fear so fierce in someone's eyes. It hurt me that she was losing it over a memory. I grabbed to hold her, but she screamed more at me to stop. I didn't know if I should force her or let her move away from me. If I did let her go, would she be afraid of me forever? I couldn't worry about myself, I had to help her. I grabbed her hard and pulled her on my lap, not letting her get away, "Joselyn!"

She pleaded more, "Please, stop. You don't have the right."

I held her firm in my lap with one arm. I pulled her face to mine hoping she would see it was me, "Joselyn!"

She blinked at me for a second; like it was coming to her, who I was, but then the fear came right back, "Please don't do this."

I had to get through to her, "JOSELYN!!!"

It was like she finally saw me. Tears were filling her eyes, as she realized that she was here with me; that what she saw wasn't real. The sadness and shame showed on her face, "Oh, Tyler."

I pulled her close, wrapping my arms around her, hushing her, "It's okay, Joselyn. It will be okay now. I have you and nothing will ever happen to you again. I promise you."

"It was awful."

He rocked me in his arms, "Don't think about it."

Joselyn:

How was I ever going to get over that? The flashes were still going through my head. I jerked as they repeated over and over in my thoughts. Tyler's arms were so strong that you would think he could stop my body from trembling; I knew he was trying, but gradually that nightmare was being hauntingly remembered. I clung to him trying to secure myself in a place that I felt safe... in his arms.

54

It was very hard to walk the kids to the house that I used to call home. I didn't know how I would react the first time I saw Ryan, but it was guilt. Not anger, not hate, just plain old guilt. Why did I feel like that; this all happened because of me? Was this all happening, because I wanted the family life and ultimately he didn't? Did I disgust him after having a baby? I found myself searching for any indication that he may have given me after having Jared, then Terra, and finally Haden. He came to the door holding it open, and he tried to hug each of them as they walked in. His eyes met mine, as he yelled back at the kids already in the house, "Guys aren't you going to say goodnight to your mom?"

They all came running back out, and hugged me at the same time. This was going to be very hard for me. I let them go, kissing them over and over. I glanced back to see Tyler sitting on the front step watching us. I smiled slightly as they walked back in. I looked up to meet Ryan's gaze again.

He seemed worried, "I am really sorry, Jos."

I turned to walk away, but he spoke again coming out of the house, "Hey, thank you for letting me have the first night. I missed them."

I stopped not turning around, "You're welcome."

"Hey, do you want a coffee or something?"

I finally turned to him confused, "Coffee?"

"Yeah, Jos, this is killing me."

"Coffee?"

"Anything. Just... can we talk about all of this? I mean we were together before you ended up in the hospital."

"Because of you."

"NO, it wasn't. You wanted to be with me. Don't you remember?"

239

I glared at Ryan, and then glanced back at Tyler. He stood up, and took a step down. I could hardly breathe, but I was able to respond, "I don't remember it that way."

"I swear, Jos. You wanted to make this work. We were going to discuss holding off the divorce."

"No, I wouldn't do that. I didn't deserve what you did."

"You are bringing that back up. It was so long ago."

"Our lives are a lie. You never stopped seeing other people. You weren't happy with having children."

"How can you even say that? They are my life, and you know it."

"Yeah, well now you will have the time to prove it."

Tyler was walking my way. He knew I was getting upset.

"So, are you two living together?"

"No..., yes..., I was afraid to be alone."

"Afraid of what? Wanting to come home?"

I heard Tyler, "Joselyn, are you okay?"

I shook my head and walked towards Tyler. He took my hand in his, as we walked back to the house quietly. I sat down in the kitchen looking out the front window at the house. Tyler stood in the doorway watching me. It was getting on my nerves. He had to know this was going to be hard for me.

"Joselyn, I was thinking..."

I turned to him confused. Was he going to lecture me for what just happened?

He tried to grin, but it looked like a grimace. He sat with me at the table taking my hands in his, "I know this has got to be horrible for you, but I was thinking that I really don't know how you feel about me staying here with your kids across the street."

He has been through hell, and all he was thinking about was me. Me, he loved me. I couldn't help myself all I could do was smile at him.

"What?"

"You are thinking about my kids?"

"Yes. I don't want them to hate me for taking their mommy away from their daddy."

I leaned forward pulling him in for a kiss. I really did love this man. His mouth turned to a grin that was full of mischievousness, "So what are you thinking?"

"I think I don't really want to be alone."

Full of determination he said, "Well… if that is the case then I will make a bed on the couch."

I grimaced, "Why are you doing that?"

He raised his eyebrows, "Um… we gave Jared and Terra a key. What if they show up early?"

I sighed with satisfaction that he was thinking of everything I hadn't thought of yet. He kissed my hands and walked out of the kitchen.

As I was getting changed he knocked, "Joselyn, are you okay?"

I opened the door, "Yeah, why?"

"The door was closed?"

I laughed with a sigh, taking his hands in mine walking back out to the living room, "Just an old bad habit."

This… being here with him… was awkward, but made me happy. We would have to learn how to do this together. He moved quickly up behind me speaking softly, "You can't wear stuff like that to bed."

I furrowed my brows, as I turned around to look at him, "Why?"

His hand went to cover his eyes, "Because you are very sexy, and sometimes Zeus has a mind of his own."

"Zeus?"

"Do you have a better name for it, because it pretty much is in control of my life when it comes to you?"

I shoved him to where he had made up a bed.

He pushed himself up to rest against the back of the couch, "If you want to be forceful with me Zeus is up for that too."

I shook my head lying down the long way and resting my head on his lap. His fingers glided through my hair, as we watched TV.

"Zeus?" I said out loud in a commercial.

He laughed, "Did you think of a better name?"

"No, but a god?"

He laughed, "Yeah. Like I said… he rules my world when you are around."

I rubbed my hand against him to test his theory. He only laughed until I cupped him and caressed him. It didn't take but a minute and I laughed, "I guess you are right. Zeus it will be."

I pulled my hand away from him and he groaned, "You are going to leave me like this?"

"Yeah, talk to Zeus about it."

241

He sat there quietly as we watched TV. I was almost dozing when he begged, "Joselyn, you have to help me with this."

I went to glance up at him, but Zeus was definitely in the way. I giggled, "I was wondering how long you would make it if he was in charge."

He put his arm over his face, so I got up crawling over him. I pulled his arm off of his face, so I could kiss him all the while grinding my body against his. He was shaking his head, "I don't want you to..."

I kissed his face making my way to his ear, "I don't think it will happen if I am on top. Do you want to try?"

I felt those warm strong hands glide against my thighs, and he moaned a yes to me as we kissed. I felt his hands glide under my panties as he lowered them; I stood up so they would come off quickly. I was standing over him looking down. He slid his boxers off before I knelt back down over him. His hand came to caress me, touching me where the heat of my desire was already throbbing. I pressed to his hand more as I kissed him eagerly. Pleading with a growl, "Now, Joselyn, I can't wait no..."

Giggling I licked his earlobe, "Come get me."

Pulling me to him with his arms wrapped around me; down... down... until I felt him fill me with Zeus. He gasped as I trusted forward to engulf him completely. His body took over instinctively, as it thrust into me repeatedly, rising with each plunge. I felt as if I was riding him into the great unknown, and he was taking me there with each pleasurable blow. I was his completely, and this man was mine for the keeping. My mouth remained open against his to take in every breath he let out. I didn't want to miss anything he could give me. His lips sucked in my bottom lip only to trap me with his teeth holding me there, "Argh," and then he let my lip go. I grabbed his face wondering what was wrong. I tried to look deep into his eyes but they were scrunched in a painful way.

"What's wrong?"

He was trying to breathe but his words came out desperate, "Help me?" His air gasped and shuttered.

"Are you in pain?"

"Yes!"

"Why?"

"I waited too long... shit."

I moved to him more and quicker trying to help him, as his face pressed against mine in agony, his mouth open tracing my face. He cringed and started to moan. I moved slower and he gasped, "What... oh shit. Is something...."

"Shhhh..." I kissed his face tenderly, as I gripped his shoulders to move to and from him forcefully. "It's okay, Tyler."

His eyes came back to meet mine with tenderness. Our mouths connected as we slowly moved together. His arms wrapped around me and held me lovingly. The pain went away from his face as the gratification came. I wasn't having flash backs, but I was having an eruption like a volcano, which seemed to be oozing everywhere. Moans and sighs were escaping me, and Tyler's mouth came back to me, "You okay?"

I was okay the way he was talking about, but I wasn't sexually okay, because the pleasure was almost unbearable. I could only nod pulling myself closer to him. He was as thankful as I was, that I wasn't having flash backs. I felt the warmth shoot against my interiors filling me with his seed.

"Should I have done that?"

"Temporarily, I have an IUD in."

Those strong arms pulled me to him holding me firmly; his lips pressed against my cheek and words escaped him, "Playtime is on."

Pressing my face against his, I let my heart fill with joy, "Yes, baby, OH... YES!"

55

Tyler

I woke to the door being opened from the outside. I knew it was the kids. I sat up as they came in; Jared came up the stairs, "Where is my mom?"

I pointed down the hall, "The last bedroom."

He walked over to me glaring, "You slept on the couch."

I glanced up, "Yeah, she didn't want to stay here alone. She misses you guys."

He grinned at me and sat down.

"So, why are you guys here so early? Don't you have school or something?"

"Yeah, but there is no food in the house. So we were hoping to raid the fridge."

I laughed, "Yeah, give me a second; I will be right down. By the way, this is your home too. You don't have to ask to eat."

He nodded and ran down the steps. I slipped my jeans on and pulled my t-shirt over my head. I walked in pulling out stuff to make pancakes. Jared had boxes of cereal out and milk. I asked, "Does anyone want pancakes?"

Terra and Haden both screamed yeah, but Jared shook his head, "I have to go. Maybe a different day; when I plan it out better."

I nodded and started to make pancakes, "What time does everybody have to leave for school?"

Jared stood up bring his bowl to the sink rinsing it out, "I have to leave by 7:30."

Terra spoke next, "I have to leave by 8:30."

We all looked at Haden, waiting for him to speak up. He was reading the cereal box not paying attention. Jared put his hand on Haden's head, "He has to leave by 9:30. Do you want me to wake my mom?"

I shook my head, "No, I've got this."

He laughed grabbing his bag, "You may be sorry you said that. Tell mom I love her."

I glanced back as he looked up the stairs. I knew he wanted to see her, "You know she would probably love it if you went and said goodbye to her."

He turned to me, "Isn't she sleeping?"

"You think your mom wouldn't want you to wake her up? Are you kidding me? I could hardly get her to go to sleep after you left."

"What?"

"You know what I mean. Go wake her up."

He took off up the stairs dropping his backpack on the ground before taking two steps at a time. I flipped the pancakes over.

Terra asked, "Do you have bacon?"

"Um, no."

"Sausages?"

"No."

"You should really have more than one food group."

"What about Fruit or Vegetables?"

"Well, I have OJ for a fruit and we don't need a veggie for breakfast."

"Who told you that?"

"MY MOM!"

"Oh, really. I guess I will have to work on that."

She giggled. I walked over putting a couple pancakes on her plate.

"Why is she first?" Haden was talking to us now.

I laughed walking back over getting his, "Well, two reasons. One she is a girl. You always have to let a girl or lady go first. It's something we just have to do. Second, she is leaving next, so I want her to eat first."

I plopped a couple on his plate.

"Well, at least I didn't have to wait long."

I messed his hair up, shut the stove off, and watched them eat.

Terra asked with her mouth full, "Are you going to be here all the time?"

"I hope so, but it is up to your mom."

"If you promise to make me breakfast every day, I could put in a good word for you."

"Thank you, but I have to go back to work just like your mom, so I can't do this every day, but we can try to do it on days you stay here."

She was all smiles, as I glanced at my watch, "Hey, if you want to see your mom you should hurry."

I went to the stairs, "Jared, don't you have to go?"

He came running out, and almost jumped down the steps grabbing his bag, "See ya latter, Tyler."

"Bye."

Terra got up, put her dish in the sink, and then ran water over it, "Did you want me to leave it in the sink, or put it on the counter?"

"What did you do before?"

She took it back out, and set it on the counter next to Jared's bowl. She walked past me up the stairs. I knew she was heading to Joselyn. I sat down with Haden, "Did you want any more?"

"Nope."

"Are you going to go say hi to your mom?"

"Nope."

"Why not?"

He looked up at me, but with such a face; like I was supposed to know why. I didn't say anything, so he went back to reading his box of cereal.

I didn't like that he wasn't going to see his mom. I guess I could try again, "Um, don't you think she will want to see you?"

He rolled his eyes until they fell on mine. He bugged them out at me, "I am reading here."

I laughed, "Okay, okay. Anything interesting?"

"Uugh, shhhh." He glared at me, but went back to his box of cereal. I sat there tapping my fingers wondering what to do while we sat here. He slammed his hand on mine, "What are you doing?"

I shrugged, "What should I be doing?"

He raised his eyebrows, and handed me the plate, "Usually, someone does the dishes."

This little shit was going to make me do the dishes, "Are you done eating?"

"Yes." He waved the plate for me to take it. I grinned and stood up not taking the plate, but walking to the back of his chair I picked him up tickling him, "If I have to do the dishes, you have to help me."

"No, stop, no. I'll tell mom."

"Yeah..." I tickled him until he agreed to do them with me. I tried to set him in the sink to be funny, but he reminded me he was ready for school. I set him on the counter and started the water. I handed him a towel, "How about I wash and rinse, and you wipe?"

"Fine, but I am still telling on you."

"What did I do?"

"You were playing at the table when we were eating."

I raised my eyebrows, "You were done eating."

"She is going to be mad at you. I'll bet you."

"What do you have to offer?" I handed him a plate.

He glared at me, wiped off the plate, and dug in his pocket. He pulled out a super ball, and two quarters. He slammed them down on the counter, "There... what do you have to offer?"

This kid was funny. I dug in my pockets and there was nothing. I pulled out my hands empty. He got a great big grin on his face, "You have nothing to bet with?"

I held up one finger, and ran up the stairs grabbing my wallet. I took out a five dollar bill, and ran down the steps. He was wiping the next dish as I walked in, and I chuckled slamming the five on the counter.

He looked at it, and then looked back up at me, "But that is more than what I have."

I shrugged, "Well, if you are right it is yours."

He wrinkled his nose at me and glared, "You are so on. I can't wait to see your face when mom scolds you."

I laughed, "I don't think so."

We finished up as Terra came down the steps. She was going to head out the door, but I hated that she was leaving by herself, "Do you want me to walk with you?"

She looked back at me, "Why?"

I shrugged, and she waved for me to go with. I picked up Haden and set him down on the floor, "Go see your mom, but no coaching on if she should be mad at me. That has to wait, or all bets are off."

I took off out the door after Terra, "Hey, you said I could walk you."

She was trotting down the step, "You did not bet with Haden did you?"

"Yeah."

"You are going to be in trouble with my mom."

I was trying to keep up with her, but she walks like she is running a marathon and I didn't grab shoes, "Hey, how far do you have to walk?"

She stopped holding her hand up, "You can stop right there. Are you like over protective or are you a complainer, because right now I don't know what you are."

I threw my hands in the air, "Both."

She laughed, "I am meeting friends on the corner. Can you make it that far?"

I nodded and caught up to her, "So, am I going to be in trouble with your mom if I bet Haden?"

"Yes." She shook her head. When her friends came running out she turned to me, "It's your first offense, so she won't ground you or anything, but you may get a slap on the butt. I know Haden will."

I was worried that Joselyn was going to spank Haden, and it was my fault. I should have never encouraged him. I ran back to the house stubbing my toe as I ran up the stairs. *Be careful what you wish for*, is what I thought as I went through the door. I ran up the steps and walked back to the bedroom. I heard them talking and she sounded so happy. I knocked and walked in.

She was trying to keep a straight face, but I could see the smile under it, "I heard you were playing at the table?" She raised her eyebrows at me. I jumped to the bed landing on the other side of her from Haden, "That is not fair. He was supposed to wait, so I could defend myself."

"Well, go ahead then."

I pushed on Haden's head, "He was done eating."

She looked at him, "You did leave that part out."

He rolled his eyes, "Fine." He pulled out his two quarters and his super ball handing them to me. I looked up at Joselyn as I took them from him. She was glaring at me, "What is that for?"

Haden spoke but sounded beat, "We bet on it. You were supposed to be mad at him."

She turned him to her, "You know you are not supposed to bet. That is how we lose things we love."

He looked at me, "Yeah, I know."

She looked at me in that scolding look that drove me crazy, "And you are a grown up. You should know better."

"But he would have gotten five bucks."

She shook her head, "You are both grounded, and since you like the kitchen so much, your punishment will be dishes for the week."

Haden got up, "Fine, but I am drying."

I laughed, "That means I have to wash?"

He glared at me, "Unless, you feel that you were worse than me because you are the adult. You could do everything."

I shook my head, "No, you know your mom's rules and I don't."

"Fine, I should go. The bus should be here soon."

I got up, "I will give you two a couple of minutes."

I ran down the steps and picked up his bag waiting for him. He finally came down and I handed him the bag, "Do you want your stuff back?"

He shook his head, "No, you won it fair and square."

I nodded, "Do you want me to walk with you?"

"I am not a girl. Besides, I only have to go to the house. The bus picks me up there."

I nodded and watched him walk to the house. Ryan was outside waiting for him, so I went back in. I ran up the stairs and threw myself on the bed next to Joselyn, "How in the hell do you do this every day?"

She laughed tracing her fingers through my hair, "Thank you."

I glanced up at her, "For what?"

She just smiled at me.

"I mean it, Joselyn. I got scolded by two of your kids, then I stubbed my toe, and I am out five bucks."

"But I thought you won?"

"I did, but I felt bad, so I put his stuff in his back pack and gave him the money."

She laughed out loud crawling down to my foot, "Let me see it."

I pulled it up so she could see.

"I think you will live."

I put my arm over my face, "This... what am I doing?"

I heard her whisper, "Tyler, I told you this is a lot of baggage. Do you want out? I would understand, but if you could just wait until I am officially divorced, because I kind of need you right now."

That wasn't what I meant. I grabbed her feet and pulled her down closer to me, "That isn't what I meant."

She moved over me straddling me, "I am serious, Tyler."

"What I meant was that I suck at this and I think I made at least five mistakes and that was only in the morning."

She traced her hand down my chest, "What mistakes did you make?"

"First, I was on the couch. I didn't know if Jared was mad at me, because I was or wasn't in here." I shook my head, "Then I didn't have the protein with breakfast."

She was shaking her head leaning down to me.

"Next, I was interrupting Haden's reading at the table."

She grinned and leaned down whispering in my ear, "What was he reading?" Oh my god she was licking and sucking my ear.

"Joselyn, I am serious here. Next, I sat Haden on the counter, and I suppose you have a rule against that. I bet with him. I asked Terra too many questions when I walked her down the street, and..." She was breathing heavily into my ear, "You walked her down the street."

"Yeah, but it isn't like I did anything right."

She moved to my mouth and kissed me gently, "I think you did fine."

She was getting me going again and I grinned, "Really?"

She nodded as she grazed over me.

"Joselyn, they wore me out."

She giggled and pushed me over. I felt her crawl over me rubbing my back. She was the one that was supposed to be taking it easy. I tipped over knocking her to the bed. She was disappointed until I grabbed the lotion, "You are supposed to be relaxing, so it's my turn to baby you."

She pulled off her lingerie and lay back down on her stomach. I rubbed my hands together, and slowly moved over her back rubbing gently up and down.

"Tyler, what time is Mr. Jenkins coming today?"

I looked at the clock, "Shit, we have to get going." I leaned forward and kissed her back pulling her up with me and dragging her to the shower. It was hot and steamy, but I wasn't tired anymore. More like rejuvenated.

56

Joselyn:

I walked into the court room with Shane at my side, and Tyler behind me. Ryan was standing there alone. I felt horrible, but I was basically giving him everything. The only thing I was asking for was one of the vehicles, and the kids 50% of the time.

The judge asked a few questions, but when he got to the one that mattered, "So, this relationship cannot be reconciled at this time or any time in the future?"

Shane nodded, so I said no at the same time Ryan said yes. The judge encouraged him to speak his mind. Ryan pointed out that we haven't tried everything to save our marriage. He wanted to try six months of counseling, and he suggested I move back home to make the attempt.

Shane spoke for me stating that the last miscarriage that there were drugs in my system that would cause me to miscarry to which Ryan had an outburst of it not being his child. Shane insisted that this was not the first time that it had happen, and it shows in the medical records, so we feel it is unsafe to go home, and we are discussing the divorce not working on things. Shane stated clearly, "Mrs. Evans wants an end to this situation."

The judge nodded and looked up and around the room, "There is infidelity on both parties I see."

God I hated that she stated it that way.

She looked at Ryan, "Do you understand the terms?"

He shook his head no. I glared over at him. I knew that is why he didn't get a lawyer. He could play stupid.

You both will meet with the arbitration board in one week. Mr. Evans, I suggest if you don't have legal representation that you at least have a list of things that you are wanting from this.

Shane spoke up, "I think this offer is more than adequate. We would like to finalize things today. Mrs. Evans is agreeing to pay for the house and leave it to him. She isn't asking for anything from the home. She only wants one vehicle, and Partial custody of the children. It couldn't be easier than that."

She wasn't pleased with Shane, "The meeting will be in one week from today, 9 am down stairs. Everything can be worked out at that time. If everything is agreed upon I will sign."

Shane wrapped up his stuff and led me out. Tyler took my hand as we walked passed him. Shane turned on me as soon as we were out of the doors, "She is such a bitch. She is always rooting for the little guy."

I was not pleased with his wording, "Little guy?"

"Joselyn, you know what I mean. He makes it look good. Like he is home more than you, and he doesn't work as much, so it looks like he is the homebody, and you are the trashy wife. She doesn't understand at all."

"It's not that big of a deal. It's only one more week." Shane turned to Tyler, "I am sorry about this weekend."

I had to ask, "What was this weekend?"

He raised his eyebrows, "Nothing that can't wait another two weeks."

"She said one week."

He grinned, "But we will have the kids next weekend."

Ryan came out looking at the three of us. I felt horrible that he was alone. I wish he would have brought the girlfriend. It would have made things easier.

Ryan asked, "Tyler, can I have a minute?"

Tyler glanced over at him, "I don't think that is a good idea."

"Please?"

He let go of my hand and I stood there watching. I think Shane was as shocked as I was, because his mouth was completely open. Ryan stood almost four inches shorter than Tyler, and even though he keeps fit his body did not compare to Tyler's magnificent body. It was hard to see Ryan behind Tyler, but I kept seeing him glance over Tyler's shoulder. Every time he did Shane would look at me too. I just stood there glaring, because I knew he was up to something. Shane finally leaned to me, "Do you know what this is about?"

I shook my head glaring more as Tyler walked back over to us. He took my hand, and we started to walk out of the building with Shane following us closely.

"What was that about?"

57

Tyler shook his head, and his jaw locked in a gritting motion. I stopped causing him to stop. He didn't look at me, but I could see the anger in his face.

"Tyler, what was that about?"

His face turned to me with a horrendous forced smile, "Nothing. Can we please go?"

He didn't wait for me to agree so I followed him, but Shane brushed my shoulder so I would look at him. He mouthed to me 'this isn't good'.

I didn't know what to say or do; I have never seen Tyler angry before. He pulled the car door open stepping aside for me to get in. The door slammed shut after I was in. After saying a few words to Shane he got in. I stared at him as he drove, but we weren't going back to the office like we had planned. I didn't know where he was going until we were on the highway going north; we were heading to Ty's. I eased the seat back and closed my eyes. I heard his sigh with a laugh as he asked, "Don't you want to know where we are going?"

"No, I already know." I glanced at him from the corner of my eyes to see a large mischievous smile. I had to ask, "Did you call the office to tell them that court didn't go well?"

"No, but I called the office to let them know we wouldn't be in today."

"Tyler, I have three appointments today."

"Yes, and they are being rescheduled for Monday. Can I please have you today?"

"Yes, of course. You're the boss."

He laughed more.

"So are you going to tell me what that was about?"

He took a deep breath, "He thinks I am influencing your decisions. That I am keeping you by offering you benefits. He doesn't want me there for the next meeting."

"He is going to like me a lot less if you're not around."

He glanced over at me, "Why?"

I put the seat back up and leaned to Tyler, "Because there were three of us, and I actually felt bad for him today. If you're not there, and it's just Ryan and I, I won't feel sorry for him, and I won't be so nice."

His jaw tensed, his eyes squinted, and then he took a hesitant breath, "So you're okay with going at it alone?"

"I won't be alone. Shane will be with me, won't he?"

He sighed again, "Yes, he will. I love you, Joselyn."

I took his hand turning it over kissing his palm. His thumb traced my lips, as he pulled me closer to kiss me, but I pulled away, "Not while you are driving mister. It's a long drive."

He glanced at me with the most thoughtful look I have ever gotten from him, and I leaned back closing my eyes again relaxing until we would get to his place free from distractions.

58

I was correct about being harder on Ryan without Tyler there to hold my hand and keep me calm. I was a lot more determined without having someone there to hold me back. I was getting legal custody, but shared physical custody. I was perfectly fine with giving up the house for that. I didn't want him to have any legal rights to take them out of state without me saying so. I just didn't think he was safe anymore after what I believed he did.

We had a celebration when the kids got home that Friday; we were able to hang out and talk about their week. We ordered pizza, and camped out on the floor in the living room. Tyler was the biggest kid of them all bringing out a bunch of blankets. He had Jared help him prop them up so we had a tent. It was kind of like having the best of two worlds at the same time; camping, which I didn't mind, and no bugs, which I loved. We played board games until Haden couldn't keep his little eyes open. Tyler carried him for me, but I followed close. He laid him in the bed, but moved so I could tuck my baby in. Tyler put his hand on my shoulder, as I admired my baby laying there.

We finally walked out of the room, but he stopped, turned to me, and stared into my eyes, "Joselyn, do you even want another child?"

I tried to hold back a grin. I didn't until I thought I was pregnant, and then the idea grew on me, but it was the way Tyler was about it that changed my mind. I cupped my hands to his face, "With you... I love the idea of having another baby, but if you want more than one, we would have to do it right away, because I really don't want any after I am 40 years old."

He wrapped his arms around me, pulling me into him, raising his eyebrows, "More than one?"

I kissed him quickly and nodded, but pulled him back to our tent in the living room. Jared already took down part of the tent. He smiled at us as we walked back in, "Terra and I were thinking… Maybe we could stay up longer and watch movies? I could help Tyler make popcorn."

Tyler laughed, "Is that your way of asking if I will make popcorn, or your way of getting to stay up late.

Jared was very truthful, "Both."

We all laughed as they headed to the kitchen.

We settled on the couch, Tyler on one end and me on the other with Jared and Terra in between. Tyler reached for my hand, but Jared pulled it back down, "I don't think so. When we're here then you have to behave. She is our mom first."

I tapped Jared on the back of the head, "Hey. That is enough."

Jared sat up, and looked at me. He was angry, and stood up putting his hands on his hips, "For one, mom, I was kidding, but you are our mom first. I hope you remember that, or are you still going to have kids like dad?"

I didn't get that, "What did you just say?"

"Do you plan on having more kids like dad?"

I glanced at Tyler, because I could not believe what I was hearing.

Tyler sat up moving to Jared grabbing his arm, "Hey, I don't know what's eating you, but I was kind of hoping I could have one baby with your mother. It's not like you would become less important here. I like having a guy to talk to, so if you don't mind I would like to do more grownup things with you."

That wasn't exactly what I was thinking he should be asking. I wanted to know if what I heard was true, "Your dad is having another baby?"

"Yeah, with Stacy, you know that girl that keeps coming over."

My mind was wondering deep into him killing another innocent baby. I couldn't let her go through this. It wasn't her fault for my failed marriage; that was our own fault, but I didn't want him to kill another baby.

257

Tyler grabbed Jared throwing him over his shoulder, "Besides… who would I have to wrestle with?" He headed down the steps with Jared laughing and screaming. I tried to remind them that Haden was sleeping, but they were headed down to play wrestle in the sitting room down stairs. I was relieved that Tyler didn't focus on the problem; he was focused on getting Jared's mind off of the problem.

59

I put Terra to bed and headed to bed myself. In my mind I was trying to organize how I was going to talk to Stacy about getting checked out? Tyler crawled in shortly after me, "You okay?"

"Yeah, is Jared okay?"

"He is more grown up than you think."

I grimaced a look, "So, he is okay?"

"Yes, he is great. He knows things, Joselyn, more than you realize."

"So, what do you think I should do about Stacy?"

"What do you mean? It's none of your business now."

I glared at him, "Tyler, I can't just let him kill another baby."

His face became stressed, "I didn't think about that."

"What did you think I meant?

He turned away from me to get changed, "I don't really know what I thought."

I moved to him, slowly tracing my hands along his waist, and wrapped my arms around him. I trailed my lips against his back before kissing him, "You didn't think I was jealous?"

He shook his head, as he ran his hands through his hair, "No, I guess not."

I turned him to me trailing my hand along his face, "I am very happy here. You helped me to feel again, and you brought me back to life. Please, never doubt that."

He was shameful in his actions, as he pulled away from me, "I am sorry, I just..." His eyes came back to meet mine, "I really do love you."

I wanted him to believe that I was totally in love with him, "Tyler, I have one famous saying that you will want to remember, 'When you have doubt, it poisons the mind.' Please, Tyler, don't doubt me, and how I feel about you. I need you here in my life, and it scares me to even think that you are worried that I have any other thoughts."

His hands came to hold me so strong and firm, "I wish the kids were here all the time, and I wish we didn't have to have him in our life at all."

My heart raced with happiness, "If I can prove that he is the one poisoning her to get rid of the baby, and then it will prove he poisoned me. Then he will go to jail, and we will have the kids' full time; but is that what you really want?"

"I want you to stay away from him first of all. I don't want him near you." He grabbed a hold of me, "Second, I will take care of the rest if you want me to?"

I shook my head, "You know what I want?"

He was shocked that I didn't want him to take care of things. I was good at taking care of things, finalizing them. What I needed from him was the tenderness of his touch, and the moral support of his love. I traced my hand down his chest and then slowly helped him to take off his t-shirt, lifting it slowly up as I kissed his chest.

The creases on his face became very apparent with a grin, but he stopped me, turned to the door, and locked it. He glanced back at me, "After what Jared has seen, I think I would prefer to keep this private."

I wanted some privacy also. He came back to me lifting my full body. I wrapped my legs around him as he lowered me to the bed; his mouth was desperate to find mine, and we became engulfed in the pleasures of entangling our tongues. I reached down to help him finish undressing, but he stopped me by taking my hands in his. He pulled them up to his mouth to kiss them. Holding up one finger, which he slowly pressed to my lips, he inched away from me with something on his mind. He gave me one last sexy grin disappearing into the connecting room. I could hear him digging for something, "Tyler what are you doing?"

"Shhhhhhh."

"Tyler, please."

He peaked back in the room, "Are you begging me?"

"Yes."

He laughed and disappeared again. I crawled out of bed to see what he was doing, but he appeared again, "Oh, no you don't. Get back in the bed or you are going to get it."

I moved closer to the door, "But that is what I want."

He peeked around the corner, "Stop. Please go back to bed. Give me a minute."

I rolled my eyes moving back to bed sitting and waiting. He came in with a bag, and pulled out a candle, lighting it and setting it on the night stand. He glanced at me, and pulled another one out. He lit it and set it on the dresser. He lit another one setting it on the other end of the dresser. Then he walked around the other side of the bed, and put another one on the other night stand. He peeked back at me as he walked away, and went into the other room again.

"Tyler, please. What are you doing?"

He looked into the room again scolding me with his eyes, "Shhhhh."

I chuckled as he disappeared again. When he came back in he jumped on the bed lying next to where I was sitting. He gazed up at me with the cutest smile.

"What are you doing?"

He shook his head taking my hand in his, "Just making this special."

I took a deep breath as I watched him, "Why so special tonight?"

He pulled me to lie next to him and kissed my hand, "I wanted to wait for this, you know the whole dinner out, maybe a show, and then take you down to the city for a walk by the fountain, so I could set you down for a serious talk."

"A serious talk about what?"

He slid off the bed kneeling on the side of it messaging my fingers with his, "Joselyn, I was wondering if you would honor me by being my wife."

I tried to smile, but how could he ask me this? I wasn't good at marriage, "Tyler, my marriage wasn't like yours... you know happy... and are you sure you want to marry me?"

"You don't want to marry me?"

"No, it's not that. It's just that I screwed up one marriage, aren't you afraid I will mess this up?"

"Is that what you think?"

I was regretting saying it, but I was afraid that if we preceded that it would end, "Yes."

He shook his head crawling back in bed with me. He laid next to me, with his eyes directly on mine, fingers strumming against my cheeks, and his lips against mine, "He didn't love you the way you deserve. I promise to cherish you for the rest of my life if you will love and cherish me."

The tears not only filled my eyes, but they also dripped out the sides. How could I refuse a promise like that, "Yes, I will marry you."

He pulled out a ring, and slid it on my finger, "I thought you would want to see this first."

I held back a smile, as I shook my head no. I didn't care what it looked like, because the look in his eyes is what made me said yes. His nose, lips, and cheek skimmed along my skin starting with my face, slowly moving down against my neck, still further to my chest. Feeling blissful I whimpered a moan. He moved swiftly back to my face concerned that something might be wrong. I leaned to his face with mine, clawed his body with my finger tips to pull him closer, closed my eyes, and let out a satisfying moan. His mouth moved over me as light as the air from a butterfly's wing. As his mouth made its way down my wanting body, the heat rose from within as I throbbed to feel him. The slight touch to my breast with his luring tongue protruded it to him and made me tingle within. His open mouth kiss as he warmed my nipple, made me cradle his head to me. His eyes darted to mine, but my body moved to compliment the curves of his. The feel of his hands moving down my sides pulling me up to meet his mouth made me tremble. The licking and sucking of my stomach stimulated me to a shuttered state. He stopped so he could remove my panties, but quickly came back to entice me more with his tongue, slowly moving along my lower stomach up to my belly button. My body took over control, making me arch, as I felt the shattered release of enjoyment from deep within me. He moved quickly up to my face taking both hands in his to entangle our fingers, "I have pleased you already?"

He did please me in many ways, but sexually I think he was my perfect match. A slight grin came to his face, as my eyes pleaded with him for more. His lips met mine and we shared our breaths as he dove into the waters of my ocean. The pleasure was so good that my body moved to his like it was meant to be his all along. When he pushed to me my body pushed back enhancing the movements. When he moved to pull out, my body squeezed him tighter to not let him go. His moans were pleasing to me, as I whimpered with excitement. The release that I felt from him caused another eruption from me, but his hands released the tight grip on mine. I wrapped myself around him tracing his back, as his body relaxed into mine. His breath traced my face, as he moved his mouth back and forth across mine. Another slight grin grew on his face, "You are going to marry me, and I promise when we make love it will be like this. I want you as satisfied as me. Promise you will never fake it with me."

I couldn't help but smile, as I shook my head.

"So, are you faking it?"

"No, I will never fake it. If I need sex from you, I will attack you until you give it to me."

"Oh, so if I play hard to get... you will come get it?"

"If I feel the need... yes."

"What if we are at the office?"

I glared at him, "That is business. So, we will have to have a business meeting or something in the city."

"Oh, so we will sneak off to meet?"

I agreed, "We do have to be professional at the office."

He slowly pulled himself from within me, and my body shuttered from the pleasure that he had caused. He lay back looking at the ceiling, "I give you that much pleasure?"

I rolled to him tracing my hand down his chest and pressed my mouth against his shoulder, "Yes, Tyler, you are amazing in bed."

"Would you say *god* like?"

"Yes, you are *a god;* and I worship your body which is especially like Zeus."

He smiled wrapping his arm around me, so that he can pull me closer, "And you are my goddess, but if you want more you are going to have to do this yourself. I am so tired."

"You are playing hard to get?"

He shook his head trying to roll away from me. I crawled over him, but he grabbed me rolling back over to trap me with the weight of his body, "I love you, Joselyn."

"And I am in love with you, Mr. Reynolds."

He kissed my nose laughing, "So, we are back to that Mr. Reynolds crap?"

I nodded, "Well, if you are a god?

We playfully kissed until he was aroused enough to make love to me again, and again, and again. The way he made me feel when we made love gave me the desire to be with him over and over again, never hurting, never dry, and each time just as good as the first time.

60

I was walking the kids back to their father's house with their stuff in their little arms. I never wanted to do this to them, because it was so unfair, but at least I was close enough that if at any time they called me for help, I would be there in an instant. Haden held my hand, and glanced up at me as we walked to the house. He stopped at the end of the driveway. I stopped turning back to him to see why he stopped, "What is it?"

"I left my spy watch at your house. I can't wait a week to have it."

I laughed, "Honey, we can get it now or later. I live five houses down from you. You are welcome to come get it whenever you want. The only thing I ask of you is that you let your father know what you are doing, and where you are going."

"So, when I am at your house, if I forget something here... I can come here and get it?"

"Of course, but that rule to tell someone where you are going applies at my house too."

He hugged me so tight, "You are the best, mommy."

I leaned over, and picked him up the best I could, and whispered in his ear, "I am good, because you give the best hugs ever."

He laughed as we got up to the house, but Jared and Terra were still standing in the entryway.

Ryan came out taking Haden from me and set him down, "Joselyn, can I talk to you for a minute?"

I glared at him. I didn't know what he was up to, and I didn't know if I could be alone with him without kicking him in the balls. He raised his eyebrows, "Please?"

I nodded as he moved pass me down the driveway. I followed, but out of the corner of my eyes I saw Tyler was now sitting on the steps. He stood up as soon as Ryan stopped and turned to me.

Ryan cleared his throat, "Um, well, I was wondering…"

He was extremely uncomfortable, which I found irritating, "What?"

"Well, I kind of have plans this weekend, and I was hoping to switch weekends with you. They can come on Sunday night, but I have some stuff I need to do."

"Like what?"

"None of your business."

I shook my head, "I don't think so then."

"Why? What are you doing?"

"I don't know, but I might have plans."

"So, you don't want the kids?"

I rolled my eyes, "Of course I do… I just don't know if we have plans yet."

"What, you have to ask to have the kids stay there?"

"I think you should deal with your problems yourself."

I turned to walk away, but he grabbed my arm, "Jos, please, please… just this once I am asking?"

I stopped and pulled out my phone calling Tyler.

"What does he want, Joselyn?"

"Do we have plans this weekend?"

"Why?"

"He is wondering if we could switch weekends."

"Of course, but don't switch just take the extra weekend. I will cancel Bali."

"What?"

"Joselyn, I am kidding about Bali. I know you love having your kids here; tell him that we agree to take them this weekend, but it will be extra time for you with them. Don't give him next weekend."

By the time I was done asking Tyler, I was completely filled with Joy. I turned to Ryan, "I will take them this weekend with one condition."

He was pouting, "What is that?"

"That I still get them next weekend. I don't want to exchange; I just want the extra time with them."

He actually smiled as he agreed. I walked back up to the house giving the kids the good news, but my phone rang so I answered, "What's up?"

"Have the kids bring their best clothes. We have the art gallery thing tomorrow, and we'll just bring them with us. You can talk to the director, and I will entertain them."

I laughed with a sigh. He didn't mind spending time with my children, and I found it adorable. I sent the kids to get their best clothes, but I ended up going in and helping them dig for them.

We got back to the house, and I had them all try on their clothes to make sure they fit. It had been a long time since they had to get dressed up. They stood in a line in front of me and Tyler sitting on the couch. He was trying to cover his mouth to stop himself from laughing. I nudged him hard to get him stop. Jared rolled his eyes, "I don't think this is going to work."

Tyler did chuckle a little, "When was the last time you had to get dressed up?"

I rolled my eyes, "A long time ago."

I looked at them. Jared's pants were two inches short; he couldn't button his shirt, and he was holding his shoes in his hand. Terra's dress was well above her knees and it was a little young for her, but she also had her dress shoes in her hand. Haden didn't even have the clothes on. He just shook his head, as he stood there.

Tyler pushed himself up, "Okay, go get changed. I think we have to go shopping."

I glanced up at him. Did he even understand what was involved with shopping with children? I grabbed his hand, "Are you sure?"

He grinned, "Well, do you have a better idea?"

61

Shopping was quite the treat. We went to one department store where we could get everything. Tyler and Jared went off together for shopping. I was surprised, but I think Tyler and Jared got along the best. There was hope of Jared becoming a really good man out of all of this. Tyler knew more about my son than I did, and maybe he needed an adult friend to confide in. We went to get Haden's stuff first. He was the youngest, so he was going to be the easiest to dress up. He rolled his eyes and pulled at the tie and then the belt complaining, but I told him we would do ice cream after we were all done. That calmed him enough to put up with me pushing more clothes at him. We finally agreed to an expensive pair of slacks, but he liked them because they weren't itchy. We agreed with a light lime green shirt and a black tie. We would go for shoes when we met back up with Tyler and Jared.

Tyler showed up at the perfect time to entertain Haden, while Terra tried on dresses. We made it through eight dresses, but Tyler sat up with this last one, "That's it!"

Terra turned around and around in the mirror looking at herself and then at him. She finally stopped and turned to him, "Are you just saying that because you are board?"

He laughed, "No, that is the perfect one. You look like a little angel."

She smiled, "You really think so?" She was all giddy, as he smiled at her.

I pushed her in to get changed, and fell on the bench next to Tyler resting my head on his shoulder, "Thank you."

He turned to kiss my forehead, "That was the perfect dress."

I shook my head laughing, "By the way... I promised Haden ice cream, so he would put up with me."

"So, it's okay to bribe a child just not bet against him?"

I shook my head pushing him disapprovingly, "Yes, but I don't look at it like that. It's more like I get what I want by giving him something he wants."

"Bribery... I will remember it. I only wish I would have known that before. Jared wanted some pants, and he didn't want dress slacks, so I could have bribed him."

I leaned to Tyler, "If you want... you could take him to get those pants, and we will meet you in the shoe department."

Tyler glanced at me, "You don't want to look at them first?"

I shook my head, "If you feel he should have them, than I am okay with it. If you are having doubts, then I would stay away from it."

He laughed, "You trust me that much with your kids?"

"Yes, is that okay?"

"Yes, and no we are not getting the pants. They were completely horrible. It would drive me nuts to see him in them, and I would constantly want to tell him to pull them up."

I laughed, "See, you are already good at this."

We headed to the shoe department, and got shoes for all the kids. It took us another hour, and it was almost 9 pm. They were closing soon, so we went up to pay for them before heading out of the department store with all of the kids, hands full of bags. The three of them were full of chatter, as they walked in front of us. Tyler noticed the grin on my face, and he took my hand in his to walk out of the store.

We were almost to the door when Tyler stopped turning to a mannequin, "Joselyn, would you like a dress like this?"

I pulled him, "No, I am wearing the one from your work party."

"No, you would make this look amazing."

"Tyler, I don't need another dress."

A grin grew on his face, "I am guessing a size 9?"

I shook my head, as he let go looking at the tags.

"Kids, wait up. Tyler is picking out a dress for tomorrow."

They came walking back to us all giggling. Haden was rolling, "Tyler, boys aren't supposed to wear dresses."

Tyler peeked over the rack, "You silly boy. This is for your mom."

Terra gave me a really big smile, "It would look good on you."

I shook my head as he grabbed it, and went to the counter to buy it. We didn't have much time to get out of the store now, "Do you want us to go get the car?"

He shook his head, "No, just give it a minute."

We waited while he paid, and then came taking my hand in his again. The kids all laughed and started on their way again. Tyler leaned to me whispering, "I want to see this on you tonight. You know, so I can evaluate the merchandise."

I nudged him hard in the side, "Please, kids."

He laughed, "I was quiet."

Jared turned around, "Yes, but kids hear everything just like mom's and dad's do. You should be more careful around the children."

I had to laugh. He wasn't considering that he was still a child to me. Tyler shook his head laughing. Terra wasn't pleased, and then we had an argument on *us holding hands*.

All of the arguments ended when Tyler pulled into Dairy Queen. Then everyone was happy, and discussing what they were getting. The rest of the night was a breeze.

62

The next morning was a complete disaster. If Tyler still wanted to be with me after this morning, then I would have to see about getting his head examined.

I woke him first, and advised him he better get in first or he would end up with a cold shower. He wasn't eager except to pull me back to bed. I would have loved a quickie, but that wasn't going to happen with three kids in the house, especially since Terra wasn't pleased that we were together at all. After Tyler was all dressed I pushed him from the room, and went to get Terra, so we could have two showers going at the same time.

Tyler.

I wanted to help Joselyn, but I didn't know what to do that would help. I went downstairs, and sat out cereal for breakfast, and the boys came down with stomping and jumping. I watched as they inhaled their food. Haden would look at me and laugh, so I finally caved in, and I sat down with them. I elbowed Haden, but Jared scolded me, "Remember, mom doesn't like playing at the table." He glanced up at me over his box, "And if you're dressed already you don't want to get dirty."

I felt like he was the dad for the moment. I sat back and crossed my arms, "We are in a hurry; don't you think one of you should be in the shower?"

Jared got up, and rinsed his bowl putting it in the sink, "I'm first. Haden goofs around."

"Hey, I do not. I just have a lot of dirt in places that mom will check later."

I laughed again. I had a family now, and I loved every minute of it. I think there was a lot more for me to learn, and Joselyn was not one to correct me unless someone told on me. I leaned forward and asked Haden, "How am I doing today?"

"Well, considering we got stuck with cereal, and you did nudge me with your elbow, but we haven't bet on anything today, so I guess you're okay."

I nodded agreeing with him, but then he looked at me funny. It was a very serious face and asked, "You're not wearing the dress you picked out yesterday?"

I grabbed him from his seat, and pulled him to me tickling him. He laughed out, "Hey, this is against the rules; no picking on the little guy. STOP!!!"

I hugged him tightly, "Thank you."

He glanced over his shoulder at me, "For what?"

"When you pick on me it makes me feel like I am one of you."

He was confused, "You are. Mom is with you, and Dad is with that Stacy woman."

I was in shock, as I let him go. He turned to me, "Yeah, that is why we had to stay here. He is moving her in." He grinned and headed up the stairs. I knew I should tell Joselyn, but I needed her fresh for the gallery meeting. How was I going to tell her that this woman was moving into a house that she was paying for? I sat with my face in my hand thinking about how I was going to bring it up. Should I do it in front of the kids, so she doesn't over react to the news?

"Hey, is that what you are going to wear?"

I looked up to see Terra in her perfect little dress. I nodded, watching her take a bowl, and pouring herself breakfast.

"You would think you could dress up a little more if you are making us dress like this."

I laughed, "I am wearing a jacket with this."

She glared at me, "Well I guess that is okay then, but the next time you might have to get a tux."

I shook my head in disbelief. She was downright out spoken.

She grinned, "You will know why when you see my mom. You are not dressed strong enough to escort her."

I shook my head, "I do have a black suit; would that be better?"

"Yes, and I hope its Armani."

271

I raised my eyebrows, "She looks that good?"

She laughed, took a big spoonful of cereal, and nodded while chewing. I had to see for myself, so I headed to the room immediately. I did knock, but walked in at the same time. She was trying to get her shoes on, and the zipper was still down. I could see her back all the way down to her butt, which was a little exposed because of the thong underwear. I raised my eyebrow, as I moved to her, "Would you like me to zip this up?"

"Yes, I can't find my earrings. Did we get my jewelry from the house?"

I went to my dresser, opened the top drawer, and pulled out a box with earrings in it. I was saving it for something special, but this will do. I handed it to her, and then I bent down to kiss her back before zipping her up. I could hear her gasp. I didn't know if it was from the kiss or the earrings. I zipped her quickly, as she was turning to me with her hand over her mouth. Terra was right; I was under dressed to stand next to her. She radiated in beauty, as I stared into her tearful eyes, "You might not want to cry. You already did your makeup."

Joselyn:

The earrings were beautiful. They were a teardrop with a diamond at the end and they dangled just perfectly. I was speechless as he grinned, "You like them?"

I nodded profusely and trembled, as I took them out to put them in my ears. I felt his breath graze my skin just behind my ear followed by a kiss, as I tried to put them on. He whispered, "Your daughter said I was under dressed. I am supposed to put on my Armani suit."

I was surprised, "You have one?"

He laughed, "Yes, of course I do. I only like to wear it once in a while, but to please your daughter I guess today is the day."

The boys were fighting now, and Terra was standing in the hall laughing, telling us that we better get going; we were supposed to leave 5 minutes ago. Tyler and Terra headed to the car, and I went to deal with the boys. They were fighting, and Jared was messing up Haden's hair. I pulled the boys apart trying to get them to the door. We walked out, but now Terra wasn't in the car. Tyler put up is hands like he was trying to hurry me, but I shook my head, "Where is Terra?"

272

"Inside, she said she had to do something."

I went back in to find her crying in the bathroom. I knocked, but she didn't want to let me in. I continued until I saw Tyler coming up the stairs.

"Joselyn, we have to go."

I shrugged pointing to the bathroom.

He raised his eyebrows, "Tell her that we have to go now!"

I glared at him, "Yeah, because when a girl is hysterical that will work!"

He took a big sigh, "Can we ask her to please hurry. We are going to be late."

"This was your idea."

"Joselyn, I am not going to argue with you. We just need to go, so can we please find out what is wrong, and hurry it along?"

I was now pissed at him, and wanted him to back off, "Just go to the car, and we will discuss this later."

He crossed his arm and tapped his foot. I raised my eyebrows, and pointed. He huffed, but knew to walk away. I heard the door unlock, and the door slowly opened. I let myself in looking at her big huge puppy dog look, as she looked at me horrified.

"What is it baby?"

"That thing you told me I would get when I became a woman."

I felt tears come to my eyes, and I pulled her to me hugging her tightly, "I am sorry it had to happen today."

She was crying, "So am I."

"Did it get on everything, or was it just a little?"

"A little."

We got her cleaned up, and taken care of for the time being. I took her hand, and we headed out of the bathroom. Tyler and the boys were now sitting in the living room, and Tyler had one hand on each of their chest holding them down, so they couldn't fight with each other. He glanced over at me, "Everything okay?"

I nodded. He defiantly changed his tune after seeing me all stressed out.

"I called and let them know we were running late."

"Where they upset?"

He smiled slightly, "No, more relieved that we weren't changing our mind about representing them. They heard you were amazing."

273

I shook my head, "And where did they hear that?"

He grinned, and stood up pulling the boys with him, "From me, of course."

I laughed lightly, and leaned down to Terra, "Can you please go get in the car?"

She turned to me whispering, "You're not going to tell them are you?"

"Of course not, it's our little secret." I gave her a small smile and Jaden followed Terra down the steps and out the door. Haden stood there staring at me.

I laughed, "So, you had to fight today?"

"No... but we were bored and I hate dressing up."

Tyler put his hand on his head, "How about pizza and ice cream if you don't fight the rest of the day?"

He looked up at Tyler, "You are good at bribing. You got a deal."

He took off down the steps and out the door. Tyler walked up to me and cupped my face, "Are you okay?"

I closed my eyes, "Do you want out yet?"

He laughed, "No. I am sorry." He pressed his lips to mine, and I was relieved. How in the world he could still feel this way was a surprise to me.

"I am sorry, too."

"No, you didn't do anything wrong. I got pushy."

"Yeah, but I snapped."

"Is she okay?"

I opened my eyes looking into his sweet and caring eyes, "She is a woman."

He didn't get what I meant. The confusion on his face made him look like a lost puppy. I raised my eyebrows and smiled, "She got her period."

The look of horror came to his face, "But isn't she too young?"

I shook my head, "It happens at different times for each girl. I had mine at eleven too."

His eyes bulged out of his head, "Should we cancel. Is she okay? Is she getting those cramping things?"

I hugged him tightly, "No, it will be fine, just bad timing."

63

I was getting a separate tour than Tyler and the kids. He was walking from item to item in the gallery. As the director was giving me details, I would glance over at them. Tyler always made sure that Terra was comfortable, but then I would see him standing with the boys. I found it very odd that they would look the same standing the same way while they were looking at a piece of art. I would chuckle and then remember what I was supposed to be doing 'listening'. The next time I got a glimpse of them, the three boys were standing in a row. They all had their arms crossed against their chests, and one hand resting on their chins. Terra caught me looking, and I saw her noticing me. She pointed to them, and shook her head. I joined her thought process and laughed too.

Tyler.

I got the kids some snacks while we waited for Joselyn. Truthfully, I knew she was in the conference room, and I wanted to watch her. I made sure the kids all had a spot on the bench, and I walked over to the window glancing in to watch her. She was standing in front of a conference table next to an easel, but she wasn't using it. She was talking very directly to all of them, and I watched as they all nodded to agree with her. Her body was strong, confident, and direct. I loved the way she would explain things with her hands. I could almost understand without hearing her. I loved the way the top of her dress tapered, clinging to her skin, and the swing of the skirt, how it complimented her movements as she paced a little making sure to keep eye contact with each and every one of them. She glanced in my direction, but never even cracked a smile. She paced a little more, and I could see those beautiful legs with the contour of her calf that moved as she stepped. I imagined tracing those legs with my hands.

"What are you doing?"

I glanced down at Terra, "Watching your mother."

"Why?"

"She is amazing, and I love to watch her work."

"You should go in there."

I laughed, "No, she wouldn't like that. She doesn't allow me to sit in on her meetings."

"Why not? If you two are together, she should be okay with it."

I shook my head and took her hand in mine, "No, she says I make her nervous."

Terra pulled me from the window, "You would make me nervous, if you stood in the window, and stared at me like that. Let her do this."

I didn't want to move away from watching her, "But I like to watch. Did you see their faces? They can't tell her no, and I find it absolutely amazing."

"You are a dork. Let her do her job, and let's go see the third floor."

I followed but glanced back for one last glimpse. I missed having alone time with her. Sunday night was coming and she was going to be mine.

64

I didn't know if it was appropriate or not, but I had a plan and I hoped it would work out. Joselyn got the kids in the house, and I called for delivery. Haden didn't let me forget about the ice cream, so I was heading back out to get it.

"Does anyone want to go with me to help pick it out?"

Joselyn came to the top of the steps. Her face was a mixture of confusion and adoration. I smiled up at her waiting for her to tell me what it was that she was thinking, but both boys came at me, and went through the door. I laughed, "I guess I have some takers."

I loved the way she was looking at me right now, as she came down the steps. I waited to see if there was something she wanted. She moved close to me and glanced back up the stairs, but her hand grazed my chest, as her face came back to meet mine. I got the best kiss ever, and my arms acted on their own, as they wrapped around her to pull her close to me. I wanted more of this, but I felt her mouth turn to a grin, as she stopped kissing me, "You must be crazy, Mr. Reynolds."

I didn't get what she was saying.

"Don't you want out yet?"

I grinned, shook my head, and kissed her lightly on her cheek, "Nope, I am looking forward to the freedom of getting them all sugared up."

She leaned to me smiling, "Remember, the more sugar they have the more energy they will have."

I raised my eyebrows and nodded. I had to remember to not go overboard on the sugar.

While we were eating pizza the doorbell rang. I jumped up. This was my surprise and I didn't want anyone else to get it. I ran down the

277

steps taking out my wallet. To my surprised it was Mr. Williams the jewelry store owner. I stepped out of the house, "Mr. Williams what are you doing here?"

"You had ordered something, and my employee couldn't have it delivered, so he called me."

"He could have just called me."

He grinned at me, "I figured if you were having it delivered without even looking at it, it must be important."

I couldn't even believe this. It was his weekend off, and he was personally delivering the gift to me. I gave him the money and then looked up at him, "Come see me in the office on Monday, would you please?"

He was confused, "If you would just look at it I think it's perfect for what you explained."

I nodded smiling as I opened it. It was just what I was looking for. I glanced back at him, "No, it isn't about this, but with service like this I would like to maybe put the word out about your business. You know maybe some at cost advertising."

His eyes almost popped out of his head, "This is just a necklace."

I was so pleased, "But she is a very special girl, and you made a special trip for me."

"You are one of my best customers." He laughed a little, "We could make a matching necklace for the mother."

I laughed, "Come see me on Monday, and yes make that up for me."

He was pleased as he moved back to his car. I really had to think about how much I spent with him. He was driving a better car than me.

"So, what was that about?"

I grinned. She was such a controlling person. I shook my head, "Nothing. You will see in a little bit."

She glared at me, and I couldn't wipe the grin from my face. This was going to be great. After everyone was done eating pizza I pulled out the ice cream, but Joselyn chased them out of the kitchen to go wash up and get ready for bed. We would have ice cream and watch a movie. Joselyn went up to help Terra, so I started to pick up and clean up the kitchen. I was getting nervous about giving Terra her gift, but I watched for the perfect moment. The boys came down first with Joselyn, and they started to work on their creations of ice cream in a bowl. I watched out the kitchen door for Terra, and when she finally was coming down the steps, I walked over to her, "Your mom told me that you are a woman now."

She was horrified that I knew, so I quickly handed her the little box, "I thought you should have something that a woman would want."

She looked up at me, and then opened the box slowly. I could see she was torn in her feeling, because little tears leaked out of her eyes. She looked up at me again, but she was really upset. She closed the box and through it at me and yelled, "You are a dumb jerk."

She ran back up the stairs. Joselyn and the boys came out from the kitchen. Joselyn passed me to run up the stairs, but turned back to me, "What happened?"

I shrugged, "I thought she would be happy. I got her this because of the *'you know'* thing."

I didn't want to say it out loud, because the boys were standing there now, but I handed it to Joselyn. She opened it and tears came to her eyes. Shit, girls were way too emotional. Did I make her angry too? She glanced back at me, came down the two steps, and threw herself into me hugging me. I wrapped my arms around her and looked back at the boys confused. They both shook their heads and went back to the kitchen.

"Did I do something wrong again?"

She was crying into my neck, "No. You are such an amazing person. I will take care of this."

She kissed my neck, and wiped her eyes as she pushed away from me heading up the steps. I slowly followed, but only to try to understand what had just happened. I leaned against the wall next to her room listening. I couldn't make out what Terra was saying, but Joselyn was holding her in her arms talking with her. I heard her say, "He is trying. You know this isn't easy for him."

"Then make him go away. It would be better if it was just you and us."

"No, I would be lonely when you aren't here, and he is good to me."

I turned into the doorway looking at the two of them, "That's all I was trying to do. Make you feel good about..." I shrugged my shoulders, because I really didn't know how to say it: Period, or welcome to womanhood; or whatever I should call it.

Little Terra was pissed. She got out of her bed yelling at me that I was not her father, and I never would be. She was hitting me as Joselyn tried to stop her, but then something amazing happened. She wrapped her arms around me hugging me, "You are not supposed to be nice, and I am supposed to hate you. So, you can't do that anymore, because that means you are a nice guy."

I didn't say a word, but only because I was in shock. I wondered what was going on with her, as I glanced at Joselyn for answers, but she was happy and wrapped her arms around both Terra and me. I kissed her forehead, but Terra argued, "And none of that while we're around. It's hard you know."

Joselyn kissed her head, "But isn't it nice to see your mom happy again?"

She peeked up at us smiling squeezing me tighter. I wiped her cheeks with my thumb, but I still had no idea what to say to her, so I went with something very easy, "You want some ice cream?"

She laughed and nodded as we let her go, and then she headed out of the room. Joselyn pulled me back behind the door. I thought I was in trouble again until I felt her press against me and kiss my neck. I was turned on right away and traced my hands down her sides and around to her butt to pull her closer to me.

I felt her mouth turn up, and she bit my lips, "You are hot."

I agreed and begged in one pitiful look. She giggled a little before saying, "We better limit their sugar intake. Otherwise, it could be a late night."

I let go of her with a groan, but I didn't want them up all night. We headed down, and once I got to the kitchen I knew it was going to be a very long night. Jared and Haden had made themselves a brownie, hot fudge, Sunday.

We ended up curling up on the couch with Terra between us. It was nice, but my mind was completely on Joselyn. After she came on to me, I have done nothing but think... thinking about tracing every inch of her body. By the time we were heading to bed, I had worn myself out from trying to control my wanting. I crawled in next to her tracing my hand along her side as she curled up to me; but the sad part was, I fell asleep kissing her forehead good night. I felt her squeeze me tighter, but I was on my way out.

65

I really like her kids and I had my family, but I was relieved when I went out on the step and watched as she walked them back to the other house. She had a nice walk. Her hips moved from side to side the way they would if she was wearing heals. Today she was only wearing tennis shoes, but yet her hips were very luring. It must have been a very long weekend. Now she was on her way back to me, and I could see the smirk on her face. She was thinking the same thing as me. We were going to have play time. I took her hand in mine, as we walked back in. We moved up to the living room, and I was leading her to the couch, but she let go and walked back to the bedroom. She was going to put something sexy on for me. I lit a few candles and turned on some soft music. I was going to make this last all night; I had to have my fill. I looked up, but she was walking out with a laundry basket in her arms. She had a flirty grin on her face, but she shook her head going down the steps.

I leaned over the railing, "Joselyn, what are you doing?"

She glanced up at me, as she went down the next steps, "Laundry you silly man."

Was she teasing me? I went down the steps quickly after her, "Joselyn, you don't have to do that now, do you?"

She laughed as I walked into the laundry room. She handed me a basket, "It would go faster if you helped."

I shook my head taking it up the stairs. I separated it and brought the piles to each of the kid's rooms. I set them on the beds that were all made and neat now. I didn't think she would want me to put stuff away; they may need these clothes for the week. She was still busy when I walked out, but this time she was in the kitchen. I slowly went back down and walked into the kitchen. She was at the sink, but I wanted her to

281

know I needed her, so I walked up behind her wrapping my arms around her waist and nibbled on her ear.

She giggled again and handed me a towel, "It would go quicker if you helped me."

I huffed and wiped the dishes and put them away. She left the kitchen while I finished and went back down the steps. I rolled my eyes, as I watched her continue to take care of things. She came up with another basket, so I went over to her and grabbed it, following her up the stairs. I sorted things out, and she was taking them to the kid's rooms.

"Anything else? I mean I could sweep the kitchen, mop the floors, or Vacuum the living room?"

She nodded, "That is a great idea. Vacuum the living room, and I will do the sweeping."

She went out, and I headed to the living room. I was sorry for mentioning it, but now that I did, I suppose I had to get it done. I was not very happy pushing the vacuum around the living room, but as I did it, I was happy that we were getting things cleaned up. I didn't realize that it was so messy. I sat down on the couch to wrap the cord back up around the pegs.

I almost lost it when she walked over to me, standing in front of me with a little red camisole that had a slit down the front of it, exposing her belly, and sexy matching lace bottoms. After evaluating her whole body, I noticed she also had on red pumps that caused her calves to flex just the way I liked. I must have been drooling, because her hand came under my chin closing my mouth for me. My eyes drifted back up to meet hers, and the sparkle in her eyes told me she was pleased with me. To my surprise, she was *very* pleased with me and pushed me back undoing my pants. My heart raced and the pulse in my veins pumped through every muscle in my body

I was going to get lucky, and that is what I have thought about all day; being alone with my Joselyn. I eagerly helped push off my pants, and put out my hands for her to come to me, but she had a very naughty grin on her face, and leaned over me slowly crawling up my body, teasingly. I closed my eyes as she kissed me so low that it made me want to beg, but I put my hand on my chest to help keep my breathing in check. The next thing I felt was her nose tracing my inflamed rod followed by her tongue. I thought I was going to whimper, but I held it in. When her lips wrapped around me I let go and moaned which might have come out more like a growl. The pleasure she was giving me was turning me inside out and upside down. My mind was mush, but I wanted her; I needed to be in her. I reached down to cradle her head and tried to pull her up to me. She mistook what I wanted and quickened her pace and increased her suction. I yelled out her name when my toes curled, but she stopped right at the point of no return. "Argh!" as I reacted trying to stop. Her body came to mine rubbing her labia against me, while I felt a wave of relief overcome me, I jerked with an utter orgasmic release. I wrapped myself around her rolling her to the back of the couch. I nuzzled into her neck and nibbled on her ear, "What was that for?"

I loved when she smiled in that sexy way.

"I wanted to make sure you know I am thankful."

I glanced at her and closed my eyes, "For what?"

"Helping me." I could hear the confusion in her voice.

I laughed lightly, "Do you want me to mop the kitchen floor or maybe clean the bathroom? I would gladly do any of it."

She was so beautiful laying here in my arms, and I traced my hand across her stomach waiting on her reply, but she only shook her head. I nibbled her ear again asking, "What do you want from me?"

She grinned and a sparkle came to those eyes, "Everything!" She pulled my hand up to her breast, as she unclasped the front of the camisole. It knocked the wind out of me, but I knew what she wanted now.

Joselyn:

I knew by the grin on his face, and the glide of his hands, that he was going to make me a very happy woman. I scooted down as he moved over me gazing into my eyes. His fingers softly traced up the bottom of my breast carefully pushing upward until they glided to my nipple. He glanced at me again through his eyelashes just before he moved his mouth over it to place his open mouth to it. His tongue felt like velvet against my nipple, and his mouth sucked hard pulling it to him more until it was completely erect begging him for more. He smiled at me through those eyelashes, as he moved his mouth to give the other breast attention, but not forgetting the one that stood erect for him. His hand came up to warm it until the other breast had the same reaction. The way he enjoyed this, it ran through my mind that he must have been breast fed as a child. That innocent pure look when a child is feeding was on his face, as he taunted for more, but not pulling too hard. I wrapped one hand in his hair, while I cupped the other to his face tracing my thumb along his check. I love this man and the way he filled my every need.

Wanting to entice me more he scooted down further licking, sucking, and taking me all in. His mouth traced back and forth over my stomach leaving a trail of his breath gliding against my skin. My body was begging for him, and he knew it. His hands traced to my underpants, as he pushed himself back sitting up to remove them slowly. I pulled one of my feet out first wanting to roll to my side to completely curl up and enjoy the touching, but he wasn't going to quit there. He pulled my legs back open kissing my inner thigh as he moved back over me. I closed my eyes and anticipated the pleasures to come, and they came quickly.

Moving so his mouth was in reach of my sex; his warm breath glided over my tender flesh, igniting me. I wanted him; I wanted his mouth on me, but he was keeping his mouth just out of reach. On one hand it was making me crazy, but on the other hand it was making me feel desired, sexy, and downright needy. I moaned arching my back, but my body shuttered when his fingers found me followed by his tongue exploring my moist folds. Yes! I wanted to yell, but he knew without a sound what I wanted. His tongue lingered there moving this way and that, giving me exactly what I needed. I found my hips rising in response to him, wanting him to satisfy my body.

"Oh, yes. Tyler." My body was trembling while he gave me everything; his tongue, fingers, and lips. "Oh, shit." I was so close to falling off the edge into the pool of ecstasy.

Everything stopped. I wanted to open my eyes to see what he was doing, but when I felt the warmth of him push into me, my body moved to him in the most natural way, squeezing him tight as he plunged in. I heard his breath of determination, gasping, as he kissed my neck hard. We were one moving in the same direction. The goal was to submit completely to one another and fall over the edge together. Strumming to the same rhythm, my body sucked him in deeper and deeper. He grunted with each thrust, and I gasped contracting my inner muscles, gradually moving closer to that ecstasy. We fell off together tumbling down to the reality of earth. Our heart beats still strumming quickly, our lungs gasping for air, and the glorious satisfaction filled our bodies. His body collapsed onto mine boneless; my body, now made of jelly, molded to his. He pulled the blanket over us and didn't move away. We were complete as one, neither of us wanting to part. I knew he pushed away all of my pain.

66

Everything seemed to be going great for me, but somehow in the back of my mind I knew it was too good to be true. Weeks went by without any problems. I was still closing between four and nine deals a week. Tyler acted like he was the man at the office, because he loved that everyone knew we were together. I still didn't allow him to be in the room with me when I close the deal, but that was only because he still made me nervous, like I had something to prove. I should really get over that, because he always bragged me up to everyone. But still to have someone that amazing look at you with hungry eyes... it blew my mind. I had to take a deep breath with just the thought of that.

The kids were getting along with Tyler very well. He seemed to like that they challenged him. One night, when we were heading to bed, I was concerned that they were a little rough on him.

"Joselyn, it's fine. They are just kids."

"You are so good to me, and I don't like when they pick on you like that."

He grinned plopping down on the bed next to me. His eyes glanced up, as he pulled my gown up. I shook my head, as he traced his fingers over my stomach, "I think of it like this. If they didn't like me or even hated me, they wouldn't pick on me. It makes me feel like they like me around, and I seem to learn a lot about how their minds work."

"Well, that's a relief." I had a touch of uncertainty in my voice.

He glanced down where he was tracing, "Joselyn, when they give me a hard time... it's like I belong."

I threw myself on him hugging him tight.

"So, you want to pick on me too?"

I smiled as I leaned down to kiss my handsome man. It was our weekend alone and we didn't have anything planned. We laid in bed all day Saturday. We took turns running to the fridge for water and snacks, but mostly cuddled and watched movies. I never thought I would take a day off and lay in bed doing absolutely nothing, but of course you couldn't count this as nothing. We played our own little games in between movies that sometimes lasted as long as a movie.

Sunday, I had to get out of bed if nothing else but to stretch my muscles. I went down and started breakfast while Tyler was in the shower.

"MOM! MOM!! MOM!!!" Jared came storming in the front door.

"Jared, I am right here. What?

He was grabbing my hands, and pulling me to the door.

"Jared, just a minute; what's going on?"

"We don't have time."

"Time for what?"

He was frantic, and looked white as a ghost. I pulled him to a stop, "Jared, I am not even dressed yet. Tell me what is going on?"

He pushed me up the stairs, "Hurry, we don't have time."

I could see the fear in his eyes, so I thought something was wrong with Terra or Haden and he wasn't telling me, so I wouldn't freak out. I ran up the steps, threw on my jeans, and grabbed a shirt pulling it over my head, as I leaned into the bathroom, "Tyler, Jared is freaking out, and I need to go to the house really quickly."

"Joselyn, wait I'll go with you."

"He says we don't have time to wait. Just come down after you are done; I may need your help."

"No, Joselyn, wait for me."

I couldn't wait. I had to see what he was upset about. I ran alongside him, "What happened?"

"Remember when you lost the baby?"

I wanted to throw up, "Yes."

"Well, it's Stacy and the twins."

Now I was running at full speed, but my head was spinning.

He continued as we ran up the driveway, "Mom, she is doing the same thing as you did."

I pushed my way through the front door, but Ryan was there to stop me, "You don't live here anymore."

287

I shoved him out of the way, "Like you're going to stop me."

He grabbed my hand pulling me back pinning me against the wall, "This doesn't concern you."

"The Fuck it doesn't!" I pushed him with everything I had, and he tripped over some shoes in the entryway, as I ran up the stairs and into the bathroom. Stacy was curled on the floor blood coming from her. I felt horrified that he was doing this again. He came to the door, "I already called for an ambulance."

I looked up at him, "If you kill these babies, I am going to nail you to the wall; you fucking prick!"

I pushed back the hair on her face and helped her up. I grabbed a towel and wrapped it around her. I yelled for Jared, but Ryan came in grabbing her other side. We walked her out to the living room, and I pulled a blanket down around her lying her down. Ryan went to the kitchen as I knelt beside her, "I know how this feels, but is there anyone you want me to call for you?"

She must have been ten years younger than me, and she was so scared. I remembered my first loss and how scared I was. She was going to relive this, every day of her life. Her eyes were a clear blue and radiant, her skin so white and pale, her hair blonde and ratted, and her body was frail. Ryan came back out, as the first responders came through the door. I yelled at the kids to go to my house and took out my phone calling Tyler.

"I need you to stay there. I am sending the kids over to you, and I need you to stay with them."

"Joselyn, what is going on?"

"Stacy..." I smiled at her, trying to keep it with the best of hopes in my voice, "Well, she is pregnant and is spotting, so I will be there shortly. The ambulance and responders are here."

"Joselyn, come home. Let them take care of it."

"I will, but I just want to see her in the ambulance. Please try to help the kids. They are pretty scared right now?"

"Yeah, whatever you need."

I held the phone closer to me, "I love you."

I heard a breath of relief, "I love you too, but I don't like that you are there."

"I know, but I couldn't let it happen to her too."

Ryan threw something at me, "There; that is what I gave her. The same stuff you took when you couldn't take the prenatal vitamins. So if there is anyone to blame it is you!"

288

"Tyler, I have to go."

"What did he just say?"

I hung up taking the bottle of pills from the ground and looking at it. It was like being in a dream, as I wondered how truthful this could be…"

67

Tyler.

I went out the door waiting for them to come to me. I could see that Terra and Haden were crying, but Jared, well he was just pail white. I wrapped my arms around the two youngest ones, but looked at Jared for answers. He was in a daze and didn't bother to look at me, or anything else. We walked into the house and the kids all seemed to huddle together on the couch. What was I going to say to them or do for them? I remembered holding my baby as she died in my arms, and I thought maybe I understood what they were feeling, but maybe not. I paced back and forth from the kitchen to the dining room. I knew that ice cream wasn't going to fix this. I slowly walked up the stairs looking at them all huddled together. I sat down next to Jared not saying a word, but only because sometimes not saying anything at all helps.

"It was just like last time." Jared spoke as his eyes stared straight ahead.

"They will help her now." Was all I could think of to say.

After more time passed, I was getting worried about Joselyn not coming back. I didn't want her in that house alone with Ryan. I stood up, "Guys, I need you to stay here."

Jared jumped up, "We are going with you."

I shook my head, "No, I just want to make sure your mom is okay."

He shook his head, "You are not leaving us."

I was confused, so I sat back down, "It's okay. I just need to make sure your mom is okay."

He glared at me, "She's not."

I was instantly angry, "Why did you say that?"

He went back to looking straight ahead.

I was careful, "Jared, what do you mean?"

He shook his head, as the tears leaked out from his eyes. Haden got up and ran to his room, and Terra covered her face. I knew I couldn't leave them like this, so I pulled out my phone calling Joselyn. She wasn't answering. I paced down to the front door, and noticed her car gone, "Jared, did your mom say anything about going to the hospital?"

He turned so he was leaning over the back of the couch looking down at me, but was shaking his head no.

"Do you know where she would have gone?"

He shook his head. I tried to call her again, and again, and again. She wasn't picking up the phone.

I went to the downstairs bathroom and called Shane.

"What's up man? Another big deal?"

"You could say that."

"Okay, what do you have?"

"I need to find Joselyn."

"Where did she go?"

"If I knew that I wouldn't be calling you."

I explained the details that I knew, and he was going to have her license plate traced and found. I advised him to check at the hospital that was the closest. The only thing I could think was that she went to make sure Stacy was okay, and maybe something to do with accusing Ryan of hurting Stacy. It would explain her not answering the phone. I paced up and down, around the rooms, and everywhere else I could find a path. The kids seemed to be relaxing, while my temperature was going up. Why wouldn't she at least call me to tell me she was okay?

Jared moved to the kitchen, so I followed. I thought maybe he was going to tell me something. I waited as he looked in the fridge.

"Are you hungry?"

"Not really, but we should feed the kids."

He made me laugh. He was so grown up for someone his age. I helped him look, made a few suggestions, and we decided to make dinner together. I realized it had been almost eight hours since I had heard from her. It was driving me nuts, so I had to ask, "You sure your mom didn't say where she was going?"

He shook his head, and I saw them fill with water again. He knew something, and he wasn't telling me. I let it go, because I knew he would confide in me eventually. He always did. We finished making dinner, and he went to get the other two to eat. We all sat at the table, but we all just picked at our food.

My phone rang, and I almost fell off my chair running for it. I had left it in the dining room on the table. All of the kid's eyes were on me as I answered, "Joselyn?"

I could tell she was upset. I could hear her sniffling, "Joselyn, did she lose them?"

"Tyler, send the kids home."

"No. Tell me what happened?"

"Tyler, please send the kids home."

"No! Tell me what is going on."

"Hey, buddy."

I held the phone out to make sure it was Joselyn's number. Why would Shane be on her phone? "Shane?"

"Yeah."

"Why are you on Joselyn's phone?"

"Tyler, we need to discuss some things, so I really need you to send the kids back to their fathers."

"No, he is dangerous."

"It's not what you think. She is on her way now, but she wants to talk to you alone."

"No, I have to hear it from her."

"No, Tyler, she's leaving, and I am giving her the phone. You really don't want the kids to hear what she is going to say."

"What is going on? You need to tell me now."

"I am sorry that I can't. You have twenty minutes." And he hung up on me. I looked at the kids, and Jared was already pushing the other two up, and I shook my head, "What are you doing?"

Jared looked at me with the saddest eyes, "He's not dangerous Tyler."

I stood there stunned, as he led the other two out of my house, my house with Joselyn. Why would she let them go back to that house? I sat on the steps waiting for her and trying to make sense of this all, but nothing was working out in my head.

I was trying to organize my thoughts. Jared said Joselyn wasn't okay, which made Haden run away, and Terra cover her face. Did he hit her while she was there or do something to her? When I had asked Jared if he knew where she went, he was torn up about it. Did he really know?

Did she go back to their dad? It just wasn't possible. Then the flash of Jared's face in my memory, as he said *he's not dangerous*. Where was this all going?

I stood quickly as she pulled in. She was a mess, and I didn't know what to do. She didn't even look at me as she passed me, "You need to get your things and go."

I didn't move. Did she just tell me to leave? She stormed into the house and was blubbering the whole way in. I followed, "Joselyn, what happened?"

She turned to me. Her eyes were completely red, her skin blotchy and the sadness in her eyes was compelling; I remember seeing this look on her once before.

"I don't have the strength to deal with you. You have to leave."

I was angry, and yet I felt bad for the way she was feeling, "I am not leaving."

She turned to run up the steps, and I ran after her grabbing her arm in the hallway to stop her from running from me, "Joselyn."

She screamed at me, "Don't touch me."

I put both my hands on the wall around her, and leaned down to her whispering, "What happened?"

If the look on her face wasn't enough to knock the wind from me, her next sentence was, "I killed them."

I stood there frozen looking into her eyes. I didn't understand what she said.

"Tyler, I killed all of them; including your baby. I killed them."

I took a step back staring at her.

"I killed them. Do you get it now?"

I shook my head with disbelief.

"Get out!"

I backed away from her but didn't take my eyes from her. She fell to the ground sobbing. I couldn't help her, because I didn't know how to feel, let alone breathe. I took a step back, as she sobbed repeating it over and over again, "I killed them."

I couldn't leave her like this. I took a step towards her trying to stay calm, "This must be a mistake."

She looked up at me glaring and crying at the same time, "Don't you get it? I KILLED THEM!!!!!"

293

I turned and walked away confused and numb. I grabbed my keys and left.

68

My days were blank, and I didn't know where I was half the time. If only she would show up here, so we could talk about this. There had to be some sort of mistake. She must have seen something in her old house that made her feel responsible. Shane wouldn't tell me anything other than Joselyn had signed over complete custody to Ryan. I bribed him to hold off on filling them; most would call it a large donation to the firm.

"What the hell is going on?" I looked up to see Mr. Jenkins storming in. I didn't have an answer, let alone not being able to breathe. "You look like shit, and where is Joselyn?"

I shrugged my shoulders.

He glared as he came closer, "Did you hurt her?"

I shook my head, and his face turned to confusion. He moved closer, "You look like hell; you have been here for what... five days now, and where is Joselyn?"

I shook my head again. I didn't know what to say to him.

"Did something happen between you two?"

I felt it coming, the large lump in my throat with the burning sensation of closing off. My eyes watered, as I felt the loss of her. It was worse than losing my first wife; Joselyn had killed our child. I didn't want him to see me loose it, but I was well on my way. I cupped my hands to my face, "Joselyn said she killed the babies."

I heard him move in front of me sitting in the chair across from my desk, "Do you think she did it?"

I shook my head and began to sob. He stood up and moved to close the door, "Well, I would like to think not. Tell me what mother loves her children more than Joselyn. If you don't believe it, than what the hell are you blubbering for?"

295

I glanced back up at him with some relief.

He gave me a quick grin, "It might look bad, but she takes on the world and this might be something she is just taking on, Tyler. Did you think about it that way?"

I shook my head, and I felt a nerve twitch in my cheek. There was hope. He was right. Joselyn would never do anything to hurt those children, so why did she think she killed my baby?

"So, I guess when you can stop feeling sorry for yourself, you could fill me in."

All I could get out was, "Shane."

I stood up and walked out with Mr. Jenkins right behind me.

Mary yelled from the front desk, "Tyler, good luck."

Good luck. What do I need good luck for? I got in my car, and Mr. Jenkins was getting in too. I glanced over at him.

He grinned, "If you think you are the only one that loves her, you can think again."

He almost made me laugh, but I was on a mission now. I needed to find out the truth. We were heading to Shane's. He was going to tell me, or we wouldn't do business ever again. I stormed into his office, but the secretary tried to stop me. Mr. Jenkins did some good blocking, as I ran into his office. He wasn't there, so I looked down the hallway. Mr. Jenkins was stopping her by rolling to his left and then to his right. He never laid a hand on her, and I did end up chuckling, as I ran looking from office to office. I noticed all the offices were empty. I knew where they were now, in the conference room. I stormed in, "I want to know everything."

He coughed and stood up, "You know I can't tell you her business."

I raised my eyebrows, "Fine you won't have mine than." I turned to walk away. Mr. Jenkins had let her by as I walked to him.

"Did you find anything out?"

I shook my head, but Shane was behind me, "Tyler, you know I can't tell you, but you could maybe find something in my office while you wait for me."

I turned to him glaring into his eyes. I could tell he was begging me to not push anything further, "Fine, we will wait in your office, but I need to see you in ten minutes."

He grinned, "You only need five. It's a big one, so it is on top of the pile."

I turned running to his office. I opened the file as Mr. Jenkins followed in huffing a little, "What? What does it say?"

"She sees herself as an unfit parent. She admits to killing all the babies that she has miscarried. She was taking a drug." I looked at Mr. Jenkins confused, "Are we wrong about Joselyn?"

He shook his head, "Have you ever seen her take as much as an aspirin?"

I really had to think about this, and he was right. She didn't like to take anything even for a headache. I shook my head reading further. There were signed documents giving Ryan full physical and legal custody of her children. I handed it to Mr. Jenkins and he cried out, "Oh, no, Joselyn. He is an asshole; why are you doing this?"

Shane came walking in.

"What does all this mean?"

"She killed the babies. I don't think intentionally. She was heartbroken, and her hands shook when she signed those papers. Tyler, I really can't hold off much longer on filing these."

"Give me some time. Do you know what she was taking?"

"An herb that causes miscarriages."

"Did she know what she was taking?"

"She said she went to the store to get them herself."

I was confused. She was doing a very good job at hanging herself on this one. I sat down staring at Mr. Jenkins.

He glared at me, "Are you giving up that easily?"

I sighed with a laugh shaking my head, "You're right."

"Where did she get it?"

Shane shrugged his shoulders.

"Do you believe she intentionally killed my child?"

I think I could actually see tears well into his eyes, as he shook his head no. I closed my eyes with relief, as Mr. Jenkins pulled on my arm, "I really think we need to hurry before she does something stupid."

I turned to him, "You don't think she would...?"

I could see the pain in his eyes. I pulled out my phone and called Ryan.

"Hello?"

"Hey, sorry to bother you, but has Joselyn been by to see the kids?"

"No, I thought you two took off. I walked the kids down a couple of times, but she didn't answer. I didn't want the kids to go in if you two weren't there. So she dumped you too?"

I could not believe I was going to deal with this asshole, "I need you to tell me what she was taking while she was pregnant."

"I threw them at her. It's all her fault you know."

"What do you mean?"

"She got sick taking those prenatal vitamins, so she went and got those other vitamins to take. That is what caused the miscarriages. The doctors said they weren't vitamins at all. She wanted to get rid of all of them including yours."

I really wanted to kill him right now, but I didn't have time to deal with him, "Where did she get them."

"The health food store on the corner of Blake and Ringgold."

I hung up and Mr. Jenkins was probing me for information. I told him what Ryan said, but he felt the same way I did. There was no way this was our Joselyn.

We spoke with the manager about his employees and asked if any of them dealt with Joselyn. I had to show a picture because over half of them were not fluent in English. One of the little old ladies nodded and smiled. She was Russian and was just so helpful that she nodded, "Yes, No, Baby."

I glanced over at Mr. Jenkins and he shook his head and spoke up, "Security cameras?"

One of the younger boys came forward, "Yes, we keep the tapes in the back."

The owner stepped forward, "No, no, no." He was pushing us. I had to get the tapes. Maybe I could find out if Joselyn really did want to get rid of the babies. She wasn't too thrilled about having one with me to begin with, but I thought she wanted it by the time we knew for sure. The younger boy assured the elderly man that he would push us out. We got to the door, and I held up three one hundred dollar bills. Mr. Jenkins smiled and the boy shook his head and told us no, but he whispered, "Meet me by the dumpster."

I nodded and left willingly driving around the back. He came out with two large garbage bags, "Dis all of um. You bring back when done?"

I nodded and gave him the money. He smiled and tucked them into his pocket, "Please bring back?"

I nodded and put them in the trunk. I headed back to the office. Mr. Jenkins carried one in and I did the other one. We went to the conference room, and started to look through them. I couldn't make out anything and neither could Mr. Jenkins. I walked out to the front desk, "Is there anyone in the building that can translate Russian?

Tori walked up laughing, "You look like shit!"

"Why thank you, but if you don't know Russian I don't give a rat's ass."

She shook her head and walked into the room, "What do you need to know?"

I almost fell over realizing that she did.

"I need to know the dates. I need one between April 1st and August 15th."

"Just one?"

"No, all of them."

She started to put them in order, and I put them in to play. I looked at Mr. Jenkins and he was nodding, "Tori, you will get paid handsomely if you will stay with us and help."

"What are we doing?"

I snapped at her, "Helping Joselyn."

She sat down, "Anything. Is she okay?"

I shook my head and called Shane.

"Did you find something?"

"Not yet, but I need information."

"You know I can't tell you anything."

"Well, this isn't about confidentiality if that is what you are worried about."

"Okay, then what?"

"I need to know when Joselyn lost the other babies."

"Tyler, what are you up to?"

"Just... Can you get me the fucking information, or do I need to find a new lawyer?"

"I'm on it."

I hung up, and Mr. Jenkins was nodding.

After a few days of searching around the clock, I asked Mr. Jenkins to go to Joselyn. Tori went with him. They weren't gone for very long, so when they walked back in I was surprised.

"She wouldn't talk to us."

299

My heart was breaking.

"Tyler, I think maybe you should just go to her. I don't think she is eating."

Tori spoke next, "I did check the medicine cabinet and the cupboards in the kitchen she really doesn't have anything in pill form that will kill her, but I think if she did... It wouldn't be good, Tyler."

I went out barking a few orders, and we had two more tape players moved into the conference room, so we could view three at a time. The girls from the front desk came in to help us watch. Two of the agents came in and offered to take a turn. After I explained that we were looking for any tapes that had Joselyn on them, they all took turns. Next thing I knew everyone was rotating into the room to watch the videos. We had about 9 years of videos to look through.

69

I pulled up to the house with Mr. Jenkins in the passenger seat and Tori in the back. We all got out, as I looked at the house. I have never felt so much relief, as I did right now. My hands were trembling, as I walked up to the house. After three weeks of searching, we finally found what we were looking for.

I opened the door and Tori spoke, "She was in the bed room curled up on the floor."

"You didn't make her get up and eat?"

She glared at me, "I think she wanted to hurt herself slow and painfully."

I swallowed and headed up the stairs, and they followed me all the way down the hall way. I turned to stop them at the door, "Go get it ready. She won't believe us if she doesn't see it herself."

They both turned heading back to the living room. Nothing looked as if it were touched in the time I had been gone. I heard the front door slam into the wall, "Tyler?"

I stopped and turned to see Jared coming down the hall, "She won't eat or talk to me. I tried... I really tried. Where have you been?"

The tears filled my eyes; he walked closer until he was standing in front of me, and my tears flowed down my cheeks. I didn't know how to explain it to him, so I put my hand on his shoulder, "I think you are man enough to see what happened."

He nodded and looked anxious. I pointed to the living room where Mr. Jenkins and Tori were standing watching us. He looked back at me, "She didn't do what she said she did, did she?"

I shook my head and wiped the tears, "Go have a seat. I am just going to get her."

He nodded and slowly walked backed to the living room. I took a deep breath walking into the room. Tori had said she was curled up on the floor, so I looked around but didn't see her until I advanced into the room. It broke my heart to see her lying there miserable, with her face plastered to the floor. I squatted by her pulling her to me. She tried to push me away until her gaze fell on me, and I lost it as she began to sob, "Oh, Tyler I am so sorry. I killed it."

I shook my head sitting down pulling her to me. Her face came to rest on my chest, "No, my *belle Dona.*"

She was confused by my words, but I tried to get up with her. In this little time she had wasted away quite a bit. I knew she had not been eating. She was pushing me away again, "No, Tyler I can't. I don't deserve to live. I killed them."

Now she pissed me off, so I held her in my arms pulling her into the bathroom, and walked right into the shower holding her against the wall, as I turned on the water. She shook her head, as I held her under the water, "No, Tyler why? I can't live with myself. I killed them."

I shook my head, because she was making my blood boil, and not in a good way. I turned her away from me holding her mouth to the water hoping she would take some in. I whispered in her ear, "I lost my wife and daughter, please don't put me through this again. I am miserable without you."

She collapsed in my arms, and I turned her to me wiping her face, "Please, don't do this to me."

"But, Tyler, I killed our baby."

I shook my head, "If you honestly tried to kill my baby would you be this upset about it? Joselyn, I am not stupid. It was an accident, and I found out how it happened."

She rested her face on my chest as I heard a knock, "Hey, do you need some help?" I knew it was Tori asking.

"No, we just need a few more minutes."

Joselyn's eyes came back to meet mine, "Tori is here?"

I nodded, "Everyone worked together to help me find something. I need for you to come see this; and you will understand. It wasn't your fault."

She shook her head, as the tears streamed down, "I still took the pills, Tyler. It's still my fault."

I pressed my lips to her forehead, "But you didn't know what you were taking. You cannot be held responsible for that."

Those eyes... so green, so sad, and so full of worry, "Tyler, what happened to Stacy and the twins?"

I turned off the water grabbing a towel, "Stacy is fine, and they caught it early enough; the babies are going to be okay."

Moving her to the closet, I supported her weight while I slowly undressed her, drying her as we went. Her eyes stayed glued on me, so I would glance to them here and there, but the sadness in them was far worse than I have ever seen or felt. After getting her in lounge pants and a t-shirt, I wrapped her bony body in a house coat. When I bent over to pull off my jeans at the bottom, her hand traced my back. I peaked up at her giving her a slight grin, but she just stared at me. I hurried and put on sweats, but turned to her, wanting her to respond in some way. I took her hand in mine pulling it to my chest, to where my heart beat for her, and to the place that she needed to be.

She swallowed deeply; her eyes remained sad. I needed her to see those tapes right now. We needed to end her misery. I grabbed my t-shirt and pulled it on over my head. Her hand slid down my front as the t-shirt fell, finally the response I was hoping for. Her fingers spread out against my stomach; she was touching me. I pulled her into me pressing my face against her head, "Josely, everything will be okay. I promise you." I turned her and wrapped my arm around her to help her to the living room. Jared came running, as soon as he saw us, wrapping his arms around his mother. Again, Joselyn responded the way I was hoping. She cupped his head to her, and kissed him repeatedly. We slowly walked to the couch where I lowered her, and Jared curled into his mother not letting go. Mr. Jenkins put his hand on my shoulder, "Sit with her. Well, do the talking." I moved to her other side and wrapped my arm around both of them. Tori was coming up the steps with a large cup. She handed it to me, "Soup. Try to have some, Joselyn, while we explain."

Her eyes met Tori's with regret. Tori lightly touched Joselyn's face, "It's okay, Joselyn. You are okay now."

I could see the tears well up, as I handed her the cup. She took slow sips while Mr. Jenkins hit play.

Tori started, "This was the most current video we could find."

I watched this for the 50th time knowing it would be confusing for her.

"Do you have those vitamins you gave me last time?"
"No, baby?"

303

I watched as she touched her belly completely smiling, "Yes, baby."
"Okay, baby gone?"
"No, I need the vitamins for the baby."
The little old lady smiled and patted Joselyn's arm and walked back to the shelves coming out and handing them to her. Joselyn took them smiling and paid for them at the counter.

She was torn on how she felt by the way her eyes looked up at me. I traced her face, "That's not it, but that was the first one we found. There is more." I nodded as Tori put in the next one.

"This was the one previous, when you were going to have that little girl."

We watched as she happily went to the counter, "I am pregnant again!"
The same old lady was shaking her head, "Same ting?"
"Yes, I need all the help I can get. Prenatal vitamins make me sick."
"No baby right?"
"Yes," She was rubbing her belly. The lady put the bottle on the counter and smiled at her but was shaking her head, "There are better."
Joselyn smiled, "No, I just need this for the baby."

Joselyn looked up at me as the tears leaked out. I smiled at her, "One more, baby, and you will understand."

Tori put the next one in, and stood back looking at the screen. She put her hand over her mouth, and Mr. Jenkins walked down the steps to the kitchen. We had watched this over and over again to try to make sense of it all.

She walked into the store cautiously. She looked around as this older lady that didn't seem that old in this video. She stopped and watched Joselyn for a minute and then asked, "Help you?"
Joselyn smiled at her, "I am not doing too well with my pregnancy, and I need some sort of vitamin. The prenatal vitamins make me sick."
The lady shook her head, "No more sick?"
"Yes, I need something for the baby. No more sick."
The older lady tilted her head, "Baby yes."
"Yes, No, I mean I don't want to be sick anymore."
"So no baby sick?"
"Yes, no baby sick."

The older lady walked to the back and came out with a jar, "You sure no baby sick?"

"Yes. I don't want to get sick anymore."

I heard Joselyn gasp with sadness. I pulled her close holding her.

The older lady wasn't happy, "Dis get rid of it."

Joselyn smiled, "Good, because I don't want to feel sick anymore."

The lady rang it up and kept shaking her head, "You try some tea first?"

"No, if this will help I will try this."

"You know you take a lot, for it to get rid of it?"

"Okay, how much?"

"Three times a day."

She held the bottle up looking at it, "What is this?"

"Special remedy. Will get rid of it all if you take enough."

Joselyn bought a bottle of water and opened the jar, "I guess I better get started right away."

Joselyn was breaking down, and let go of Jared. I pulled her closer, "Joselyn, you didn't know."

She shook her head, "But I should have checked it out with my doctor."

I kissed her forehead. Tori came over and knelt down in front of her, "Joselyn, remember telling me that you didn't like the way the new vitamins made you feel, and you quit taking them with Haden?"

She nodded, "They weren't what you thought. The lady misunderstood you. It is very clear in the videos."

Jared took his mom's hand, "You didn't know, mom."

She pulled him closer and kissed his head, "I am so sorry."

I shook my head, "It wasn't your fault."

Mr. Jenkins walked back up and leaned over us kissing Joselyn on the forehead. "I love you like you are one of my own. You will not blame yourself for this, and I expect you to let it go. You have a week, and I want you back at work."

I looked up at him like he was nuts. He winked at me, and took Tori by the arm pulling her from the house. He yelled back, "We are taking Joselyn's car if that is okay."

"Yeah." Was all I could say. We sat there in silence with Jared on one side patting his mother's hand, and me on the other side holding her tight.

70

Six months later we were at Ray's place having our reception. She looked amazing considering how thin she was, but she was getting over the guilt of everything still. She was down to apologizing three times a day, which was much better than the 20 we started with.

I sat at the end of the bar watching the kids dancing on the dance floor; we had them full time now that Ryan had his hands full with the twins and a new wife that didn't let him get by with just sitting around. My attention moved to Joselyn; she was talking to everyone as they congratulated her. My bartender, Max, came over, "Are you sure you wanted to get married?"

I was shocked as I turned to him.

He grinned, "Well, you seem down today."

I went back to watching my new wife with admiration. I did love her, but the part that I was struggling with was that I felt like I was betraying my first wife and daughter.

I tried to not let it get to me, but now this wasn't just making Joselyn happy, it was about me too. I guess I was feeling guilty for loving Joselyn more than my first wife, but only because I was so young and didn't understand the importance of how little time we have here together. Maybe now that I knew that, I put more of my heart into loving her.

I turned back to Max with a grin on my face, "I think I am totally in love with this woman."

He laughed, "I should hope so."

I stood up and crossed the room with my eyes only on her. As she spoke to different people she noticed I was on my way to her, and everything else seemed to stop. We stood face to face; I held out my hand, "My Joselyn... we shall dance forever."

Her face brightened, as she took my hand. I pulled her close, and we glided together as the room darkened and she glowed in my arms. I thought I heard a whisper in my head, "I love you my handsome man and you will have love, now that you have let me go."

I pressed my chin against Joselyn's face, "I love you."

She pushed back, "I am in love with you, Tyler."

"Can I call you Mrs. Reynolds?"

She laughed, "Yes, Mr. Reynolds."

I knew my Joselyn pushed away all of my pain.

Other Titles by Melissa M. Marlow
Forever Yours: Series
Forever Yours   12–10
Wasting Away   5–11

Ebooks:
Push Away... 5–11

Connect with Melissa M. Marlow online @:

http://home.comcast.net/~mmmarlow/site
http://www.facebook.com/melissammarlow
mmmarlow@comcast.net